Praise for *The Dissenters*

"*The Dissenters* is an encyclopedia of all the ways bodies are imprisoned or made free—by politics, sex, power, love, death. An Egypt of the senses, mind, and heart, laid open and dissected in every manner. This book will seduce you from its opening pages and stun you with its last. A tremendous, confident novel from Youssef Rakha, assuming his rightful place on the literary stage." —**Bina Shah**

"A stylish, deftly told story about a stubbornly cosmopolitan and nonconformist set of characters whose lives set them on a collision course with Egypt's military regime leading up to the Tahrir uprising and its grim aftermath." —**Amitav Ghosh**

"Youssef Rakha is the rare writer who is actually paying attention and trying to make sense of the world while many are devolving into despair. In *The Dissenters*, revolutions and their aftermath play the chord of unsung protagonists of History—not of the ones creating and disseminating grandiose lies and killing for them, but the ones willing to create a world outside the tinted windows of power, even if that means challenging the abyss." —**Yuri Herrera**

"One of the most original and inventive writers of his generation." —**Omar Robert Hamilton**

"Here is Egypt, Cairo, 'Mother of the World,' viewed through the chameleon lives of one Cairene mother, 'a fractal of our country.' With thrilling prose and a narrative that flows as relentless as the Nile, Youssef Rakha takes us on the big dipper of Egyptian history from Nasser to now. *The Dissenters* is by turns haunted, horrifying, and hilarious. At heart, though, it's an elegy for lost revolutions, generations . . . but never really lost, not in that land of revenants. You'll end up knowing more about the real, perhaps hyperreal, Egypt than you will from many a history. Knowing, too, that love's more real still: more real than time."   **—Tim Mackintosh-Smith**

"History is bulldozed not metaphorically, but in real time and with real machines and with true ogres at the wheel. There is almost everything that we cannot save, and every day we are not just reminded of but actually see how we've been pulverized, reduced to specters. And yet, we go on witnessing. *The Dissenters* is the book of witnessing par excellence, telling not the story of just one woman or one Egypt, but rather of all of us who are of these geographies."   **—Salar Abdoh**

THE DISSENTERS

Also by Youssef Rakha and Available in English

The Book of the Sultan's Seal
The Crocodiles

THE DISSENTERS

A Novel

YOUSSEF RAKHA

Graywolf Press

Published by Graywolf Press
212 Third Avenue North, Suite 485
Minneapolis, Minnesota 55401

www.graywolfpress.org

Published in the United States of America

ISBN 978-1-64445-319-3 (paperback)
ISBN 978-1-64445-320-9 (ebook)

2 4 6 8 9 7 5 3 1
First Graywolf Printing, 2025

Library of Congress Cataloging-in-Publication Data

Names: Rakhā, Yūsuf, author.
Title: The dissenters : a novel / Youssef Rakha.
Description: Minneapolis, Minnesota : Graywolf Press, 2025. | Includes
    bibliographical references.
Identifiers: LCCN 2024028845 (print) | LCCN 2024028846 (ebook) |
    ISBN 9781644453193 (trade paperback) | ISBN 9781644453209 (epub)
Subjects: LCGFT: Epistolary fiction. | Novels.
Classification: LCC PR9375.9.R35 D57 2025 (print) | LCC PR9375.9.R35
    (ebook) | DDC 823.92—dc23/eng/20240624
LC record available at https://lccn.loc.gov/2024028845
LC ebook record available at https://lccn.loc.gov/2024028846

Cover design: Kyle G. Hunter

Cover photo: Courtesy of the author

For Labiba

I sought permission to beg forgiveness for my mother, but He did not grant it to me. I sought permission from Him to visit her grave, and He granted it to me.

Hadith Sharif, Sahih Muslim (Book 4:2129)

Citizens, if Gamal Abd El Nasser dies, he will now die reassured, for you are all Gamal Abd El Nasser. You are all Gamal Abd El Nasser.

Gamal Abd El Nasser resuming his address after an attempt on his life by members of the Muslim Brotherhood on October 26, 1954

Three Letters & a Myth

THE ATTIC

March 2, 2015: July 26, 1956

Dear Shimo:

Do you remember the disused attic on the way to the roof of our one-story house? That cramped, dust-coated space where Mouna used to keep a small safe among Baba's hardbound law books. It occurs to me now that, however often she passed it, Mouna almost never went inside.

I don't suppose you'd imagine me going in the attic either, any more than you'd expect a letter from me. You were the reason I first stole up there, while Mouna was still alive. Since then something has come unstuck in my access to time, and I've found I can experience events that happened before I was born just as well as the episodes that marked me. Mouna might be beggaring my soul for spending too much in Alexandria or she might be jumping about in a miniskirt, unrecognizable.

Either way her body is there in front of me. The door to her mind is open in a way that it never was in her lifetime. And, stepping through that door, enraptured and disconsolate, I walk further and further into her life. Living, reliving it—I'm either her or an infinitely versatile camera trailing her. Sometimes I'm both Mouna and the camera.

But—here's the thing, Shimo—the more time I spend in the attic, the more it feels like a debt to myself to reconcile you to her.

Swollen with the knowledge I've gulped down, I know I have to share it all with you. No matter how I reach out, you remain seven thousand miles away, I know. But if you were here and we had the business of living between us, how much of this stippled story could I really tell?

I marvel at my desire for Mouna, a Mouna that is and is not my mother. And, thinking again of your absence, certain as I've never been of anything in the world that you have a right or a duty to know, that you absolutely must know, I sail through the mouth of that river into the sea of her life.

Like a bridal wraith I see the girl she once was haunting the bedstead, one hand hovering above her groom.

In its lined broadcloth pajamas the portly figure lies on its back, arms crossed over chest like a dead pharaoh, ensconced in a lattice of sunlight. She brushes his nightcap: no response. She whispers, nudging his hairy hand. When she plucks up the courage to slip her hands under his shoulders and pull the man snarls and she flinches. As he begins to snore again his motionlessness is such that she backs out of the door, unnerved.

She wants to wake him to ask what to say when her sister arrives. The marital apartment is in Shoubra, the same neighborhood as her father's house, so the sister who lives in the same building won't be long now. She will find her still in her wedding dress, bedraggled and bruised but dry where she should be bloodied.

Amna knows that, since this is her sabahiyya, her eldest sister, Arwa, will show up demanding the family's sharaf in the form of a stained piece of cloth spread over the bedsheet in the marital bed. The staining is, of course, the responsibility of Mansour Effendi, the forty-year-old husband she had only just met when she arrived at this apartment the night before. But she knows she is the one Arwa will question.

In all things Amna's mother, Bara Hanim, walks behind her eldest daughter like a blindfolded water buffalo, which in the six remaining girls' affairs makes Arwa the despot of the Wahib Abu Zahra household. Amna is the third youngest, the most recent to be married by a crack of Arwa's whip.

Last night, in his final bound for the fugitive hard-on, the bookkeeper had seated her bodily on the dresser, bared one Alphonso mango–like bezz, and slowly parted her thighs. He was fully accoutered except for the trousers, long johns, and underpants piled over his glossy oxfords, the tassel of his tarboosh primly combed to one side. Even his eyewear in place.

While the schoolgirl blushed, horrified at first, he alternately suckled and lowered his gaze, burbling *Allahallahallahallah* as he rocked to and fro.

This went on for twenty minutes, punctuated by desperate tugs at the enormous bulbul dangling in state. When her suppressed smile finally registered, he recognized it as a sign of amusement. Then he availed himself of the bathroom—for bed.

The buttock Mansour Effendi had clasped during the evening's debacle smarts badly. But while she sits cross-legged on the rococo sofa in the hall, braiding her hair, it is over her knees that Amna is brooding.

This is the last term before the Baccalauréat examens, and Amna has been absent for a week. She didn't hand in her devoirs to Madame Estaban, the science teacher, who is sure to have reported her by now. Amna worries Soeur Laurette will make her cross the playground on her knees, la principale's favorite punishment. The pain doesn't frighten her so much as the humiliation of walking around with flaming welts beneath the skirt of her uniform like a misbehaved child.

Now I see her under Mansour's high ceiling, vaguely regal at the center of the sofa. A compact shape utterly unaware of its gorgeousness.

Her huge hazel eyes with impossibly long lashes stare dreamily ahead. Her long neck is so flimsy you could crush it between forefinger and thumb. The dress, creased, is in all the wrong places on her torso, as if she wore it with the seam to one side. Its glittering train covers one thigh, spotlighting the orange-tinged nudity of the other.

Over the gray plush of the sofa and the black and white tiles below, the chiffon on brocade trails all the way to the brown trunk overflowing with her wardrobe like a disemboweled carcass. Her auburn hair shades half her face as her hands weave mechanically. She is tiny.

Lying back on the floor of the attic at the top of our house, I see her. Her face crumples as she thinks of those welts, her snub nose swelling over fat, pursed lips. And I almost hear the plea forming in her head. It is nineteenth-century French but broken. And it falters before the steely stare of the elderly French nun.

I see the casuarina-flanked sand of the playground, the arch above the staircase into the Moorish citadel-style building. I see her in white shirt, white skirt, a navy blue tie resting on her cleavage under the unforgiving sun. Her pigtails hang over her bowed head while she waits on the steps. But no sooner does the image take form than she is back in her marital apartment, standing before Arwa like a child being reprimanded.

Carrying herself like a septuagenarian at thirty-five, the large, plain sister has curled one hand and is tapping it irritably with the other. A helix of gold snake bangles on each of her wrists jingles mutedly meanwhile.

—But what was I to do, wennabi, ya Abla Arwa?

The tapping quickens as Arwa grumbles, glaring at her little sister. The black cloak covering her immense bulk shimmers over a fuchsia sack dress. Below the mauve écharpe around her head, a thick portiere of jet-black hair hangs over penciled eyebrows.

Together with excessive kohl this gives her small, dark eyes a hard, inanimate quality. But there is no way you can tell she is thinking of gold—the gold her late husband's cousin, Mansour Effendi's mother, Hagga Hafiza, had pushed into Arwa's lap. Alluding to the groom's exceptional penis size, Hagga Hafiza had winked and bitten her lip while she did.

—A maiden bride untouched on her sabahiyya, Arwa wails, who ever heard of such a thing? And the man, mashallah, so well endowed by reputation. What, Lord, can we say to Wahib Bey?

For three years, since the declaration of the republic, Arwa has been referring to her father by his supposed title.

—And even if the Bey is appeased, she goes on, what will the Omda say?

Amna cowers at the mention of her eldest brother, Umair, the educational failure who, since he oversees the village into which her father's estate has turned, has taken on the title of village omda.

By now the debonair only child of herculean height and hawkish features has frittered away the family fortune. When the young republican regime starts taking over private property, he has hardly anything left for it to nationalize.

—And the man, mashallah—what lies will Mansour Effendi's family spread about us now, Arwa carries on.

It is Amna I hear, a while later on the same day. In the tactful Arabic of sixty years ago, she's asking Abla Arwa whether it might be better if she eats before scrubbing the kitchen floor, as her abla says she must. Amna has not slept a wink and, now that she has faced her sister, she can feel how hungry she has been.

Then I see her in a petticoat on all fours in the kitchen, sobbing while she scrubs.

Later, four years after the revolution when it is over and I am ready to move along, I recall that it was Mouna who drew my attention to the Jumpers. At first it was professional interest that drove me: a reporter on the trail of a scoop. But it soon felt like something much bigger, much more personal than journalism could ever be:

Women of all ages and circumstances stepping over windowsills and leaping across balustrades, unaccountably killing themselves in the thick of protests and lies.

By 2012 I won't be as interested in the revolution itself as all those women—thousands of them spreading out of Cairo to Alexandria and Suez, all the demonstration hubs, one after another testing the destructive power of gravity—for no apparent reason.

Tipped off by the mother he lives with, the seasoned journalist doing some extra work: I did not yet realize what the attention she paid the Jumpers would end up doing to her.

Their story feels like the boat I've taken down the river of the revolution—one officer out of the presidency and, past the election and ouster of a sheikh, another in—but where has that cyclical course delivered me?

In the cramped, dust-coated attic where I've been lying back to gulp down knowledge, Shimo, it feels like a debt to myself to convince you of how like the mother you resented you really are. How your revolution against her was a version of her revolution. To tell you of her as I saw her in the last four years of her life, and of the sixty years before that as they're revealed to me. To tell you of the revolution you missed. But perhaps most importantly of all to tell you of the Jumpers. How strange it was that they existed, how frustrating that no one paid any attention to them except Mouna.

She was still alive the first time I visited the attic, five days after I brought her home from the hospital.

Mouna insisted I drive her myself—in the Burakmobile. Remember the heart-shaped scratch on the bumper, which you called Bug Wing? I stowed the stretcher in front of the back seat where she lay. Everything went smoothly at first, but then at the U-turn she skidded sideways and slipped half onto the floor, exposing her legs. When she asked me to help her and I pulled over next to a fruit stall, that was the first I saw of the transformation: it was unlike her to make a request without invoking either God or His Messenger.

—Don't look too harshly on the cripple you've been burdened with, ya habibi, she said, almost without emotion. I promise you it won't be long now. Besides, these legs aren't even worth looking at now. Imagine seeing them in their prime! Only a behim and the son of a behim could fail to covet them.

Suddenly she was laughing, as much as anyone lying paralyzed in a VW Beetle can laugh. She had the same look you used to give me when I teased you about your boyfriends.

—Don't you doubt it, son of Amin. It wasn't just famous artists they tempted. C'est vrai! Forget this decaying carcass you see in front of you. You would've gone deranged from a single glimpse.

I don't suppose I was wide-eyed so much as thin-lipped, hearing this. Something in her voice released the weeping clockwork which the last four years had been steadily winding. Only three weeks prior she'd been in good health. Her body was frail and ruined, but whole. Yet just that morning the registrar who'd been following her case, coordinating the work of three different consultants, had patiently taken me through the cardiological and orthopedic procedures she'd undergone, explaining that due to age and hypertension—diabetes, too—no more surgery was possible.

—Her condition is stable for the time being, the young man sounded apologetic. But if internal hemorrhage were to recur or if the medication fails to prevent the reemergence of hemothorax—he broke off, looking down timidly.

Suddenly I was struggling not to sob in the car.

Later I thought maybe what had dammed up my tears since the Cataclysm was knowing how resigned she would be to her death at seventy-six, a devout believer. As if her being okay with it would make it okay for me too. Not that she'd blasphemed enough in that moment to suggest she'd given up hope of an afterlife. But what she said made it clear to me that, whatever she herself felt, for me her death was not okay.

—Bas bas, bas bas, I heard her rasping when I was driving again. Don't cry, light of my eyes.

It was another five minutes before I could turn on the ignition.

—A life is only worth as much as a life is worth, she went on. Besides, you've been a good son.

At first I assumed it was a lapse, all that godless talk of putrefaction and desire. But I was near her for the rest of the day and she did not perform salah once. She was lucid, almost in her element. Even her hearing seemed to improve, but her elaborate way of speaking now omitted religious references. At night I listened for the sotto voce invocations I'd heard her repeating for decades. Nothing.

The next day I asked as casually as I could whether she wasn't going to perform salah.

—No, she said simply, giving no explanation.

There was an overtone of some kind—defiance or distress, perhaps simply disillusion—but it was so subtle I could just barely detect it.

—Do me a favor, will you, habibi, she added after a while. Find me a book by Ihsan Abd El Quddous. I'm sure they're hidden away somewhere here in the house. Will you look for the sake of your Mouna?

I don't know if you can imagine, Shimo. Mouna hasn't touched a nonreligious book since before you were born. Whimpering with joy and grief, I begin to scour through the bookshelves, Baba's filing cabinet, and the oddest piece of furniture in the house: an ancient mahogany secretaire with marble top and satinwood interior. I'm searching not just for what she wants but also for a black-and-white photograph in which she looks young enough to be my daughter, an image that's been haunting me since she came out of the hospital. It's not much bigger than a playing card, and I know she has never housed it in a photo album.

I find it. On the back is one line in her hand, which has not changed fifty years on: *At Serag and Samira's, celebrating Amin's release. May 26, 1964.* I slide it next to the ID in my wallet, so it can be with me wherever I go.

I find the photograph alongside a similarly sized, framed print I don't remember seeing before. A black-and-brown lithograph, signed

Aziz Maher, Egypt's best-known artist of the sixties. I plan to ask Mouna about it, but in the sound and the fury of her dying, I forget. The lithograph shows her face at more or less the time of the photograph, executed with an expert but unfeeling naturalism. The face is instantly recognizable, pretty as anything. But its mischief, its ingenuousness, the shadow of that bitter look of hers that hangs over it—everything that makes it hers—is omitted. I leave it where I found it.

I find the books, too, yellowed and brittle underneath the sensational drawings of couples kissing on their covers.

Five days later I will force Mouna's eyelids down and ease the wedding ring off her finger. I will remove her neck support, slip off her stud earrings, and unlatch the antique gold watch she called Ramona to slide it off her wrist. And from the moment I return to her room with the books till I do this, not once will the television be turned on. For the rest of her life Mouna will be absorbed in the starry-eyed, politely sexual romances of her youth's best-selling novelist.

By the time her eldest sister visits again, six weeks later, Amna Abu Zahra will have accrued all kinds of reasons to be pleased.

Grateful that her maidenhead, her life's capital, was not squandered on the stodgy knob who cut short her path to university, she is pleased she managed to minimize her mother-in-law's encroachment by saying just one thing. In the first week, while arguing about whether or not she was too spoilt for her son, Hagga Hafiza bellowed:

—You do not honor your husband's manhood!

—But surely, Neina Hafiza, she responded, in a savagely steady voice, nothing I'm capable of doing could ever undermine Mansour Effendi's manhood in society's eye.

No one has dared force her to do housework since. The gangly lady arrives twice a week with two little girls from the village, her white Ottoman veil over her face. She raises it above her head, still standing, and in a mournful voice orders the girls about the house, sighing and biting her lip while they work.

Sometimes, in the evening when Mansour has returned from the diwan, the hagga arrives with different helpers. A barber-quack suggests electrifying his balls. A Quranic healer makes him swallow a piece of paper with a holy verse inscribed on it in deer musk. An herb dispenser in a wheelchair almost burns down the house. In a cloud of incense, Amna is made to rub her face with the blood of a rooster freshly slaughtered by her husband's hand.

Yet, through all this—*Allahallahallahallah!*—the monstrous member will not budge.

Amna watches, awed and disgusted by turns. With true feeling for the man she marvels at the way he submits to each new humiliation. He is barely twelve years younger than Hagga Hafiza, who is more superstitious sibling than mindful matriarch. But she needs virility's vindication and her hold is strong.

Though he's a religious bureaucrat, Mansour is a believer in modern medicine. The doctors have told him there is nothing physiologically wrong with him. They assure him he need not be mad to consult a psychiatrist, psychiatry helps all manner of human beings, but what if someone from the Prime Minister's diwan where he works were to find out? What if it turns out he is mad?

Amna is pleased she can use her marriage to live as she likes. Most of the time she has the apartment to herself. Using the only piece of furniture that made it over from her father's house, a yellowish mahogany secretaire with marble top and satinwood interior, she resumes her études from home and, once she discovers she can, she begins to go out unchaperoned. A virgin playground, Cairo configures itself around her.

She is distantly pleasant to Mansour Effendi, who appreciates her keeping his secret. He probably knows about her outings, though she is always home when he leaves for and returns from work. They don't speak beyond necessity, never spend time together, but what money she asks for, the bookkeeper gives.

Her purpose in leaving the first time is to explain her situation to Soeur Laurette, who on seeing her in an elegant halter-neck dress with a wedding ring on her finger proved shockingly ingratiating. *Je suis sûr que tu trouveras ton chemin, ma fille!* Since that afternoon, Amna wanders the streets of her school's upscale, young neighborhood. She moves on to the modern cafés and the cinemas in the weeks to come.

Apart from the occasional whistle of admiration, no one bothers the petite madame with hair like Gina Lollobrigida's in *The Wayward Wife*.

The trottoirs, as she will continue to call them till the end of her life, are wide and shady. And after that first day her heels are never too high for walking comfortably, with poise. She keeps away from Shoubra for fear of being spotted by an Abu Zahra, but there is more for her in Heliopolis anyway.

It is there that she manages to reconnect with her former classmate Susanne Qansuh. And within days the two of them are accompanying Susanne's older sister, Lena, to Cairo University, where Susanne is studying at the Faculty of Law, all the way at the other end of town. Amna's never been anywhere as exciting as that campus cafeteria.

Most of all Amna is pleased a dark and scruffy young man is paying her attention. He is genial but jittery, with an abrupt manner and a bleat-like laugh. Less than ten years her senior, what's more, he is slight enough not to look like a titan when she stands next to him. His physiognomy recalls one of those frighteningly real faces painted on wood panels that have stayed with her since a school trip to the museum. Aren't they supposed to belong to ancient Roman or Greek mummies from Fayoum? People call him Aminov. Through Lena Amna finds out he is a law graduate named Amin Abdalla Amin.

She finds out that, just like her, he is the third youngest of many siblings in a middling family, the only one to go to college.

Amin shares an apartment with two other law graduates, and all four hail from the same cluster of small towns around Dekernes, east of El Mansoura.

—Yaah, Amin-n-nov, Susanne and Lena's svelte sibling Fouad stutters when she brings Amin up over bottles of Spathis, taking a sip of the fizzy lemonade before he goes on. He's a comm-m-munist all right.

Fouad Qansuh is training to be a pilot—Amna calls him *ya Captain*—and he cuts a dashing figure despite his speech impediment.

—But he's one of those cr-r-rackpot communists who can't get their act together, Fouad smiles now. They say the secret organization Aminov belongs to has three m-m-members all told. I'm given to understand they are l-l-loyal to the French Communist Party, the tw-tw-twerps. Fouad's smile is enchanting. I'd be careful, ma chère.

Amna has been told communism is haram: a conspiracy started by Jews to block the mercy of the All-Merciful. But this communist is neither Jew nor Nazarene, and she feels he is truer and more merciful than any halal-observing man she's met.

Amin never uses the word, anyhow. What he talks about is a place where everyone is free and equal, where no one is forced to work in order to eat and science reigns supreme. This place, he calls Socialism.

—No, he tells her emphatically when she asks, true Socialism does not exist in either the Soviet Union or the People's Republic of China.

Amna is most reassured when she finds out he hates Egypt's own communist organizations, the biggest one especially: the Democratic Movement for National Liberation known by its Arabic acronym: HADETO. Amin really hates HADETO.

If he's opposed to all the communists in the world, she reasons, then he can't really be a communist himself, can he. Who's going to pay attention to a three-member organization anyway? So long as he doesn't bear arms, which he doesn't, Amin will be safe.

As far as she can tell there are hardly any communists among his friends. Amin has friends from the Ikhwan—even then, ya Shimo, that's what the Muslim Brotherhood was informally called—as well as Young Egypt fascist friends. He knows royals-turned-chauffeurs and itinerant knife sharpeners. He knows waiters at the kind of hashish-smoking establishment called a *ghorza*, which really means *stitch*, where the radio plays Quranic recitations with the range and power of opera and men bring their own Lebanese Flower to smoke over molasses-soaked tobacco in earthenware water pipes.

No, no. Amin can't not be safe. But, being a married woman—she remembers, and it hurts—what does it matter if he is safe or not?

In Mouna's last three days the house fills with well-wishers. They are mostly Khalto Faiza's progeny, but there are also paternal cousins of ours and the daughter of her late friend Siham Gad. That's Tante Semsem's full name, you realize. I don't know if you ever met her daughter Gamila, named after the Algerian militant Djamila Bouhired, just as you might expect an Arab nationalist's child to be.

With Gamila, Mouna cherishes the memory of her soulmate. The first to lend her money when they met at Ain Shams University. And, when Baba died forty-four years later, the last to leave her side.

The woman was a lifelong somnambulist, but the condition had ceased, apparently after menopause. Then it returned abruptly at the age of sixty-seven when one night Tante Semsem stepped out of the house while eating rice with the angels and sleepwalked to the October Bridge exit outside her apartment building, where she was run over by a minivan. For months Mouna had analyzed and re-analyzed the incident, forcibly making it demonstrate the wisdom of divine power. But by her deathbed it is Gamila who speaks of God's mysterious ways.

The other visitors—mostly women, all in hijab—Mouna receives more coldly. Especially after they find out she has abandoned her salah.

I can tell from the way her eyes move. She abhors their small jihad. The threats, the promises, puerile rites of cleansing and bene-diction. Instead of bags of fruit, boxes of chocolate, and bouquets of flowers, they come in with booklets of prayer, Surat Yasin and Ayat Al Kursi, incense sticks, electronic rosaries, sermons on memory sticks.

While she still can, Mouna laughs in their faces. Later she grunts and turns away, pointing to the door of the room with her chin. Those who still won't leave, I have to drag by the arm, murmuring *Thou guidest not whom thou lovest, but Allah guideth whom He will* while hustling them out.

In all of a month Abid has come once to the hospital, twice to the house. On his second visit I catch him, having propped Mouna uncomfortably up, trying to steer her through the motions of salah. Clearly furious, eager to protest more forcefully, she only has strength to groan.

Abid has money, I remember, yet he hasn't paid a single guinea toward the greatest expense in Mouna's life. If not for her savings and the check you and your partner sent, I could never have afforded the hospital bill. Abid has carefully conserved his material resources, but now he is saving Mouna's soul.

And all over Egypt it is like this: people observing the rituals to improve their solvency with Allah while defaulting on what human loans they can.

Coming up from behind, I punch him on the head as hard and as quietly as I can before I ease her back down and rearrange the pillows the way she likes, kissing her cheeks.

Outside he hisses, cradling his cranium and glowering:

—She's not in her mind. She wouldn't want to die an infidel like you know who. Aywa, ah! Nor do I want her to.

—Why don't you torture the khara out of her till she utters the Shahada, I spit. Isn't that what you do for a living?

—Nour, he starts in a hurt tone.

—Kossommak, ya Abid!

At night there is no one. Me, Mouna, and the photograph.

And that is how it will be the afternoon she surfaces to sing a few couplets of the Sayyid Darwish song "Ana Hawet." Through some miracle, from now till I start making phone calls, no one comes. A faint smell of piss complements the stale incense and a lingering rose fragrance wafting around. I tell her she has a pretty voice and she tells me she loves me. Then she closes her eyes.

—I can smell sea salt, she breathes. My toes in wet sand.

She is still conscious when I bring her soup, which she eats with unusual appetite, remembering Baba.

—Nour, she whispers urgently while I wipe her mouth, was I very unfair to him, you think? Tell me honestly, start of my happiness, toil of my tummy! You think I let him down before he died?

The next time she surfaces the sun is going down. Her usual anxiety restored, she fumbles about in bed. Then she says something she hasn't said in at least two years:

—Any news of Shimo, son of Amin?

The last time you came up was when I told her you'd had a baby girl, back in January 2012, and she consented to seeing some videos of Nadja. A year before she'd started to grumble when I mentioned that the revolution coincided with your wedding. But, remembering her policy of silence, terrified of her desire to see you, she quickly cut short the tirade.

Gazing into her face now as she asks about you, I can see the look by which I've always identified her. Grief, hatred, and letdown. Bottomless letdown.

I hear a car brake violently after she falls unconscious again. At dusk she stops breathing.

I have no idea why I postpone making the phone calls that will fill up the house and set off the mortuary formalities. By midnight I have slipped under the covers beside her, sniffing the sweat on her neck, playing with her earlobe, feeling her warm flesh go cold while I doze.

I think I hear the dawn azan much earlier than it is supposed to sound. The world, spaced out, is speeding down some derelict highway in time. And long before my attic visions start, Shimo, I am thinking it is time that happens to people. We talk about having and saving and wasting it as if it is ours to work with, but really it is we who are time's property. It molds and meddles with us, changes us without our knowing, so that one day we wake up with no idea who we are. And suddenly the life we've lived is no longer ours.

Like someone about to pray I get up and head to the bathroom, but instead of the ritual ablutions that precede salah I strip and step under the ice-cold water. Barely dry on the veranda, I light cigarette after cigarette, feeling nothing but the satisfaction of thick smoke filling my lungs and nicotine charging my nerves. I seem to remember the moment as it happens, smoking on the veranda in the early hours of March 2, 2015, right after Mouna died. As if I lived that moment before, exactly as it happens.

When I slip back in next to her—I will never forget this—Mouna is no longer there. Something else lies in her place. It is familiar and benign but it isn't Mouna. Of all that happens in the last week of her life, this has to be the hardest moment.

Three days later when Mouna is no longer there and I first think of moving out of the house, I will climb up to the attic for the second time. And, lying on my back, I will have my first image of Mouna before I was born.

It is crisp and crystal albeit in black and white, and it comes with its date and venue clearly marked: August 10, 1963, at Masr Train Station. The main one in Cairo. Remember when you asked me why, even though it only serves city, it was named after all of Egypt?

On my back in the attic I start living Mouna's life vicariously, Shimo—either her or an infinitely versatile camera trailing her. Sometimes both.

During my third time in the attic I see the Cataclysm. I can't quite understand it yet, though I recognize it immediately—not just from hospital records and conversations with doctors but from the way Mouna talked about the fennec fox the day President Abd El Fattah El Sisi took office, back in 2014.

I see the Cataclysm unfolding in the neighborhood of Agouza, and it sparks my desire to know how—from being the mother you and I knew—Mouna could end up there. And, to find out, bit by bit, in whatever order unstuck from chronology, I will come back up to the attic, again and again.

By the time Amin overcomes his timidity and sits at the same table—three weeks after they first lay eyes on each other—Amna has already met all kinds, lookers and talkers and mystery men. They've told her things about Gamal Abd El Nasser, the mustachioed, charismatic young officer who led the coup that sent King Farouk yachting away to Italy, then managed to lock up the Ikhwan and place the older officer who became the country's first president under house arrest. Nasser was a bikbashi, which is what the rank of major was called then. But maybe you know this already? How much recent Egyptian history do you know anyway?

This coup alone claims credit for the ongoing withdrawal of the British after seven decades of occupation. But for four years the Ikhwan who want Islamic sharia, the monarchists who want British-style constitutional democracy, and various army factions have been cockfighting over control of the country. That, anyway, is what it looks like to Amna. And it makes her laugh to think of those stern faces on the necks of roosters headbutting each other in a sandpit.

By now the feather-flecked dust is settling around the lone rooster who's managed to rally the fellahin around him. Egypt's ancient peasantry? The fellahin are whistling for Nasser, looking at the properties of Jews, Italians, Greeks, Armenians as their divinely ordained loot. Neither democracy nor sharia can stop Egypt's first-ever homegrown Zaim.

Even I am no longer sure what that word means, Shimo. Zaim. Not so much leader as chief, chieftain. Warrior, deity. A boss who puts loyalty above competence. It's hero and idol but also avenger, destroyer of rival and traitor, punisher. By 1956, that's what Nasser has become for the fellahin and those who identify with them. Among the young men Amna's met, three ideas are making the rounds.

Some think of the bikbashi as a lowborn brute who will end all civilized life in the valley of the Nile, that infinitely kindhearted watercourse that, if you kept it clean, kept you provided for, as they say. Though they can't seem to decide whether it is modern colonialism or Islamic conquest that defines *civilization*.

Others say he is the spunky spirit that, rousing her out of her slumber, will revivify the motherland. But the fellahin with whom the motherland is identified have never had a political vision of their own, and without either Ikhwan or monarchists it's unclear what that revivified motherland looks like.

Still others feel Nasser can only be an instrument of the inexorable forward march of progress, the liberation of peoples.

Amna herself can't make her mind up what to think about him.

And that is why, on their first outing alone—to the Zamalek Aquarium Grotto, in your favorite part of the island neighborhood, Shimo—Amna asks Amin what he thinks. They've just come to the first aquarium through a wooden arch over a lily pond, birds chirping, and so far only the sweetest compliments have parted his lips. At the mention of Nasser's name he stops with his back to the glass. His expression changes so abruptly that Amna balks. She considers apologizing.

—That turd, Amin sputters, unconcerned with the romantic intensity of the moment. That impudent turd who'll stop up progress in every direction.

—I didn't realize—

—He will worm his way to power until he is idolized, won't he. To become chief of all chiefs, leader of nations, Immortal Zaim! That's all he wants, the postman's son, the psychopath. And what do they think will happen to this country when his little education is elevated to scripture, when his little man's conservatism is consecrated?

—But haven't the HADETO people announced their support for him, ya Amin? She manages to overcome her shock just enough to keep the conversation going. Isn't he giving the fellahin land and doing other things they like?

—Those traitors, Amin roars. Those lily-livered patriots, puerile populists, useful idiots. Do you think they count for anything anyway? When you support an insular ignoramus like Nasser, Amin winds down in a lower voice, still sputtering, you betray not only socialism but the very meaning of democracy. HADETO, indeed!

Amna turns to the miniature ocean in front of her, a fright like cold fingers digging into her neck. She can see it. She doesn't have a full-fledged visitation, as she will learn to call them—nothing like what will afflict her later on in life—but in her mind's eye she can make out what she recognizes as the source of this fluttering and need to hide, this icy helplessness piercing her skin. It manifests in a split second and lasts an even shorter time, but it's vivid enough to remind her of when she saw it before, when she was nine years old.

Amna never articulates it at this point, not even to herself. But had she been asked what that fright looked like, she might've described a giant housefly. Less like a fly than a hooded crow, she might've said, but clearly an insect. It has bulbous compound eyes so large you can see the furrows separating out their ommatidia. It has zigzagging, translucent wings and a proboscis like a deer horn dagger, blade-rimmed and silver. The wings flutter nonstop at unimaginable speed. The outsize eyes pulsate in their sockets as the thing wheels, cawing. A sharp, shard-filled sound of which Amna might've said, *If being instantly frozen had a sound, this is what that cawing would be.*

Where she and Amin are standing a spot of sun illuminates a narrow triangle. Its base below the glass tank in front of them, its tip by their feet.

For a while all she can see is water, then a dwarf lantern shark rears its jaws from behind the diminutive marine forest, coming straight at her. Amna gasps, gulping before she smiles. She doesn't look back at Amin until, cutting short his apoplectic tirade, he steps forward to take her hand, which brings his face into the light.

His grip is rough, awkward, but there is such grace in his eyes that, caring nothing for propriety or being a married woman at seventeen, Amna rests her head on his chest. And the moment Amin slides his palm into her armpit—there is shelter in the gesture, a sense of being contained she has often yearned for without knowing it—Mouna knows.

She knows she will tell him everything. She knows it won't make him want her less. And, should he propose to her, he would mind neither the lack of a dowry nor the run-down condition of Wahib Abu Zahra's house.

—Mouna, he whispers, beaming. My Mouna.

It's the word she will prefer to Mama when she finally has a child of her own. It means nothing, but it is how that sense of being contained has changed her given name. What Amna becomes when an intense young man falls in love with her. She closes her eyes.

The girl hasn't heard of Tolstoy. Four years later, after she has graduated in the absence of Amin, she will watch *River of Love*, the Egyptian adaptation of *Anna Karenina*, at the Downtown Cinema Metro. And she'll weep over Faten Hamama as the unhappily married young woman in love with the young police officer, Omar Sharif.

But already on their first outing, she can sense she is one more incarnation of a celebrated character. She knows she's living out an archetypal moment that will take her not just farther than the Aquarium Grotto but farther, much farther than being happily married to a man infinitely more suitable than Mansour.

Nuzzling up to Amin's bony chest, Amna half remembers what brought on her insectile fright. The picture of her life she will show Amin is not yet complete, just as Nasser's picture is still to form through wars and iniquities no one in the country can anticipate. Something is still to come, the climax in the storyline.

A girl before a minuscule shark suffering a premonition of disaster while she falls in love. This is the way the world starts. With a joy never before felt. In the smoky, musky odor of a crackpot communist's chest.

—:•

After Mouna's no longer there, no longer breathing, I am next aware of myself in the passenger seat of a white van. The van is indistinguishable from a service microbus except for its pristine condition and shaded windows. It is called the Vehicle for Honoring Man.

In the internecine traffic, it takes five hours to traverse the fifty kilometers from Maadi to the Abu Zahra cemetery. The village is just outside Shoubra, at the point where the countryside begins to creep into the city and alter it.

At one point I look beyond the hand-shaped amulet hanging from the rearview mirror, and we are crawling in the shade of a stretch of bridge. A tortuous passageway; except for an uneven mesh of brightness, nearly black. I have the feeling I am on a haunted-house ride at some funerary fairground. The hawkers juggling packets of tissue paper, the street kids clinging to wing mirrors, the wailing women in black robes—they're here to startle and horrify. Dancing to the horns' grim concerto, they rear up into the light. Then, just as imperceptibly, they blend back into shadow.

As we slide out of the maze onto more evenly lit asphalt I can no longer tell if the faces belong to beggars or pedestrians. Like Rembrandts in a zoetrope they are rotating across the windscreen, stately and dignified. It is as though they summarize whole life paths, going by, their destinies literally written on their brows. And the life paths they summarize are all Mouna's. I'm convinced. Somehow Mouna has lived all those lives. They are shoddy and grueling but she has lived them, not letting on for a moment how punishing they were.

I gaze back at the amulet. *Alf baraka*, I hear her utter one of her mantras in her distinctive tone. A thousand blessings, yes? Baba has been fifteen years dead by the time Mouna sheds her religiosity, and already I am chaperoning her to the grave.

Egyptians have a credulous habit at funerals. There are always too many pallbearers and, whether they're aware of it or not, some of them will always speed up, forcing the others to keep pace, so that to any random pallbearer—sometimes to onlookers, too—the box appears to be gliding independently of human hands. Then they say the deceased must've been a good person, their coffin was impatient to convey them to the small piece of heaven reserved for them underground. And they smile happily as if there were no more need for grief.

In Mouna's village the underground rooms where bodies are deposited box-less are built into a knoll on the outskirts.

Surrounded by the four army conscripts assigned to his service, Abid's stocky, gym-toned figure is ahead of me on the climb. He is walking sideways with his arms stretched to the eau de Nil fabric draping the coffin, almost touching it but never quite, the light on his thinning hairline making it glow green. When the procession speeds up abruptly, he trips. His minions nearly trample him.

Now, tittering as I look up—are they, too, laughing at Abid Bey?— I realize I've given up the race. The coffin is a long way ahead now. It is so high above it might be some heavenly being alighting in answer to the prayers of all those upturned hands.

The sky is overcast. Black birds circle a mud brick dovecote in the distance. Underneath it is the neighborhood of Shoubra, just visible past a dark sliver of highway. For a moment, recalling with disbelief that I am forty-five, I take in Mouna's place of birth, that knobbly motherboard of grueling destinies. A mosquito makes me slap my ear, hard, but I miss it. Then I snuffle, treading dust.

At the entrance to the Fatah Mosque annex, back on Road 9, I am lined up next to Abid and three other male close ones. The hall to which we lead is a hothouse of red carpeting and bright yellow. Inside it the nonstop echo of the amplifier chases holy verses through the air. And, stopping to salaam by hand, one by one, unsmiling men in suits are filing into their range.

Mouna attended women's theology classes here for years on end, but at first I have no sense of her presence. It must've been on this stretch of pavement that, when I was six or seven, she took the vow of hijab.

Mouna once owned a huge wardrobe of miniskirts and sleeveless blouses, Mad Men dresses, backless gowns. Clothes that, as I stand here in the dusty breeze, I seem to remember paired with exact and extravagant hairstyles, though there is no way I could have seen her wearing them.

In the seventies the headscarf wasn't as ubiquitous as it was to become, nor were we as attuned to immodesty. Anwar El Sadat, the second head of state to stay in power till he died, hadn't yet declared himself the Believer President, though he was already forging alliances with the newly oil-rich Wahhabis across the Red Sea.

As I thrust my hand forward, now, it occurs to me that by adopting the millennium's most popular confessional badge right after giving birth to Abid in 1976, Mouna was Sadat's model citizen.

She would take to fasting twice a week all year, doing her salah sitting or lying down when she was too ill or weak to perform the motions. Starting when Abid was three, she would go on the hajj three times, and twice as many times on the little hajj called umra. That's how—never mind the French she kept speaking—Mouna became a hagga before you were born.

I think Baba felt it as a betrayal, this reversion to religion. He wouldn't have thought of abandoning us: me, her, and baby Bido. But I think he resented her certainty that the concealment of her body except for her face and hands was necessary or desirable. And, together with her *petty bourgeois ambition*, it made him resent his life.

She would come home from the State Information Service Press Center with a white headscarf wrapped round her face in a tight circle. And if he happened to be there and said something like *Nice hair*, she would launch into an unrelated attack, *Like you were ever any help to me, Amin*, haranguing him about having no religion, wanting his wife to be a sharmoota. Then, angrily, emphatically, as though teaching the whole world a lesson, she would perform salah.

At seven or eight years old, for me, those were horror-story episodes: as long as she was on the salah rug, I could not call out to or come near her. For the duration of the ritual she was beyond reach. Her unfeeling features filled the medallion formed by the scarf, and the flowing robes made her shapeless as she moved with mindless regularity.

I could only think of the demons that torture dead souls. Not only in hell, as I overheard her telling her girly intime Tante Hudhud once, but apparently also in the grave, wherever they were disposed of underground.

Live Quran piercing my ears, now, I see her as I've seen her a million times trudging up the steps past the gate. She's wearing the pious-mama uniform that makes her look twice her age: Gulf-style black cloak; light-colored headscarf tied loosely under the chin, not wrapped with pins as before; and large square handbag to go with clunky clogs.

I actually see her. She's moving with ponderous piousness, projecting a beatific calmness into what faces cross her line of vision.

Amna leaves the Aquarium Grotto in a reverie. That evening after a messy session of Unani bloodletting, she walks into the bedroom to find Mansour naked on his side. In the faint light from the hall she can only see his paunch like a full jute sack drooping over the mattress. For the first time since they met the morning of the katb kitab—the writing of the book: drawing a marriage contract, in case you've forgotten what that means too—sympathy is flowing out of her. But when she bends down to touch his shoulder she trips over the rug. Her hand grasps his arm as she tries not to fall.

And with the same fear of a half-remembered future she realizes she has not touched Mansour since her first morning in the apartment. She thinks he will growl again but, resonantly, he whimpers. She goes on scrambling until she has settled next to him, legs crossed. Slowly she begins to pat his shoulder, duplicating the gruff grace with which Amin took her hand.

As she slides down something in the window catches her eye and she looks past the prostrate heft to a half-moon. It is chalk-white and large, larger than she's ever seen the moon at this stage. And seeming to tell her, *Aywa, you're right to be afraid, ya Amna*, it gleams dully in the starless sky.

When she finally falls asleep Amna dreams. She dreams she is alone in a courtyard, Amin Abdalla Amin's fashionably dressed wife. It's like a tramway station but infinitely bigger, this courtyard, with canopies, kiosks, columns, and benches, tracks set in ducts as deep as an Olympic pool with huge huffing trains so long you cannot see the end of them. It is noon, heavy heat and humid breath. The light and shade are harsh and dappled, the colors either washed out or too bright.

She knows she's going to Alexandria—where she has been twice in her waking life, both times before her marriage to Mansour Effendi, always traveling by automobile—and she knows it should make her happy to be married to Amin and on her way to the sea. But she also knows that Amin is indefinitely absent and that this time the sea's summons is sad. Her presence in what she eventually identifies as Masr Station, which she has never seen, marks her involvement in something ghastly over and above the prospect of sea spray. Certain of the reality of that thing without knowing what it is, it no longer surprises her that she has been weeping inconsolably into her handkerchief.

In the background, over the hooting and heaving, Abd El Halim Hafez—her favorite singer, by now the star of both love and pro-Nasser music—is singing a song she has never heard before, in praise of the brave bikbashi.

The words make no mark, but the tune frazzles the nerves in her body and makes her weep even harder. It enters not through the ears but by tearing straight into her abdomen, rhythmically rending her solar plexus with a mixture of guilt and grief, shame, loss and letdown. It all has to do with Amin or her being his wife or his not being with her where she is, and Amna suffers it all in her sleep.

By the time she wakes the next morning she will have shed all memory of what she suffers. But, like the lantern shark and the name Mouna, like the shelter in Amin's chest and her sympathy for Mansour, the dream too is my genesis. Even if it's too accurately prophetic for any awareness of it to remain with the dreamer, this song of experience has already toughened her up.

It feels right that I should be in the place where Mouna spent more time than anywhere to take her consolation, so close to our one-story house. But after the endless grip-and-girth parade I am tired of open palms.

When at last it is over, when the handshakers have gone and the sweet-voiced reciter has been paid, I leave Abid and the male consolation takers on the steps without a word. I do not bother to swing round to the women's section to bid salaam to Khalto Faiza and the females. Tugging at my tie, peeling off my blazer, I sprint to the Burakmobile and, in the steadily dwindling traffic, drive northwest across the Nile to the farthest all-night Cilantro's I can think of.

It is midnight in Mohandessin by the time I settle into a kind of berth fashioned of the curvature at one end of the space. Frank Sinatra is warbling in the background, and, backdropped by the Mustafa Mahmoud Mosque, the arresting face of a woman your age flashes right in front of me as she's on her way out.

Occasionally, a face encountered by chance promises the kind of wholeness over which a man at forty-five realizes he is nothing but a mound of shards.

She is sparrowlike, dark, her pointed face balancing lithe curves and an avian timidity at once humble and haughty. Dressed all in black, she evokes not Mouna but the gorgeous fennec fox that, on Mouna's insistence, back in March 2011, we wound up burying in the garden by the mango tree.

But before I've fully registered what's happening the woman is gone. Coming into my line of vision is a teenage girl who has slid her Blackberry under her hijab so it hangs fastened to her ear, though she is no longer speaking. The sight reminds me of Mouna saying *abortive modernity*. Along with *sectarian cesspool* and *idol worship*—one of Baba's refrains, remember? But until March 2014, while telling me how the Jumpers had changed her, Mouna had never uttered the expression, not once.

And gazing at the girl, Shimo, I suddenly see them. They're everywhere I've looked for nearly three years now. In the mayhem of pedestrians and vehicles warring for space. In the haphazard parking and the cratered asphalt. In the calmness of bikers balancing gas cylinders on their heads. In the microbuses' wrath. In knife-marked delinquents dispensing garlands at car windows. And in niqab-clad women precariously poised behind Vespa drivers, their legs to one side while the things galumph through stalling traffic. Even in my editor in chief's voice when he lies—its pitch rising ever so subtly, its tempo dropping—I see the blank, stricken faces of the Jumpers.

I look out past the teenager. This is not Agouza. But, thinking I was shaking off the funerary rites, I've wound up at another of the deceased's haunts. Tante Hudhud lives just across the street from here. Surely I saw her at the condolence ceremony? More vivid in my memory is Mouna dropping by her house on her way to or from this mosque complex, so far from where I took her consolation yet so similar. I picture her handing in our annual zakah money at the collection office, accompanying her working-class connections to the charity clinic, taking off her shoes on the threshold of the women's prayer zone.

After the army decided to let us stage an open-ended sit-in in Tahrir Square, Shimo—no one was going home until Mubarak stopped being president—regime cronies began to organize counterprotests.

That's when I first heard the expression *honorable citizens*. They were honorable citizens while we at Tahrir Square were traitors, you understand. The spot they chose to rally was outside the Mustafa Mahmoud Mosque. That's where they vilified and orchestrated offensives on us. And it really amused me how troubled Mouna was by their choice of venue. Everyone knew the protesters gathered there were idlers and thugs in the employ of policemen, politicians, businessmen. But I wouldn't have thought they could so completely unhinge her faith in a favorite spot.

She still hadn't declared her support for the protesters I was risking my position at the newspaper to be among. But those protesters' archenemies were enough to rule out the presence in the mosque's vicinity of any angels or saints. It made her question where she'd been handing out the portion of her money God prescribed for the poor.

—Alors, she managed to articulate one morning after I found her

33

gabbling and trembling on the veranda. *Those dependents* at Tahrir Square are foreign-funded conspirators, bon? Their aim is to bring down the state, as the official channels keep saying. Our Lord still looks on them more kindly than the sharmoota's sons in Mustafa Mahmoud, n'est-ce pas?

—That's why you look so bothered, my lovely. But, Mouna—

—Imagine praying there for so long. Imagine thinking of it as so full of baraka!

—I guess that means no God-fearing person ever worked at the Mustafa Mahmoud Mosque in the first place, I said, barely containing my giggles. Pity about all that zakah, then.

—Don't you dare start with me, son of Amin!

For a moment, as I burst out laughing, I thought she was going to cry.

Then she gave one of her all-purpose French sighs: *Hein!*

—It wouldn't be your fault anyway, I said.

—But I used to feel such calmness in that mosque. However can an evil place inspire such ghastly calmness, hein?

Arwa will not visit again for six weeks, and then only to announce that the Omda is making the journey from the saraya. That's what Arwa calls the Abu Zahra village residence, just outside Shoubra, never mind how unpalatial it is. The Omda is leaving the saraya for the house of the newlyweds in Shoubra itself. By now Arwa is sure Mansour Effendi has a problem, something she has suspected since the day she took hold of Bara's ear and started hissing, like the Quran's Sneaking Whisperer, making the mother desperate to marry Amna off before she too fell into the well of wrongdoing:

—A schoolgirl Amna's age got pregnant. Because her family didn't find her a suitable husband. A schoolgirl Amna's age got pregnant, Neina. Her picture was in the newspaper. A schoolgirl Amna's age!

Last week she had the Omda pay Mansour Effendi a visit at the diwan where, surrounded by large, armed men in galabiyas, the groom confessed to temporary difficulties he had neglected to mention, he insisted, because they were temporary. And he was in the process of dealing with them.

It figured. Not even putting up a fight, the groom's family had paid full bride money without receiving any dowry. They not only provided the wedding jewelry, Amna's shabka—two shabkas, in fact, though no one knew of Arwa's—but also paid for the weeklong wedding and furnished the apartment as well.

It was this that made Wahib Bey bless the union, postponing the fuss that must be made about there being no actual loss of virginity.

Mansour Effendi's family has been so accommodating because they have something to hide.

Yet Amna knows nothing about this while she plants her lips on her sister's brow at the double door. Her eyes making one last, envious tour of the interior, Arwa steps out almost as soon as she has arrived. Asking if Amna is pure one last time—Arwa has been following Amna's menstrual cycle by phone for some reason—she announces that the Omda feels it's time to visit and is on his way.

Now Amna is doing a pirouette toward the tombstone radio, an Arvin marvel she values above all else in the apartment. The wooden object, somewhat larger than her torso, sits on the Victorian console by the salon door. Amna has placed it opposite the mahogany secretaire where she has taken to writing Amin chatty, chaste love letters signed Mouna, which she burns unsent.

Humming the tune of "Ana Hawet," speeding it up to make it cheerful, Amna belly dances her way to the console. A girl in love. She fiddles with the knobs in search of a love song, but all that comes forth in the metallic timbre of midcentury telephony is orotund oratory and histrionic applause.

The high, edgy voice is familiar, but it takes Amna five sentences to figure out that this is Nasser making a speech. To her chagrin it is being broadcast over and over on both channels.

—That is why today I signed, and the Cabinet approved, the following law. A decision by the President of the Republic: to nationalize the Universal Suez Ship Canal Company.

Nasser is quiet while the people explode.

—In the name of the nation. But there is too much noise for him to continue.

—In the name of the nation, he repeats. The President of the Republic. Article Number 1: The Universal Suez Ship Canal Company is hereby nationalized as an Egyptian public limited company, he starts.

But the cheering is so intense it sounds as though he's already wrapping up. Amna can tell there will be no love songs on the radio today.

An impudent turd that will stop up progress—she balks again, willing her body to go on dancing while the applause winds down.

For a split second the nonstop noise maker turns into an actual tombstone above which the insect-like bird is fluttering. This time she can smell something. An ancient, rank odor, full of fear. So that when Nasser's voice comes back to read out the rest of the Suez Canal Law, a clack of jaws is all she hears.

She manages one last swing of the hips as she kills the broadcast. But it is half-hearted, mournful.

Amna cannot know this is the day her new life starts, the day the canal dug for khawagas with fellahin sweat and blood comes home to the fellahin. There will be war, but Nasser will emerge the stronger. There will be an exodus of practically all Egyptians other than the fellahin. She doesn't know that, thanks more to Nasser than to anyone else in this world, her next ten years will be a decade in hell. But the day is soaked in that ancient, rank thing and she can tell. By the time she sits at her secretaire, the giant fly of two weeks before is again circling her hair.

That day both panels of Mansour Effendi's door must be open to admit the Omda. Having gone down on his knees to undo the latch on the permanently closed panel, the bookkeeper rises with difficulty. He steps back citing a litany of welcomes, gesturing with his hand. He trips and steadies himself, trips again. Without a word the squat man-mountain looks ahead, inert, a dinosaur at the marital threshold. Two black-clad crones hang by his shoulders like a flaccid pair of wings.

Looking on from a distance, Amna wonders about the crones. The one on the right stirs up some blocked-out memory, a tightness in the midriff, she doesn't know what. She has risen from the secretaire to greet her brother. As if taking leave to go over and kiss his hand, as she knows she should, she solicits the Omda's eyes. He betrays no sign of recognition. Amna stops in her tracks.

Modestly dressed in a Chanel-style suit, her hair in a bun, her peachy cheeks are already stress-flushed. A scaled-down vision of domestic decency.

Framed by the worked-wood doorway, the Omda looks like a power-pressed version of the Bey, the height squashed into girth. He affects neither the baladi finery of his henchmen—who are conspicuously absent—nor the European effendi ensemble his father and brother-in-law display. Over what looks like a white shirt that comes down to his ankles, he wears a genuine Savile Row blazer of striped gray flannel. His sweat-drenched turban is wrapped round a tarboosh, not the usual skullcap.

With his elbow against the glazing, one hand is reaching for something in the jacket. A gesture on pause. Gold Swank cufflinks complement a Rolex Oyster above the scented handkerchief in the other.

At this point Umair is thirty-eight, the same age as the Zaim, who looks both younger and older than his years. With his brand of sartorial fusion, his Godfatherly cool, Umair too is outside biological time. Maybe that's not what you'd expect him to look like, someone who's been to London and Paris as well as Sudan, who's built a harem and sired an army, who's killed over twenty peasant souls with his own hands. He looks almost generic, like a comic-book character or a heathen god. Feudal ferocity personified.

Fear takes hold of Amna gradually, after the still frame dissolves into Umair's hand emerging with a Smith & Wesson Model 36 revolver. Grimy gray, almost square in its chunkiness. He places it flat on the palm of his Rolex hand, then moves it to the other. He keeps moving it from hand to hand as he responds to Mansour Effendi:

—May your house be full, good man. His voice is a deep, dry monotone. Rest your feet, I am happy as I am. God willing, I have come to reassure myself of the well-being of our daughter Amna.

She's breathing in gulps, the tension in her sugar-doll shoulders easing momentarily. With a groveling grin, Mansour Effendi takes a step forward, almost crashing into the Omda while he begins to say something.

—But I have reason to worry, Umair cuts him off. And Amna's shoulders tense again.

In the cramped, dust-coated attic there is barely enough room for one person to stretch out on the floor. But on Mouna's penultimate night, I stride up there and, baring my nether half, lie back in what room there is.

With an effort of mind I push away my baby sister, strike through the easy, chaste affection, the wan protectiveness, amused admiration. I break the unseen manacles that bind and keep us apart, so that with the force of desire I can picture your dough-colored skin, the violin of your torso, the nipples hardening through your T-shirt while you text braless on a summer night.

I suppose I remembered the scene that brought about your estrangement from our mother so many lifetimes ago. Can you believe it's barely been five years since you left the country? I remembered the scene and resolved to break ranks with reality to stage my own private revolution, in its honor. Anyway it is your absence that draws me up there. And my need to break free of all that gives order to reality.

If there is anyone on earth who can understand this, it is you. The revolution had brought us even closer in my heart than we were at my Cairo University graduation when you were four and, raising you in my hands, I blew on the back of your neck as you took my diploma from the professor handing it out on stage. So many years later, when the revolution fails to change the world, my body and your memory are all I have.

This is my way of reaching out while Mouna is still here: a kind of contact ritual.

For a month now my body has been made of wood. I feel parted from myself, and I don't want to recall the past or project into the future. I want to reinvent the world so that, for a moment while Mouna is still alive, I can return to myself in your company.

It is not just that I miss you. I miss not wanting her to die.

Forcing food down her throat and collecting her excrement, giving her Valium and morphine. Every hour it is more unbearable knowing I can't keep up these routines. Not going in to work, wrangling with cabin fever.

Well-wishers are still showing up daily, and I am tired of entertaining them, people who can never know Mouna, who will never have an inkling of what happened to her for as long as they live.

I hate Abid for his evasions and lies. I notice I don't hate him for what he did to my fellow protesters, only for what he's done to himself through the years. Seven decades after the official abolition of titles, in the interior ministry policemen are addressed as bey regardless of rank. Grieving for my little buddy Bido, I hate this thirty-nine-year-old bey's regimented piety, his fake concern, the cold, inviolate violence that lines his face.

I miss you, I hate Abid, and I reflect on Mouna's destiny. I reflect on her destiny in the light of the revolution. Or perhaps it is the other way round: Mouna's destiny tells me why the revolution has failed.

It tells me why, within four years of one military president for life stepping down, a new military president for life is already consecrated. And while that happens no one notices women are jumping out of windows.

So it is not just that I reflect on her destiny or that wherever I look I see the Jumpers.

I can't sleep much but every time I do—always next to her on her four-poster bed—I open my eyes to the same thought: Mouna will be no longer. And so while she still is I want to do the impossible, if only to neutralize the shock of all the impossibilities that overtook the last four years of her life.

That is why it's neither Aya nor any other partner, actual or possible, that I choose to focus on. Only you. That, and the fact that it started with you right here. You leaving the country, the revolution, the Jumpers, the Cataclysm—it all started with you up in the attic on the way to the roof, Shimo.

But in the end no matter how much I obliterate, the world stays as it is. The comrade, the surrogate daughter whose arrival in the world when I was fourteen felt like a gift, remains haram. Admired but stubbornly undesired. I can only miss you.

Yet as my hand glides down I am involuntarily summoning another. And before that other, to my alarm once I recognize her, my faltering hardness immediately takes heart.

In black and white she stands, a diminutive figure, leaning forward and looking up. With childlike concentration she sticks out her tongue, the specter of a smile dancing about her temples. Her go-go boots are arranged one over the other, bare knees bent at different angles, the front one in line with her pointed chin. Her hands on her hips accentuate the breasts pushing up through her polka dot dress, framing her haunch. Nothing moves me more than the thought of my lips closing in on the heart-shaped face below her towering chignon. The round lips, the dimpled cheeks, the enormous eyes . . .

They say that, after it is sated, the male animal is always sad. As though doing penance, I go straight from the attic to Mouna's bedroom.

When I walk in she is reading, holding a tattered paperback with her one remaining good hand, balancing it on her fractured hip to turn the page.

The morning after she came back from hospital, I hauled Baba's architect's lamp up from behind his Arabic Olympia typewriter in the basement and clamped it onto the table by the side of the bed. In its sharp light her animated expression belies how hollow her cheeks have become, how emaciated the rest of her body with so much broken bone and ruptured tendon.

Examining her in silence, I can see her face is not heart-shaped but triangular, with jutting jawbones where the plump cheeks should be. One eye is permanently half-closed. The other seems much smaller than I remember it. The rare hazel of the irises is diluted and darker, nearly brown. Her nose has doubled in size, and her lips hang shriveled over the flattened chin, straight and expressionless.

It shocks me how meager she's become. Mouna was always small, but now she looks like a portable stand for the massive neck support over her shoulders, a human accessory. Something in the way she reclines seems to mimic her posture in the picture. Her lopsided joints and her bandaged, shaved head; her feet propped up on cushions; her sagging, heaving chest. A macabre echo of the image that moved me.

Still, at least she is reading. She's been reading since she came home from the Salam Hospital on the Nile Corniche, and that's good.

A hip replacement, open aortic surgery, and two weeks in intensive care. But, even as death beckons, there's not the slightest inclination to worship. The event that sent Mouna to hospital that final time, which Abid, lying, calls *the accident*, had been very serious. That's why I call it the Cataclysm—the way the deluge is referenced in the Bible. Because it restarts creation. Anyway, since it happened Mouna has not recited the Fatiha, uttered the Shahada, or held a holy book in her hand. I know you'll find this hard to believe.

Our mother on her deathbed, religionless.

Behind his horn-rimmed glasses, the bookkeeper's eyes are darting from the Omda's blank face to his wife's and back again. By the time she gets his attention his posture will have slackened. Already his grin is solidifying into a frown of disgust.

—With your permission, Umair points back with his thumb, moving neither his eyes nor his head, these good women shall have some time alone with her. Tayyib?

Amna's cheeks flush deeper as she battles to make contact. A vision of tormented beauty. The shoulders, the vulnerable neck, the tight waist, and the diminutive haunch. She's no longer breathing while Umair stares her down. She shifts her weight from one foot to the other, lips drawn, hazel eyes enormous. Desperate enough to seek out Mansour Effendi's eyes. But, registering his doming dumbness, she turns to one, then the other of the crones. Now as later they are hard and dry, bulletproof.

—It is not my place to say, Mansour Effendi, Umair lets out, still motionless. But you may leave the house for half an hour if you wish. God willing, we shan't be longer than half an hour.

Umair looks at Amna then. For the first time since his appearance he cranes his neck, the shadow of a smirk ever so slightly arching his handlebar mustache. Inadvertently she looks away, unable to handle the Omda's attention now she has it.

And I am so wrapped up in her face I don't see Mansour Effendi's portly frame making its egregious exit, positively back-bent. I don't notice the Omda signaling to his wings with four fingers as it passes, nor the wings detaching till they have snapped onto Amna's arms. What I do notice is Amna being led into the bedroom like a drugged inmate. The unamplified afternoon azan rises through the shuttered windows, a miracle of melody. But I don't hear it till I see the light from the shutters spreading in such a way that it makes the bedroom cavernous, like a psychotropic substance savaging the scene.

And not until it seeps into Amna's nostrils do I smell the rank odor of ancient, unwashed flesh.

In the psychotropic cavern, without a word they seat her bodily on the edge of the bed, pull her panties past her Baby Doll pumps and deftly part her thighs. Raising her skirt over the suspenders above her knees, they press down her shoulders as if to prepare her for copulation in the valedictorian position.

Upskirts, I can't help thinking. Schoolgirls. Stockings. BDSM? Tiny teen!

Meanwhile the Omda, still blank faced, is closing both panels of the door on his own. He has replaced the Smith & Wesson in one inner pocket. Fishing a BBB Bulldog pipe out of another, he sits on the rococo sofa under the high ceiling to load and light it.

In the pornographic cavern, she's too dazed to struggle against being manhandled—womanhandled, lifehandled—to the cooing call to prayer. She doesn't know what's happening but she knows she'll tell it to Amin. She'll find out what it is then tell him, and he will understand no matter how hard. But when her hair hits the mattress, eventually to come undone, the light shifts again and she identifies the face she sighted.

I see the terror stiffen, then loose and jiggle her body. I follow the contortions of her face.

To the cooing melody miracle, rank flesh in her nostrils, Amna is reliving a time when she had no breasts. Barely eight years ago, when she had neither breasts nor a period. She was placed in the same position that day, held down screaming with them parted, her knees above her breasts while she lay on her back, the glint of a metal object bobbing between her thighs.

The woman on the right, the one who stirred up a blocked-out memory at the door—she was crouched down as now, her face enclosed by the U of Amna's groin, as if poised to eat out her charge.

The woman was no younger then, no less rank. Her odor was ameliorated not by Virginia Gold pipe smoke but by myrrh and frankincense. The Abu Zahra household's regular sheikh was reciting the Quran, sheer braying. For some five minutes the woman stared into the cerise baby hamster that was Amna's vulva. She scaled the muzzle and the limbs with one hand so she could cut them clean with the other. Then, to the braying Quran, she came down again and again, maiming the precocious creature. Bringing forth cascades of gore.

In the psychotropic cavern, in the pornographic cavern, this time there is no paring knife in the woman's hand. She uses two fingers that seem to detach from the rest of her body, like dead twigs reanimated. It takes only a second. Then, on the sheet placed under Amna, folded thick—how come she never noticed it?—there is a small amount of blood, much less than last time.

There is also less pain. No giant housefly or self-erasing flash-forward. Beyond that moment of recognition, hardly any fear at all. But that isn't why she has been quiet. Apart from her mournful squirming, an involuntary reaction, Amna has been totally quiet. But it isn't for lack of either blood or pain.

It's because no one told her the pellicle could be perforated without a prick, losing her life's capital in female company.

It's because she really, irrevocably lost that capital. Even if he chooses to marry her, she has nothing now to give the one she loves.

It's because they ripped her off on the one thing they'd brought her up to value.

It's because she has imagined that moment and she always imagined it differently. She imagined the pain enfolded in an embrace, a sense of being contained balancing out the infraction. She imagined a weight on her breast, and a smoky, musky chest interfacing with that weight.

In our one-story house there is a disused attic that can only be reached through the landing on the way to the roof. You must remember it. For your upcoming birthday your boyfriend had given you a battery-powered toy and, because your room was too close to the other two bedrooms to feel private, you waited till Mouna and I were asleep then went up there to try it out. You had miscalculated.

The dawn azan sounded a few minutes into your frolic and, unaware that it had woken Mouna, you made no attempt to muffle the buzzing of the smooth silver object, which looked like a bullet or an egg. Mouna was on her way to the bathroom. In those days if the azan roused her she got up to observe the dawn salah. The gasps that escaped your breathing must have suggested an emergency, but I've always thought she might never have noticed if not for the noise your buttocks made as they brushed the floor.

When she opened the door your knees were above your breasts, a string of liquid like a rat's tail slithering up your mound of Venus. Your panties were hanging off one of the heavy books by your head, and the hem of your nightie flapped rhythmically over your belly.

At the time you were days short of twenty-seven, the sexiest person I'd ever seen live. But Mouna swears she mistook you for an ugly old crone. Your face, she said, looked ghoulish.

In the faint night light from below, I wonder how much she actually made out, how much the shock impressed on her. I don't know if she ever discovered the source of that steady, buzzing drone. I simply see her gaping. And it occurs to me that under the circumstances she might've screamed, making a point of waking me—to shame you. She might've bent down to slap or pull you up by the hair. All she did was step back out and close the door behind her. But in her haste she slipped and crashed into the balustrade. I woke all the same.

Not that I could've stopped anything anyway, but I wish I had realized what the incident portended. A couple of months before, Mouna had finally identified the source of her searing bellyache: a uterine tumor, huge and sprawling but thankfully benign. It hadn't been a fortnight since she had her hysterectomy and she was still feeling sorry for herself. Now she stopped talking to you. I wondered how long it would take for the standoff to end this time. You were both so stubborn, even with my mediation it could take weeks for one of you to grunt a greeting at the other after a scene. And this time Mouna's silence seemed to come from a deeper, graver place.

More than once that week, while she pretended you weren't there, I took you aside, weighed down your shoulders with my elbows, and looked into your eyes:

—Tell me, wennabi, virtuous sister. The other night when our mother backed away from the attic as if she'd seen a giant housefly, did you manage one last climax before she hit the floor?

—I see that's all you rack your brains over, big brother. My climaxes. Maybe you'd do better to think about someone else's for a change?

You spoke in that savagely steady voice, loud enough for her to hear. But even as you swaggered away I could see you turn crimson. If I could've told you how endearing that little extra color on your cheeks was to me then, how much more tenderness it made me feel for you. But we'd taken on those rival roles three months or so before, as soon as I moved in: big brother and virtuous sister. I laughed with you at Mouna's horror, too. But it never occurred to me she might be feeling the weight of her own life when on Abid's next visit I overheard her mutter to him:

—That curb-born sister of yours. Had she been purified like a respectable family girl, I wouldn't have lived to see her so derailed.

He was nodding sagely when I walked in, but I knew she couldn't mean what she had said. Your not being cut was hardly unusual for a city girl—even city girls of Mouna's generation were mostly spared—and anyway she was against the practice as a rule.

She had never commented on you being the only girl in both extended families who had never at any point felt the need to wear the hijab. Of course, since before I first moved out—a few months before Baba died at millennium's end, when I was thirty and you were seventeen—the two of you hadn't stopped fighting.

There was your drinking and bhango smoking, all-night raves, magic mushrooms in the desert. There were your boho chic outfits and alien cosmetics. Then the profanities that clung to your tongue like gum. *Deen keda*, your catchphrase, especially. Because while there is nothing obscene about either *the religion* or *of it*, together the two words make a gloriously insolent blasphemy.

Since the age of twelve you'd wanted to finance yourself. To her relief, even though you spent the night out of the house as often as in, for practical reasons you never quite managed to live alone. But you'd always wanted to and she'd commented on the disgrace that would bring on your father's name. I remember because her mention of Baba especially infuriated you. Little did she know you were so sick of this country you were already saving money and applying to US PhD programs. Gathering references, taking tests.

How often had you brutalized strangers who voided filth in your ear or tried to touch you. For this you wound up once in the hospital, thrice at police stations where if not for Abid's name you would've been harassed for real. Each time Mouna nearly had a heart attack.

Abid might've been the khawal you and I disliked for being an officer at State Security. A husband never seen in his wife's company and a father whose two small boys were worse off than soldiers under his command. But he was also the only one of her three children who, having *completed his religion* by marrying, had stayed married and had two boys—even if she never got to see them.

Now I know it wasn't the sacrilege of you gyrating to the call to prayer that stunned her into her fall. It wasn't the shock of seeing you on the floor, the buzz echoing off your groin, or the scandalous scent of your sex. What stunned her was the sight of your knees above your breasts, a glint of metal bobbing between your thighs.

—⁘

When she has recovered enough Amna emerges from the cavern in dishabille. Except for her stockings she is barefoot, and she treads so softly on the black and white tiles no one can hear her approach. The azan has ended. The light is sober. Even the street has gone quiet.

By now the crones are at the door, waiting, but the Omda is still smoking his Bulldog on the sofa: Budai in a bed of plush. Looking up as he exhales a vortex of fume, all at once he finds the bloodied wraith floating over his head.

—The family's sharaf, he starts to say.

But he never finishes his sentence.

When the two women left the room Amna's mouth was gratingly dry and she started sucking on her thumb to moisten it. The sputum under her tongue was pleasant, her throat begged for it, but she did not swallow.

Bending over to gaze into Umair's face, now, just as he utters the *f* in *sharaf*, she ejaculates the thimbleful of spit onto his forehead. The force of the assault makes him wince. Spit dribbles into his eye. It soaks his moustache, wets the stem of his pipe.

Cumshot, I'm thinking. Facial, femdom—humiliation.

The thick skin of his face, close shaved, was stone-smooth when he arrived. Now it's crisscrossed with grooves like a hilly landscape with fallow fields. He looks apoplectic or pleading, depending on which part of the terrain you tread. He looks helpless and hollowed out. His first expression of the day.

—You dirty little—in high staccato. The family's, he begins again, no longer deep or dry, no longer monotone. Tayyib!

In the leaden, lumbering way large people have of getting up, he's leaning on the sofa's arm to stand. By the time he makes as if to slap her Amna has raised her skirt, stepping back to give him a better view of her lower half. A little blood, rust brown, has coagulated on her thigh. The rest is streaming to her knee like a drying brook.

Deliberately, she dips two fingers in the source. They come out bright, alive with shrieking redness. She brings them to her eyes, as if communing with the color. Then she steps forward to press them square onto his lips, so nimbly he has no time to recoil.

—Bas bas, bas bas, she rasps. The family's sharaf.

The crones are still made of stone.

—Magnoona! Umair is expectorating, wiping his mouth with the back of his hand and vigorously, violently expectorating. Magnoona!

He pretends his foot is stuck so he can look down. He won't admit it to himself, but when he turns to her, he faces something he'd rather never have to see.

While he finally finds his feet, casting the pipe aside, he has reminded himself of the loaded pistol in his pocket. He knows he can kill her with impunity. It would upset Wahib Bey, perhaps—the money it would cost to keep it quiet. But he would no longer have to look at her. She could be buried in the village before nightfall.

—The family's sharaf? Amna asks in the same emaciated voice. Wennabi?

He knows it can be done, yet the look on her face tells him she knows it too. And doesn't give a tarboosh's tassel.

It is this look that sends the Omda off. The grief, the hatred, the bottomless letdown on his little sister's face. He can't bring himself to touch her, but no coherent sentences are forthcoming. So, after several more attempts at harsh words he picks up his pipe and wipes his face with his handkerchief. He mumbles *Magnoona* one more time, shoos away his crones, and chugs out. As if to quarantine the inmate, he closes both panels of the door behind him. But the look on Amna's face remains.

It is there when Mansour Effendi returns and she confronts him, not patting him on the back when he breaks down. It is there when she packs her trunk, arranging with the doorman to bring the mahogany secretaire to her father's. It is there when Arwa comes jingling in, followed by Hagga Hafiza with her white veil. No one can do anything about it. And when she arrives at the Abu Zahras' in the middle of the night and in an absolutely unthinkable provocation bursts straight into the Bey's bedroom to find him sleeping and switches on the light screaming, *Wake up*, the look on Amna's face is there.

The bridal wraith who spent her wedding night without sex or sleep has genuinely stopped caring. And it terrifies him. Too shocked to beat her for waking him, Wahib is astonished when he notices her making eye contact, addressing him in a tone she has never used before:

—I will not stay married to that eunuch. You're welcome to kill me if you prefer. But I will not go back to that house, ya Baba. D'accord? I will be divorced from Mansour.

I don't suppose Amna is aware of what is happening, but the fact that Umair and Arwa have done this to her with Wahib and Bara's blessing makes her invincible. Her time as a young wife and meeting Amin have given her some knowledge of the world, some confidence. And now that she has lost all respect for her family it is easy to state her conditions. She isn't afraid anymore.

Amna will tell herself it was Amin's love that enabled her, against impossible odds, to leave the marital house and go to college. Without pretending to be someone's wife, to live as she liked. But it isn't Amin's love that frees Amna. It is two twigs digging into her in a marital bedroom-turned-pornopsychotropic cavern, the day the Suez Canal comes home to the fellahin.

From that day till their last, Amna will look both the Omda and her Abla in the eye, wordlessly telling them to eat khara, feeling only a vague repulsion in their presence. The hazel above her snub nose bores through Bara's fleshy cheeks and makes Wahib's aquiline nose quiver. To make it more acceptable, they will all call her a magnoona. They know she is no magnoona but she shows them something they'd rather never have to see. She shows them what she thinks of them—what they are. And it terrifies them.

—⁘—

In the relative seclusion of our one-story house, right after Mouna found you in the attic, you decided to celebrate your birthday. Bringing all your friends along. The boyfriend who had given you that toy among them. The hilarious, wiry singer with dreadlocks named Zengy—have you been in touch with him at all since you left? Everyone arrived at sunset, just as Mouna was leaving for a long evening class at the Fatah Mosque. I remember two androgynous figures in denim overalls carrying a cake that spewed firecrackers at the halved blood orange of the sun.

By the time Mouna came back you'd all banded together under the mango tree—I counted eleven of you—passing a bottle among yourselves in the dark. When she stepped through the gate Zengy was doing a handstand with the spliff in his mouth. Right behind you the cake-carrying pair, who turned out to be a couple, were rolling on what grass there was, passionately kissing.

I'm sure she could hear the music and the voices but she didn't pay any attention at first. She was heading to the door when she glimpsed something out of the corner of her eye. I could tell because she abruptly turned her head, then she stopped and looked hard. I held the smoke in suspense. Mouna sighed, audibly, then resumed her quiet shuffling—outside my line of sight.

Suddenly there was this roar, *Shaimaaaa*, and she was running at you as I'd never in my life seen her run, sprinting like some Pious Mama superhero with her cloak flapping behind her like a cape. And I cracked up so much I bent over and slapped my thighs.

—You, I remember her turning to me at one point. You should be ashamed of yourself.

Before you'd had a chance to get up off the floor—as though in a film, the music ceased—Mouna was hunched over picking things up: bags, hats, individual shoes, substance stashes wrapped in foil and cellophane. She would briefly inspect the item and spit before hurling it as far as she could over the hedge. Whenever she bumped into someone she would glare, pushing or pulling them in the direction of the gate.

—If you want to be a sharmoota, be a sharmoota, she was telling you with relative calm, her voice the only sound now. Be the biggest sharmoota in the history of Egypt, ya habibti. Just do it away from here, d'accord? Don't let your sewage stink up my house.

That night I found out you'd already been accepted to the PhD program of your heart's desire—computer science at Stanford. You were just waiting for the visa to come through. You hadn't told anyone, not even Zengy. For fear of jinxing it, you said. You were supposed to leave in August, four months from now.

—But since I've been kicked out of the house, big brother, I guess I'll aim to be there as soon as I can.

We were across a kitchen table at Zengy's, past four in the morning. The trap musician looked crestfallen standing by the door, saying nothing apart from *Can I get you anything, Nour* at five-minute intervals. And every time I tried to hug you, you bristled.

—You don't have to do that, I said, you really don't.

On my way to Zengy's I'd packed you a suitcase of clothes, just as you had instructed. In the next two weeks I would bring you another three cases and two huge boxes: *the essentials*, you called them. I would inform Mouna you were doing a PhD in America. And, though it left her speechless for a little while, she seemed resigned. But I didn't believe you would never come back.

—Mouna was crying her eyes out when I left, I said now. You know how much you weigh in her balance. She didn't mean to—

—Call me a sharmoota in front of all my closest friends? Call them sewage and tell me to drain them out of her house?

—You must've realized how offended she would be by people taking drugs and making out there. It was as if you were testing her, ya Shimo.

—Deen keda, you said, and your voice trembled for the first time. I was testing to see if I existed, ya Nour. For ten years I've lived with Mouna as an adult. Since Baba died. And for ten years the only thing she could see was a spoiled little slut—a kind of Westernized embarrassment. But you know what? I think I've figured it out now. Since Baba died she's just resented me, hasn't she? I mean, I don't know much about Mouna's life before I was born. She's supposed to have struggled for her independence, right? Stayed faithful to the man she married against her family's wishes while he was a political prisoner, then devoted herself to bringing up her children. Like a true Egyptian woman. Being a mother as a mother should be. A fucking matriarch. A medieval-minded matriarch, big brother. And so she looks at me and she sees something lesser, something privileged and irresponsible, incapable of motherhood. Something she was far, far too good to be at my age. But, you know what I've figured out? I'm actually the thing she was too cowardly and self-hating to be. I am the woman that—bowing down to religion, burying her head deep in the khara of all that subjection and subservience—Mouna could never be . . .

That night when you finally let me hug you, it was longer and harder than ever before. You gave me the implausible privilege of soaking my shirt in your tears. And, though I truly hurt for your sadness and fear, there was something uniquely gratifying about that. There was an intimacy, a mutual need that would come to feel almost like making love.

Your moving back into Maadi would not come up again. Though you could tell how much I wanted you to see Mouna, to make some kind of peace after that garden scene. It grew more and more urgent as your departure drew near, but that only fueled whatever it was that made you want to leave before you saw her. So that by the end, though you never quite cut me off, we were playing cat and mouse across Cairo.

I kept my promise of not discussing you with her. She never asked about you, that's how upset she was. But every few days I volunteered the information that you were safe. My tone had stayed apologetic since she saw me laughing, but now there was real sorrow in the way I looked at her and she saw it.

At the end you gave me a general idea of when you would be traveling, never the exact date. You point-blank refused to let me drive you to the airport. I suppose you were scared I would take the Burakmobile straight back to our one-story house off Road 9 and frog-march you into her bedroom?

—But you know I hate goodbyes, big brother, you would tell me the first time you called from California, three days after your phone went dead. Do you have any idea how painful that would've been?

While she stays at Wahib Abu Zahra's, Amna speaks her mind even to the Bey. Until Bara Hanim dies suddenly in 1957, Amna gives her long, merciless lectures on truth and justice. She incites her younger sisters to rebellion, shows no respect for her brothers except for the youngest, Mahmoud.

She doesn't really attend classes again—Soeur Laurette is confused by her unexpected reappearance, though all too happy to let her graduate—but she promptly sits for the Baccalauréat and passes it. Starting once the war is over in November, she takes the tram daily from Shoubra to the newly opened University of Ain Shams in Heliopolis. Where she has been accepted at the Faculty of Arts' French Literature Department. She hasn't told anyone, not even Amin. For fear of jinxing it, she says.

No one gives Amna money, but neither does she ask for it. She is the one who supports herself through college—first from the sale of her shabka, then from working as a French tutor—eventually becoming the only one out of seven Abu Zahra girls with a degree.

After lectures she spends time with Amin and her friends. She can come home when she pleases now she has told Bara Hanim that, well, if they prefer, she'd be happy to move out. It is too late to be rid of her, she knows. They'd rather her *wily waywardness* than people talking of a daughter of Wahib Abu Zahra's living alone with her hair undone. By the time she does move out of her father's—already a divorcée—Amna will have obtained a husband of her choosing.

By then Amin has invested the few hundred guineas' inheritance his elder brother forked over in a house off Road 9 in Maadi—a whitewashed cube with a crescent-shaped veranda that looks like a beach chalet except taller. Like a signpost on the road to Helwan, it is the only residence within several kilometers' radius. Who would've thought, looking at the spottily paved desert all around, that within ten years it will be first among equals and, within twenty, one of a handful remaining davids resisting the goliath of apartment blocks replacing the villas and bungalows of Maadi's original treed avenues?

As yet our one-story house is barely furnished, but Amna is eager to move in with Amin. She is a third-year student, then—a junior. And she has been divorced for a year and a half.

I know we never had much to do with Mouna's siblings except for Khalto Faiza, but you'll know Khalo Mahmoud from the way she talked about him. The policeman who died in a train accident? That was right after Bara Hanim died. He was only thirty-five. But it wasn't the only reason she loved him so much more than the others.

It was Mahmoud who volunteered to release her from that hold, once he realized what was going on. Biding their time, neither Wahib nor Umair did anything even though they realized how easy it would be to persuade Mansour Effendi to let her go. One day, wearing his police uniform, Mahmoud paid the bookkeeper a visit at the diwan.

—Our girl sacrificed herself for your manliness, he said eventually, smiling his policeman's smile, even though God knows her marriage was never consummated. Mahmoud paused, giving Mansour time to nod. We're happy to let you off all that would be due if you respond to our request for an official divorce. Deferred payment, alimony, expenses: we'll let you off all of that. But the very least you can do is respond to our request.

After the funeral, I dream of evil activists gliding through the streets aboveground, leaving behind spuming puddles of blood and excrement. Sometimes I see myself hunched over by the mango tree. You have just left and I am butt naked, howling with pain or desire. The look of grief and letdown is on your face, not Mouna's.

And I am so wrapped up in that look that, when it is over and I am ready to slip in next to her, I merely contemplate her face. Bending over her, neither touching her nor weeping, I stare into the vanishing wrinkles, the knots coming undone, shape-shifting outlines.

I do not know it yet, but before too long I'll be back in this room to look again at her body's resting place, empty of her now, and wonder: can these four posters really be the mythical bed on which, at the end of August 1958, Amin Abdalla Amin deflowered Amna Abu Zahra without having to break her hymen?

I do not know yet that this will be the moment I come to time after time, harrowed and hung up on history, my mother young enough to be my daughter tolling my libido like a bell. And if that sounds like an implausible conjunction, Shimo, it is because implausibility is the substance of the story I am resolved to tell.

I would stay wrapped up indefinitely, too, except that Mouna's astral body—something like that anyway—now appears to me on the bed. And, summoning back the Rembrandts in the hearse's windshield, rearranging her lineaments into a map of the world, her face changes as I gaze into it. Instantly, over and over, I realize she is reincarnating. As I stare down at the bed her avatars supplant each other at speed: grieving widow, betrayed lover, secret agent. Frustrated career woman, enraged daughter-in-law. Reborn mother at forty-four.

I can hardly believe she is this old when she has the daughter she has always dreamed of, light of her eye and last grape in the bunch: the sweetest and dearest.

Eventually, through a moment of peace when she looks young, almost unsullied, Mouna rests on the gleeful apostate avatar. It's as if, still there on the bed that no longer contains her, she is using her insensate face to tell me that all has ended well.

Over decades, instead of suffering the Bara and the Arwa within her, she had become a contemporary, correct copy of them. In that capacity she presided over a small tribe of our relations for fifteen years after Baba. She organized the money pools called *cooperatives*: ten participants each pay a thousand guineas a month for ten months, say, and every month one of them gets ten thousand. She advised on medical and religious matters, lent a hand in child-rearing, shared doctors' and butchers' phone numbers. And she pulled what strings she could to get fresh graduates jobs or obtain official documents through wasta.

But on her deathbed she could hardly recognize the close ones for whom she'd become the provident matriarch. Now her insensate face is telling me that, thanks if not to the revolution then to the Jumpers, the feisty French student returned at last.

In our house there is an attic where I follow in your footsteps, Shimo, doing penance once I am sated and sad. Suffering the premonition that tomorrow will indeed be the last day. Sleeping by the corpse when tomorrow comes. And, the day after tomorrow, watching the corpse washer strip and scrub its unbending contours. Foaming water in the crooks, the clefts, all the shame sites.

With Mouna's passing, I tell myself, the story has come full circle. The story of the revolution and how it changed her, which you missed, but also the story to which that railway image from 1963 belongs. And which begins to play out in my head the minute I go back up to the attic after the funeral.

If anyone can understand this, honestly.

I've lived here since my divorce in January 2010, Shimo, moving back in just in time for the climax of your lifelong feud with Mouna. I'd moved in not planning on staying longer than a few weeks, but it was left to me to comfort her when you suddenly moved out, and again after you got on that plane without saying goodbye. When I ended up staying longer and longer, I told myself it was to take care of Mouna. Then I told myself it was because I was depressed. But I was making excuses.

I suppose what the revolution did to her would've made me stay anyway. But the truth is that at some level I knew my marriage had failed because I was this woman's son. I'd moved out of Maadi just after meeting Aya, though we didn't marry until three years later. I was convinced I was free of Mouna when I did, but once I had a real partner I expected the same desperate, broken love Mouna had given me, and when I got something different I grew cold. A small but inexorable part of me had been determined to disappoint Aya exactly as Baba had disappointed Mouna as well. And, without once articulating it even to myself, I decided that staying on with Mouna was the remedy or the punishment I deserved.

With her passing I can finally look forward to moving along with my life—not just leaving Maadi—but only once I've told you both her stories. So that you too know about the Jumpers. Maybe one day you'll read my letters to your daughter, telling her they're from the uncle who became his own mother. Who, scraping the underside of the Egyptian revolution of 2011, realized this is what it was about.

The story has come full circle, I tell myself. And, thinking of your absence, certain as I'd never been of anything that you must know, I'm hunched over this keyboard writing you like a desperate correspondent filing a report directly from the battlefront.

A middle-aged man lost, going in circles around the women who have made me. And only your reading this holds any promise of arrival.

Your loving brother,
Nour

THE VERANDA

February 11, 2011: August 10, 1963

My beautiful, darling Shimo:

Four years after the revolution when I'm ready to move along, Mouna's insensate face is telling me that, thanks if not to the revolution then to the Jumpers, the seventeen-year-old who barged into Wahib Abu Zahra's bedroom shouting *Wake up* had returned at last. But, knowing where that girl would take the mother I love, how grateful can I be for her miraculous arrival?

Mouna and I didn't know it while we were burying the fennec fox, but by March 2011 the Jumpers were already throwing themselves out of windows. There would be hundreds of them as time passed. Starting in 2012, they take up Mouna's energy now that the stars of the movie *Revolution* have all let her down. Ya Allah, how absorbed she has been in that movie, the medieval-minded matriarch!

You've been estranged from her for nearly a year when the protesters first gather in Tahrir Square. Of course you assume she is against what's happening. The one time we talk I try to tell you. Something is changing in Mouna and she is turning to the demonstrators' side. But you shut off the moment she comes up, the way you always do.

—Nour, you groan, I don't want to know.

And from your voice I can picture the mortar of impatience hardening your cheeks. There is just no way I can explain that you do want to know, that you absolutely must know. When she encountered the Jumpers it was so natural and predestined, it felt as though she was simply stepping back on a road she had momentarily strayed from. Except the diversion had taken fifty years.

As she weaves through Masr Station, bleeding while she weeps, Nimo has the impression that at some point in the past she dreamt what is happening to her now. She dreamt she was carrying a black leather bag three times the size of her usual purse and rushing to the platform on her way to Alexandria, Amin Abdalla Amin's news-writer wife. Though in the dream she didn't know it was Susanne Qansuh's distress signal that was dragging her there, she could feel the humid heat of a summer noon exactly like this one. She knew she was going because something ghastly had happened.

Now she is consciously crying. For the child who would've been three this year and the uterus coming apart in her tummy and the hymen not broken by Amin. For the slight her body had borne when she let herself be seduced by a stranger. For the beautiful, stuttering boy now bloated and fish-eaten at the bottom of the Arabian Sea. And for the girl who introduced her to both of them, the terrifically unfortunate girl lying there in the clutch of rigor mortis, her sister broken beside her not knowing whom to call.

Over the hooting and the heaving she can make out Abd El Halim Hafez crooning some Nasser adulation, and his voice rakes up a disgust for her bleeding body that has been getting worse and worse since the operation she had four years ago. It wasn't exactly a coat-hanger affair, but it might as well have been.

Nimo doesn't know it is less than a year before Amin returns from the Wahat Prison, out in the middle of the Sahara, where he is serving ten years with hard labor. She doesn't know the person to return will be someone other than Amin. But, fatigued, frustrated, fed up with feeling unclean, she is no longer sure if she is crying for his absence or her infidelity.

In the first few weeks after Amin is gone, before her sister Faiza and Faiza's two children move in with her, Nimo wonders if Our Lord might be punishing her for not taking His rules too seriously. Especially when she realizes she is pregnant—what would it take to actually keep the baby? As she calculates her expenses, counting on her fingers with childlike concentration, the material meaning of her situation manifests.

With Faiza's destitution weighing on her conscience, wherever she goes she can smell Amin's indefinite absence as clearly and as hopelessly as a decomposing cadaver. For two years she suffers it so pervasively that the day she can place her hand on Amin's cheek for real, it's as if she is touching an absence. A notion of home and togetherness that is entirely abstract. A lie she told herself, called Mouna.

By the time she sees him—his first visit by anyone—Nimo has graduated and, with the aid of an army wasta courtesy of her intime Semsem, quickly found employment on the third floor of the newly opened Maspero headquarters. The Radio and Television Union to be, which she liked to call the Round Building. The biggest, quirkiest edifice she had ever seen in her life, which looks like a wedding cake in a nightmare.

Nimo works as a translator and news writer at Sawt El Umma, Voice of the Nation, which notwithstanding the first TV broadcast in July 1960 is still the nerve center of Egyptian media. And it's taken her this long to make that visit happen. Slowly maneuvering her way up the power pyramid through ever more meandering paths. Patiently seeking out information about *that group of incarcerated intellectuals.* Cautiously bringing up her situation with an older employee, a high-up secretary, the head of the news writing department.

Until one day she found herself face-to-face with Sameh Khairy, the man who started Sawt El Umma eight years before. And unsure whether his long-awaited summons would be about Amin, it rattled her to be standing before him.

She had never suspected there could be a working space this large for just one man, much less on the same floor as herself. Nor had she so much as glimpsed the room that housed Sameh Khairy's three secretaries, which led into his own. Even the secretaries' room was twice as large as the newsroom where she and six other people labored day and night with their indelible copying pencils over sheets of yellow, unlined paper. She waited for nearly an hour before the double door closed behind her. And it was all she could do not to goggle, stepping in.

Persian rugs submerged aureate furniture around an awfully elaborate desk. Hanging from the ceiling like a bad deed, an oversize crystal chandelier gave the impression of being inside a study at the royal residence, Saraya Abdeen.

Nimo registered a subtle difference, though. This wasn't so much an actual palace study as a peasant's idea of what a palace study looks like. A peasant who had ransacked palaces, it's true. But a peasant nonetheless.

—Sit down, ya Amna!

It was the same melodramatic baritone, at once soft-spoken and impassioned. It could be folksy or imposing as needed. As if for the first time, Nimo noticed it was also fake, wondering how in so many ears, in Semsem's ears especially, it could ring so true.

She was more distressed to see the legendary voice emanated not from the pensive, personable face she had always imagined but from the thick bovine features of a bald troll. A peasant who looks like the behim he tends, she caught herself thinking.

—So you want to visit a man, Sameh Khairy was saying. A man by the name of Amin Abdalla. A man by the name of Amin Abdalla who is locked up in the Revolution's dungeons.

Unsmiling, the Sawt El Umma director was obviously in less of a hurry than he pretended to be. But at least it's about Amin, she thought. He is getting there.

—A man who is a known communist, an enemy of our blessed Revolution—

—Ustaz Sameh—

—I haven't finished, ya madame!

She swallowed and looked down, the words *peasant* and *behim* looping percussively in her head. Her desperation became burlesque. There had been such pent-up unease that the abrupt admonition released a coiled spring and she was no longer intimidated, no longer in a state of supplication.

The rumor—probably started by the Mukhabarat themselves—was

that offices and houses, even streets were monitored for dissent with sound-recording equipment. Whether or not that confirmed it, it was a fact that even in his office Sameh Khairy spoke Socialist Union, as she called it: that strange new tongue.

But it was the nonchalance with which a glorified news reader could eliminate a man he didn't know that made her want to laugh. A man who was transparently his moral, let alone intellectual, superior. Then, having stamped that man's death warrant while leching over your thighs, your hips, your bust, the glorified news reader can go on to tell you off for interrupting him. This was so funny that when, evidently to make up for snapping at her, Sameh Khairy took a fraternal tone, she had to make a huge effort not to laugh.

—You have been working here in this grand new building for only two months, Amna. Yet in such a short time you have proved yourself to be a credit to the Revolution. That is why I have come to think of you as my little sister.

His beady eyes all but popped into her bra as he said this.

—I speak for your good alone, Amna. And I am telling you your work, your position in society is on the edge of the abyss. This man you want to visit, you must never vouch for such a person. And not just for reasons of self-preservation but also for the love of Egypt and by the dictates of patriotic sentiment. No, no, you must never vouch for him.

Releasing a laugh into her cupped hand, Nimo appeared to be retching. She sighed.

—However, Sameh Khairy continued after the shortest pause— and now Nimo felt he was mentally undressing her in earnest—as your older brother, but only as your older brother, I am aware that, a scourge and a sinner though he is, this man is also the husband to whom you owe loyalty and devotion . . .

She must've missed some of what he said after that. The next thing she knew they were both standing, facing each other on the way to the double door. On the pretext of a warm salaam, her hand in both of his was being made love to. Then he was leaning over her, his lips grazing her neck before she managed to slip out.

—Anyway, you have the number you will call. Major Ramsey, he knows. I am confident you understand. No one must ever hear of this. I am putting my neck out for my little sister. But I am also confident this is the last we shall hear of the man named Amin.

Not until she was in the corridor did Nimo feel the tears trickling off her jaw.

Later, four years after the revolution is over and I'm ready to move along, I see Mouna as I did at the time it all started. She's looking like a Russian doll in the flower-patterned, tent-like wimple she wears over her nightie so she can pray in bed. The morning paper is open in her lap, the small television on the dresser loud enough to reach the Corniche.

Since January 25, the first day of protests, Mouna has been following the news, replacing her daily diet of Syrian soap operas and celebrity preachers with images of the young flooding the streets and talk of a new age. It isn't as if she's suddenly become politicized at seventy-one, but unarmed protesters in the thousands forcing the police into hiding make her think.

Not once in fifty years has she felt it necessary to oppose the authorities. She's never liked the way things are run. Often she's actively hated people in power. But her logic is—who is she to question a whole country's fate? If you're privileged enough to have a life free from sickness and want, you should give thanks lest that life be taken from you. *God never told us to change the universe*, she used to yell at Baba.

Now the casualties, the asphalt crawling, and the old patriotic songs sound like practical prayers for a changed universe. And, watching, she marvels at the thought of Him answering them. She knows the older of her two sons is among the protesters while the younger schemes to have them shot. For hours she finds herself staring, petrified, at the screen, in turn grieving and ecstatic.

By the end of the third day of protests army tanks are rolling over the pedestrian crossings to take charge of Cairo. Halfway across town she cannot know they are shielding her forty-one-year-old son from police fire. But when she sees the boys and girls climbing astride the tank muzzles, chanting, Mouna grows emotional. More emotional than she's ever been listening to bearded fanatics speak of Allah's mercy, or imbibing the implausible tragedy of a fair young widow in Damascus. Too emotional to speak.

And in her speechlessness it dawns on her that God might be just as interested in righting wrongs as He is in displays of piety.

It is a cold February that year, especially cold among the scant furniture on the bare tiles of our house off Road 9.

Mouna has taken to using the same small copper tray Baba made his coffee on. Did you ever get to see that ritual of Amin's? Instead of his hourglass-shaped kerosene stove and conical coffee pot with a long handle, the tray now carries a saucer of cottage cheese and a little glass of tea. The tea glows amber where she places it, a half-moon of flaky, Lebanese-style bread hanging over the tray's handle.

Black tea dust boiled in water with a spoonful of sugar must taste of her old age. But coffee makes her heart flutter, she says. She takes medicine for hypertension as well as her type 2 diabetes medicine, and she can't stand her heart fluttering too much. Sometimes in the course of breakfast she will put on Baba's Wayfarer glasses to read the papers, her snub nose cockled, her large hazel eyes enlarged behind the thick lenses. But mostly she just gazes at the half-dead Alphonso mango tree—the only one in our tiny, grassless garden, which no longer bears fruit.

She eats fast, not out of gluttony but for fear of slacking, as if at any moment something unspeakable may happen that requires her full attention.

Every day before I make my way to Tahrir I see her shuffling out of the kitchen to the sunny corner of the veranda. Her thick woolen nightie is held up by a muslin écharpe wrapped like a sash under her bosom. Her hair, drained of all color, is racked in a heap above her head. A pair of white long johns is tucked into men's socks over the rubber slippers on her feet.

Back bent, Mouna dodges the rubble as she sets the tray on a plastic stool in front of her bergère, directly under the ten o'clock sun.

I forget when in the last year or so the eighties-style bergère that used to be her throne was placed there, looking the worse for wear without its footrest. It's facing away from the gutted section of parapet so she can pretend the veranda is still intact. The parapet collapsed so loudly it muffled the dawn azan, and you must remember how deafening that is. It collapsed without warning, giving her her worst scare in years, but whenever I've brought up fixing it, she's doggedly postponed the chore.

—I'll call in the builders, she keeps saying, as if speaking of arch-angels that might be asked to fix our fates. My builders will do a bet-ter job than anybody. Just give me some time to find the number of the contractor I trust.

And once again, hearing her, I think of her second bout of visitations—that's what she really calls them: *visitations*—because it was the parapet's collapse that triggered it. Removing the rubble would remind her. But, pretending there is no rubble there, she can just deny to herself that she's been visited. All she has to do is dodge it, make sure her seat is facing the other way.

A whole decade had passed. Long enough that she'd forgotten her first bout when the visitations struck back two weeks after you left. Once you phoned from California I'd told her, and she'd been acting cool. Perhaps it was the effort of pretending she didn't care.

The visitations only returned for a night at first, but when the para-pet broke a week later they stayed for a full, three-month term. I had been sworn to secrecy the one time she talked to me about it when they first hit, a few months after I moved out in 2001. After ten years I too had almost forgotten. But I had some idea of what was happen-ing when I saw it.

You said it wasn't till Baba died that she started *going full medieval*, right? Now I know it wasn't so much your turning seventeen as his death that brought on her entropy. The evisceration that was his sec-ond indefinite absence—his infinite absence—made her question the point of her life.

That's when she sold her BMW E39, the last and swankiest in a line of royal blue conveyances she'd owned and operated since she learned to drive. It was within a year of your birth in 1983, her becoming a driver, which she did to set herself even more firmly apart from her walker husband. Who—true to his communist convictions—would go on cultivating the rodeo skills required for using Egyptian public transport well into old age. Not once did she touch a steering wheel after he died.

She'd been in a middle-class reverie since at least 1986, the year she settled for early retirement the better to devote her pious-mamahood to money and maternité. Raising you like an exotic flower while she went through the motions of worship—with ever more fanatical gusto. Embarking on one pseudo business venture after another. Buying and selling land, transportation, currency. Renovating real estate. She was always calling in the builders.

She could busy herself to distraction after Baba became a lawyer for the Saudi multinational the Umayya Group. Never mind Abid's Jeep Cherokee. It occurs to me for the first time that if not for that career move you would never have gone to the American University in Cairo or got your long-distance MA.

After 1990, Mouna grew so mellow her look of letdown all but disappeared. Never to return in force until she found herself arguing with Abid about whether Amin had died an infidel, then admonishing you for your wayward ways—*fatherless floozie* that you'd become!—the true extent of which she would never have the courage to take on. Decades of worship had not prepared her for the anger and the anguish of bereavement. Nor for the loss-lucidity that rudely shook her out of her reverie, made her see.

Nor, against fear of disgrace in this life and torture in the next, could her children provide relief.

Nour might be the sanest man in her life. That's how she thinks of me despite my marriage to Aya Mandour. A sane mind and a clean soul. But, whether in terms of heavenly credit or practical living, I was a lost cause, now, wasn't I.

And, correct and caring though he acted, she could only see Abid as a state-of-the-art miniaturization of her late brother, Umair. Or worse: her second handler from the Mukhabarat. With his athletic physique and clichéd good looks, Abid was a younger version of the person she called the Newspaperman. She might deny it even to herself, but she knew in her bones that boy would always be an aberration, not of the same benign substance as Amin. It must've boggled her mind even more than his siblings' how he could turn out that way. But there was no denying he had.

As for her exotic flower, it had grown into a man-eating mandrake. Now there was no more money with which to drown her sorrows in value propositions. But, worst of all, there was no Amin to argue with. Unbeknownst to her, the very purpose of Mouna's life had actually been to refute Socialism. To surround the puritanically left-wing political prisoner she'd married with a well-heeled and Allah-fearing Sadat-era family, never mind how he felt. Now this purpose was wrested from her bra where she had kept it, like a peasant woman's cleavage-purse, for decades on end.

Unlike the parapet, Mouna's initial collapse would be gruelingly gradual. But if it hadn't happened in 2001, nor would her 2011 transformation. Four years after the revolution I am forced to the appalling conclusion that only Amin Abdalla Amin had enabled Amna Abu Zahra to stay a believer. He had to die before she could reinvent the world one last time, plucking God out of it to fulfill her destiny.

It was late, very late, and freezing. There had been a small party. Bottle upon needlelike bottle of Greek brandy over kabab and live oud. Amin recited Abbasid love poetry while couples discreetly embraced in the haze. Amin's intime Medhat El Tetsh was there with some wannabe fashion model from Tanta. His other intime, the aspiring architect, talented painter, and inveterate hash head Selim El Mawardi—ginger, freckled, Scottish-mothered, millionaire Selim El Mawardi—looked jubilant as he set up his own portable shisha so he could have his mazag among drinkers.

Mazag. It was baffling enough for the not yet twenty-year-old Nimo that this word should mean both *mood* and *good mood.* Why must there be a foul-mouthed khawaga sucking on a rubber tube to draw it out of a water-filled beaker too?

But the sight of Amin in company would torment her the most in the years to come. How deliciously raffish he looked reclining on that throne-like acacia-wood bench at the far end of the veranda. A Coutarelli cigarette in the corner of his mouth and a small glass of brandy in the palm of his hand. The carefree sprawl of his limbs belying the smallness of his body. How happy.

Oddly, as it seems to her in retrospect, by the time the three men appeared everyone had managed to leave.

Nimo remembers neither their arrival nor their departure. She cannot bear to think of their departure. Only the sight of Amin, in the same tweed three-piece he had been wearing all evening, standing by the bench talking to them in hushed tones. Scarily serene. His body compacted into so little mass you could plausibly mistake him for a stray plank jutting out of the armrest. Nimo was perversely reassured to notice that, tucked into the small of his back, his fists were clenched so hard you could almost hear the muscles creak.

Amin large on the bench, Amin shrunken by its arm. That's what she remembers, along with embodied fright. Together with the life-destroying troika waiting in the cold while she helped him to pack a small bag and watched him splash his face with water, gathering himself to go.

Only the man in the middle had spoken at all. Bespectacled and oddly glamorous-looking in a striped Mao suit, he was one of those hair-proud men with a permanent scowl like a comment on their Brylcreemed mop not holding out against baldness. But he was incredibly courteous. He had introduced himself as Nabil Nabil, then respectfully declined the invitation to step into the house or have a glass of tea. Now, careful not to make a noise, he murmured to the pair of overcoats on either side of him, facing the spot where no one had yet planted a mango tree.

Could there be a moment when Nimo slipped out and stood swaying in that same spot, gazing up at them in terror, or did I make that up?

She remembers being puzzled that the two men wore sunglasses even though it was dark, wondering briefly if something was wrong with their eyes, whether it could be the same affliction of the senses that kept them so forebodingly silent.

While they waited, she remembers, the azan sounded. Even then, five times a day, you could hear an azan from our house. But, crossing a huge distance and not so rudely amplified, it was mild and mellifluous. It didn't exactly comfort her, but it blew away some of the steel wool of bewilderment, making it possible to concentrate on Amin, to stay with his face as it showed not fear or dejection but exasperation. The same incredulous look it had worn whenever he railed against his HADETO comrades.

And when, emaciated and almost totally bald, he is finally standing by the bench again, Nimo will see his face has set permanently into that exasperation.

In their four months together, from September to December 1958, she had quickly realized that his hatred for the Zaim was that of a betrayed lover for his beloved's seducer. The bikbashi not only profaned the cause but also prostituted its champions. Amin was furious with them for letting themselves be prostituted.

In Abu Zaabal, in the Tora Prison Complex just outside Maadi, and in Alexandria's Hadra Jail—all places where he stayed on his way to Wahat—he was to watch them chanting Nasser's name like a prayer even as they died of broken necks and severed spleens. Worshipping the wrathful god that smote them right through the moment of being smitten.

He was to see his future and theirs redeemed not for the sake of truth, justice, or the dictatorship of the proletariat, but on the whim of a fat Slavic buffoon named Nikita Khrushchev. The Soviet Secretary's visit alone prompted the mass release from Wahat, Shimo.

He was to be royally vindicated in his opprobrium, first by the pulverization of the whole communist movement in Egypt, then by Egypt's humiliating defeat in the Six-Day War.

This, Nimo will imbibe. Amin's decade-long and very costly disillusionment, which leaves him apolitical and—except for her—alone. She is part of it. And so you could reasonably conclude it is her fear of the consequences that keeps her away from politics from the early sixties on.

The only other politically active people she knows are Selim and Medhat, and they were both arrested at their houses later on the same New Year's Day. You could see their future even then. It's true Medhat will manage to become a surgeon against the odds, albeit with enough paranoia and resentment for a whole class of medical graduates. But Selim—hedonist, gregarious, profligate Selim, with twinkling blue eyes and a face exuding youth—will give up both architecture and painting, ending up frailer than an octogenarian at thirty-six, plodding around bleary and inert, without job or family.

Even in her twenties Nimo is a practical and realistic woman. What happens to her husband and his friends is enough of a cautionary tale. But the truth is she just finds it laughable. Her interest in dignity is one thing; it won't have quite the same weight after New Year 1959 anyway. But the spectacle of otherwise happy young men giving up families and futures, even lives for something as abstract and unconvincing as a khawaga's idea of how the world should be feels puerile. It feels ungrateful and male in the way that Umair is male. Holding the world at Smith & Wesson point.

Still, hiding her true motives, Nimo learned just enough politics to be able to massage his manliness. Which, apart from the gruff tenderness that could make her the happiest woman in the world, consisted of his sense that he was politically right. While out at the Ain Shams

Faculty of Arts, at the Cairo campus cafeteria, or at her seamstresses' and coiffeurs', she would forage for news or information that helped to prove his theories.

It's been proved that the 1954 attempt on Nasser's life was a stage show to get rid of the Ikhwan, for example; or, *A French magazine published a report on Jews being forced to give up their Egyptian nationality before they left the country under duress.*

And, holding on to it till one of those nights of unbearable constriction when he fell silent and seemed to lose the capacity for sitting down, his limbs diminishing, his muscles tensing so phenomenally they chafed her ears, she would release the information as if by chance, back it up with its source and watch for the eventual deep breath.

In a short while—sure enough—she would see the upsurge in twitching that always presaged distension. Amin would cross his legs and, smiling, launch into conversation. At such moments it mystified her how accurately his body reflected his mind. His expansiveness prompted expansion in space as he sat back, less and less jittery while the fire found words. She felt triumphant.

Led by a formidable Ain Shams geography student named Semsem, her college and later work friends took to calling her Nimo. But in her four months with Amin she had gloried in being Mouna. It and the child who would never be were the dearest two things he gave her, and within a year of his going she would lose them both.

The child, forever. But the name—she was to regain it by a one-woman effort of will when she became a mother and her first child learned to speak. That's why it hurt her when Abid switched to the standard *Mama* he's insisted on since the age of fourteen.

Mouna was something she valued. After she moved in with Amin, she felt transformed by the name.

They lived well. Amin could bring in a reasonable amount from one-off jobs for the big law firms—the Qansuh sisters' famous father's included—which were busy sorting out the minorities' fast-changing finances and arranging for the rich, then the less rich, to leave. He spent lavishly.

He brought her Vanity Fair cigarettes, pink and blue like her friend Lena's. Which she could smoke with the Turkish coffee he made her from dark-roasted Brazilian beans. Such smooth, flavorful coffee was like liquid silk. But she preferred his stumpy white Coutarellis.

He bought her sunflowers and chrysanthemums, strawberries and champagne.

He handed her twenty guineas every time she went shopping at the freshly nationalized Jewish department stores.

And he kept telling her stories while she learned to cook for him. Folding vine leaves over herb-spattered rice, soaking garlic-toasted bread flakes in beef stock, easing marinated rabbit legs into boiling oil.

He told her of Verlaine's love for Rimbaud and Diaghilev's for Nijinsky, of Sartre's open relationship with Simone de Beauvoir, of Diego Rivera cheating on Frida Kahlo with her sister and Kahlo returning the favor with none other than Leon Trotsky.

He taught her the difference between an internationalist and a Trotskyite, the secrets of Sufis and psychoanalysts, the humor in the rhymed prose of medieval Arabic kama sutras, and the quirky mathematics of dialectical materialism.

And he nitpicked over everything, from Umm Kalthoum's purported lesbianism to Mrs. Mawardi's Scots stinginess.

Riveted by these world-widening, morality-mauling mawwals, Nimo was left floating in a kind of cinematic cloud where even Our Lord's rules were null. She half believed they could live up there forever, the two of them, never having to obey orders.

Amin's voice reverberating in the echo chamber that was her cranium, she began to perceive a different world in each new recipe. A unique universe with its own structure, connected to one or another of his mawwals. She found these culinary revelations as soul cleansing as her infrequent performances of salah. Even though much of the mawwals' actual content was meant to be soul dirtying, being in the rule-proof cloud felt more spiritual than either.

Over the next seven years that cloud's relentless precipitation into acid rain will bring her back down to a rule-ordered earth more terrible than the one on which she found Amin. It will demonstrate to her just how necessary it was, if you didn't feel shame when you were expected to, to actively pretend you did. Eventually it will drive her to the rigorous religiosity she is to stick with till she comes on the Jumpers. But not yet.

In their four months together Nimo did suspect that—like Arwa's for what she now thought of as the Abu Zahra Correctional Facility for Girls, or Nasser's for the baby republic—God's orders must be followed to the letter if you wanted to survive. Besides, in Arwa's and Nasser's case it was a matter of getting past earthly obstacles. But in God's case the test was the Day of Resurrection. *That day mankind will issue forth in scattered groups to be shown their deeds.*

Still, it was enough to believe in God's mercy to feel safe. *Merciful* was His name. It was enough to recognize that the theology written by the omdas and the Nassers of the past did not necessarily reflect His will. Which just might be Amin's skin on hers, the heavenly interface with which she had been gifted.

Partly because she deduced it was very wrong but mainly because it didn't cross her mind that it might be worth doing, Nimo had never masturbated. The trauma of circumcision and the discomfort of menstruation were enough to put her off that area, although she had occasionally sensed pleasure there from a distance.

Since childhood she had embraced the notion that being naked should elicit shame, the magnitude of which doubled when she considered the hair growing around the now lipless fissure between her thighs, and tripled when she thought of warm pee cascading over it. But, even when Mansour Effendi undressed and leered at this part of her, she had never felt shame.

To her amusement now Nimo discovered she was not shy. As long as she was alone with Amin the shame she knew she should feel but didn't intensified her excitement. She momentarily flinched the first time she found her knees above her breasts, but it was easy to see there was no metal in the vicinity. And she hardly blinked when she felt the weight she had always imagined on her chest.

Next to Mansour Effendi's Amin's bulbul was tiny but—never mind its wakefulness—she found it more approachable. She could hold and stretch and stroke it without having to stifle a laugh. She could even stab the underside of its tarboosh with a knuckle-hard nipple, unselfconscious. Listening for an electric exhalation, she could close her mouth over all of it without repugnance. It also had the capacity to grow dramatically, which fascinated her. It was solid enough to make their bodies one.

Nimo relished the ease with which she could make it big time after time. The paradoxical power she felt over him when, unable to contain his passion, he'd pin her down and let it fumble and fulminate.

With his breath on her stomach she grew to admire her curvy compactness. The citrusy scent she detected on herself smelled delicious blended with his fresh sweat. She thought she could see herself as he did, her hazel eyes and auburn hair, and for the first time in her life she felt beautiful.

Half the time wine or love's cupless drunkenness colluded with her surviving nerve endings to bring her to some kind of zenith. She didn't worry too much about whether or not this was the female orgasm her friend Lena Qansuh had explained about giving herself and having a man give her, or whether it was going to happen the next time.

They spent hours entwined in the spacious cast-iron bathtub he'd had installed, having splash fights and singing duettos. Wet hands clutching armpits, tongues cavorting in locked mouths.

The evening Hosni Mubarak steps down—after eighteen days of complete standstill while the army keeps the peace, but you must already know that—I walk all the way from Tahrir Square to Maadi, stopping every so often to snivel into my hand or cheer the flag-waving revelers going in the opposite direction. For nearly three hours while the sun goes down, I can think of nothing but Mouna's joy that God has responded to the prayer that is the revolution.

Yet when I get home she isn't sitting up under the blankets, as I've been picturing her, squinting through her old Erika glasses at the dresser where the squat twenty-one-inch Toshiba is tuned to Al Jazeera. She isn't making supper downstairs in the kitchen. Or, with the bathroom door half-open, performing her ablutions for the evening prayers. She isn't even chittering on the landline to either of her two surviving intimes. Girly, dusky Tante Hudhud and butch, almond-skinned Tante Fifi. Did you know she called them *the cat and the dog*? Neither of them knows where she is when I phone.

To make sure, I scope out the whole house. The roof, the attic, the three bedrooms with incredibly high ceilings. The hall that opens out onto a veranda adjoining our circular sliver of a garden. The narrow corridor that leads to a kitchen at one end of that hall. That enormous bathroom at the other end. And, down the three steps by the bathroom door, the dark, spacious, semicircular netherworld below ...

Her smartphone is switched off as usual: she never remembers to take it anyway. I ask the garage attendant next door and the owner of the corner shop opposite. I phone Abid and Khalto Faiza. No one has any idea where she might be.

With mounting panic I wait by the gate, feeling the night chill as my sweat dries. I picture her, hunched and frail in her cloak, blanking out in the middle of a busy souk. I picture her blindfolded in the back of a limousine, a knife tip pricking her abdomen while, shaking, she mutters devotions under her breath. But most of all I picture her sprawled crookedly on some sidewalk, her head dangling over the curb, dried blood in splotches all over her face.

I forget when it last rained, but there is a fresh puddle by the moldering slice of sidewalk where Mouna used to park her BMW alongside our hedge. In the light of the corner shop, it reflects the way into the cul-de-sac where our house stands. But every time I turn to it I see her mantled head, stiff and bloodied, hanging over the edge of a grimy sidewalk. I guess I grow tired of pacing and looking out. So, like a fortune teller consulting a crystal ball, I crouch down and brave the sight that, though as yet only imagined, will be my ultimate reward for introducing Mouna to the Arab Spring.

Then something marvelous happens.

Superimposed on that chilling image, a petite figure begins to edge into the jagged frame. Below the neat bonnet that marks it out as a woman, it takes me nearly a minute to recognize the face, which though not smiling is at rest, almost free of creases. A magazine-sized flag flutters by one ear. The shoulders are in a straight line, the gait confident. Making brisk progress. Once I've registered the moss turtleneck blouse, an ocher trouser skirt floats into view.

—Ya Allah, I whistle as I look up, ecstatic at her lack of headscarf. My mother is a movie star.

—You're home early, Mouna trills, the premillennial warmth of her voice restored.

Now my mother is smiling for real: an expression utterly unlike the baraka she used to project going about her devotional duties. I haven't seen such peacefulness in her face since before Baba died. She stands waving her flag, then she steps over the puddle that no longer shows her dead.

—I couldn't stay home on a day like this, now, could I, she says. Besides, I just took the Metro to Kasr El Ainy and walked to Tahrir. C'était incroyable, ya Nour. *Hold your head high, you're Egyptian,* we chanted. But it wasn't just a chant, you understand. It was real.

One evening not much later I come home from the office to find Mouna and Tante Fifi at the dining table. Hunched over two block notes, as Baba would've called them, they are silent. Except for the Tiffany-style lamp Mouna has placed in front of them, the hall is in darkness. Plumes of smoke from what I take to be glasses of tea are dancing over their heads. The localized rainbow glow gives them an atmospheric quality, like figures in a movie or a dream. For a moment it's as if I've walked in on a secret meeting of some tiny communist organization like Baba's.

Under the table Tante Fifi is gently rubbing Mouna's thigh. And, while not touching her intime in turn, Mouna doesn't try to remove her hand. They are wearing lace-trim galabiyas, the colorful faux-fellahin apparel I will grow to associate with septuagenarian *engagement*. With shipshape bonnets and Dr. Scholl's sandals, a vision of left-wing chic.

—Salamat, I cry out, but neither of them can hear.

So, doing my mock tai chi, I sneak up on them and, with a twisted face, thrust my head between them and whistle.

Mouna gasps without looking up from the piece of paper in front of her. With three tiny breaths through pouted lips, she mimes spitting into her cleavage to exorcise the fright, still not looking up.

—Aren't you a senior editor at *Al Oruba*, ya habibi? Tante Fifi barks in her abrupt way, not waiting for me to reply. Aha, then you'll be able to help us with this work we're doing.

—Planning to overthrow the Military Council, ya Tante?

—But isn't the Council only temporarily in power?

The stout woman keeps interrupting herself while I pace around in the dark. Mouna goes on scribbling.

—The only thing Hosni Mubarak did right since he became president thirty years ago. Can you believe it was thirty years ago, Nimo? That's quite a bit older than Shaima, isn't it, may Our Lord prolong and protect her.

Reluctantly, as it sounds to me, Mouna grunts her *Amen*.

—Anyway, the only thing Hosni Mubarak did right was agreeing to give up his rule in such a short time. But, being a military man, by law supreme commander of the armed forces, aha, who but the Military Council was he going to hand the country over to? Now it's true the gendarmerie haven't been too good to the revolutionaries still on the streets. Though it is hard to avoid the question, aha, should those dear children, my darlings, be on the streets still? And isn't that the way of all soldiers? They have promised to hand over power to democratically elected leaders by Our Lord's baraka. Now we might like or dislike them, we might be against the constitutional amendments they're proposing. Whoever thought I would ever be heard saying *constitutional amendments*, Nimo! But it's the truth that they protected the revolutionaries from Mubarak's police and his cronies' thugs, aha, those ugly baltagis. And on that basis—

—Let's hope they keep their word, ya Fifi, Mouna switches her off.

I recognize her domineering cadence: the tone with which, without threats or promises, even as an adult she could make me do her bidding. Funny to realize I never heard her use that tone with you. All through your years of fighting, it was her other, long-suffering tone—the one full of self-pity and piety—in which she chided you.

Mouna's dom power is so warm and glowing that, even as I remember my own suffering, I would happily float back out to the times I was her filial sub, one by one. But she is looking up, and as I turn to her I discover I've been mistaken. There are no glasses on the table, of tea or anything.

White and pungent, the smoke is rising from Baba's seashell Murano ashtray, which I haven't seen since he died. I watch in amazement while Mouna picks up a half-burned cigarette, which she brings to her mouth and curls her shapely lips around. It's the brand Baba used to smoke through the eighties and nineties: Kent Deluxe 100s. As far as I know, before now Mouna has never smoked in her life. But there is such grace in the way she does it I can't help gritting my teeth.

—Alors, she says, the fumes rarefying her face, will you stop bouncing about and sit down?

When Tante Fifi is gone I find Mouna sitting up under a fluorescent green bedspread, her profile silhouetted in the bedside table lamp light. The flower-patterned salah-wimple is folded over the armchair—she's no longer praying in bed. Like some stuffed mammal carcass, the little thing she calls her *télé* sits lifeless on the dresser. She has a newspaper in her lap, her glasses gobble up a third of her face—but her eyes are elsewhere.

Mouna is unaware of me while I watch her, a smile unfastening my lips. Because she's doing something I haven't seen her do since my teens. She is counting. With childlike concentration, performing complex arithmetic under her breath. Bending fingers and mumbling as she translates people or days into sums of money. Or perhaps into votes, now. I watch for a long time until, sensing my breath, she turns to me, her face drained of its earlier gravity. And as I bend down to kiss her forehead I can smell tobacco.

—Enjoying all those cigarettes, I wink. We ought to get you some cognac to go with them.

—If only cognac wasn't haram!

At the dining table I peruse the block notes in private. Of the two of them, I find, one lists individuals and groups that the Nimo-Fifi duo plan to persuade to vote no in the Military Council's referendum on constitutional amendments, to be held on March 19.

Not only because the amendments the Military Council is proposing will give ghastly power to the army, Nimo has written in her dainty hand, *but also because those sheikhs and jihadi breeders are campaigning for a yes now, and we must demonstrate to them and the whole country how small and insignificant they are. We must show the whole world that when Mubarak used to threaten us with a religious state in order to stay in power and rob the people, he was bluffing. For, respect and love and cherish our beliefs as we do, we also say there is no compulsion in religion, sadaqa Allahu'l Adhim. In Egypt, where different beliefs have always coexisted and folk have always worshipped by choice, there can be no such thing as a religious state. Besides, Egyptians are sick of the military state that was foisted on them by Nasser, under which they have suffered in different ways for sixty years. We must oppose the Military Council's amendments in order to show we are saying no to both the military state and the religious state . . .*

Out of all this I want to underline *jihadi breeders*, the phrase she used to describe the Ikhwan and their secret or reformed allies. Mouna may be a pious mama, but she sure can't stand political Islam.

Then again—I don't know it yet, but—this bundle of scribblings will be forgotten, totally, down to the over-legible phrase *Long live the Revolution*. By morphing into the definitive Jumpers' Log, it is the other, thick block note with a blue cover and yellow spirals that, along with the iPad Mouna hasn't acquired yet, takes on significance in the next four years.

That evening it sinks in, though. Since stepping over the puddle in our little cul-de-sac, Mouna has transmigrated into an earlier avatar. And even if I had realized where this was taking her, the spectacle would still have been impossible to resist.

Within weeks now Mouna loses enough weight and gains enough posture to shed the pious-mama look and go about her new, revolutionary rituals with vigor. Never mind the maimed and the martyred already squatting in our mother's head. Seeing her like this is a gift I cherish to the point of letting myself fall into dysfunction. None of this would be happening if words didn't take up with her again, I can tell. Her life's nomenclature changing anew.

Already I can see how—positively, negatively, by force, by choice—words have marshaled Mouna's biography.

Sharaf undid her first version of herself and, by putting her husband in prison within months of their marriage, *Socialism* cut the second short. For this she hated Nasser. For breaking up the life story she had started to tell by living it, depriving her of being Mouna just as soon as she inhabited the name.

But notwithstanding Amin's vitriol, for thirteen years from when they met till she had me, it was a catchword of the Zaim's that she kept secretly safe. *Dignity*. It was both the opposite of sharaf and the halal part of communism. Abdel Halim Hafez's voice rhetorically asking whether this land belongs to us or to khawagas in uniform. Dignity meant villagers back at the saraya standing up to the Omda, unafraid. The children of the rabble reading political philosophy in public libraries. And all these women tearing off their veils and raising their voices, going out to earn their livelihoods unchaperoned.

If anything could justify the ignominy of a man being sodomized by a trained German shepherd—if ever there could be a reason to make people spy on each other en masse, forcing them to file reports with the

Mukhabarat on pain of dog rape—dignity was that thing, that reason. But since nothing could and nothing came of it but defeat, dignity had to be replaced with *baraka*.

Still, not until she had her second son in 1976 did Mouna's words incline Islamically. *The womb tie* was her theological pretext for presiding over a tribe of our relations like a mob chief, displaying the kind of pious cynicism that drove the new, Sadati bourgeoisie. *Observe the measure strictly* was the Quranic edict by which, through the seventies and eighties, she periodically dabbled in the black-market dollar trade. *So that Our Lord will bless what He has given*, she would remonstrate, haggling with business partners.

In 2001 her fright returns. The crow-like housefly she almost saw on her first outing with Amin has evolved into a furry Afreet. A brown, featherless bird with a face like a fox's and umbrella-like, webbed wings. Bat-like, for sure, but in some ways more like a giant housefly, with bulbous compound eyes and a proboscis like a deer-horn dagger. In 2001 it turns her nights into punitive fandangos, and by the time you leave in 2010 the words are weak and wicked enough that it returns.

They have lost their momentum, voiding all projects of meaning and life of the meaning that is having a project. Time passes. Then one evening Mubarak steps down and—not just to Mouna, right?—it feels like an absolute miracle. A once familiar word takes on incredible substance then.

Revolution.

It used to be a euphemism for *coup*, some mangy military animal surreptitiously supplanting his predecessor, ready to start a civil war so he can be zaim for life. Now that Mubarak's been ousted, however, it has enough power to wire her up for a different order of project:

—To participate in my country's destiny. Aywa! Et pourquoi pas, son of Amin?

——⁘•

By 2012 Mouna has completely forgotten that in 1963 her close friend Lena Qansuh jumped off the roof of the Hotel Cecil in Alexandria, crashing head first into a parked horse-drawn carriage and dying while the horse reared, neighing.

Mouna was twenty-four when this happened, already better known to herself as Nimo—the name her best friend Semsem had given her, in the absence of Amin—and she found the shock debilitating.

Because of her sister Lena, who was an alumna, Amna's classmate Susanne Qansuh had been her way into the Cairo University campus cafeteria—a full two weeks before she even heard of Amin. She wasn't yet Nimo when she went to meet Lena for the first time in 1956. On the way Susanne told her in confidence to be extra nice to her elder sister.

—A Swiss doctor whose specialty is mental illness examined Lena and said she had something called *manic depression*, she told her. He gave her newfangled pills that Papa spent a fortune on obtaining from abroad, but Lena refuses to take them.

Susanne tried to explain it was a kind of melancholia that could nonetheless cause jubilation, but all Amna understood was that her classmate's sister was tara-la-li, as crazy people were called—you've heard the term—mimicking a jingle. She went with her metaphorical boxing gloves shielding her face. But, seeing the glamour-puss version of her classmate, Amna gulped. She gulped less at the beauty than the sheer collected grace with which this magnoona carried herself.

No wonder insanity was synonymous with music. Tara-la-li. When within two minutes Lena leaned over Amna's shoulder and, winking in Susanne's direction, whispered, *She told you I was mad, didn't she?* Amna knew she had made a friend.

Even though Lena was one of exactly seven women who attended Amna Abu Zahra's wee wedding, the young wife didn't see that much of her slightly older friend. Semsem hated her, that was partly why. But Amna was busy with her own madnesses.

After she found Lena on her knees fumbling with Amin's fly—Amna had stepped out for some fresh mint from Road 9 so they could all have tea—Lena never visited again in Maadi. Amin wouldn't have been averse, exactly. But happily Amna arrived just before his shock subsided. So that while Lena genuflected to his bulbul, her hands reaching for its bed of balls while she looked up at him, his arms were still in the air, palms open over his head like a revolutionary trying not to be gunned down.

Amna could feel her hedgehog body furl, keratin-hard spines bristling out of its hide. She coughed, loudly, then said nothing while Lena ran out.

A week later there was an apologetic crack-up outside Amna's lecture hall. Full-scale self-hating hysteria. Amna had put down the phone every time she heard Lena's voice, and now the girl was grabbing at her foot to kiss it, offering to throw herself at a speeding vehicle for her pleasure. Amna had to crouch down and take her in her arms to end the scene. *Mon chou*, she called her then. *Mon pauvre chou.* Lena liked it so much it became their nickname for each other.

Since that day in 1958 she has found unique distraction in Lena's company. After Amin went to prison especially, through long phone calls and aimless drives in Lena's own private automobile—always unplanned, always full of sordid on dit—Amna could engage in repartee-with-swearing and talk sex. She could make fun of the Egyptian Radio Elders, as she called them. She could even consider altogether dropping religion. Once she asked Lena, *But isn't all that haram?* And the girl instantly retorted, *Nobody knows anything about God, mon chou.* There was such freedom in the look she gave her Nimo envied her lack of concern. But they rarely spoke of the big issues. Having forbidden the mere mention of financial help from Lena on pain of *cutting all diplomatic ties*, she could pour out her day-to-day heartache without constraint.

Amna will remember this when she sees the dead girl's sister, Susanne, when the sort of meta grief that flares up once a loss is shared forces her to recall her dead friend. But eventually she will forget.

A few years from now, pretending Lena never existed—which is what she will carry on doing till she drops out of her awareness for real—Amna won't have to continue dealing with the four-tiered grief she's feeling as, uncomprehending, she steps onto the second-class coach bound for Alexandria: for Amin, for the child, for Fouad, and now his sister.

But all the same, while she tries to lose herself in the novelty of the seat, the narrow window, the rails, the pleasant chugging and the changing view, the thought of Lena brings back more shades of envy. Because the girl, who is only twenty-eight, has everything Amna can imagine wanting besides freedom from religion.

She has a name that evokes the Asmahan song "Nights of Delight in Vienna" so well it always pipes a waltz in Amna's ear.

She has the Circassian beauty of her mother Nazlı Hanim's ancestors, white-marble skin and flesh like Turkish delight, hair soft and thick as a mink fourrure.

She has a mink fourrure.

She has a degree in law, a policeman fiancé as handsome as he is solvent, a villa in her name in Heliopolis.

She even has her own pink Dodge La Femme, which she drives around town like a movie star.

And she has an indulgent papa. Not an abah like Amin's cloth-merchant father or a baba like most city folks'. But a proper, plosive papa who used to be not a bey but a basha—a real one—before Nasser abolished titles.

Ali Qansuh is so famous in the legal profession he is known simply as El Maître. Though a landowner with connections to the Saraya, he has managed to keep his law firm and most of his Cairo property by calling in favors with friends in the army, never missing a chance to declare loyalty to the July Revolution, and taking the humiliation of being called Sayyid Ali instead of Ali Basha in his Fabian stride.

For a time too brief to scratch Amna's memory, everyone is called *sayyid*. Effendi, bey, basha, rayyis, usta, ustaz. All will become sayyid before, jumbled and reconstituted, the old appellations are rapidly reborn. Later in life she will remember the word only as a humorous form of address for Amin, after his release.

And that is how, on her way to Alexandria, Amna cycles back to all that is wrong with Lena. Not the fact that she can go a week without sleep, jumping red lights and speeding into watermelon pyramids. Not even her drinking habit, or the eagerness with which, when she can get her hands on it, she snorts cocaine.

Lena's voice is sex appeal and her body odor is Chanel No. 5, but she takes lovers at random. And her lovers often speak insultingly of their time with her. Which drives her to make long convex cuts like layered crescents in her thighs and pelvis with a paring knife, so that she bleeds and hurts and looks like she has an extra, giant koss when you make love to her. Like she has two or even three of them, one inside the other. And in certain, patrician-playboy circles she is called Lena Matryoshka if not, with an aristocratic delight in working-class commonness, Lena Kossain.

Seven years before Lena died, during her second week of lectures, Amna met a different friend. She arrived on campus to find a ring of students shuffling about the Ain Shams campus gate, unable to get in.

Some military official was visiting, she had understood by the time a senior security man stepped out to announce that entry would not be permitted until His Excellency left the premises. He was a doddering old man with a gray Nietzsche mustache and a loud, lordly manner.

Glancing at the Ramona-model Bulova wristwatch Amin had given her, Amna was about to turn back, giving up on the day's lectures, when suddenly a wiry figure in a pencil dress and a sun hat almost as wide as she was tall strode straight through the gathering to the old man. With a confidence that belied her size, the girl took off her hat, stood on her toes, and whispered something into his leathery ear. And, taking one step back to look at her in momentary disbelief, the security man suddenly straightened his back and saluted, immediately opening the gate.

While the students filed into campus something possessed Amna to catch up with the girl and tap her shoulder. As she stopped and turned Amna dreaded the expression on the girl's face when she saw her. But it was just an impish smile.

Winking while she introduced herself—*Siham Gad: Semsem, as in sesame, aywa; Arts, geography*—she took Amna's arm.

—Tasharrafna, ya sett Semsem. I am Amna—

—Amna? No, you're not, you're Nimo.

—Nimo?

—Amna's too old. Plus, you look like a Nimo, wouldn't you agree.

—I am at your service.

—You look like a Nimo and you are studying—no, wait, let me guess. History?

—French.

—Mais bien sûr!

—Or should I change that too?

—You should never change la langue de l'amour. Even if you look like history. I went to the Mère de Dieu in Garden City, you to—

—The Sacre-Coeur in Heliopolis.

—Enchanté. Now, Semsem nudged her new friend, I believe you desperately want to know what I told His Excellency out there.

—Ah, wennabi, ya Semsem!

—We are short like each other, Semsem removed her hat again. So I'm going to tell you.

She didn't have to stand on tiptoe to reach Amna's ear.

—*His most exalted highness Field Marshal Gamal Moftah, Chief of the General Staff, tells you to let the students in immediately. He sent me, a student, so as not to attract attention. Long live the Revolution!*

By now Amna was doubled over, laughter making her face wet. *Stop,* she tried to say, but Semsem was perfectly deadpan, as she always is when she delivers her medicine.

—I just gave Nasser a different surname. I didn't even say which general staff this field marshal was supposed to be chief of.

—I just hope he doesn't get in trouble for disobeying orders, Amna managed to interject when her convulsions began to subside.

—But he's only about three steps away from everlasting rest, Semsem said, and the convulsions resumed instantly. How much trouble can you be in at this stage.

And so it continued: Semsem exercising her stand-up talent, Amna learning to laugh. But, also, in the course of it, Semsem abetting Amna's interest in dignity. Encouraging her to muddle that up with ambition, so that she can pursue her career while Amin is in prison and still feel she was fighting the good fight.

With hindsight it seems almost scripted that Semsem should turn out to be from Shoubra.

In El Assal, the Shoubrite neck of the sands already notorious for the kind of hatchet wielder by whose name—*baltagi*—all Egyptian thugs are known, there was a motherless only child whose father turned his back on the work of collecting protection money to become the best-known plumber in all of North Cairo. Gad El Sersawi sent his daughter to the Mère de Dieu, too, but she soon met a Sersawi second cousin, a skilled baltagi named Anwar whose fingertips knew exactly how to install brittle, tiny lightnings under her skin.

At fourteen she persuaded her father to take Anwar in as an apprentice. At fifteen she gave herself to Anwar, then convinced her father to let him marry her. At seventeen, having figured out he had been sent by her paternal uncles to punish their renegade brother—though she still couldn't imagine life without him—she persuaded her father, Usta Gad, to kick him out of the plumbing business.

That's when Anwar started beating her. He would wrap her hair around one hand to make a kind of leash and, pulling her down by it, let his fingertips do their work. Enduring this, Semsem gasped and groaned just as she had done while he pleasured her, not because she confused the horror of his beatings with her body's happiness but because, knowing what she knew now, she felt she deserved them.

At eighteen she watched two of her maternal uncles hold Anwar down while the third cut his throat like a sheep's on Eid El Adha. She had expected she would turn away. But she felt nothing while she made eye contact, keeping it till his face dissolved in jet swirls of blood.

Anwar had emptied a sachet of white arsenic into Usta Gad's morning tea. She had seen him hide the substance without knowing what it was. She had tried to warn her father, and Usta Gad had laughed and kissed her forehead, telling her Anwar wouldn't dare. But when he died in the hospital the next day she knew what had brought on that strange bout of diarrhea and vomiting.

Semsem arranged for the penalty. Her paternal uncles wouldn't admit they had ordered the murder, but neither would they avenge it. Her mother's family, though not exactly their rivals, had ongoing vendettas with the Sersawis and they were glad to oblige. Semsem had never liked her maternal uncles—their humors did not mix with hers—but she knew she could depend on them. She didn't know she could depend on herself not to turn away.

Her mother's brothers were glad to take over Usta Gad's shop, inheriting equipment and personnel in return for a yearly emolument she will go on receiving until her eldest uncle dies in 1968. His funeral will bring her back to Assal for the first time in ten years, then.

—Don't think I'm going to pay my respects, she will tell the then-pregnant Amna. No, I have to be there to make sure they'll place him firmly underground!

There was no love lost when they helped her to move to a modern apartment in Abbasiya, back in 1955. She took along her younger, unmarried aunt, whom she found a kindly shop owner husband within months. Though no one from Assal attended the wedding.

It wasn't exactly upward mobility, Semsem's need to reinvent herself in this way. Like her marriage to an impoverished aristocrat from Garden City—younger than she was and so, by her own self-fulfilling prophesying, guaranteed to jilt her for a younger woman of better family—becoming a middle-class orphan from Abbasiya was a way to fit into the new country she believed Nasser had sired.

Later in life Semsem will become one of those intense bareheaded widows of the left, as Mouna will disdainfully call them. Odd ones out among the hordes of pious mamas in hijabs.

Mouna could always see that, for Semsem, Nasser was nothing but a kind of überbaltagi starring in the countrywide, grown-up version of her childhood mythology. But to her credit—Mouna saw this too—Semsem was never cynical about embracing the brave new republic.

Besides, without her best friend, how could Amna have survived from the day Amin was taken away to the day she managed to visit him?

Amin had been dead nine months when the visitations started. A week or so after Tante Semsem stopped coming in daily to check on Mouna—for nearly a year after 9/11, Tante Semsem would be wrapped up in the life of her son Nidal, a religious type who lived in New York City. But wait—you must remember Cairo's pandemonium in those days. The shrieks, the shimmies, the schadenfreude.

It's when we shared a joint for the first time, you and I. Your plump lips curling around the cardboard tip, I saw your wide-eyed surrender to THC. The wind coming through lifted your uncombed hair. And I was noticing that on your face there was not a trace of fear. I felt no guilt about introducing you to cannabis, but there was something about the way you took to it, the innocence and the eagerness, that made me wonder. I could never have guessed I would live to see that same something in Mouna.

We drove around Zamalek listening to "Independent Women," by Destiny's Child—in those days you couldn't stop talking about *Charlie's Angels*—and you got so high you thought the whole island was a spaceship, my car a little shuttle touring its interior.

—You know what, Nour, you said, giggling. I think Mouna should try some of this. I know she doesn't smoke but, deen keda, she'd love it!

I bet you don't remember that.

In reality Mouna's life was narrowing to a furry Afreet only she could see. A brown, featherless bird that looked more like an insect. She could hear and feel and smell it. A burning brimstone smell straight out of the firepit. It was odious how it replaced her husband's odors while jihadis were spectacularly reinventing Islam.

Every day the Afreet landed on her head after dark. No matter how far she ran within the house, past the garden onto the street or— once—all along Road 9 to the Metro station, it would stay till first light. Never mind how vigorously she shook or beat it off—leaping, yowl-ing, self-slapping, expectorating, crushing her face into the carpet—it went on tormenting her with headache and hyperthermia. It pricked and burned and kneaded her, mocked her hysteria, fusilladed her fu-selage. It tempted her to unthinkable horrors, planted ghastly hexes under her tongue. And it left her sleepless and suicidal, with crinkly skin and canceled eyes.

A psychiatrist, then another prescribed Xanax and antidepressants, brand after brand, but it was no good. The Xanax incapacitated her and the SSRIs gave her palpitations, preventing her from sleeping during the day.

For three months Mouna's nights became episodes in Jahannam. She grew convinced this was the gift of the Zabaniya—that's what the Quran calls hell's angels, virtuous sister—and started muttering that God was purging her of her sins while she was alive so that she could go straight to heaven once she died. But by the time the Zabaniya were done with her, you'd think she was already half-dead.

With the word *revolution* driving her, ten years after that, it isn't just that Mouna has a project again and all her endearing qualities are back in force. The earnest self-importance, the coyness, the curiosity. The childish insistence on standing up for what's fair.

It isn't that, with all those dusty cassette tapes in her recently resurrected boombox, which she carries by the handle from kitchen to veranda to table and back again, humming along while she multitasks, she is now listening to folk music. Rough, raw, gut-wrenching mawwals from the southern highlands of Upper Egypt. The opposite of Halim.

It isn't even that, most days from now on, she wears kohl and perfume, looking both spruce and spry.

It's that she's reversing our roles.

For months after I moved in with her, I had daily left and come home while Mouna stayed. Except to go to the Fatah Mosque—once or twice a week—she almost never left the house. Often, when I had the energy and she was in the mood, I kept her abreast of the politics and scandals of post-9/11 Cairo.

I don't know whether or not we talked about Obama coming to Cairo to tell Egyptians how great Islam was, back in the summer of 2009. But I remember telling her about Egypt's BMW man in 2004. After falling out with Hosni Mubarak's elder son, Alaa—compulsory partner for anyone doing business above a certain profit margin, at that time—that man's rhino-thick torso started to appear on all kinds of computer screens. Butt-naked. Pumping the supple, orgiastic form of a star belly dancer. *C'est vrai? And you can see her without her clothes on? Our Lord save and protect us!* His private videos had been leaked on CD.

Now Mouna is the storyteller. She's the one who goes out and comes back with news. She's too wary of Cairo traffic to think of driving again after ten years, but that doesn't prevent her from intensively, impressionably rediscovering Cairo—trailed by her sidekick Tante Fifi—while she seeks to participate in her country's destiny.

Even when she gradually slows down till she stops going out completely and returns to the veranda in the summer of 2014—by which time I'm all over the streets again—I remain silent while she spins Mouna mawwals.

Strange now to think that, while the revolution has given our apolitical, apathetic mother energy and agency, it is depleting me—the journalist who thought he was making a career out of seeking the truth, the self-aware dissident, the man about town—to the point that I depend on her for information.

One day in the summer of 2011 I can't fend off sleep in the morning having stayed up all night, so I don't drive to the office till I wake up after dark. I'm in charge of my own section of the newspaper and, because of all that's going on—like any state-supported workplace my office is overcrowded anyway—for now I can get away with two or three hours at night, just as long as I clock in and out every day. And, once I fall into that routine, beyond those two or three hours I never leave the house.

I suppose I'm getting what I came back in 2010 unconsciously looking for: the kind of womb-like isolation where nothing is required of me, where to be loved and cared for doesn't mean having to do anything for anyone. Your leaving, then the revolution hadn't given me a chance to be that way, but now I can?

Except that it really scares me, this. It's as though I only exist through Mouna, my faith and drive dependent on her remaining engaged. Until

I realize it isn't just my own atrophy that's unsettling—it's the revolution itself. It's been long enough to think about what it means and why. I am beleaguered. At no point have I imagined Egypt without Hosni Mubarak before he was dead. People dared not even imagine him dead. Now, alive, the war hero who'd been president for thirty years is in jail and, lo, everything looks and feels exactly the same. A little worse, actually. A lot worse.

In Tahrir Square I had believed I was making Egypt a place where you could have lived without constantly planning your escape. Now more women than ever in my lifetime were being gang-raped in public. More were covering up or being made to wear the niqab, and just as many were being killed by husbands or fathers or brothers, plain and simple—killed, the way Mouna's eldest brother, Umair, killed peasant girls when they got pregnant out of wedlock. How many times did I catch myself feeling grateful that you weren't here to see it! Mubarak was bad and the revolution brought down Mubarak, but does it follow that the revolution is good?

When I spoke to Abid at the time of the sit-in he was adamant that *hog-tie the economy and foot-fuck security* was all mass protest could do. Now I have the creeping suspicion that, unthinking as his response was, the khawal was right after all. Mass protest has restored Mouna to a fuller, feistier self and that's a major achievement right there. But if things end up being the same or worse, sooner or later Mouna too will feel bamboozled—her preeminent project predoomed—then who knows where she'll go.

To have believed in something. A partner, a revolution, a god. To have believed and then ended up naked and bruised by the wayside.

Writing you now it staggers me how Mouna raised us never to make a noise in the bathroom, any bathroom, lest we disturb the dirty djinn that dwell around toilets and drains. How that could fit with her saying, *Only a behim and the son of a behim believes what he cannot see with his eye or touch with his hand*, I have no idea.

More fondly than I ever did while she was alive, I think of her sprinkling imaginary salt over your head while she burbled the protective suras. Or, like a Jedi under attack, fending off the evil eye by splaying the five fingers of her raised right hand and staring hard ahead of her, jaws taut. Those ancient and irrational signals in which her body spoke, it is they that will spider-crack through my scalp when I see her laughing on her deathbed.

The close ones mounting a soul-rescue mission on her account— never mind how not close they will have turned out to be—they will be *selling water in the water carriers' quarter.* You must've heard her saying that proverb. Reminding her of duties she knew infinitely better. Calling her back to a subtle realm in which she was infinitely more at home.

They will be unaware that, by the time Mouna dies, she will have journeyed through four years of revolution. The last and perhaps the only true project of her life. She will have seen, in Hosni Mubarak's place, first, Mohamed Morsi—*Egypt's first civil, elected president,* apparently, though he was just a representative of the Ikhwan—then, a year to the day Morsi was sworn in, the military man who led the Ikhwan's ouster: a kind of neo-Nasser called Abd El Fattah El Sisi.

Hunched over a battered iPad with Baba's thick Wayfarers on, she will have seen this Sisi run for the presidency practically unchallenged and become absolute arbiter in a few months. After people, hundreds of people, died in a matter of hours on the asphalt. She will have seen the revolutionaries turn into fiends and fuckups. Besides *sharaf, dignity, baraka,* and *revolution,* there must've been a million words sequestered in the space around those battles, but in the end none of them could make a difference . . .

On July 19, 1962, an Egyptian passenger plane coming from Hong Kong via Bangkok crashed into the Sankamphaeng Mountains in Thailand. All twenty-six people on board, including eight crew members, died.

At Sawt El Umma the task of reporting the incident fell to the mysterious young belle who had arrived a little over a year before, and who—some insinuated—was either having an affair with Sameh Khairy or being groomed for one of his friends.

Nimo was given three hours to compose the text for a three-minute news broadcast. Because they had arranged to have lunch at Groppi's, Nimo spent most of that time with Semsem. And, less because she agreed with Semsem's view that the plane crash was an imperialist conspiracy by the enemies' intelligence agencies to show up the Zaim's fledgling aviation than because she felt it would go down best with her boss, this was how Nimo wrote it up.

Her first lie.

That week she was summoned to Sameh Khairy's office again, but this time, to her astonishment, the bald man had come to the door to welcome her in.

—Star, he sang out the English word in a faux–Humphrey Bogart voice, smiling broadly and bowing as he kissed her hand. Superstar!

On July 28, 1963—exactly twenty-four days after Sawt El Umma's tenth anniversary—the same flight, this time coming from Tokyo via Bangkok, crashed into the Arabian Sea instead of landing in Bombay, where it was due for the third of four stops on its way to Cairo. Fifty-five passengers and eight crew members died.

This time Nimo had nothing to do with conveying the news, but like every other news item of significance it was phoned into the State Information Service before it was broadcast. While she was scanning the stack of newssheets, one after another, her eye caught the name of the pilot.

Fouad Ali Qansuh.

Nimo hadn't seen Fouad for years. Now as his winning smile formed in her head and she dropped the whole stack, she could barely prevent herself from kneeling, slapping herself, and wailing like the professional mourners hired for Bara Hanim's death. She had joined them one whole evening, wondering why Bara's loss depleted her reserves of safety even though they had never been close. It was worse now.

The premature death of Susanne and Lena Qansuh's sibling felt like her own bespoke punishment for presenting Flight 862's first crash as an imperialist conspiracy. The lie for which she had been rewarded. Even though what happened with Aziz Maher should've been punishment enough.

Sameh Khairy had taken her in person, his little star as he'd been calling her since the first lie she authored successfully went on air. He had just had her transferred and officially appointed to a more vital but less visible part of Nasser's hydra of hype, the State Information Service Press Center.

A week later he phoned to say he'd arranged a meeting at the new Shepheard's Hotel with *that renowned genius Aziz Maher*. He had told him all about her intelligence and beauty, he explained, and the artist couldn't wait to meet her. Mainly for fear of sounding stupid, Nimo didn't ask what the artist might want. Though, thanks to Sameh Khairy's powers of suggestion, she was sure this was a reward, an opportunity she mustn't jeopardize.

And so the two of them were chauffeured in the Sawt El Umma director's state-bought black Cadillac DeVille. Next to her in the lush back seat, his hand patted her shoulder and wriggled down her arm until it came to rest on her thigh. But, seeing her recoil and pull her skirt down, Sameh Khairy quickly disengaged, coughing as he pulled back the little curtain to look out of the window. Saying nothing.

In the course of her full, fully vocalized confession to her dead friend, Nimo was to explain how much more he would turn her stomach when she finally realized it hadn't been for himself that he wanted her. For now she was only mildly surprised when, barely ten minutes after the three of them were seated, he excused himself with a gratuitous grin, declaring that Aziz Maher could always give Nimo a lift back to work.

—That was how the sharmoota's son stepped away, she would tell Lena, posthumously. Just like a licensed pimp!

But then there was the other sharmoota's son waiting by the Shepheard's Nile view with champagne, canapés, and a smile so cool and clear she couldn't help diving into it. That one was no behim. He was the country's best-known painter, and clearly master of his craft. Two minutes of doodling with his fountain pen and her likeness materialized on the menu with stunning verisimilitude. Together with the statement that he had never heard a radio broadcast more powerful than the one she'd written, that pushed her into his thrall.

As they spoke she noted that Aziz Maher's views were identical to Sameh Khairy's. He believed in Nasser, his mission, and his enemies. Or he didn't believe any of it but pretended to, because it was good for his art and his appetites. He had a potentate's appetites. *Art requires a trouble-free life* was his refrain. In any case he was actually fluent in French, so they conversed in the kind of Franco-Arabe Nimo had often used with her intimes. This made him feel closer than he was.

He was the tallest, whitest, most athletically built suitor she'd ever had. And he didn't seem to mind that she was already married or that her husband was indefinitely in prison. He behaved like a suitor. Unlike Sameh Khairy, he only ever had kind things to say about Amin.

Three weeks later all that remains of Aziz Maher is the print he's given her, sole artifact of her agreeing to model for him, which she will tell dead Lena she knew perfectly well was a euphemism for niquer. What she did not know and could never have suspected was how this vision of gentility might go about doing crac-crac once he had her receptive and ready.

His spacious Zamalek studio was the most modern interior she'd ever been, though it was somehow also *Thousand and One Nights*-ish. Straight-lined black furniture and whitewashed brick walls with ancient-looking draperies and antique smoking implements. Collectibles from all over the world and originals by Egyptians—Mahmoud Said, Tahia

Halim, Abd El Hadi El Gazzar—she was still to learn were the nation's greatest artists.

All that remains is the print and the image it captures: the moment she became his mannequin.

She's been reclining nude on the low palm-frond-and-cowhide Sudanese divan onto which he hoisted her since before he revealed her orange-tinged topography, rubbing and kneading, adulating her. While he squats shirtless a few steps from her, his buttocks on a small table or a footstool, wielding a twig of charcoal into a huge sketchbook, looking like a day laborer earning his bread. Like some scaled-down odalisque dragging on a sebsi—she could've sworn she knew that's what a Moroccan kif pipe was called—which he's just refilled with tobacco and soft hashish.

—Voilà! Do you like the incense, ya amari?

He's always called her *amari*. Not *ya amar* but *ya amari*, making it *his*.

But why does she want to laugh? Things have grown so fluid they are bleeding into each other: sandalwood into chocolate; the long metal pipe into a rubbery erection; sweat-streaked stubble and sooty fingers into orange blossom and bated breath.

She's not sure whether this is the effect of hashish, Aziz, or Jacques Brel. She's always loved Jacques Brel. It's as if "Ne me quitte pas" were playing not on the gramophone but through some tiny phonograph in her head.

Each time it comes on she is surer than the last that the words, the notes are microscopic fish swimming in and out of her pores. Like Aziz's sweat, everything smells slightly of sea salt. But although she appears to be swimming Nimo is flying because the fish, the colors, his tongue in her crotch have transformed her into her favorite bird, which she knows by its onomatopoeic Arabic name: *hudhud*.

Now her beau chignon is a fan of dark-tipped golden feathers, her cul incroyable a magnificent blast of black and white plumage. When she moans what comes out is *oodoodood, oodoodood, oodoodood*.

That's why Nimo barely notices when, in the midst of the act, she becomes aware of a burning ache in her backside. For a while it is part of the florid fluidity of what's going on, an extension of one or another of the myriad sensations that have stopped time. But then she begins to recognize it.

All her life Nimo has suffered intermittently from constipation. It sobers her to remember this, the magic hemorrhaging out of her system. The worst is when you're beyond the point of no return but unable to keep going because the burning ache is such—but that burning ache is exactly what she's feeling now. She can smell neither sea salt nor orange blossom water but something ironlike and tinged with—khara, actually.

As her hazel irises swivel about and her body shakes with the effort of sitting up—Aziz having mistaken this for excitement, his stabs speed up and intensify—she can see that her knees are above her breasts, a thin string of blood trickling between her thighs. Dripping from the place where her body meets Aziz's, it is staining the edge of the divan a purplish black. Nimo notices then that, while her stunted labia are slightly parted, Aziz's long, willowy penis is halfway up her behind.

And when a moment later she pushes him off, gathers her clothes together, and runs out without a word, she encounters not so much resistance as mild shock, a vaguely mocking disgruntlement she can only understand as that of a dissatisfied customer.

Even later—three weeks to the day after she met him, when she resolves to thank him for the print of her face she found on her desk without a note—it takes nearly a month to get hold of him on the phone. And then he sounds so haughty and high-handed she abandons the thought of paying his Zamalek studio a surprise visit.

Some of the gossip will have reached her. Not only about her being Sameh Khairy's *private assistant* but also about Aziz Maher's women. The many nubile morsels he needs to consume, and whom Sameh Khairy sometimes finds for him. Though she is grateful that no one has dared say anything in her presence, for fear of the same Socialist Union connections that would be ready to punish her the minute she upsets the powers that be.

It won't be hard to prove herself virtuous in the next few years.

None of it affects her as much as that moment when, having understood what's happening, she tries to make eye contact. Aziz can see her buttock, her bezz. He can see his penis slithering out of her. But she might as well be a blow-up doll. And he doesn't have the remotest clue that, for the duration of that moment he is nothing but an intractable turd she is laboring to discharge.

A Vision of Lena

A lithograph, as they call it. Hand-printed by the artist. Nimo doesn't know where the nude sketches went. After three months three years three decades, the lithograph tells her not that she's beautiful but that, however beautiful she may be, she must continue to suffer from constipation. Only a magnoona would keep such a thing but, magnoona or not, she's keeping it. She's keeping it because it captures the thing she could've been, the model, the mannequin that she was with her extramarital lover. A mannequin has no innocence or bitterness. A mannequin is cold, colorless, almost nonexistent. However can its image bring on such ghastly rainbows of heat? All of a sudden it is noon and Lena's figure appears in strips and clumps as she bounces off enchanted glass, in and out of mind, beyond time. So long as she's not a corpse. And yaani Nimo can't not see the beauty of her friend, Lena's literally deadly beauty, knowing how impatient Lena is to be erased from her own memory. Grief is not being with Susanne while Lena and Fouad are gone. It is not even Lena being gone. Grief is the hurt of the man and Nasserism. The endless hypocrisies that have seeped in and out of Nimo, befouling every last one of her founts. Grief is her inability to tell Lena of them. But, El Maître and Nazlı Hanim having left the country, now she just pictures Lena on her recuperative trip, which is only the summer vacation painted black or anyway the color of infinite absence. Having lost something so dear it is worth a thousand worlds and their hereafters, Nimo pictures her friend waiting with Susanne till the two of them and their elderly nurse Dada Ghalia are out of the Agami beach chalet and in the Raml Station apartment. Nimo pictures Lena in that quaint bluish building wedged between El Nabi Danyal Street and the Greek Hospital, within the same polygon of alleyways as Cavafy's. Here the Hellenic-speaking Alexandrian brought back visions of male beauty into which to dissolve, then wrote his poems in solution. Though to listen to Semsem one would think he was not an Alexandrian at all, nor even a homosexual, but a foreign conspirator intent on poisoning the virility of our Arab youths, rendering them unfit to join the battle for national glory. Maybe Lena knows the poem herself, *tu chercheras en vain d'autres rivages, la ville te poursuivra*, the one about never being able to leave. Amin showed Nimo the Arabic translation but it's the French that she has learned by heart. And it's clear to her Cavafy was a truer Alexandrian than any Upper Egyptian immigrant of future decades calling himself an Alexandrian, whatever Semsem has to say about it. Nimo pictures Lena waiting until Lena has settled into Cavafy's polygon of alleyways, a ten-minute walk from the Hotel Cecil at Raml Station. However can it still be there, that French villa-style cube opposite the Saad Zaghloul statue where, so Amin told Nimo, Cleopatra's Needle used to stand? The balconets that frame its mullioned windows, the shiny cresting atop its roof walls, however can they continue to exist in Lena's absence? Grief is not being able to tell Lena how Nimo hadn't felt so much as a breath on her knuckles when all of a sudden there was this handsome gentleman, this stud. He was not simply making love to her, he was mixing magic with degradation, placing his manhood in—bas bas. Her reward for brainwashing the people. The price of being called a superstar. To be a sharmoota, anyway sharmoota enough to make Lena proud. And Lena no longer there to say bravo, mon chou. Lena, who actually killed a man by her beauty and promiscuity, should be proud. *Où que je tourne mes yeux, où mon regard se pose, je ne vois que ruines celles de ma vie gâchée.* Nimo pictures her friend slipping out early in the morning while Susanne sleeps, wearing only a bright shift dress and no underwear. Lena walks fast, cocaine-confident in the sea breeze. And while Susanne sleeps she suspects nothing more than another pigeon at the window, not a scrap of Qansuh anywhere in the archives. Susanne dreams of a tabby-sized tiger scuttling down the narrow steps. Now Nimo pictures Lena sashaying through the revolving door, an impossibly voluptuous teenager greeting the liveried Nubi bellboy with the long tarboosh before she steps into the pretty little ascenseur that will take her up, up, all the way to heaven. Her beauty stops everyone, but no one dares stop her. Nimo pictures her climbing the last flight of steps and opening the roof's little gate. She smokes two cigarettes while she paces in search of the perfect break in the cresting for her gorgeous cul to rest, the angle from which to view her favorite city, *la ville qui te poursuivra*. Her perfect calves dangle while, seated on top of the world, Lena dreams of strolling in enchanted sea spray with an old man who's Fouad. It's Fouad but he's as old as El Maître, because he's lived to the ripe old age everyone had expected of him. Lena's strolling along this same sea-struck Corniche, laughing, her arm in his—engagé like a nineteenth-century couple—while all around low-flying planes swoosh through the trembling azure over the turquoise headscarf of the sea. It's this headscarf that she aims for, like the Gezira Club swimmer she is. Of course she understands the water is impossibly far—she knows what she is doing—but it's on the turquoise that she trains her eyes after she lifts herself up and teeters, unafraid. Nimo pictures her dress coming off forthwith, her flesh radiating while she zooms down so that she glows brighter than the sun. For a moment Lena is a comet or an angel, a piece of Our Lord's light in the morning sky. But by the time her head cracks on the metal side of the carriage driver's perch, collapsing the hood and startling the horse enough to overturn the whole carriage, she is once again the promiscuous woman about town. Cold and colorless. A mere cadaver. Her remains must be scraped off the asphalt and her identity guessed at—she was once seen with her dada, but already Ghalia and Susanne are scaling the streets distressedly searching for her—then taken to the morgue. And after three months three years three decades all that remains is a print, n'est-ce pas?

On March 20, 2011, some Egyptian aircraft must be crashing somewhere while everyone gathers at our one-story house.

Abid and the two strangers who arrived with him watch from the veranda while, cradling what looks like a stuffed toy with prodigious pointed ears, Mouna stands gazing up at them in terror. Two men flanking a third on the veranda while she sways hunched under the mango tree, her slippers half buried in grass-sprinkled earth, one side of her drenched in blood.

It's the kind of thing that only happens to someone as spiritual as Mouna—whatever *spiritual* means—but, as I'll come to think of it, in time, it's also a numinous intervention to buffer the bad news. *I was checking for mites*, she'll explain. And it's true she's mentioned clearing the narrow strip of garden behind the house. But what drives a reborn life-lover to a space she hasn't been in years exactly in time for a bleeding fennec fox to literally drop on her head?

—She was not dead when I took hold of her, she'll keep saying, having instantly seen it was female.

But the fennec dies before Mouna has summoned up her first scream.

There is a rusty old antenna jutting out of this side of our roof. Somehow propelled from the unfinished residential tower opposite, it seems the fox has impaled itself on it then managed to wriggle free, tripping over the edge just in time for Mouna's head to cushion the fall. What are the chances?

In my childhood it used to be that you could occasionally spot a fennec or sand fox by the side of the desert road—not on the upper floors of Maadi skyscrapers—but by the time you were born, Shimo, even in the desert they'd started dying out.

Gray, arm-length boughs, some of them detaching and sliding down when she inadvertently hits the mango tree branches, hang about Mouna's shoulders and bonnet as she walks toward the veranda in a daze. It is still light out and, clasping that impossibly cute thing to her bosom, rocking it like a baby, she is visibly sobbing. Without being a pious mama again, somehow, she has aged back the years she has let go of since Mubarak stepped down.

In their identical black suits and aviator sunglasses, the two State Security clichés alternately bend over the slight, hard figure of Abid Abdalla to whisper in his ear. This is the first time he's shown up since the start of the revolution, and his presence feels like a bad omen while I grapple with a pail of water and a long spade. Panic. Because I'm thinking it would be the end of the revolution if the Military Council won. At least a sure sign that the revolution is failing. It would mean that, when Mubarak said it was either him or the Islamic Republic of Egypt, he was not bluffing. It would also mean that, aside from its conflict with the Islamists, the army has ruled by consensus since the time of Gamal Abd El Nasser.

I put my pail down, pilfering glances in their direction, cursing the lieutenant colonel under my breath. I mark out a spot and sprinkle some water onto it, softening the earth with my spade. Then I pick up the shovel to dig.

That's when you appear suddenly, jumping up and down in the mud I've created. Your pigtails and your smile overwhelm me. Because, even though I remain forty-one, you're not twenty-seven but nine. A restless, skinny figure dancing about with your arms. Your body is only just beginning to take on its present shape, but your eyes and cheeks are almost perfect circles.

—Can you get out of this mud please, Shimo, I say in my big-brother voice, before I realize I'm weeping.

—But why do you look so glum, ya Nour? You jump faster, laughing and sticking out your tongue. Nour, why do you look so glum?

So I step in the mud and lift you bodily—you don't run away from me, you're not even upset—but the minute I touch you, the minute I realize you're not really there, I feel such pain in my upper abdomen that I begin to retch.

I'm hallucinating my baby sister but not the pain of being here now, seven thousand miles away, unable to communicate with her.

Apart from army and police cohorts in and around the state-supported press—here's the thing—I don't actually know anyone who will vote yes in the referendum. Yet when the final count proclaims the revolution's defeat on Mouna's little télé, it is not a bolt from the blue. Not even she seems shocked as she takes in the information:

Seventy-seven percent of the vote is in favor of the constitutional amendments proposed by the Military Council and supported by the Ikhwan.

Abid leaves half an hour after I smooth the last layer of earth over the fennec's body. By now you, too, are totally gone. And it seems the disquiet of the dead creature is negating what our minds know: that practically one hundred percent should be opposed to said amendments.

—Bas! That's enough, I can hear Mouna rasping as she prepares to cite another proverb: *Better the catastrophe than waiting for it.*

Now the ripples of my anxiety settle while I walk around the house. Huddled together under the covers, Mouna and Tante Fifi sit up and grope until I hand them a lighter and ashtray. They will spend hours smoking and snuffling in the bed's invisible canopy, speaking of the dead darling and the country's flanks being run through. Touching with a passion I will not understand till after Mouna is dead.

But already it occurs to me that, like the portents and premonitions we have always reshuffled in our sleep and our waking dreams, the fennec arrived at our garden not from another place but another time.

Just as expected, things will keep degenerating after the March 2011 referendum. By New Year 2012 the Ikhwan's tide has filled parliament with mosque idlers, baltagis, jihadis, tuk-tuk drivers, black marketeers, and procurers of short-term girl brides for elderly men from the Gulf. The people's choice, apparently. MPs whose only qualification is that they have long beards and zebibas—those fungus-infected raisins of dead skin on their foreheads, you've seen them—apparently from rubbing against coarse rugs while they're wet in salah.

Mouna calls it a dark cloud, referencing rice-husk-burning season, the noxious smog that overtakes the city for weeks on end after rice is harvested every autumn. And she seems to lose momentum until, one morning in October 2011, I find her gabbling on the veranda again, writing furiously in her blue and yellow block note. When I ask what she is writing about she turns to me:

—Voilà, she says. Even if this is pure coincidence. Even if it's always been the case. If one in ten news items is about a woman falling from a balcon or a roof or a window, isn't that worth investigating?

From that day on—in the company of a twenty-two-year-old Kasr El Ainy Hospital nurse named Monica Younis she grows insanely attached to—investigating is all Mouna seems to do.

I too begin to scout the relevant emergency wards a few months after that. I stalk the security guards, pestering friends and relations for contacts, following what leads present themselves through word of mouth. I'm not allowed to publish a word of it, but I do my work as a journalist.

By the time Tante Fifi leaves Mouna alone on her quest, I will have spoken to eleven spouses and office workers who were witnesses. They all agree it is abrupt, without prelude or explanation. Their otherwise normal wife or coworker at an otherwise ordinary moment will simply step over the edge. The women tend to jump from the highest floors, yet few of them die immediately. Limbs break, skulls split, swaths of skin come off the tender jelly of unprotected flesh, but once they hit the asphalt the women will often be conscious, in pain.

At hospital some Jumpers are taken to be victims of riot control. Often they are so shocked by their own behavior they play along with that fiction. Sometimes they make up fictions of their own about how they leaned too far while hanging out the washing or how, cleaning, they tripped and tumbled while reaching under the sill. The doctors believe them.

Some Jumpers are called while they're preparing to leap. When that happens they respond normally, they can carry on a conversation to the point when gravity takes hold, but no matter what is said it never stops them. Later they'll explain they were in a trance for as long as it took to execute the vault, feeling it was the most natural thing.

They are in a trance, they say, but they can never tell when it starts. No jolt occurs, no change in perception. The action follows from whatever comes before it like a page in a flip book. Objectively the image doesn't fit the sequence, it belongs in a different and demonic narrative, but the trance makes it so that the woman can experience it as a link in a chain.

—⫶—

As she weaves through Masr Station, on her way to Alexandria, Nimo has the impression that she is on a spiritual journey, a pilgrimage within like the ones saints are said to go on periodically. Sometimes it'll be a Miraj like the Prophet's ascension through the seven heavens. But more often it is to visit a fellow Sufi long since deceased or impossibly far. That is what it feels like to Nimo.

The train is a giant mechanical snake crawling along the iron road.

The train is a locomotive tomb for transporting pretty young women to the afterlife.

The train is a dry riverbed spattered with a soup of blood and tissue. It runs from the highlands of the south all the way down to the northern seashore.

That is why, sitting stiffly by the window in the wood-and-velvet coach, fanning herself with her cloche hat, Nimo can see almost nothing of the cabbage and cornfields that flit past, the billowing galabiyas at station stops, or the facades of rare colonial architecture elsewhere on the way.

She is busy reliving the two incidents that, like a snake or a tomb or a riverbed, have slowly brought her to this moment.

The only time Amna manages to see Amin while he's inside is during Ramadan, in October 1961. The visit takes place in a nondescript hall within the Qanatir Prison compound, empty except for two guards and an officer waiting in the corner. With piles of sandbags where the tables should be, a grotesque memento of the cafeteria where they met.

The prison is bustling everywhere, the guffaws and coughs of the wretched echoing nonstop, but this space seems to muffle all noise, just as it slows down motion. When Amin emerges in his soiled navy uniform, barefoot with a slight limp, she can tell he's been hurt in ways he didn't know were possible. For the first time it dawns on her how wrong she was when she thought he couldn't be a real communist and no one would pay attention to a three-member organization.

Amin is gaunt and guarded. But when he takes her hand his grip is rough, awkward. And there is grace in his eyes when he looks at her, jittery and genial, undeniably himself. For what feels like an hour they are silent. Then his lips are brushing her ear.

He says, *How can I ever make amends?*

He says, *Thank God for you!*

He says, *I got a ten-year sentence. If you want to start over you have every right to a divorce.*

There is profound shelter in his presence, but it's excruciating.

He goes on saying things, but now they don't come through. As the meaning of that last statement condenses, she gradually becomes aware of rage taking hold of her body, replacing all the other emotions. She barely knows what she's doing as she pulls her head away from his ear, takes half a step back.

—You dare? He catches hold of her hand just before it hits his face. You dare say that to me, son of Abdalla? She snatches it back and thumps her own chest. You dare tell me I can divorce you?

—I need you to know I wouldn't blame you, that's all.

—A little too late now, don't you think. Besides, you know where I was coming from when I married you. Are you taunting me about my background now?

—Mouna!

—The officer who arranged this meeting said it was a very special favor for my boss. I might never be able to visit again.

—You won't.

—So you know I won't and you're still telling me I can divorce you.

—Amna, he sighs.

Amin may be gaunt and guarded, but it's him. Although she has never seen him weep, not once, she recognizes him the more once she notices a fat tear hanging by a thread from his lower lip.

—Yaah, ya Amin!

Now he smiles. It's the sad, the incredibly sad smile that will become his trademark look, in time, but she doesn't know that yet. He smiles and fumbles in his pockets, lost for body language. Until he fishes out a roll-up and, flourishing it with a nod, walks over to one of the guards, evidently to ask for a light.

Her eyes rove round the hall for a moment before Amin reappears with a cheap wooden chair like the ones they use in baladi cafés. He positions it below her backside before he crouches by her feet like a peasant at the Omda's, with his back to the wall. He slides down and thrusts his knees up to adjust his balance in a single fluid movement she has never seen, but which is clearly second nature to him now.

Now Amin smooths out and lights his cigarette, shrugging apologetically as if to say, *I wish I could offer you one.* He looks like a day laborer waiting for work on a bend of the Corniche. She wants to draw his attention to the fact, she thinks it'll make him proud. But he's inhaling so voraciously she decides to leave him to it.

Forget salah, she tells herself instead. He never even fasts, my little infidel. But perhaps it's permissible not to fast when you're in jail?

Any moment in Nimo's life could conceivably be in Ramadan. And of course when it's daytime in Ramadan and she doesn't have her period, she cannot eat, drink, or smoke. Not that she resents the fast, which she's performed unthinkingly since the age of twelve. She just needs coffee and cigarettes more than usual that day. It's been a cold morning and the hall is bare, but Nimo is hot and clammy.

Something about the trip to El Qanatir, normally a sortie de vacances, made her mouth parched in a way that brought back the day, some two years before, when she rang the doorbell in that ordinary-looking Manial building. It wasn't Ramadan then—and she'd had some water—but there was a different reason she couldn't eat.

With something of Frankenstein's monster about him—as if his misshapen face and huge hands had been cobbled together from metal, leather, and glass—the man who opened the door did look like a butcher. She gripped Semsem's arm as he turned to her, a lewd smirk like the kingpin holding up his unnaturally tall frame. He wore pajamas, and the room onto which the door opened looked like the hall of a family apartment.

Stepping through the next doorway without a word, he motioned for them to follow. Nimo was surprised to walk into a middle-class salon, as if to be entertained as a visitor. But the man bent over the sofa and, groping, unlatched a secret door. He opened it without pulling away the sofa, squeezing behind it and motioning for them to do likewise. Once inside he closed the secret door behind them. As if by magic now, he was wearing a white coat, complete with surgical gloves and mask.

It was then she saw the surgeon's table with all manner of saws and spikes neatly positioned next to a kitchen stool by what looked like a stretcher, not a bed. There was a sink to one side, a blinding lamp above her head and a kind of mantelpiece with differently sized beakers along the wall in front of her. Smirking still, the man asked her to remove her clothes and lie down under the sheet.

—I hope you haven't eaten anything, as I requested, he said.

—She hasn't, Semsem snapped, as if to say, *Get on with it.*

—Good, he murmured, busying himself with the anesthetic. Very good.

When she came to Nimo was unafraid except for a strong sense of her knees having been above her breasts. Cutting through her grogginess was a searing pain that seemed to disconnect her pelvis from the rest of her body. She could barely feel her legs anyway, but it was as if her pelvis had been replaced with some alien and abhorrent prosthesis. She was grateful to find she was alone with Semsem.

On her way out, the Frankenstein monster was in the armchair by the main door, in his pajamas again, listening to some invisible radio over a glass of tea. Semsem paid him and noted his instructions; then he bid them wait while he rummaged in a small cupboard to one side. He came back with a paper bag, which he handed Nimo along with a valid-looking prescription listing an antibiotic and a painkiller.

—I thought you might like to keep it, he said, smirking lewdly again.

As she peeled the paper she could see a rusty lid. Pulling, she found she was holding an all but broken specimen jar containing what looked like a flayed mouse in a soup of blood and tissue. For a moment an intense nausea overpowered the pain in her abdomen.

As she watches Amin smoke Amna recalls how, leaning on Semsem, who held her up by the armpits much of the way down the stairs, the first thing she did was stop at the nearest juice shop for a tall mug of sugarcane juice. It was already evening, and Manial's crisp, early-morning emptiness had given way to a lugubrious and dusty congestion.

She needed that reinvigorating sweetness, which she guzzled in two drafts while staring at the fetus in her handbag. Then she bent down, placed the specimen jar on the asphalt and gently nudged it so it rolled over to the middle of the road. She drained another mug of sugarcane and watched as a car tire smashed it to pieces, turning her dead homunculus into a barely perceptible stain.

As she weaves through Masr Station—or is that just me time traveling in our disused attic?—Nimo's mind wanders forward to the day Amin is freed. Carrying the travel bag she has brought into work in preparation for staying the night with Susanne, Nimo doesn't know she is seeing the future—only to forget it in time for when it happens.

They are standing somewhere familiar, perhaps on the veranda in Maadi, and she is looking at him while he tries to conjure up some of the grace that used to soften and curve the rigid lines of his physiognomy. His face remains hard.

With a glance he used to flood every last scrap of her in that rough, redolent tenderness of his. Now even as he holds her face in his hands he cannot invoke enough of it to sprinkle one little toe.

Later, four years after the revolution when I'm ready to move along, I see Mouna as I did at the time it started over. June, July 2013. She is looking like a stick doll in her faux-fellahin outfit, so bony has she become. Wearing her Scholl sandals and one of her lace-trim galabiyas, her freshly dyed hair in a bun or bonnet and her eyes kohled like the Prophet's, she has a silk foulard over her shoulders for when she needs to cover her hair.

For a long time all through winter and spring, while the Ikhwan carry on shooting themselves in the foot, Mouna has been poised for a second revolution. By June 2013—my forty-fourth birthday—it's been a year and a half since that Kasr El Ainy nurse was gone. And for half a year a comic cold war between Islamists and the rest of us has threatened to turn hot.

Not that Mouna and I know it is abetted by State Security, though come to think of it how can we not? Every party that can conceivably work against the Ikhwan is working against the Ikhwan. The fanatics embarrass them, the electricity company stages power cuts to foment anger with them, the media strews fear of what their catastrophic lack of experience will bring about. Even the revolutionaries denigrating Islamist violence have started speaking well of the police.

All this might have been voluntary, I suppose. But the beggar women at busy intersections calling out hysterically to the stalling cars, *They will strip you of your clothes and burn down your houses*—no way that's on their own initiative. Still, whatever the deep state is doing, a lot of people are ready to kill to get rid of the Ikhwan. But almost as many are ready to kill to keep them. And even if she has to delude herself about the role of State Security, having the Islamists to blame for the Jumpers' deaths keeps Mouna more or less sane for now.

Every day on my way out I see her carrying her coffee and cigarettes to the newly fixed veranda—she still takes her hypertension medicine, but even with cigarettes coffee doesn't seem to affect her heartbeat now—where there is no longer any debris. When she finally agreed to mend it, she replaced the plastic stool with a Bauhaus coffee table and had the bergère reupholstered. Sitting straight-backed in front of her no-longer-gutted parapet, she begins to run her finger over the touch screen as she sips, daintily blowing smoke.

Do you know the term for the dance a headless chicken does before it falls dead, *the spirit's sweetness*? The idea is that the spirit is too sweet a possession for the body not to try to hold on to it when it's time to part.

After her story with the nurse I think something like this happened to Mouna. A mania of mundanity afflicted her. There was all the work on the veranda, but then she threw in paint jobs and replaced pieces of furniture, going about the work with such focus and speed you could see a shadow of her businesswoman self peeping through. She seemed unduly euphoric while she attacked stores and wrangled with contractors. But you would've known at once—she was grieving.

It was as if she managed to substitute ecstatic energy for the rituals of mourning, which she would've performed with professional aptitude and acuity. She didn't fall catatonic when the chicken dance was over, but she drew closer than I could've imagined to the Cataclysm. As her energy ebbed, Baba loomed for a moment. She had a sleepless night or two, wept over her supper, hissed. But by December 2012, the surge had passed.

Monica settled down to oblivion. And Tante Fifi went to live with her only son and his wife in Sharm El-Sheikh. The move had been on the cards for years by then, and, after Monica, Fifi must've felt it was time to make it.

—But yaani c'est la vie, n'est-ce pas, son of Amin?

Only that hail of shooting stars went on cascading round Mouna's head. The Jumpers.

The day Sisi appears on TV to dismiss President Mohamed Morsi and end the rule of the Ikhwan—he is flanked by every possible religious, political, or community leader—I happen to be on the October Bridge, on my way home from an asinine interview in Heliopolis. There is a traffic holdup and I'm crawling patiently along, alternately fantasizing about an Aya look-alike and wondering what might be going on with Mouna.

I do not know she is home alone, reminiscing about the last two years while she sits cross-legged in her four-poster bed, her iPad and block note beside her. For once the small télé on her dresser is turned on again, but with the sound off so she can listen to herself humming the Sayed Darwish song "Ana Hawet." She's doing it at an even slower tempo than the original, turning it into a kind of lament while, with half an eye, she watches.

In the middle of the screen a small man in khakis is surrounded by all the army's standards, as if swathed in them. With the red and white and black of the republic preponderating, a black beret dwarfs his unremarkable face. Mouna watches that face going from right to left while, lips strained, he reads from something unseen below two little microphones overhanging at chest level. Leaning on it seems to press down into place not just the little podium but the whole world. And it only takes her a second to identify another Nasser installing himself into Egypt's hardware.

It's as if she knows everything already, then. The violence, the violations, endless inflation to fund megaprojects. Hunger and hopelessness in the army's country.

She can tell he's saying all the right things—about the media, the economy, human rights. And she won't be surprised when his first move turns out to be a New Suez Canal. But it hurts her—it *wrings her belly*, as she would've said—even harder than dead Jumpers. By the time the new canal is inaugurated in August 2014, she will be on her way.

For a little under a year before Sisi is elected president, there will be no end of explosions and assassinations. Mass arrests—executions. As far as Mouna is concerned, relief about the Ikhwan's departure cannot make up for that.

The people she associates with these days are mild and mannerly revolutionaries, not half as worried about the Ikhwan's wrongdoing as the way Wahhabis talk on TV. She feels no connection with them. And, from now on, whenever she hears them or others hailing Sisi as the country's savior—sincerely, half-sincerely, spontaneously or by order of State Security—she will remember the sight of that face reading the script, going dumbly from right to left, right, left, like a pendulum bob, the arms like the edges of the clock case. His speeches mark the hours.

And who can survive a future as unending as the history of the July Revolution? Will anybody live to see that pendulum stop?

That day I am nowhere near her till early evening. Then, my anxiety rippling while she grows catatonic, I hover around the bed trying to talk to her. She spends hours there, neither gabbling nor trembling but completely unresponsive as she stares at the ceiling, pointedly awake.

Long before she explains to me what is happening, Shimo, long before the hallucinations start for real, I can tell she is having some kind of vision. And no matter how hard I try—without your tempting me up to the attic, before slipping in next to a body that is not her—no way I could begin to guess what it might be.

For a long time now Mouna has been quiet. There's nothing wrong with her on the surface. She spends time on her iPad. She talks and is talked to. But her heart isn't in it. Though she still takes care of herself, she is quiet, subtly zombified.

I'm grateful we still spend time together, as we used to, telling each other stories. Because that's the only way I can tell she's struggling. Sincerely, strenuously struggling to latch on to some revolutionary focus other than the Jumpers. By now Mouna is convinced she needs to rid herself of the fixation that's cost her both her intimes, her social prestige, and a good half of her mind. But she can't seem to break free.

Strange now to think that, until the Cataclysm, Mouna was still doing her salah. It feels unbelievable to me, but so does everything that happened before all those people were killed at the Rabaa El Adaweya Mosque square.

For far too long at that Nasr City intersection—and, simultaneously, in one other spot near Cairo University, at the other end of town— Islamists who had felt empowered or represented by the Ikhwan will have set up camp in protest of their overthrow, demanding the Ikhwan leaders' release from custody and crying coup d'état. They will demolish sidewalks and barricade themselves with sandbags, set up *defense committees* that function like checkpoints, and send out little machine-gun-brandishing patrols. Anti-Islamists caught among them will be secretly buried after having their fingers chopped off.

But, even before this is made public, people know the Qaeda front-man Ayman Al Zawahiri has pledged allegiance to the Ikhwan president. Islamist leaders have already called on military personnel to defect to a Free Army like Syria's. So when the Ikhwan declare they can stop ongoing jihadi operations in Sinai with the swipe of a smartphone screen—just release our leaders and we'll do it, they say—even the most Islamist-sympathetic revolutionaries are ready to give up on diplomacy.

Still, it takes two weeks for a contingent of army-backed riot police to move in and, after a whole day of tear gas and loudspeakers, protesters start firing at the riot police. That's what interior and defense ministry leaders have been hoping for, it seems. Because, despite safe passages and alleged good intentions, by the time it is over there are nearly a thousand corpses at the site, almost all of them belonging to male Islamists.

People speak of the asphalt changing color, the ubiquitous mud puddles from shopkeepers hosing down the asphalt to make the dust settle being viscous and bright red.

August 14, 2013, when this happens. All over the world now Abd El Fattah El Sisi has a massacre on his hands. But in Cairo the deification dance has started. His image crops up everywhere, sunglasses under army cap—even in the dark. Talk shows extol his talents. Astrologists foretell his glory. Sheikhs compare him to God's prophets. Billboards beatify him. His likeness appears on pendants and chocolate wrappers. Women swoon while he delivers cloying homilies. And it devastates her.

Even more than the death of a thousand men, the rise of a new Zaim devastates her. She's convinced that enough women will have died jumping to expiate those deaths. But what about the future of the country?

How it crushes me to think of her somehow aware of the Cataclysm even then, impelled to run for her life and not knowing how.

For a few days she seemed to win her struggle. Without so much as mentioning the Jumpers, she was involved in the buildup to the Second Revolution, as the June 30 protests really were called, long before it was clear they would lead to the rise of Sisi. She helped to collect signatures for the nationwide petition to overthrow the Ikhwan, coordinated the martyrs' families' marches in Heliopolis—where the main demonstration was held. She sounded enthusiastic telling me about it. We went together. And for a moment or two that day I thought I glimpsed the Mouna of February and March 2011 sashaying around the haunts of her youth. But by now she was a consummate enough revolutionary to know: if the police weren't attacking it, let alone actively protecting it, as they were doing now, it could not be real.

Later in the month Sisi will go on air to demand *a mandate from the people to fight terrorism* and, in the form of brief but loud displays of patriotism on the streets, receive exactly such a mandate. Then the Second Revolution will feel even more fake to her, and its fakeness will redouble her distress.

The harder you looked now, the more the zombie came through. Not just Mouna's zombie: the Second Revolution felt like a shadow, an obverse, a parodic likeness of the first. The millions who took part in it—driven not by dissent but fear—were like the living dead. They were more honorable citizens than revolutionaries. And, sensing their hypocrisy and terror, Mouna was reminded of Amin abruptly leaving a party thrown in his honor when he came out of prison in 1964.

That day, he told her, he felt as if he'd come out into a Cairo whose inhabitants had been replaced by mutant look-alikes unaware of what was wrong with them.

In August 1963 Nimo is only twenty-four. Semsem is the comic in her life, Lena the immoralist. And, although she feels wizened enough to be two hundred and forty, both are still teaching her.

Except that Semsem can't seem to discuss anything anymore apart from the Aswan High Dam. Never mind apocalyptic flooding if it's ever bombed—the Nuba erased, the end of agriculture, an entire Abu Simbel temple relocated—Nasser's megaproject will put the imperialists in their place. By now Semsem is actually getting humorless.

And Lena is, well—Lena's no more. Still, through the two of them Amna Abu Zahra is settling into sixties Cairo.

Time and again, since she was parted from Amin, Nimo has desperately missed being Mouna. To soothe her pining she would recall Mansour Effendi's bedroom, so that she might remember the grief, the hatred, the letdown of those days. But however much it hurt she still longed for the triangle of sunlight on the floor of the Aquarium Grotto, across which she might savor the ring of her Amin-given name unsullied by all that would follow.

Since seeing him for the first time after they were parted, she has felt grateful for being the childless career woman into which his absence turned her. She has happily inhabited the role of the young worldly woman who can never mention her husband, who did so well at Sawt El Umma she was transferred to the State Information Service Press Center, closer to the political kitchen as they call it.

The purpose of the center is to control where foreign journalists go, what they see, and who they talk to, on the pretext of providing information and assistance, including glorified fixers like Nimo. Who enjoys the company of French speakers so much her new position feels paradise-perfect.

Every month her body still revolts against the flayed mouse in the specimen jar, it's true. But every month she feels more identical with the persona her femme-baltagi friend has given her. And so the earliest shoots of cynicism are being grafted onto her maturation, spliced together with ambition, anxiety, and a capacity for ingenuousness that will stay with her no matter how many times she loses her innocence.

Time and again, since meeting Aziz Maher, she has felt that only a return to God could resolve these endless contradictions. Only Our Lord, the Lord of all of us, can bring her all together, mentally.

Although she refuses to acknowledge it, with all that Amin has opened up to her and her Abu Zahra–whetted sensitivity to injustice, Nimo can see that a deity who permits slavery and places even free women in sexual bondage to men, a deity who commands that all but his followers be conquered or killed is not so much an all-powerful as an all-petty god. Venal and small-minded, more interested in sect than spirit and keener on ritual than right. It'll take her another ten years to become a pious mama in hijab, but already, in her psyche, none of that makes Him any less crucial to her well-being.

Because His rules spare her all kinds of moral confusion.

Because He makes this life a mere rehearsal for a better one.

Because His mercy turns pain, which is predestined and inviolate, into purpose, which is freely chosen and can be changed.

Because no matter how invisible, how contemptible she is, He can see and redeem her.

Because by worshipping Him loudly she can be as venal and small-minded as she likes, knowing that people will approve of her regardless.

But I'm no longer talking of my mother, am I. I'm talking of the Mother of the World. Surely even you know that's what Egypt is called, dear sister. At moments like this it seems as if Amna Abu Zahra is a fractal of our country, her biography a variation on its history, a version of the same story.

As she weaves through Masr Station her mind wanders forward to the sight of Amin standing by the bench; I'm definitely time traveling in the attic, Shimo.

Fists not so savagely clenched behind him while the evening azan traipses mild and mellifluous into the veranda, he's in the same tweed trousers and plaid shirt with brown leather braces he was wearing on New Year's Eve, 1959. Yet she can barely recognize him.

—Amna, he sighs. But his smile is a rictus. She knows he won't be calling her Mouna again.

—Yaah, ya Amin!

—I came straight from the graveyard, he says. Not explaining how, upon his release over a week before, he felt an inscrutable urge to visit his birthplace. He figured the journey from Wahat was long enough anyway.

But he just says, *From the graveyard. I was in the family graveyard in Dekernes.*

The most chilling part: he is no longer jittery. It's as though he's been surgically modified for stillness. Even after a general amnesty is declared in December and he no longer has to be home for the police guard to come and stamp his post-prison document twice a day, he will have regained only a fraction of his restlessness.

Nimo used to think of Amin's black irises as tiny tinted windows she could look out of to a world where she was the person she aspired to be. College-educated, independent of water-buffalo hanims and fake beys, no longer a virgin anywhere in her body.

But no matter how long she gazes into those irises, after his stint in prison they remain brittle buttons. If anything they reflect the same young woman working miracles of perseverance to fend off penury and penises straight back.

Before he was taken away Amin could be sulky and neglectful, he could occasionally act callous, but she had never doubted his desire. Now, while his skeletal body slowly returns to normal, while the scent of musk comes back to his chest, she must grow used to his lack of interest in her body. His reluctance to come into bed with her. His remaining flaccid even when she's close enough to feel him inside her and can smell orange blossom water on herself.

She can tell something's wrong the day of his return, when she runs a bath for him and he doesn't lean over to kiss her neck, as she's expecting.

It's been four and a half years, but he doesn't start to undress her.

He doesn't quote from the Song of Songs while slowly encircling her left bezz or, like a frog catching a fly, jab his tongue out to lick behind her ear.

He doesn't circle her waist with his arms and slowly pretend to fall backward into the water.

Nimo is waiting for him to do one of those things. To do anything that could serve as her cue to collapse and confess her liaison with Aziz Maher, which felt very recent though it was three years before.

She was waiting for a cue at least to tell Amin about her pregnancy. How, within three months of his being gone, she had her knees above her breasts one more time while glinting metal rid her not of a clitoris or a hymen but of the seed of his back. How that seed had dwelled in her flesh and started to grow inside her while he was gone. And how she had wanted to keep it so badly that shedding it felt like dying.

But Amin just stands in his threadbare pants and his wilted skin, all kinds of previously unseen bones poking out at her like armor, and a strawberry-shaped scar deep in the small of his back. When she says she'd better go and prepare the food in the hope that he'll protest her departure, an involuntary expression of relief overtakes his averted eyes.

It's a new expression, this. An expression she will learn to identify. At the obvious level it says she should leave him alone, he's too drained and dusty to play, but deeper down it tells her she is no longer welcome in the world he inhabits. He has suffered so much he no longer has the courage to let in anyone at all.

Eventually it strikes Nimo as craven, this capitulation. His post-prison silence feels soft and spineless—so Nimo tells herself, with all the misogyny of a true Abu Zahra—like that of a marah.

Nimo has often wondered why in Egypt the Arabic word for *woman*, the one used without incident in all other Arab countries, should be an unequivocal insult even to a person it technically describes. But in her disgust with Amin the word froths out of her without her noticing.

Marah.

She doesn't know that's how they taunted political prisoners when, with white-hot skewers on their thighs, they forced them to belly dance: *Say I'm a marah, say I'm a marah!*

In time her anger brings back all her harshest thoughts about him, without the humor. His risible rhetoric, convoluted convictions. The criminal carelessness with which he threw out their future for nothing.

Still, thanks to the way his face turns helplessness and despair into a kind of solace, miraculously, all those French existentialist concepts he spent hours explaining to her in vain start to make sense. Hell really is the other person's face. Especially if that other person is your husband. The burden of free choice is unbearable. Till the godly secret quits the mortal frame, each one of Adam born must remain utterly and unalterably alone.

Sensing the ridicule and rejection, Amin clams up even more. Even as he gets better, coming into his own again, he is disinclined to confess to a person he now sees as a petty bourgeois placeholder, a pretty piece of historical furniture, prone to no end of superstition and greed. Already he can tell that, notwithstanding his intellectual guidance, Nimo is bound to give in to the religious demons lurking at the threshold.

Neither of them says much, but Amin's contempt for what Nimo stands for begins to balance out her disgust with his impotence. Immediately she's convinced she too cannot let him into the world he wasn't there to share in. Whether it's Lena's passing or Faiza's pauperization, Sawt El Umma or State Information, she will have to keep the vagaries of his absence to herself. Including the precipitation of the cinematic cloud he used to conjure up in her mind—their four months of happiness.

In time all memory of the cloud will disappear, but for now its diminishing presence marks an ugly equilibrium.

It's a disappointment to both of them. An insidiously deep and gnawing disappointment that will gradually replace desire as the principal component of their love. And so, from a tiny blackish pinprick in the fabric of their togetherness while they're standing in the bathroom, the rift that spells a lifetime's unhappiness begins to grow.

Amin is in the basement he has cheaply converted into a private slog pad after planting the mango tree. He is writing one of those impossibly pithy affidavits in the nineteenth-century Arabic Nimo can never quite understand. Half standing over his stainless steel desk in vest and pajama trousers, loading a sheet of paper into his Olympia typewriter, his face is spotlit by a brand-new architect's lamp. He looks oil painted in the dark.

—I have some news, ya sayyid, she yells as she barges in, excited about massaging his manliness again after so many years. On very good authority, too. Yaah, she starts chuckling. You're going to love this.

And while he sits back down on the lab stool, turning to her with one hand on the keys, Nimo goes on to announce that HADETO leaders have voluntarily liquidated the organization on the understanding that all members would be automatically admitted to the Socialist Union, only to be told that this illustrious merger of revolutionary forces was but a misunderstanding on their part.

—The handful of former prisoners already chosen by the secret police will indeed become members of the blessed party, she impersonates a Sawt El Umma news anchor. But the rest can either swallow a shoe or come back inside for some more buggery-and-beating.

It's been nearly a year since his release. His silence has dissipated, and so has her contempt for his capitulation—momentarily. He has recovered enough weight, libido, and twitchiness for her to recognize him. Now his passivity, the failure of his manliness to respond to her desire alienates her even more. She cites some place-names and dates as she plays with his earlobe, waiting for him to buzz.

But apart from a peck on the cheek and one of those incredibly sad smiles he's taken to giving her in the last few months, the harsh sound of the Olympia's keys is all she gets.

Now the memory of Mouna's voice ringing *If one in ten news items is about a woman falling from a balcon or a roof or a window* brings me back to the time I went after the Jumpers. Early on I could see they were her ultimate murder mystery. The best seller she would devote herself to reading and maybe even authoring, in part.

Because, whether or not these women truly were choosing to die, Mouna was determined to see the iblis behind their demonic destinies held responsible. At first it was easy for her to identify that iblis with the Military Council, then the Ikhwan. But as things got more complicated and she began to lose her faith and eventually also her optimism, she couldn't help seeing that it wasn't just officers and sheikhs who were to blame but even dissidents, even revolutionaries themselves.

Her inevitable conclusion would be that the Egyptian People are responsible, the entire People embodied by the male population . . .

Right now I can only think of Mouna's story as a string of mawwals, those rough and riveting mini sagas that are one of three colors depending on their subject: white for moral and spiritual instruction; green for nature, virtue, and benevolent love; red for human vice and destructive passion.

Like any mawwal, hers would start with the ancient and mysterious call *ya lail ya ain*. I can see now these words invoke not so much *night* or *eye* in themselves as the night of the soul and the source of all vision. They evoke consciousness and its opposite, life and what happened to Mouna.

So begins a life story or a country's history, Shimo. I can no longer tell what kind of tune my rababa is picking out. For already this *Life and Death of Amna Abu Zahra* sounds like the revolution's mawwal: white for religious rebirth, green for the promise of meaning, red for the truth—in blood. And more and more the revolution itself looks like history's précis, its delusions and disappointments making a tricolor map of modern Egypt.

Then again, whichever way I draw my bow, the rababa plays a dirge for the Jumpers. Woman after woman dispensing with the delusion that righteous rhetoric can bring on glory at no extra cost. Woman after woman using men's failures and her body to write the ultimate description de l'Égypte. Because to tell you of Mouna's death and life is inevitably to mourn those noble unrevolutionaries, unknown soldiers in Egypt's battle for atonement. And I wouldn't blame you for thinking of it as a totally fictitious fight, but it's what Mouna believed and what she used to salvage meaning from the wreck of her life. They defied the patriarchy, the piety, the people. And they were her secular salvation in the end.

Within weeks of her passing, the Jumpers begin to take hold of my life. They become the kaaba that, if we are to think about changing the country without deceiving ourselves, we must circumambulate. The tragedy being that no one's noticed them and, since their numbers have dropped again, no one will.

I marvel at the symmetry of their encroachment, the perfect arch their numbers would describe on a line chart over time. They soar with Mubarak's fall at the start of 2011, peaking midway between 2012 and 2013, and three years later plummet with Sisi's rise. It's as if the more women die, the more hope there is. As Mouna would quickly explain, the women didn't jump because they believed men's lies. They jumped because they saw men's words and deeds for the unforgivable wrongdoing they were. Consciously or unconsciously, they died to tell the truth.

Within weeks of her passing, I remember that it was Mouna who drew my attention to them. And I want you, I'm asking you, to hear her own voice telling their story as she lived it. Will you have a little patience for once?

Always,
Your Big Brother

THE MYTH OF THE HOLY JUMPERS

When the night comes in, I sit thinking of the Afreet.

The time I used to spend with Fifi or Monica or the others. None of them are around now. It is March 2014 already as I sit here talking to you, ya Nour. And, calling that sheikh's ouster a revolution, they're holding sham elections so another officer can be zaim, imagine. No one is around and there is nothing, nothing to be done.

So I just go out on the terrasse in the dark. I go out on the terrasse and I sit in front of that tragic tree. It looks éthéré behind the parapet. Not dead, but dead. Tu sais, not alive. A ghost tree. When the night comes in I sit in front of it, a ghost looking at a ghost.

I sit in front of the tree and I think of that little hospital in the Pyramids where so many things come together it is like a castle in a fairy tale. Or I think of a high roof in Agouza, above where our friends Serag and Samira used to have that beautiful balcony on the Nile. Such a sweet Sudanese couple.

They were both doctors, hein. And so incredibly cultured, ya Nour. They were here for a few more years before moving on to London to continue their studies. Never to come back. The building is still there.

I don't think I was ever on their roof, but when I picture a hudhud looking golden and glorious in the evening sun I find I am drawn to it. Then the hudhud leaves the prophet Solaiman's shoulder and flies south to the Queen of Saba. While I sit picturing the rat nose and the bat wings and the fly eyes that used to make a magnoona of me. I even grope around my memory for the sound the Afreet made. Its smoldering smell.

The fear and the fever—they too come back, not the way they were the year Amin died, when those jihadis flew planes into two big buildings in America. Now they're like taps I can open and close as I please. I can even replace the Afreet with the hudhud in my mind, you know why, ya Nour?

Because after a dozen years I know the Afreet is the hudhud, the hudhud is the Afreet. And, whichever face it's wearing, I know that two-faced thing is me. But do you know who it's thanks to that I know, after a dozen years?

Neither the revolutionaries nor the honorable citizens, neither Morsi nor Sisi. Neither Shimo nor Amin.

It's thanks to the women who have jumped to their deaths from roofs and windows since the revolution. Whether they knew it or not, to repent of the country's wrongdoing. I can see their faces as I talk to you now, habibi. A hundred and twelve of them I knew by name. You can find them all in the blue block note, look!

66. Khadiga Mohamed El Gallad, 43, Abbasiya

67. Mai George Samih, 21, Rodha

68. Alia Maged El Batroni, 39, Zamalek

69. Aisha Zakariya Hamed, 62, Sayyida Zainab

70. Ferial Said Nini, 50, Dokki

71. Amal Ibrahim Tawadros, 27, Shoubra

72. Soha Hassanain Hesham, 32, Nasr City

Bref, since the day the Military Council took over, women had been jumping out of windows. Journalists didn't report it because a new historical trajectory had started and it would make everyone's life better, they kept saying.

The children were being killed in the streets. The police were in hiding and nobody else had weapons, so only the army could be killing the children. But all they wrote about in the newspapers was how the army had protected the people, leading this historical trajectory.

And I'm thinking: But everybody's lying except for these women. Even the children being killed are lying. All those Muslims who pretend that supporting the sheikhs on the ballots is doing God's will—they're lying. And that is much worse than forgetting your salah. Even if they were committing incest or worshipping an idol that wouldn't be as bad as what they are doing, I'm thinking.

Because when you commit wrongdoing you are offending Him, c'est vrai. But you're not pretending He can't see who you are. Then once there is a moment of reckoning and His mercy permits it, you can repent. If you have it in you to seize that moment. He will forgive you. But when you've spent years—decades, centuries—mechanically following the rules while you lie, then you imagine you're fooling the All-Knowing One, non?

And I'm thinking: A thinker who's a warmonger. A sheikh who's an extortionist. A doctor who's a drug dealer. An intellectual who's a spy. A zaim who's a mass murderer. Or even a revolutionary, Nour. A revolutionary who's a wannabe celebrity, a career activist who doesn't know and doesn't want to know, giving lectures on the virtues of selflessness while people die and countries crumble at his feet.

A whole country made up of people like that.

When there is a moment of reckoning and Our Lord's mercy permits it. When there is a revolution, by the truth of the Prophet's splendor. And instead of seizing it with a view to repenting of their lies, everyone just goes on lying. The thinker, the man of God, the doctor, the intellectual, the zaim. The revolutionary who proclaimed its coming and the honorable citizen who denied it.

What does it then take for that country to be saved? How many mothers and sisters and wives must offer up their lives to make up for all those men's lies? How many women must be struck by spontaneous suicide?

It is March 2014 and they're holding elections again, having killed a thousand people in one day. Mais oui, they wanted the sheikh back, those people. They were murderers and jihadi breeders. But to a kill a thousand of them? Still those in charge are brazen-faced. Either they're talking about correcting the revolution's trajectory or claiming nothing went down at the start of 2011. That the Ikhwan's overthrow is the real revolution. And they're holding sham elections so the officer who's taking over can pretend it's democracy.

Gamal Abd El Nasser died in 1970 and we're in 2014, non? But it's happening again now. And nothing to be done.

So, while I sit thinking of the Afreet, I try to work out exactly when everything turned ghastly. It was after I met Monica Younis, and I know I met Monica Younis in July 2011. But when exactly, I am never sure.

First there was the storming of the Israeli embassy, then the Copts were run over right in front of the Round Building. On ground that sliced layers off my feet, as they say. Copts' heads crushed till they were flattened and stretched like in a Tom and Jerry cartoon. But by then all hope was gone. For Monica at least it was. And I went on struggling, first with the army men and then with the Ikhwan. I went on struggling even though I, too, could already see.

The wrongdoing was deeper and heavier than anything Mubarak could've done. Anything Nasser, Sadat, *and* Mubarak could've done. And yaani I could see that wrongdoing. Even if my heart was full of confusion and I wasn't sure what to do. I imagine I could see before Monica, before I even knew about the Jumpers:

No one was going anywhere, the revolution made no difference, nowhere. Nothing.

Because it hadn't been seven months and once again the problem was Palestine, that same old graveyard. Not the people living in Egypt. The day Mubarak was deposed and we chanted *Hold your head high, you're Egyptian*, I had imagined we were making our destiny. Changing the life that we lived, at last. Not being stumps or stooges. At last not worrying about other people's problems so we could avoid facing our own.

And now I saw this behim and son of a behim climbing up the pipes and the balcons like a clothesline thief. To pull the Israeli flag down. And I felt our destiny was being made for us the same as always. That it wasn't to make our destiny that we revolted against Mubarak. It was to give sheikhs and officers an excuse to turn us into stooges and stumps again. To worship new idols of the false gods we'd embraced since 1956.

The Turban and the Tank!

It felt like planes flying into buildings. Like Amin dying all over again.

Hold your head high, you're Egyptian. There was no difference between this and *With soul and blood, we ransom you, Palestine*, or *Freedom, Socialism, Arab Unity*, any empty slogan. It was just a chant. Because it wasn't about anything real anymore. And we, pretending that pulling down the flag was as good as liberating Jerusalem. That not being at war with Israel was the root of all our problems.

It felt like Socialism and the Student Movement. Siham Gad, your Tante Semsem, ya Nour. People who hated Sadat in the seventies and haven't stopped complaining about *normalization* since. Just because he got back the land Nasser lost in 1967 and made peace. Then I started wondering. Between me and myself, I was wondering, *What if* we normalized relations with Israel? Since Sadat went to the Knesset, haven't we normalized selling our daughters to Wahhabis who will buy them and sending our children into oil bondage in the desert? However can relations with Israel be worse than everything we've normalized, hein?

After I met Monica the children were murdered again and again outside government offices. The revolutionaries. They were arrested and beaten and given military trials. Their futures fouled. But again and again they went at the police and the gendarmerie and the baltagis with the same unthinking righteousness. While the Ikhwan took over parliament, then the presidency. It was as if they were dying so the Ikhwan could. Of course the idea was the end of military rule and free elections, civil leaders and human rights and n'importe quoi. But I could see.

No, of course. I didn't realize it yet. But already, by July 2011, dead women's stories were all the hope I had.

WHITE

There is a proverb Amin used to say: *The cat loves no one like his strangler.* When I met Monica Younis I could tell befriending her would make me that cat. I remembered the last time I'd been one, after your father died, when I took on the burden of two big families on top of the burden of my children. Not that the girl was evil or deranged, but something in my heart told me her end was bad.

I feared for Fifi more than myself. The whole story had to do with the Copts and you understand how protective your Tante Fifi gets of her folk. Monica herself wore a headscarf. She looked like somebody who never thought of herself as anything but Muslim. But even so, because her mother had never converted and I imagine because of her name, Fifi thought of her as a Christian like herself.

But I feared for Fifi because I could see she was falling in love with her, whatever religion she was. And yaani I was right. Fifi stopped leaving the house once Monica moved on. We had maybe two normal talks after the girl's burial. That was—what?—February 2012. After that, every time I ask Fifi to come with me she's too ill, she says.

If I go to visit and I try to drag her out she gives me this stare, ya Nour, a stare so empty, so totally indifferent and at the same time so enraged by its indifference that it wrings my belly every time. Then, in a voice so small it sounds like a puppy run over by a microbus:

—Aha, if only I entered the convent when I thought of it as a little girl. By the life of Our Lord wouldn't that be better?

It was as if she blamed me for the girl's destiny. I kept trying to cheer her up. Then one day her hotelier son and his wife came in and took her away. Almost like a kidnapping. Her daughter-in-law has always loved her. They'd been begging her to go live with them in Sharm El Sheikh for years, now she was older and all alone here. But Fifi had always said no. That March, just over a month after Monica jumped out of the window of *El Akhbar* newspaper—right behind where you work on Press Street, ya Nour—I imagine she finally let them.

Monica was being interviewed about Maspero. How her uncle was puréed under an army tank there. A forty-year-old father of three uninterested in demonstrating, present at the site only because he's scared for the well-being of someone. *Kind, generous, one-of-a-kind Khalo Raymond*, as she kept telling the journalist. Whose Nefertiti she was.

—He called me Nefertiti because she was the prettiest woman ever born. So he said. And a queen too. Because he was special, she told the journalist. You know, whenever we walked together we held hands. Ah wallahi. Since I was a little girl. He called me Nefertiti and I loved holding hands with him.

I don't know why the journalist asked her to come into his eleventh-story office instead of going to her himself, as journalists do. I don't know why they were doing another Maspero story in February 2012, nearly four months after the massacre. But that is how, sauntering to the window during a pause in the conversation, Monica jumped.

She spent only two days in a coma. In that time her face looked strained, as if she was in pain or distress. But once she moved on—I was there only minutes later—all the suffering was wiped away. She was smiling, I swear you could see her smiling. Her moon face lit up while her blue eyes were still open, dark skin like a newborn's. And looking at her lying there with Dimyana fainting by the door, Fifi banging her head against the wall, and the wails of several other women rising, you would've thought she was fourteen.

Actually she was twenty-five. And every time I brought up the Jumpers, it was as if Fifi blamed me for the fact that she would never get older.

In the end Fifi and I never had a fight. But, even on the phone, we've spoken very little since the day she left. She had never believed the reality of the Jumpers anyway, though as I was telling you by the time we separated I already knew. With her falling into my arms every two steps while we went to bury the girl, I knew the Jumpers were more important than any other part of the revolution.

If we had real statistics I bet you anything that the number of Jumpers is exactly equal to that of the revolution's martyrs. According to my calculations, at their peak in the summer of 2012, no fewer than five cases went down every day. Every day! Besides, when Monica told me about it in July 2011, it had already been going on for five months. And yet it wasn't until Monica's funeral that I was sure.

And I said to Fifi, I said, *Fifi, what is this? How come all these women are jumping?* And she said, *In a crapper! The world doesn't lack for curb-born harlots, aha, especially when they're crazy enough to kill themselves.* She was laughing. That would've been the end of February. I had managed to bring her over to Maadi for once and she had perked up with coffee and cigarettes till her mazag was sweet enough for laughing.

—But seriously, Fifi says. As I never tired of telling Monica herself. This is just a coincidence. It could be anywhere, anytime—

—Bas bas, I said, and showed her my newspaper cuttings and the Kasr El Ainy Hospital records the girl had smuggled out of the director's office and photocopied for me.

Official records from the country's biggest, most official student hospital, non?

Then I went inside to get my blue block note. And by the time I came out Fifi had sunk again into the darkness.

By then there was no more confusion in my heart about the Jumpers. But to what degree was the girl moving on because of her sad love story? I'd only just found out about that—from Fifi, through Fifi's sobs and stares and across the darkness she kept sinking into—in the week after the funeral. I hadn't had a clue before.

I was getting fixated, as you say. I would get even more fixated when I realized that every one of those women had a sad story in the buildup to her jump. Not always a love story, but always involving a man. And always a man at a protest, you understand.

The Jumpers were like the revolutionaries' reflections. Except they were the original pictures, the revolutionaries corrupted copies of them. They were the truth to the revolutionaries' lies. The only possible historical trajectory, albeit a terminal one.

And Monica's funeral was when I grew sure. It hadn't been two weeks since seventy-two young men died at Port Said stadium. Members of one of those groups of football supporters that call themselves Ultras.

They were in Port Said to support their team. For weeks after the funeral I thought of those boys' mothers and their futures. Sometimes I thought of the baltagis who swung machetes at their backs as they ran, trampling each other in the dark. But every time I thought of them I thought of Monica's life.

The cat loves no one like his strangler. When Monica moved on I thought again about being that cat. How the first time I became one I didn't do anything useful. I didn't participate in my country's destiny. I was strangled all right, but for what? If anything I helped people live out their lives exactly as they were always going to. This time, through the Jumpers, maybe something meaningful would come out of it.

It was the week before Ramadan, in the summer of 2011. The fifty-ninth anniversary of the July Coup. They tell you if you call July 23, 1952, a coup, then you sound like the Ikhwan. Our Lord have mercy on your Tante Semsem! But a coup is what it was, Ikhwan or Jesuits. Especially now we've seen what a real revolution might look like. It was the week before Ramadan and there was a small field hospital outside the Omar Makram Mosque.

That's how Fifi and I came to be in the same place as Monica. We worked with doctors, communist friends of your father's, and wealthy big names who believed in the revolution. But you already know all this.

Every Friday there was a millioniya, a million-strong demonstration on the country's official day off. And on each of those holy days some revolutionaries or State Security agents stayed on in the hope of starting a sit-in.

Until, on July 8, while you were skulking here like a spinster, they finally did start one. They had all kinds of demands, from a minimum wage to the trial of Mubarak. It was small and smelly and had no point to it whatsoever, once you thought two minutes. But it blocked off half the city and put livelihoods on hold. Revolutionaries we trusted told us it had been planned by State Security—may your evening be a happy one, Abid, my son!—for the sake of turning people against the revolution. That worked. Revolutionaries told us it was infiltrated. Agents befriended protesters and made them do what they wanted. Besides, the weather was ghastly.

You remember how the revolution was timed to shame the interior ministry? How it was staged on January 25, Police Day, the day the Ismailia Station officers held out against a siege by the English army in 1952?

D'accord, on July 23—National Day, the day those military balta-gis took over the country later in 1952—real revolutionaries of ours decided to forget Tahrir Square and march on the defense ministry in Abbasiya. No State Security genius could've matched their behim-brained imbecility.

Because it wasn't the army they got going against them but the army-loving neighbors, with bludgeons and machetes, with skew-ers and cables as well as baltas. There were the usual interior minis-try plainclothes men and the sharmootas' sons who work for them. There were the usual anonymous honorable citizens. But mostly there were locals fed up with *those dependents*, as they call them. The boys told us how they found them blocking every possible way out of Abbasiya.

It was late afternoon and we were at Omar Makram delivering sup-plies. A white mountain of gauze and cotton bandages. We had been promised a professional nurse that day so we decided to wait, drown-ing in our sweat and cursing the father of whoever thought of staging a sit-in at this time of year.

But when the girl arrived we thought our hopes were justified.

Later we found out that Monica Younis was an independent vol-unteer, bien sûr. She came on her own to help at field hospitals around Tahrir whenever she had time. The nurse we'd been promised—a lazy woman who looked not much younger than Fifi and me—we didn't meet until the next time we went to that little hospital in the Pyramids. The one I am always thinking about these days, remember?

The Allende Hospital. Named after the Chilean doctor-politician, aywa, because he was one of the heroes of your Uncle Medhat, who it belongs to: Amin's old surgeon friend Medhat El Tetsh. Until recently he was still treating revolutionaries for free. But that's not what made his enchanted little hospital special.

As I was telling you, ya Nour, Allende is like a castle in the middle of a forest in a fairy tale. Which, visited once, keeps you tethered to it for the rest of your life.

Fifi had had a cyst removed from her armpit there—in 2007, I think—I imagine because her doctor was looking for a cheap place to operate. But—the totally deranged thing, hein?—I remembered going to see her there when I ended up in the same hospital three years later for that ghastly operation. When they took out my womb, hein? By total coincidence. I imagine my surgeon was a friend of Medhat's who also worked with him.

Fifi in 2007, me in 2010. And in 2011 we were both there together for the sake of the revolution. The nurse we'd been promised worked at Allende now, but the girl we mistook for her too had worked there for nine months between 2008 and 2009. Monica Younis. She had started after Fifi's operation and left before mine. But it was the same hospital. Incroyable, mais oui. But maybe not surprising. Even if we don't see this all the time, all our lives are connected. Non?

Bref, Monica belonged to that enchanted race with very dark skin and very blue eyes. She was short and small in loose-ish clothes under her headscarf. Her legs curved inward like a bombé table's. Her hips were full but a little too hard-edged. Her chest was flatter than you would think it should be. All these detectable défauts, but even from a distance you could tell she had a body to drive a man deranged.

Then she comes closer and her face is a moon. And you think, Alf baraka. You think it again when you see she isn't shy so much as polite. Polite and always laughing, with this very slight lithp that's barely there but shows more when she's emotional and entrances you anyway, every time there is an *s*. And her laugh, ya Allah. Something about the way she moved and the way her feelings showed on her face, something innocent but skittish made her trop, trop sympathique, ya Nour.

We had barely salaamed when the screaming started. There was a commotion and the gendarmerie moved to surround us, but only from a distance. You understand how they routinely storm field hospitals like they were jihadi hideouts. This time they just stood in formation. Then the boys started coming, all cut up and bleeding.

All of a sudden where the white mountain had been there was this red marsh. For a sweet distance the ground was blood-logged. Red berets over khaki uniforms in a wide, wide circle wherever you looked out, and those ghastly gun muzzles at the ready.

—Maalesh yaani, Fifi kept growling at the gendarmes, and of course not one of them even glanced at her. Even if you didn't hurt them yourselves, her voice grated as she projected, how could you let them be hurt like this? Your own brothers!

By sunset it was all gone. The spray, the suture, the hope. You couldn't see the color of the cotton wool. You couldn't see the blood-orange disc of the sun dipping into the rooftops in front of you or the blue of the sky darkening behind you. You couldn't even see the faces of the boys you were tending to. Only the red and the black, and then the gashes, the deformities. There was a smell of sweat and iron. There was still screaming. And in all this world and the next—shall I tell you?—the only sweet thing was the new nurse's laugh.

One after another the boys were bandaged and medicated. They were taken to hospitals or sent home. Those we couldn't be sure would not be arrested once they got past the circle of gendarmes, we kept with us. The army didn't just beat up and torture children now. It didn't just forcibly undress young women and paw them between the legs to see if they were still virgins! It also gave them military trials.

But the girl like the moon, the unbelievably mignonne girl kept all this in the background. Fifi's tongue stayed out even after the weather cooled! We drank dusty tea in plastic glasses and used bits of cardboard to fan our faces while we lit up. She too smoked. The girl. She worked like a bee, methodical. But she laughed and smoked and swore, however timidly.

—And what's your name then, ya habibti?

—At Kasr El Ainy they call me Mona, ya abla, she said.

Imagine being called *abla*, like an older sister in the sixties. It made me happy to realize people still seriously used that title.

—But my name is Monica, she went on. Mama tells people she called me that because she likes Monica Bellucci, ah wallahi. But it's because Santa Monica is her patron. The mother of Saint Augustine, this saint. You must've heard of her, Abla Fifi? She's the patron of difficult marriages, the conversion of close ones to Christianity. And dis-appointing children. Ah wallahi! Mama only likes Latin names, she who has the most Egyptian name in all of history. Dimyana. Mama is not an Orthodox Copt but a Catholic, though, Abla Amna. She follows the Baba of Roma. As for my baba and me . . .

He died when she was eight. He was barely forty-two. He'd been working in Wahat for four years, too far to visit more than twice a year. Monica lived with her mama, her khalo Raymond, her khalo's hot-tempered wife, Safa, and their sweet-tempered daughter, Nesma. They lived in a two-story, two-appartement family building in Ain Shams. You'd think she didn't have time to grow too attached. But that girl loved her baba. She was tara-la-li about him.

Mohsen Younis was a graduate of Alexandria University. By everyone's testimony a clever civil engineer. He got work in Alexandria, but he stayed less than a year. For two years he managed his family's furniture works in Domyat. He was clever at that too. Efficient and affable. A legend in mathematics.

And it seems he was a ghastly jeune premier all his life. But there was something uncomfortable about him. He liked nothing, hated nothing. He ate and slept, but he could do without food and rest. He prayed, he socialized. He did everything that was expected of him, but you could see he did it without heart, without ever being inside it. He never traveled or went out. Never drank or smoked or watched the football. Never read the newspapers or listened to the radio. He worked from morning till evening, and when he was done he went home to wash.

Then one day he declared he was in love with a girl. All of a sudden like this, at the start of his third year back in Domyat. He wanted, was going to marry her. Which would've been happy news if she hadn't been the daughter of a merchant and shop owner in the gold market. Everyone knows the gold market is all Coptic.

So, when Mohsen pronounced her name, no one could believe their ears. A *blue-bone*, as the Copts are sometimes called, mais oui, derisively. Three years older than him. And he such a straight, strict boy. Besides, he was rich enough. He could have his pick without sectarian strife. But it was no caprice, Mohsen Younis's love for Dimyana Abd El Messih. Not that you could shut people up about it if it was.

Within days the gossip revealed they had been seeing each other since his sister's wedding when they met in the gold market, long before he went to Alexandria. There had even been hanky-panky at that stage.

And so the Muslim furniture-making patriarchate went on high alert. It seems Mohsen's father and eldest uncle spoke to him just the once. Together and severely. The oldest furniture maker in town, a distant relation, summoned him three times. There were threats. There were pleas. Blood spilled when Mohsen's eldest brother cornered him by the bandsaw and spoke badly of Dimyana. Then, silence.

Monica knew less about what happened to her mother at that time. They were never as close, she said. And her mother was never as good at telling stories. What she did know—but Fifi and I knew that too, without her telling us—was that Mohsen was a bigger problem for Dimyana than Dimyana was for Mohsen. It's not haram for a Muslim man to marry a woman of any faith, you understand.

But for a Christian of either sex to marry a Muslim. Even without converting. They are excommunicated. Men are all right as long as they don't mind never going to church again. But girls, ya Allah, imagine what can happen to a girl. And so they ran away—*eloped*, as they say in English. And by giving up his future in the gold market to go with them, Dimyana's younger brother, Raymond, saved her life. That's one of the few things Dimyana did tell her daughter. That the goldsmith could only rest content with disowning her knowing a man of his blood, a true Christian, would be present in her life. Otherwise, Dimyana was convinced, he would've had her killed.

They wound up in Ain Shams. I've never been to that bit of town. You tell me it's the site of a pharaonic city? In my mind, at that time—eighty-three, eighty-four—it's a kind of cross between Shoubra and Heliopolis. An old and quiet Heliopolis with fellahin inhabitants, like Shoubra now.

Raymond apprenticed himself to a local car mechanic and attended a night school attached to the church. Mohsen became a freelance carpenter until he found work at the Arab Contractors, the huge contracting company founded by Osman Ahmad Osman, remember him? Nasser's henchman and Sadat's in-law, tres bien.

That was the year Dimyana gave birth to Monica, eighty-seven. The job took away all Mohsen's time and energy. For the first time since Alexandria, he totally stopped carpentering. But he felt responsible for a wife and a future and he did not mind. He programmed himself to stick with it because it paid so well but, no matter how well it paid, Dimyana was programmed to spend it.

You know what they say about Domyatis. But Mohsen was never a miser. He wouldn't have worried about money had Dimyana's expenses been *just* excessive. In truth she was a total magnoona. Raymond had managed to graduate from the Faculty of Commerce, and Mohsen found him work in the same company a few months after he was appointed.

By then Raymond was already married with a daughter, Nesma, a sweet, shy girl only two years younger than Monica. He would have two sons, one after the other, much later in life. When, a year into working at the same company Mohsen and Raymond resolved to buy a bit of land and start building, at every stage they had to conspire with Safa to save the money required.

Their two-story building was as much as they managed before Dimyana, like a snake charmer, found ways to draw l'argent to herself again. An objectionably multifaith house. There was one Muslim family. Even if the mother didn't wear a headscarf like her daughter. To keep the neighbors in the dark, Dimyana slipped out of Ain Shams when she wanted to go to church. What they still couldn't understand was how *those* three could be related to the other, obviously Coptic family that lived in the same house with them. Directly, as they seemed to be. No one tried to explain.

Nineteen ninety-five in Ain Shams. The parked vans, the rubbish mounds. Dim facades behind patterned car covers and wet mud.

A girl, eight years old, is gasping for breath on the stairs of a two-story building. A girl who has her baba's good looks and her mother's nervous energy. She's just been told that baba won't be coming to visit when he's due.

When will he be coming, then?

Not for a long time.

Why won't he be coming?

His work has taken him even farther from Wahat—is what she's been told. But in her heart she knows she won't see him again. And alone on the stairs she is gasping.

In truth Mohsen's work had taken him back to Domyat, where he hadn't been once since he left. His father was alive. So was his eldest uncle and even, at ninety-two, the furniture patriarch who had summoned him.

At forty-one Mohsen was planted underground after a funeral that was trop, trop tranquille. And left there.

A steel beam had impaled the back of his neck while he was checking limestone deposits where foundations were being laid for an overpass. It was no one's fault and Dimyana was compensated forthwith. Not that the lump sum lasted two months, but she was still receiving a pension when Fifi and I met Monica.

And yaani *there wath nothing to complain about, there wath no one to complain to*, as Monica was spluttering still. You'd think she didn't have time to grow attached. But she loved her father to the degree that she learned to pray as he did. Even though she attended a school attached to the church. There were so few Muslims there that religion class was free time. Despite Khalo Raymond's objection that Mohsen himself wouldn't have liked this, Monica loved her baba to the degree that she started wearing a headscarf as soon as she had her period.

With a crucifix on her forehead Dimyana swore that, as a baby, Monica had been baptized. Monica swore that she believed Dimyana with a Quran on hers. Then they glowered at each other.

No, Mohsen never knew of her baptism. As she swore to Dimyana that day, she did believe in Our Lord the Messiah. But she also believed in the mercy and the light of the Prophet, Our Lord the Father's Last Messenger. Which made Dimyana swear at her.

Not once did Monica blame Dimyana's prodigal proclivity for ending up a mere diploma holder. Though she was the bright daughter of a wealthy civil engineer. Never even did she blame Osman Ahmad Osman for the way she ended up: a Muslim dependent on the church's wasta for a modest nursing appointment at Kasr El Ainy.

It was the week before Ramadan, and I don't think she thought she would see us again. But we were knowing and loving her, and loving her more the more she told us of herself. Piecemeal, between tasks. She always talked by retail, not in bulk. And it made her stories come in and nestle in the head.

At the end of that ghastly day we went and ate sausages—imagine doing that! In bread rolls so thin the sandwiches look like bananas, you know the kind. It was one of those baladi restaurants Fifi loves in Sayyida Zainab. With the tables set on the trottoir among pedestrians and motorcycles and giant speakers playing Sufi chant.

All that hot sauce and cola would give me tummy trouble for days, but by the life of the Prophet I was like somebody eating his last. Besides, Fifi's mazag was sweet and she kept patting Monica while we talked, gitchi-goo-ing and gentling her. We were talking and weeping till three in the morning with the streets awake and noisy as noon. Minivans and mule-pulled carts did the twist alongside us. People fooled and fought. While the moon with a body to make you deranged laughed her entrancing laugh, ya Nour.

Still, there had been so much blood and iron that day. Maybe I was opening up to her because I needed her laugh to get away from all the gashed and gouged-out body parts sticking to my eyelids on the inside.

We met in Tahrir to follow up the next morning. Fifi wasn't there because it was a Sunday and she had to go to church. You know your Tante Fifi. She's never been devout but sometimes she has to go to church. Maybe it took seeing Monica alone to be sure about her.

While we arranged our meeting on the mobile, I noticed she didn't call it *the Square* like our revolutionary friends. They had managed to drop the name everyone was attached to as if it didn't have anything to do with the place. In its stead they came up with such an archaic socialist cliché. So corny, so de blé on young tongues. But Monica called it Tahrir like a normal person. And it made me open up to her more.

I loved her. I loved her because she called me *abla* and had legs like a bombé table's and worked like a bee. I loved her because, even though she didn't graduate with the same kind of *licence*, she got her diplôme at my university. And I loved her because something about her reminded me of when I was young. She didn't remind me of myself especially. But she was both ardent and arduous and totally ta-ra-la-li in a way that reminded me of those times. So I loved and I trusted her.

And I didn't stop trusting her even when I understood there were things she told Fifi and not me. Just as she told me things she didn't tell Fifi. I understood much later this was why Fifi never caught onto the reality of the Jumpers. Except when I was present—then she was talking to me, and it might've looked to Fifi like she was *taking me according to the size of my mind*, bon?—Monica hardly ever mentioned them to her.

Bref, we met in Tahrir and I was sure. That was the day the Allende Hospital first came up. Monica's best friend still worked there as a lab technician, she told me. An albino young man who had been her colleague at Ain Shams. Called Ahmad Mahdi. She was telling me about Ahmad Mahdi and she mentioned they'd been colleagues at this small private hospital where she worked in 2009. He was very religious, this *sun's enemy* named Mahdi. True supporter of the Islamists. But he was a friend she could count on.

The field hospital felt quiet and content without white mountains or red and black marshes. Monica and I sat in plastic chairs borrowed from a baladi café in Garden City. Sipping iced mineral water and fanning ourselves with folded newspapers. She told me she had stayed the night at her ward because if she went home later than eleven there was always a fight with Dimyana.

—If only she knew what Kasr El Ainy nurses get up to before sunset, she said. Sometimes even before noon.

—With the house officers?

—Or the consultants. Or management. Or pharmaceutical company agents. But mostly with patients or people posing as patients who come in, Monica went on. And sometimes—

—Bas! Enough now, I sighed. C'était incroyable, non? But it made her laugh. Ya Allah, ya Monica, I—

—It wasn't easy to keep out ya abla. They think if you're not with them you're against them. But now they know me. I'm not in but I'm not in the way.

Monica spoke dreamily, her eyes looking out as she went somewhere far in her mind. Then she was quiet. For a long time she stayed in that far place. She leaned forward in her seat with the plastic bottle between her knees and her hands on her thighs, swaying slowly right and left, left and right. Then I too started thinking, lulled by her swaying like this. And the thought scared me:

Maybe that's where the revolution should be. Not in the palace or the square, not in the protest or at the ministry. But on beds, behind doors. Among the nurses and the patients all people eventually become.

That was the scariest bit, because I didn't know where it came from. That we all eventually become patients and nurses. And when I could see us, the Egyptian People all together, everyone was naked, embracing. It was a millioniya but instead of chanting or marching or raising signs—shall I tell you—it was group sex. Forgive me, Our Lord, wennabi forgive me. Because I wasn't even asleep when I saw it. Then Monica roused me all of a sudden.

—To be completely honest, she said, her back straight and her voice springy again, my problem is not what they do. Her laugh dissolved into that innocent expression that made the moonlight brighter every time. If a person wants to do something wrong or haram, who am I to judge that person. My problem is why they do it.

Now her eyes narrowed and her hips tensed. And from then on you could hear her lisp very clearly:

—Most people think when you do something haram it's because you enjoy it. So you risk God's wrath because you just can't help yourself, it's too enjoyable. But to be completely honest, I think God will forgive anything if it's enjoyable enough. Ah wallahi! It's when something is not enjoyable that God gets angry, I think. That's why I have a problem with my colleagues at the ward doing what they do. It's never because they want to, only because they're getting paid in some way. And if they get caught doing something, it's never because that thing is wrong. Do you know what I mean, Abla Amna? The police go after beggars and prostitutes. But it's never because begging or prostitution is illegal, only because the officers in charge haven't been paid. Once the officers get their cut of something it doesn't matter how illegal that thing is. And that's what it's like at the ward. As for my problem with the ward—not just the ward, I have the same problem with torture and wasta and bribery and all the things we revolted against here in Tahrir—it makes everyone a beggar and a prostitute whether they want to be or not. It's like we're locked up in a colony of beggars and prostitutes. It's like we don't have the choice to be anything else at all. Abla Amna, do you know what I mean?

And again, ya Nour, I caught myself thinking:

Not in the palace or the square but in the bedsheets, where people embrace or come close enough to embrace.

And for the first time since that February evening back in 2011 when I found you waiting for me outside the house, ya Nour, the suspicion entered my heart. Maybe those in charge are not to blame. The government, first Mubarak and now the Military Council. But even Sadat and Nasser. Even Nasser. If people behave like beggars and prostitutes no matter where you put them, what can anybody in power do about that? And why expect anybody in power to behave differently? Besides, how is a revolution that deposes a president ever going to remedy that kind of sickness, hein? That's what I caught myself thinking.

Monica was saying she had something to tell me. I had been listening with half an ear while I thought. Now as she said, *Those casualties were all women*, I realized with a jerk that somebody else had noticed the Jumpers. She was telling me about the terminal trajectory that was the only truthful history going down.

Now all of a sudden the revolution itself changed. It wasn't that I felt differently about participating in my country's destiny. But hearing this girl, this beautiful girl talk about her work and the Jumpers, all of a sudden that destiny looked more complicated than I could ever imagine. It wasn't a kindhearted watercourse going unconsciously down from Upper Egypt to the Mediterranean, innocently. Which, if you kept it clean and used it sensibly, would keep you healthy and provided for forever. No. What was going down was an evil enchanted train. A snake, a tomb. A mass grave.

Monica had been seeing it herself at the emergency ward. She had barely been there a year when the revolution went down. But that was enough time to have an idea of how often it happened. Almost never? And now, starting on February 11, the day Mubarak was deposed, they started arriving. Two, three, up to ten every week.

They came with broken bones and bleeding necks, their heads halved and their chests leaking. Women of all ages and circumstances who had stepped over windowsills and leaped across balustrades.

—Ah wallahi, Monica said again, looking so innocent that the sight of her wrung my belly.

And before seeing them at the Kasr El Ainy Hospital, at the Zainhom Morgue, at five hundred hospital rooms and mosques and graveyards, I knew. I just knew this was the beginning of the answer to all my questions about the revolution.

GREEN

My mother used to say, *Love's mirror is blind.* My mother was a hard woman. Love never played any role in her life. Even her love for her children was rationed and regulated. Ninety-nine percent for the boys, non? Our Lord forgive and have mercy on her. But, whatever her intentions when she said it, there is truth in that proverb.

When Monica's father died Dimyana and Safa expected her to mourn him like any other girl, by grieving and being depressed. But Monica did not cry too hard. She did not seem despondent. Raymond wasn't someone who talked much. And though shocked by Mohsen's death, he kept silent. Only he understood that, because she was so attached, Monica would mourn her father by keeping him with her while she grew up.

So goes Fifi's telling of the story.

He died when she was eight.

At ten she made a portrait of him with a ballpoint pen. Dimyana and Raymond thought she captured him exactly.

At twelve, wondering where the blood on her undergarments came from, she was sure he had a better explanation than her mother.

By sixteen—Our Lord pardon Fifi, *aha*, and me for repeating this— she imagined she was with him every time she thought about conjugal relations.

For fourteen years she chased his spirit down the winding alleys of Ain Shams. Without friends or sweethearts, she spoke to him in her sleep. When she prayed to the Messiah she saw his face. When her nose touched the salah rug she smelled him. The breeze playing with her hair was his fingers. Water drying on her skin, his breath. Ain Shams coiled around her feet while she chased his spirit, for fourteen years.

At twenty-two she was Nesma's maid of honor at the Cathedral of Our Lady of Egypt in Nasr City, not so far from Ain Shams. That was the summer of 2008, right after she started working at Allende, when she was still working her way toward an official appointment at Kasr El Ainy. But by then Mohsen's spirit had become a person and she was in love.

His name was Andrew Mansour. A reincarnation of Mohsen. And, like Dimyana for the spirit he reincarnated, Monica was the secret love that brought out his *tendresse tranquille*. She knew that was there from the first glimpse, his *tendresse tranquille*. It made her eyes laugh. Except that, unlike Mohsen, Andrew could not marry a girl not of his faith. Besides—this was the tragedy of it—he was already half-married when they met.

At nineteen Nesma has agreed to a *salon match*, as we used to call them. Because they're made in the living rooms of people's houses. Safa arranges with a boy's mother at church for the two of them to meet. The boy is twenty-five, a computing graduate from Mattariya. I am not sure but I imagine his work is like your sister's. He has a sister and a brother in America and—as with so many Copts—the long-term plan is for him to join them there. With a good young wife. That plan has been carried out now, but at that point the groom is still looking.

Of course Safa is worried that Monica, who's had no suitors though she is older and in truth prettier than Nesma, might give her a bad eye. And yaani Monica has been advising Nesma against salon matches. She believes in love, ma jolie fille. But Safa thinks it's because she's jealous and has envy in her heart. So the first few times the boy and his mother come by—his father is dead so he doesn't come with them— she makes sure Monica isn't around.

Nesma still tells her cousin confidante. Monica has a secret meeting place Safa doesn't know about: right below the roof in their two-story building, there is a tiny studio. It is empty, forgotten by everybody who lives in the building. There are days of the week and times of the day when Nesma knows to meet Monica there without even arranging for it. There is a couch and a small bulb, but they rarely light it.

So when it is time Nesma pushes the door and jumps onto the couch to find herself in Monica's arms in the dark. Like always.

Then, *Tell me*, Monica says.

Nesma has this giggle that always ends with a snuffle, leaving a tear or two glistening on her cheek. And today she giggles so often while she talks that by the time she leaves the studio her face is soaking. *He is handsome*, she tells her. She wants him to find her pretty. *He is respectable*, she tells her. She wants to have his children.

—The only thing—at this point Nesma stops giggling—he is a bit, you know how, ya Monica, mechanical.

And she gives that look of childish chagrin, a mixture of panic and pained impatience. She hopes that deep down he really likes her, she goes on, because he seems to be one of those people who can't really show it. The day they drove around in his Daihatsu Terios listening to the just-out Amr Diab album, *Wayah*, Nesma tells Monica. That was the happiest day of her life.

When he took her hand—pardon me, Lord—his knuckles between her fingers made her feel more than all the boys who had surreptitiously kissed or caressed her combined. His Terios has blue and green stripes like a shirt. It has tinted windows and armor bumpers and the biggest speakers she has ever seen in a car. All illegal, she tells Monica. But Andrew has friends in the police. Then, giggling violently, she tells her how ready she is to go in the bedroom with him.

And once Monica hears this last bit she is truly happy for Nesma. As happy as she would be if she found her own life's partner. Until she does. Because, a week before Nesma's engagement party, Monica meets Andrew Mansour.

I'd never heard of this among Christians or Muslims, but it seems Raymond and Safa decided to throw a preengagement party. It was a small affair in the family appartement in Ain Shams. Not on the roof or outside.

But it was a proper party and family members came from Domyat. They came from Tanta and Alexandria and Minya. Safa couldn't not invite Dimyana and Monica. And, making an exception for the party the way they do these days, Mona wore her black-brown hair in a gleaming chignon over a sleeveless robe de soirée that came to above the knees.

At the end of the meal Safa and the boy's mother remembered a small disagreement about how much the groom should spend on the shabka and they started quarreling. Safa lost her temper. She was shouting and Raymond was embarrassed of her. *Mother of Mercy*, he kept muttering under his breath. While he turned gray with embarrassment. As he patted and apologized to the woman, giving Safa hard looks, he was turning gray. Until Dimyana took the woman aside to placate her and Raymond sat Safa down. Then the bride asked the DJ to turn up *Wayah*.

Everybody started dancing in a circle.

Alors, this is the moment Monica stops dead. At this relatively late stage of the party while everybody is dancing to the canned voice of the pop star. *My eyes in front of his eyes / This is more than I dreamed of / This is the day I've been waiting for*, the canned voice is singing. She stops dead because she notices a quiet male guest in a very shiny three-piece with a pink papillon and a high col.

He is being pushed and pulled to join in the dancing, though he does not want to dance. His suit is so shiny it looks like it's made of rayon. He seems only a little older than Monica. Maybe not as pretty as Mohsen but with bulging muscles and a square jaw, a different kind of jeune premiere. But his voice and mannerisms are identical to Mohsen's. And the thing about him is—he is just as désengagé, on the outside of things.

By this quality Monica identifies him.

The male guest seems just as taken by Monica as Monica is taken by the male guest. More than once others notice him staring at her, unaware of the noise and the nosiness. And her blue eyes stare back.

So he leaves the group to make her acquaintance. And when they salaam his thumb strays onto her knuckles and between her fingers. Again and again she seems to hear Amr Diab singing of lifelong longings satisfied, impossible dreams come true, and the feeling is so intense that she has to excuse herself and rush out of the appartement once he turns. To lean on the balustrade and gasp. She is breathing.

For fourteen years a girl has been gasping for breath on the stairs of a two-story building. Now, as she closes the door behind her, this girl is breathing at last. Both her baba's good looks and her mama's nervous energy are catching up with her, making her beautiful and terrified. It had been so long since she last truly breathed that she hadn't realized it was possible again until it happened. And, knowing its possibility lies in the hands of a complete stranger she just met—this ghastly happiness, the wholeness and the hope of it, the total freedom she feels terrify her.

When she has calmed a little Monica knocks on the door so she can go back in. Loudly, to be heard over Amr Diab. Inside—very strangely, it will later seem to her when she finds out about it, but very reassuringly too—only the male guest who changed her can hear.

But it is Khalo Raymond who opens the door, smiling tiredly and with infinite kindness as she'll remember him that day. Looking all of a sudden very gray, very old. But Monica does not dwell on how Raymond looks. Once past him she lets herself be found by the male guest again. And together they sit sipping the marriage sherbet on the smaller of the two cabriole sofas in Safa's extravagant salon, too close together, too gone in each other to be talking or aware of others.

People keep coming to talk to the male guest. Many try to pull him away from Monica. Winking and nodding, they give him awkward, admonishing looks. It's like, by sitting with Monica, he's doing something wrong or neglecting a duty.

It would be clear to anybody. But the reason the male guest is in such high demand doesn't hit Monica until Nesma comes over in her pink mermaid gown. And Monica notices it is the exact same color as the young man's papillon. But she doesn't have time to think about this because, with a look of childish chagrin coming through her heavy makeup, Nesma is standing over the two of them.

—I hope you're, you know how, ya Andrew, enjoying yourselves, she says, glaring at one after the other.

And—before she gets up to hug her cousin and break down in what everyone will pretend are tears of joy, before she holds Nesma to her breast and whispers her congratulations in her ear, apologizing for *keeping what's yours from you for so long* and sobbing loudly again then hiding herself behind laughter—when Monica sees Nesma giving her that look she nearly slips off the cabriole.

Because only then does it descend upon her. And it is like a light but it is dark. Because it is clearer than anything.

He is the groom.

There is a tree in Mattariya, an ancient sycamore not far from a pharaonic obelisk. It is called the Tree of the Virgin, because during their flight through Egypt its shade hid the Holy Family from Herod's men, who were sent to kill them. L'Enfant Jésus was soiled and dusty from traveling in the desert. And when La Sainte Vierge rested her head on the tree a spring of water emerged from the ground with which she could clean her bébé. Then the earth drank the spring's water and the balsam grew for the first time.

Andrew Mansour lived around the corner from that tree. And yaani he was religious. More focused on Christianity than Mohsen could ever be on Islam. Fifi said she knew the type. Though she imagined he was not above sinning. And when Christians sin, Fifi swears—because they're brought up to feel all such relations are unclean—they are a hundred times worse than Muslims!

He was so carnal, Monica told her, that afterward he would flagellate himself with chains. His back and shoulders bore the marks. To him Mary and Joseph sitting under the sycamore with the holy bébé were as real as his mother and little sister waiting for a tuk-tuk under the old acacia farther out. While they were together he kept telling Monica how the tree's bark could cure any illness. How it made childless women pregnant. Even brought people back from the dead. So, even if his religion allowed it, Monica doubted he'd marry a girl who was confessionally suspect however much he sinned with her.

Besides, they both loved Nesma. This was why neither of them considered calling off the wedding. In spite of what started going down later that very night, after the preengagement party. I'll have to fast three days to beg Our Lord's pardon for telling you this, ya Nour.

Nesma was in bed waiting for the phone call she got from her betrothed every night before she went to sleep. The two little boys were arguing about the groom's pompadour. Was this the same haircut one of them planned on getting? Raymond was savoring a bit of gâteau. Safa was still shouting at Raymond. While on the floor, in the dark, the night of Nesma's preengagement party, Monica gave Andrew her maidenhead.

It seems that before she left with Dimyana she had managed to whisper to him *The last door before you get to the roof* and point up.

When Safa saw Nesma glaring at her cousin, sitting with Andrew, she found Raymond and started shouting at him. While Monica was still crying her rumored tears of joy. Safa had forgotten about the quarrel with her in-law but she used the same voice to shout at her husband. Now she lost her temper again, she totally lost her temper, saying, *This marah with a popped-out mind and her Muslim offspring.*

And not knowing what to do Raymond died of embarrassment. He looked old and gray enough to be dead. Because, though she didn't utter their names, it was clear who she was talking about. Besides, they were close enough to hear. So was everybody else. Dimyana pulled Monica by the arm and rushed out.

I don't know at what point Monica had managed to point up, saying, *The door before the roof.*

It was as much information as Andrew needed. After driving his family to Mattariya he raced back. Parked a few streets away and walked to the entrance. If somebody saw or heard him he'd pretend he came back to see Nesma, so he explained to Monica later on. But nobody saw or heard him before he pushed the door in question.

Monica never for a moment doubted her desire to give herself to this man. And—please, Lord, forgive and have mercy on her—not for a moment would she regret it. It happened in very difficult circumstances but it had to happen forthwith. Once they met, it had to. Then and there. I imagine they were both totally clear about this.

They weren't unafraid but they weren't able to acknowledge their fear, so involved were they in what was happening. He too had waited a lifetime for her, it seems. In the studio he held her on the couch and cried for a long time. Then he apologized for wasting her future.

He said, *Where had you been?*

He said, *You smell like the Tree of the Virgin.*

He said, *I know it feels like Our Lord's heaven, but it should be our last time.*

Then he promised her he would only ever have relations with another woman in order to have a child. And, though he kept telling her she had to look to her future, she promised him she would never have relations with any other man at all.

Love's mirror is blind. My mother was a hard woman, but there is definitely truth in the proverb, mais oui!

For four months in 2009, a stylish figure appeared often at Allende Hospital. A young man with bulging muscles and a square jaw. Stylish in a very baladi way. Who, though affectionate and attentive, very polite too, seemed strangely désengagé. Sometimes he came every day. Other times he would be gone for a week. He never came on Sundays or Fridays, very rarely on Saturdays.

And, though the lab technician always knew when to expect him, he showed up at different times. Very early in the morning or in the middle of the day, sometimes at closing time. There was no particular pattern to his visits. But there were so many of them that, for patients and staff—who in that small place were a little like a family, anyway—the stranger became a familiar sight.

No one ever noticed that he always came during the shift of one of the nurses, maybe the most popular one. A dark beauty with blue eyes. Who, though some people claimed she was a Christian, was always in hijab.

Others pointed out that if you only bothered to ask Mahdi, you would know. The stranger, whose name you probably already know is Andrew, happens to be the nephew of Allende's only long-term patient, the former teacher of the hospital owner Doctor Medhat El Tetsh. A childless widower in his eighties. Who's been in a coma since he had a stroke in 2007.

Puffing and squinting, Mahdi ushered Andrew into the old patient's room. There was a door inside that looked locked. It was generally locked. But when Andrew came, it would be unlocked for a moment. So that, taking what flowers or fruit he brought in with him, he could step into a tiny space like Monica's studio.

A kind of miniature hospital room with a sink. On the bed the beautiful young nurse would be waiting. After the hour or so they spent together, Andrew, then Monica would slip out. If there were flowers or uneaten fruit, Monica would leave them by the unconscious man's side. Then the door to this little space would be locked again from the outside. Mahdi usually exchanged a word or two with Monica before she resumed her duties. While Andrew went back to his life.

Andrew would stride in and without word or salaam begin to undress. Then, stark naked, he would kiss and undress her in the same breath. There was something implacable about the way he did this. Like a train, tu sais? You couldn't stop him! And in truth she wouldn't have wanted it any other way, but it worried her. His silence, his efficiency worried her. Because it was a little like going to the toilet, she thought. Until it came to her mind that it was also like prayer.

In May 2009 Monica moved to Kasr El Ainy. Since getting her diploma she hadn't stopped looking for work or wasta. There was no way she could tell Andrew she had finally found an appropriate appointment.

In the year and a half they were seeing each other, Andrew would sometimes be absent. He had bought a SIM card just for her. Which he slipped into his phone when it was safe to talk. Monica would message that number as usual. If there was no answer within twenty-four hours she understood he would be gone for a while.

When Fifi and I met Monica, Andrew had been gone for three months. His longest, which worried her. It didn't worry her but it drilled a hole in her mazag. And this hole kept filling with mind-movies. Actually that scares me now, ya Nour. Because, even though I can think of the Afreet calmly now—shall I tell you?—the hole the revolution has drilled in *my* mazag is filling with mind-movies. The Ikhwan, the dead bodies, and already, in 2014, another officer becoming zaim.

Bref, the mind-movies made Monica all the more desperate to see Andrew. It wasn't as easy gasping for breath again now that she'd known what it was like to breathe. Nobody could notice, so lovely and cheerful did she remain. But if you looked hard enough you could see she was crushed.

She could've pretended to take an interest in her cousin's life, to find out what was keeping him. But in the two months he was gone she felt very far from Nesma, who no longer came to the studio at the appointed hours. The one time she bumped into her on the stairs, Nesma hugged and kissed her with even more warmth than usual.

—I have so much to, she started saying—but instead of *tell you* she said *do*. Now that it isn't so long before, you know how, ya Monica, we go to America.

Together with the mind-movies the encounter saddened Monica. It saddened her to the degree that she couldn't bring herself to ask after the newlyweds. Because it wasn't just the last two months. And yaani it could be accounted for by the change in Nesma's life, her moving out of Ain Shams, becoming a wife responsible for a house and je ne sais quoi. But Monica could not deceive herself.

She felt far from her cousin not because she was betraying her but because she couldn't tell her about the most important thing in her own life. While, sensing a force beyond her control, Nesma took the opportunity to keep away. Dimyana and Safa were just clueless, non?

But it seems Andrew too was deranged and despairing. Because, even though they still couldn't keep away from each other, after he reappeared in August 2011 they did not meet as much. Their meetings were more and more somber and they spoke less and less, it seems. They had to be careful. They had to be more careful than when they met at Allende. There was no safe place for them now. You understand what it is like for paramours in respectable society, though this was clearly much worse because of the scandal.

But still they could've met more if they had wanted to. After Raymond died in Maspero—that was October, hein—very little was said in the family. But in their hearts everybody blamed Andrew for his father-in-law's death. Only Nesma could honestly absolve him. Andrew disappeared one last time to finish the immigration procedures. Which Monica knew were underway though no date had been set. In truth they were not to speak or see each other again. Ever. Raymond's funeral was the end of Andrew and Monica.

In December 2011 Monica said goodbye to Nesma at Safa's but she managed to avoid seeing Andrew altogether. Or he avoided seeing her. Because without either of them saying anything they both realized there was too much grief now.

His decision was more difficult for him than anybody, she knew. But it was probably for the best for all of them. Besides, he didn't want anything to shake his determination. Even more than before, Monica didn't want to disrupt his life.

They had been together exactly twelve times since Allende. Five times in an unused appartement belonging to Andrew's father in Abbasiya. Three times at Andrew's unmarried friend's in Heliopolis. Twice in Monica's studio. Once in Kasr El Ainy. Once at Andrew and Nesma's in Mattariya. And, in spite of the silence and the somberness, in spite of the lies she had to tell and her fear of getting caught, it gave her back her soul every time.

Still, by the time she understood he was immigrating she did not feel she had any objection to the plan. Even between her and herself, she accepted Andrew and Nesma's disappearance without resistance. She was grieving for her khalo but also for what the revolution had come to. And the thought of life being about breathing, not gasping, tu sais. That thought no longer convinced her.

Her mind-movies had passed into insomnia. And yaani this is another thing with the Jumpers. After the mind-movies they're afflicted with impossible insomnia.

These days it is reassuring, c'est vrai. The only reassuring thing. Because I sleep like a full jute sack. Don't I, son of Amin. But I saw for myself how ghastly was her insomnia. How weak and éthéré it made her. Like she was glowing from within. It looked like she was blooming, but the light was consuming her. Only Fifi and I knew.

Every time Andrew disappeared Monica took to spending time in the studio, but in 2011 she spent more time there than ever before. She spent whole nights recalling their first time together. Not reminiscing, you understand. Slowly, painstakingly recollecting. Sometimes she brought other times they were together into the studio with her.

But usually it was just that first meeting. Lying back, she would live again every little detail. Every sight, sound, smell. Every little twitch and jerk. Every sigh. Whole nights.

That was the start of her insomnia. What thoughts she savored overnight came back to torture her in the day.

In the weeks on weeks when she yearned for the tiniest bit of dream but could not fall asleep, when her body withered and her mind loosened and the thought of being alive grew harder, all kinds of sensations from the studio raided her head.

They came not as memories but as grotesque echoes. Like twittering demons or doubles from Jahannam. The caress that was like balsam on her skin became a pressing iron. The grunt that put warm joy in her breast became cold fear. Even the face of her beloved took on the look of a mythical beast.

The day Raymond died, Monica spent the night recalling one of her last talks with him. Their last political talk, it seems. In the morning and from then on she couldn't be sure whether they'd ever had this talk in truth, whether it was a hallucination. A memory she invented herself. Or the first dream she'd had in months.

She told me this herself.

They were walking down an alley they both liked in Ain Shams. It was late afternoon. A quiet time. They were walking, just the two of them. Calming their nerves before they went back to Dimyana and Safa and the two boys making enough noise for four neighborhoods. Then Raymond decided to stop for a shisha. It wasn't so much a café as a stand.

Monica had been telling him how it saddened her to realize that people were still surprised by Mubarak's fall. As if Egypt didn't deserve anything good. And Raymond had been silent for so long she doubted if he'd been listening.

Now all of a sudden while rearranging the burning coals over the tobacco with a pair of tongs he looked at her again.

—When you forget something well enough and then you see it, he said, taking his first pull on the shisha, then that thing really surprises you.

—You mean the revolution was—

—A reminder.

—A reminder of something we forgot, ya Khalo?

—A reminder, ya Nefertiti, of what we can remember.

Monica gave him a perplexed look.

—Mother of Mercy, Raymond sighed, bringing his face right up to hers. Ignorance is bliss because the memories—he straightened his back so he could pound his breast with a half-drawn fist, too hard—they hurt. All the time when we are ignorant, ya Monica, it's because we forget.

Then he pulled deeper on his shisha.

—So you think we had it in us to remove Hosni Mubarak all along?

—If we can remember, Raymond wheezed. Shisha smoke came not out of his mouth and nose but, it seemed to her, out of his eyes and ears, his head. If we can remember a time when Hosni Mubarak is not there, then we can remove the mother of Hosni Mubarak.

I imagine she wasn't sure what to make of this. Was it a statement about politics or life? Then one day it occurred to her that if Andrew hadn't reminded her of breathing she would never have known love. She would never have had her reunion with the father whose death made her gasp. Perhaps the revolution and her love story were the same . . .

The thought of the hole in Monica's mazag scares me because her mind-movies are exactly like mine. They are nothing like dreams, those mind-movies. For one thing they always come while you're awake, usually when you're least expecting them. And they happen outside time. I spent my youth longing to be free of time, mais oui. But it only ever happened during these horror shows, ya Nour.

Besides, they have the strangest subjects. They are not about her and Andrew, for example. They are not about Mohsen, Dimyana, or anybody dead or alive she knew. They are not about corruption, dictatorship, or anything anybody revolted against. Losing her maidenhead. Spending time on the ground in the dark. Being Muslim and Christian at the same time. They are not about any of these things. But in a strange way they are always about all of them.

Sometimes she smells tear gas. Not like she smells it now but like the first time she smelled it. You understand the terror of first smelling tear gas. The suffocation, the burning. Nothing in the world to convince you you're not dying. Of course all it takes is a gulp of air to be well again. But in the mind-movie the gas is totally undetectable. Monica doesn't know where the air is clear. She controls her panic enough to stagger away, trying out different places. But however far she goes she is still dying. And all around her people are on their backs like cockroaches sprayed with insecticide. Or they're staggering about, their arms outstretched like zombies. As she glares at the horizon it dawns on her. All the air in the world has turned into tear gas.

Sometimes she hears a slogan, say, *The people want to bring down the regime*. First it comes as real chanting, like there is a demonstration within hearing distance. But then she moves away, the sound of the demonstration keeps fading till it disappears. And still she hears the same slogan. Peddlers cry it out instead of advertising their wares. Passersby yell it at taxis and microbuses instead of their destinations. Teenagers taunt each other with it while they hang about street corners or kick balls made out of socks. Domino players and shisha smokers at the baladi cafés keep saying it as if it was a joke or a comment on the political situation, showing all the appropriate reactions. Eventually, when she opens her own mouth to inquire or complain, she realizes to her horror that she is no different from anyone else. *The people want to bring down the regime* is the only thing she can say.

Sometimes she is running. Surrounded by others running alongside her. With them but feeling alone. Nobody can help anybody. She is panting and coughing blood and her feet—unbearably painful—are oozing pus. But she knows she cannot stop. At first she doesn't understand why, then she remembers that, for years, for centuries, this has been her life. Every morning she has a mound of stones to throw at a group of armed men in uniform. The stones never hit their target. But, together with all those who are running now—each with a separate mound—she must keep throwing until the men in uniform raise their arms and start shooting. Then, propelled by the singular fear of being shot at, everybody turns around and runs. She knows she will not stop until the night makes people blind and then she will be lost to the world until morning. When, crouched by her mound of stones, she starts throwing again.

RED

When the night comes in I sit thinking of the Afreet. Sometimes I think of the little hospital in the Pyramids where so many things come together. A hospital is a place where we see our lives connected, mais c'est vrai. So I try to make sense of the progression of events while I'm not seeing mind-movies or worrying about Jumpers' insomnia.

It was the week before Ramadan when I met Monica. After Eid things stayed quiet for a time before they turned ghastly again. In that time Monica and I made the rounds. We said we were delivering donations but in truth we were looking for Jumpers. It was as if we had discussed the theoretical part and we needed to do some fieldwork.

Monica didn't want to take me to Kasr El Ainy Hospital because of the surgery professor she worked under. Most Jumpers were in Kasr El Ainy. But he was watching her. She had brought it up with him, a loyal sharmoota's son, hein. She had brought up the number of women who came to Kasr El Ainy after jumping out of windows. And knowing she was a revolutionary he had chided and threatened her. Even issued an official reprimand against her, just to complicate her life.

One night he stepped into the room where she sat alone and locked the door behind him. Then he told her, and he was very calm and polite while he did. He held her by her arm hard enough to make it blue and he looked in her eyes, calm and polite.

—I know you people want to drown the country more than you've already drowned it, he told her. But if I find you spreading rumors about women and windows again, I will personally make sure you are placed in a military jail.

So, what research she did with me, Monica had to do away from Kasr El Ainy. She had connections in many private hospitals, though. And in each one of them there were Jumpers. Allende is where we went first because Mahdi told Monica there was an elderly one there.

She was my first Jumper.

Ommo Sabry

She cleaned the toilettes at a little pension off Talaat Harb Square. But it emerged she was childless, even though nobody knew her by any other name. It seems this was her life's fancy. A boy from her belly called Sabry. No papers were found to identify her. So no one knew how old she was, though the assumption was that she was in her late fifties. But even the man she had lived with for twenty years didn't know. That was the Tahrir traffic stop's Kleenex man. They stake out territories. But I'm sure you know this better than your Mouna. There are beggars and peddlers and valet mafias working with the police. They have their own hierarchies. Among them there are those who are powerful and those who are not. Ommo Sabry's unauthenticated husband was powerful. His name was Abd El Nasser after the Zaim, and people called him Nasser. He was famous for his arm-length mustache and his fish-filthy tongue. It seems he dispensed drugs as well as handkerchiefs. When they took him to hospital they found nearly a hundred one-gram heroin packets in his clothes. But he'd been working with State Security, I imagine. Because he wasn't questioned about the incident. And, though the heroin was officially seized, he was never tried for possessing it. Besides, Nasser disappeared at the same time the police went into hiding. He had come back with them. Helping with more heart than ordinary honorable citizens. Ommo Sabry never knew about Nasser's two young wives, his duplex in Mohandessin, or the wealth he had piled up in real estate. He kept it all from her so he could make her work and spend on him. Even when the revolution started ruining him, he just complained there was no traffic in Tahrir, first for eighteen days and then for weeks at a time. But he never told her how much money those squishy-teezed khawals were losing him. The day before Ramadan when the gendarmerie came, Nasser led the honorable citizen batallion that helped them. At the end it emerged that he had been lost in the scuffle. On the landing down to the dysfunctional public toilettes, two stray protesters were hauling him off a nineteen-year-old girl in hijab. A girl who had nothing to do with anything, it seems. But, thinking her *one of them*, Nasser had hurled himself on her and pinned her to the ground. Tore her skin and bit the flesh off her cheeks.

She was an unconscious, bloodied heap by the time they found him. But when on noticing them he went on violating her—Our Lord safeguard and protect us—they picked him up and kept hitting his head against the steps until he too was unconscious. Then, leaving him for dead, they ran. Nasser's skull was cracked and he was badly concussed. He had one broken rib and one fractured shoulder. After a week in hospital he was back on the asphalt as strong as a horse. Three weeks later—like all Jumpers, without cause or warning—Ommo Sabry stepped out of the pension and took the creaking ascenseur to the top floor of the building, then she climbed two flights of stairs to the roof. Ommo Sabry had a cut on one of her lungs and a hemorrhage in her brain. She was on life support but it would be removed at the end of the week. The doctors had no hope for her. Her face was bandaged but the bandages had come off and underneath it was like pickled turnip with beetroot smeared all over it. It feels strange now. Because I already knew this was Medhat El Tetsh's hospital. But until I saw the salade that was Ommo Sabry's face I didn't think about being there before.

Laila Magdy Samir

I saw her at a field hospital in Tahrir. The day they stormed the Israeli embassy. Exactly two days before the tenth anniversary of those jihadis flying planes into buildings in New York. She was thirty-seven. She looked unharmed lying on her back on the trottoir. Laila Samir had jumped from the seventh floor of that ghastly monument to bureaucracy opposite the Omar Makram Mosque building. She had been in Tahrir all day, for the millioniya. This was the first millioniya without Islamists in a long time. It proved there were enough of us. But then those children went and broke into the Israeli embassy and the army stepped in again and—pas bon, ya Nour. God knows how she got into the government building on a day like that. When they found her by the Omar Makram statue she looked miraculously unharmed. But her neck was broken and her heart had stopped. Fifi went home early that night, yelping, *And, maalesh yaani, what's wrong with Israel? By the life of Our Lord, aha! When you live in a deadly crapper like this, what in the world can you say is wrong with Israel!* I'd been seeing Jumpers every week since July. Laila Samir must've been my—what—thirty-fifth, thirty-sixth? And she wasn't a friend. Though I'd met her on and off on revolutionary occasions. But, aside from Monica, of course—shall I tell you?—she's one of the three Jumpers I can't help thinking of every day. She was a renowned architect before the age of thirty. Egyptian American, because she spent half her life studying and teaching over there. And because she didn't feel secure as a Christian with only Egyptian citizenship, why not? But she came back to stay in 2009. With her American husband, a famous professeur of political science. He was even more excited about the revolution than she was, though she felt he was seeing it through tinted glasses. But it was her brother she had a fight with. The Student Movement icon Fady Samir. He was very close to your Tante Semsem. We used to know him a bit too. Such *heavy blood* and pretension, mon Dieu. He had joined the January revolution, of course. He had even started one of the five thousand parties that sprouted like fungus in the first few months. But it seems he had also renewed his nonparty alliance with the Ikhwan. First, Laila found out he was voting yes in the March referendum. She reluctantly accepted his explanation that it was to appease the Military Council for the sake of stability and moving ahead. But when the Copts first gathered in Maspero to protest their treatment, it emerged he was informing on them. This was a secret, of course, but Laila had her sources. She was assured it was her brother who tipped the sectarian mob that went at the Coptic protests ahead of the army. Because he was on the Ikhwan's payroll. That Maspero attack wasn't as spectacular as the main event four months later, though the same number of people died. And while she didn't set out to expose him, Laila cut Fady off. Afterward she acted normal. Once, only once she broke down and spoke of going back to America. Her husband didn't understand why she was so disgusted with her country and her people. Or how she could talk about her own *Christian minority* in terms more derogatory and offensive than anything he had ever heard in his own country. She used very foul language, but until that day in September there was no sign of anything wrong. And she looked unharmed. Her hair in a bun, her lovely Upper Egyptian face serene. Eyes closed, of course. But you could see she had the same bold beauty as Sophia Loren. With a mole above her lip. No trace of blood or pain. And yaani elegant, tres elegant in her tight tailleur. It wrung my belly to admit I was looking at a corpse.

Mariam Mohsen El Daly

This was the daughter of one of the Daly brothers. The business-man family, aywa. She was only nineteen. But her mother, who died in a car accident in 1998, had fallen out of favor early on. Because of this, the girl's father didn't care too much for her. She ran away from home in 2008 and nobody looked very hard. Ill-omened little thing! White as a khawaga's daughter. Delicate as a cigarette paper. Pretty as a lily. Monica had met her when she was brought into the Kasr El Ainy emergency ward in June. An overdose of—I don't know the names of these things. Not Tramadol. Tramadol is what she was ad-dicted to. They never saw each other after Mariam left the hospital. But Monica recognized her. After she left home she stuck with her Cairo American College friends. Even if she wasn't going to school anymore. But one after another the rich Egyptian and the expatriate American families grew tired of her. Within six months she was living with an unemployed sound engineer with an American mother, Adam. She thought they were in love. He taught her to take drugs, then taught her to deliver them. To help with expenses, he said. Some of the men she delivered drugs to tried to take advantage of her. And to help with expenses even more or to get more drugs for herself, Mariam let them. At first she thought Adam didn't know. But then she noticed he was sending her to get drugs more often than to deliver them. When she did this, she noticed that the men who had them expected what they were getting from her. Then she heard him on the phone. It was early in the morning while he thought she was asleep. *You can have her over-night*, he was saying. For such and such an amount. She heard him. And, like a sleepwalker, picked up a few things and left the house. He ran after her, but it was no good. Nobody knows for sure whether she returned to him or how. She jumped from the fifth floor of a residen-tial building right next to the Safa Hospital. Witnesses would say there was a young man with her in the appartement. Who drove off in an old and battered BMW as soon as she hit the ground. Now strangers were going to haul her into the hospital. But a male nurse smoking a ciga-rette on the stairs noticed and came running to stop them. Just as the three of us stood outside the hospital checking the names of the revolutionaries we were to visit before we went up. If they carried her wrong it could kill her, the nurse said. She was squirming spastically but stiff as a frozen thing, rasping and screeching every time she took her breath. Looking down, Monica recognized her forthwith. Fifi and I went in to talk to somebody about saving her while Monica squatted by her side. Till the moment she moved on, Mariam was lucid. She called me setto, imagine that! Not mama, not tante. But setto. She was totally paralyzed. Breathing gave her pain. She looked at me without turning, and she spoke quickly in one go so as to keep the pain to a minimum. *Setto Amna*, she said. I don't know when or how she learned my name. *Will you put your hand on my forehead wennabi ya setto? I want to know if I will feel anything there! Aywa aywa, like this*, she said. After five minutes her neck snapped. An orthopedic surgeon had had a look. Very carefully. And before he left he said she'd be all right. But by the life of the Prophet this is what happened. I put my hand on her forehead and after five minutes her neck snapped. Like it had been held by a thread. The girl didn't move and, except for my hand there, nobody touched her. We thought we heard a tiny crack, then it was over. My hand was still on her forehead when they came in to take her away.

When the night comes in I sit thinking of the Afreet. But night and day now I dream of Serag and Samira's building. The roof comes after me. With this hole in my mazag, other than my mind-movies it is the only thing I see.

Everything else pushes me away and the roof draws me to it, but it is so persistent sometimes I think it too must be a mind-movie. I was never on that roof but it comes after me. It is like I know it well. Its shape and size, the calmness of being on it. The pattern of the tiles, the height of the parapet. The beauty of the Nile from on high.

And when I'm not seeing a mind-movie and the roof isn't coming after me I think of the Afreet. Or else I think of an enchanted little hospital named Allende. Of a lily-like Tramadol addict, a world-class architect, a childless cleaning woman known only as Mother of Sabry. I remember one particular day I went to one of those hospitals and saw three people there in the corridor and the sight of them clinched something in my mind.

There was a young nurse, clearly someone who wears the niqab. But on the job, when she had to be in uniform, she used a surgical mask in place of her face veil.

There was a young footballer who had come straight from the playing court. But he had a beard that reached to his belly. Their lips look so animal without a mustache, non? And there was a baby's handprint of a zebiba between his eyes.

Then there was a young man impeccably decked out in a very expensive-looking suit, reasonably bearded. But he wore a white Afghan turban on his head.

And the thing they clinched in my mind was that, as Egyptians, as Muslims, it isn't just that we imagine we're fooling the All-Knowing One, pretending to be pious while we behave like beggars and prostitutes. It's also that we can't even be who we are without disguising ourselves! You can't just be a nurse or an athlete or an office worker—you have to have a niqab or a zebiba or a turban besides.

I thought of Amin telling me that in this part of the world modernity had been aborted before it was properly born. *People think they've been born into the present,* he'd say, *but in truth they are stuck in the womb that's the past. The catastrophe is that, being creatures of the present in spite of themselves, it's their superficial, silly, small idea of the past that they're stuck in. Nothing real.* And for the first time in my life I understood what he meant. The term *abortive modernity,* for the first time I understood that term.

Then I thought: However can there be a revolution if the people are in fancy dress?

But I think of Amin and my life too, sometimes. All these years gone. And yaani usually it's the Afreet, c'est vrai. But sometimes when it's neither a mind-movie nor the roof, the thought of my life takes me to that ghastly time in October 2011. When the Copts went out to demonstrate for the second time. And the leftist icon Fady Samir found new ways to inform on them.

Our Lord forgive your Tante Fifi more than anybody else for this. Because if not for her I wouldn't have gone there at all. Or seen what I saw that day.

I imagine that whatever happened, Monica would've jumped. But maybe the hole in my mazag wouldn't be quite so deep.

Ignorance is bliss. And *the imbecile woman's son lives longest.* But Fifi knew the Coptic protest leaders and she was feeling proactive and protective of her folk. We went twice. On Tuesday, then on Sunday. Sunday, October 9, aywa. A day or two after Raymond and Monica had their alleged political talk.

Not that I knew about the talk they had at the time, but I was thinking the same thing. Never mind a time when Hosni Mubarak is not there. Never mind a place where it is safe to be Christian. Reminders had been dissolved in acid and nobody could remember anything at all. Just as nobody remembers how we got to this revolution. Or why we have to watch again while an officer gives sentimental speeches and they hold sham elections to make him zaim for life.

Bref, it started the way it always does.

Wahhabis or jihadis or ordinary Muslims had gone and torn down a church in Aswan. Christians across the country waited. First the Aswan governor said no church had ever existed on the site. Then he said it had been illegally built in the first place, implying that whoever tore it down had a right to do that, ya Nour.

So people decided to camp out in Maspero again. Not just Copts, you understand, but mostly Copts. Angry Copts.

They decided to stage a sit-in where they'd been gathering for protests. But the gendarmerie and the riot police killed six of them the day they gathered. This was the return of the riot police, by the way. With the gendarmerie, they killed six while dispersing the sit-in on Tuesday. And that is how Angry Sunday came to be. Angry Sunday was the Coptic version of Angry Friday, tu sais, which started the eighteen-day sit-in that brought down Mubarak so many lifetimes ago.

On Tuesday we were there early, before the red and the black. The gendarme who was caught bragging about shooting Copts dead in that YouTube video, remember? Honorable citizens were congratulating him. When we got there he hadn't arrived on the scene. Small processions kept spilling onto the main streets. Which were strangely empty. It was overcast.

Never in my life have I seen so many crosses in the Cairo sky.

Wood and iron and plastic crosses of different sizes and proportions, but each the height of a human being or taller. And the light making them all dark gray against the light gray of the sky. Like the procession in that Ingmar Bergman film about Iblis in the Middle Ages. The young men chanting as they raised them above their heads, tramping where the cars should be. Gathering like gluey fluid into Maspero, with only the crosses rigid in silhouette above their heads. A sight.

Everywhere there were pictures of the Messiah, of Baba Chenouda, and the Mother and Child. Saints and priests unknown to me hung up in the air or at eye level. But the real icons were the faces.

For half an hour or so, while crowds gathered around speakers and the sky got back some color, Monica and I trailed Fifi while she greeted them. There were priests and community leaders, altar girls. Engineers and lawyers and electricians. Taxi drivers, icon painters, bureaucrats. There were revolutionaries and window cleaners. Some of them stood on pedestals with microphones in their hands. They made statements.

They were statements like nothing I've heard in my life. Monica was a little dazed even as she smiled warmly. Confused by the sound of one-half of her slandering the other, I imagined. And, between smiling sheepishly but victoriously and palming Monica's shoulder, Fifi didn't object to what was being said.

It's an honor to be called an infidel by a Muslim.

The Muslims are our guests here in Egypt. Either they behave themselves or they get out.

A bunch of thieves and charlatans, they must leave.

Islam? Islam? What kind of religion is Islam?

Egypt belongs with the Messiah as do all true Egyptians.

Strangely, as it seems now, Fifi and I never discussed these statements. I imagine it was just understood that they were a reaction to the bigotry of the governor and the army, let alone the Ikhwan. But I imagine it would've been ghastly for either of us to repeat or consider them. So when Monica started to say, *What were they saying out there,* we quickly changed the subject.

She respected that we were avoiding a discussion once she realized, ma fille. We didn't find out about the dispersion until midnight. We were so busy after we left. Fifi growled, weeping for an hour. But, when the big march was organized for Sunday, there was no question about not going back.

At the last minute Monica phoned to say she wasn't coming because she had a shift at Kasr El Ainy. She did really have a shift at Kasr El Ainy, but she was going to miss it anyway. Through Safa she had found out that Andrew, deranged with rage, was joining the protest march. She spoke with Nesma that day. From her heart she commiserated.

Monica tried to reach Raymond but his phone had run out of battery, it seemed. Between the church where he attended mass in Heliopolis and the baladi café where he spent time in Ain Shams, Monica went looking for him. No one realized until much later that when Nesma told her father that Andrew had set out to Maspero, the old man was so worried about his son-in-law he decided to go after him.

Fifi was having tea with an Anglican clergyman near her house in Garden City and she said to meet opposite the Shepheard Hotel. On the Corniche. The march had set out from Shoubra. Some protesters had reached the October Bridge intersection. But already, as I set out, I was more anxious than I would be going to even the most perilous protest. While I waited—shall I tell you?—*the mouse was playing in my bosom.*

It was dusk by the time we sat side by side in the back of the taxi. Going down the Corniche from the Shepheard to the Round Building, I was looking out the window. The sky is always pretty at this time of day, but in autumn and winter it is magnifique. So I was looking at it out of the taxi window, sitting there with nothing but a bonnet on my head and bits of my arms and legs uncovered after all those years.

And all of a sudden it came to me that this was a journey I'd made before. From the Shepheard to the Round Building, from the Round Building to the Shepheard. Especially in a car. It was my life's journey.

And I thought: C'est vrai, it is. But it's the journey of a life I left behind. A life before I was visited by the Afreet, before I took the hijab, before I even had children.

Then it came to me that making this journey again now could give me back that life. Not the life itself, of course. But its value, its meaning. Sitting in the taxi like this, going to join a Coptic protest march with a bonnet and bits of my arms and legs uncovered.

It was the last calm thought I had all day. Because the mouse hadn't been playing for nothing. The girl, ma pauvre petite, was there. I didn't know, but I could feel her. Fifi kept crying for no reason, before we saw anything bad. She didn't know either, but in time she told me she too could feel her. Even before the taxi stopped at the crossroads, saying there was a roadblock and we would have to walk the rest of the way. We could feel Monica, her horror and her sorrow.

The sky was magnifique. For a moment it was like walking back to work from a break in the vicinity on a busy day. Fifi's arm in mine, you understand. Engagé. How many times had we done that? This time there were no shocking statements. More Muslims were there, I imagine. Muslims who were sympathetic. The talk was of rights and rules. The law not being followed by those employed to enforce it. The need for a civil government that isn't Wahhabi or jihadi.

I imagine the youth groups had objected to *the black galabiyas*, as they called the clergy. It seems the compromise was for the priests to be quiet and keep their congregations quiet about Muslims.

There were hymns and anthems. There were chants of unity. But even though Maspero felt safe and cheerful, the anxiety, the sorrow stayed with us. Not that being in a sorrowful mood could make it less horrifying when all of a sudden we heard the sirens. And saw. The riot police officers looming, then the armored vehicles. Military armored vehicles. And everywhere people clapping and praying or swearing.

The gendarmes especially were rabid. They had always been vicious but I'd never seen them so determined. Like the bad guys in an action film out to kill as many as possible. The only thing slowing them down—that they're looking for important good guys to kill first. Blocking entryways. Storming appartements. Wielding machine guns at the doors of radio and television offices demanding: *Any Christians here?*

You know the area is full of media offices. Near the Round Building. The gendarmes were storming these places demanding Christians. I heard it with my own ears. We were resting at the Deutsche Welle radio. Or were we hiding, in truth? We were in a dark room at the Deutsche Welle office, a Muslim and a Copt with lots of others keeping quiet. But for some reason the gendarmes didn't search this particular appartement.

Later we found out that, while this horror was going down, the newscaster on national television was calling on honorable citizens to come to the aid of their army and help it fend off the attacks of protesters, foreigners, conspirators—Christians.

But how to explain this, light of my eyes? One minute there is singing and talk of the rule of law, the next men in uniform are shooting. Aiming for people's heads. You'd think they were shooting pellets or gas canisters, but they're shooting live bullets. To kill. I saw it with my own eyes.

While people run for their lives the armored vehicles chased them down. From one side of the road to the other. Like bumper cars at the fun fair. They chase them and they run them over.

Sometimes they run over cars to reach them, pulping the cars. Then they run over the people running for their lives. Grinding them. Like they were so much scrap iron. Molding their heads and their spines into grotesque shapes. Military vehicles, aywa. While the gendarmes looked for Christians to shoot point-blank indoors and the riot police aimed for people's heads.

The sky was dark by then, and the streetlights made everything orange and gray. Like the red and black of that ghastly day before Ramadan but worse. Much worse. I saw it with my own eyes, tu sais. Everything was orange and gray.

After I met Monica the children were murdered. For a while in August and September we made the rounds in calmness. But soon enough the Israeli embassy was broken into. Things happened. Then Monica was crouched swaying among grotesque shapes. In that bluish room that appeared in all the pictures, remember it? Where they lay like horror film props. Dead Christians.

It was the first room we entered. She looked up and saw us forthwith. Like she had been waiting. She was not crying. She did not frown. But she was swaying nonstop. I don't remember how we reached the Coptic Hospital in Azbakeya, Fifi and I. Or even why we went there. We hadn't spoken to Monica. We hadn't even mentioned her. If somebody had asked we would've said she was in Kasr El Ainy doing her nursing shift. But we found her and it was as if we'd known she would be there. As if we had come for her.

People stood with their phones in their hands taking pictures. People screamed and swore and ran around slapping their own faces, shoving each other, butting the walls. One woman laughed hysterically. Another took hold of one dead man's shoulders and shook them. Violently. There was that smell of sweat and iron. Sheets covered everything except the faces, but they covered nothing in truth. Hymns played in the corridor.

Fifi crouched down next to Monica while I looked at the shape closest to her. I had never seen Raymond but I recognized him. His upper half was normal, though clearly dead. His face neither flattened nor folded. His lower half was all but severed at the waist. And where the legs would be there was only a reddish pulp. You could see bits of it through the soiled sheet that covered Monica's right arm as well. She looked from Raymond's face to Fifi, then up to me. A while later a toned young man in tears came into the room. I guessed correctly that this was Andrew.

He crouched on the opposite side of the corpse, put his hand on its shoulder and went on crying. Monica looked to him too. But in all this time her expression did not change for an instant. Even as Fifi held her. She never stopped swaying. Eventually I bent down to kiss her. When she turned to me, the sheet slipped off her arm and I saw she was holding hands with the corpse.

THE ROOF

February 11, 2015: October 1, 1970

My Shimo:

Four years after the revolution, Jumpers begin to appear all through our mother's life: Lena Qansuh, then another friend of hers named Naila El Sayigh, and eventually also a third, Habiba Marzouk; Omayma Abd El Wahab, who went and gave her consolation at Halim's house after he died in 1977, then climbed to the roof of the building and jumped; Arwa Saleh, the Student Movement icon who jumped out of her close ones' apartment in 1997.

It dawns on me that the January Revolution wasn't the only time they were staging their occult operation . . .

But already you're making a joker sad face, the way you would when your eldest brother pleaded with you to appease the mother you had crossed.

—The medieval-minded matriarch that begat us? you're saying. The reactionary?

And even though you're genuinely scornful, your smile is so beautiful there is no trace of bitterness in your eyes. It still amazes me how impassive your face always remained, but at the same time how implacable. Giving me the finger while you continue to wave your arms at her, the rage barely ruffles your expression even as every last facial muscle quivers. Or I hear you tell her, in a voice that could never be so steady if it wasn't savage, *I'd rather die than become you, ya Mouna.*

But now that Mouna's gone you're saying something different.

—Deen keda, you're saying. Predicating salvation on femicide is such a male-behim thing to do, ya Nour. You're the one person who could've stopped Mouna's death and now you're suggesting it was the answer to Egypt's problems? Besides, is that schizo schema of being in your mother's mind really all the sense you've managed to make of the world?

But I did not make up the Jumpers. Even if you think I've gone mad, Shimo, you will know. I would've done anything to keep Mouna alive. And the world from turning into this interminable consolation-taking. From the soles of your feet to the top of your head, I'm sure you will know. Yet how to make someone float on the surface of the truth rather than drown in its fathomless depths?

Femicide is one thing—I am not predicating salvation on anything. By the time she told me about the Jumpers, even Mouna didn't think there was going to be salvation. Anyway, not here, not in this life. Beyond repentance for its own sake, in her last few months the Jumpers meant nothing to her. She no longer thought anyone was killing them, either. Just that they were the country's way of accommodating a truth the people refused to see.

And if I speak admiringly of those women, it's because Mouna made a true myth of their story. A few new chapters of my Genesis. How can I help sharing the truth she saw in those people's tragedies? But if you asked me what truth that is, I would have no idea what to say.

All I know is my grief for our mother has freed me from the lies I'd been telling myself about who I was. A truth-seeker, a lover, a revolutionary—I could never be any of those things if I didn't understand that I was an Egyptian woman's son. Only by finding out how the story of her life is the history of this country could I know who I am.

And now that this is happening, I feel I can start to live on my own terms at last. Without the shame, the loss, the bottomless letdown of being the kind of man she had to endure. Do you understand me, darling sister?

During my second time in the attic I saw the Cataclysm unfold in the neighborhood of Agouza. That's the way I came to know how, from being the mother you and I knew, Mouna could end up there, in the wildest chronological order. But however often I came up, I could see nothing else of Mouna's time after the revolution. Of the last four years of her life, the attic had nothing to tell.

Four years to the hour since she took the Metro to Kasr El Ainy to join the masses celebrating in Tahrir, Mouna takes the Metro to Dokki and starts making the relatively long trek to the Agouza Corniche, at the opposite end of Zamalek island. She's been drawn to it for a year now, but she couldn't say why she is headed to this particular building in Agouza. The one where her Sudanese friends Serag and Samira celebrated Amin's release in 1964.

Once again I'm not there when she steps out. It's been a few days since she had any sleep, I know, and she's had time to study the phenomenon of her dreams merging into wakefulness since it started in November of 2014—the dreams are mostly about Monica Younis. She panicked briefly when she realized she couldn't control the phenomenon. But perceiving it to be part of her destiny, the more she eased into it, the less it bothered her. Sometimes she even relishes the experience.

Through the Metro ride only the chant *Hold your head high, you're Egyptian* echoes through her head, alternating with the tune of the Sayed Darwish song "Ana Hawet" in an unpleasantly fast tempo. When she emerges onto Tahrir Street in Dokki the sound fades as the noise of the traffic gradually replaces it. It is late afternoon and the breeze is getting chilly, but walking will keep her warm.

Mouna wasn't confident she would know the way to her destination, but her feet take her there automatically. They navigate a path in the mayhem of pedestrians and vehicles—the chaotic parking, the bikers, the mad microbuses, niqab-clad women behind Vespa drivers—while she keeps her eyes on the steadily darkening sky.

For an hour and a half, while the sun goes down, she delights in the sense of homecoming building up inside her.

At some point Mouna realizes that people have been walking with her. People she has often thought of and ones she has totally forgotten. All kinds of people. And it occurs to her that this might be the purpose of the journey she's making. Bound for her dewy, fluttering arrival at something written in the world unseen.

It doesn't feel at all relevant that no one else can see her companions. Or that they appear both idealized and indistinct, the way they might in a painting. It doesn't feel relevant where they come from—holding her hand or locking arms with her, engagé like nineteenth-century couples—or where they go once they're no longer walking alongside her.

No sooner is one gone than the next materializes. She is conscious enough of passersby to keep her voice down and not gesture too flamboyantly. Though people still shoot her quizzical and derisive glances as they go by. The smirks just make her laugh, though. The smugness of guiltless murderers.

—The blindness, she rasps to one ghost companion, mon Dieu.

Much later in my visions—I guess this would've been my twentieth or twenty-first time in the attic—I see Mouna on another roof. And it makes me aware of myself in a way I haven't been before. All I've seen of her life so far takes place in my own prehistory. And I'm so engrossed in recording it that I'm not aware of myself till I encounter her admonishing me for naming my car after the Prophet's mythical steed. Then I remember she was named after the Prophet's mother.

Her name was Amna and she called me Nour—the Prophet's attribute. I also fell in love with and married a much older woman at my life's start. And for the first time since before the revolution I recall that this was why I jokingly called my Volkswagen Burak when I got it in 1990. Mouna admonished me, but not too seriously, because it could also be interpreted as my seeking the Prophet's baraka.

That is the transition point in my visions. When I sleep that night I dream. I cannot remember the dream, but I wake to the image of a giant egg, which I know is a person's shaved head from behind. I know it is ominous, too, but somehow I also know seeing it is a good sign. There are people all around, benign and baleful bedlam watching an impossibly large, impossibly august procession from on high.

The year is 1970, as I eventually realize. And it dawns on me I've crossed a new threshold in my attic visions. I've reached the start of history with my birth on June 12, 1969. From now on I will be a factor in the life I am reliving.

Nimo—as Mouna still thinks of herself—has barely made sense of her whereabouts when the inauspicious occiput appears. Rubber-smooth and immobile, it's like a weather-polished skull among the scree of furry, wiggling heads. Immediately on seeing it she's palpitating, dreary dryness creeping on her throat.

The Newspaperman watching the end of the world from the exact same venue as her? By sheer coincidence?

Nimo is on the roof of the Socialist Union, the squat cube overlooking both the Nile and Tahrir that, forty years on, she will watch the revolutionaries set on fire. She's roughly at the center, wedged in the human rock face so that, without straining her neck, she can see the apocalypse on both sides:

Men balanced on the scaffolding of the tramway wires overhead to watch, looking so comfortable and secure they evoke arboreal monkeys at rest. Marchers chanting slogans and gendarmerie on horseback. Black headscarves being torn and white handkerchiefs waved a hundred at a time.

She is watching, the tension building since Ustaz Nafi, the head of the Press Center, announced they were being driven in buses to where they can pay their final respects. Herded across Cairo like privileged prize cattle of the regime ranchers.

The sensation of history unfolding is in her body again. Only this time she appreciates what's happening. She doesn't yet realize how much it delights her, but she knows this egg-like head is making her hyperventilate. It was all she had to look at every time the Newspaperman addressed her. He had always spoken with his back to her, his mechanical monosyllables seeming to emanate from bone.

It had always brought her heart up into her throat, as now. Newspaperman memories drip onto her brainpan, torturing her scalp. But all she has to do to neutralize them is remind herself of what's happening:

Four years after the end of the war—the disastrous war of 1967, the one that eviscerated any patriotism she might've had left, any belief in dignity—Nasser is dead. The Immortal Zaim has shuffled off this mortal coil. C'est vrai! And the biggest crowd she's seen in her life is processing through the streets to mourn him.

As she stares at her Mukhabarat handler from a distance, Nimo recalls that wearying week at the height of summer, three years before. While two-thirds of the male population remained unheard from fighting the Israelis in Sinai, daily Sameh Khairy would announce sensational victories for the Arab Army, *Our artillery has brought down ten more of the Enemy's planes,* his football commentator-cum-religious preacher's voice reassuringly hysterical amid military marches and patriotic songs.

We listened, too, Nimo is thinking. Only for a bucket of cold sewage to be emptied over all our heads while Sameh Khairy tendered his resignation.

The truth was that Sinai was fully occupied. The Israelis controlled everything on the eastern shore of the Suez Canal. Our planes had been bombed before they had a chance to take off, our artillery instantly incapacitated. Those who hadn't been killed or taken prisoner were tramping homeward in the sand, starved and terror-stricken, stripped of all morale. For months after their return, whenever they noticed their uniforms, people were to mock them at bus stops.

And so, having *suicided* the army commander Abd El Hakim Amer, his life's intime—by then *suicide* had become a transitive verb, so many dissidents were dead!—Nasser decided or pretended to decide to step down. Then, instantly, the people appeared to fill the streets in protest. He made a speech as dramatic and calculated as any since 1956. And for hours on end the people begged, urged, ordered him not to leave them. Crying and cursing hysterically, obscenely riffing on phrases from the speech.

—But the sharmootas' sons are hirelings, Amin kept sneezing, in a rare moment of after-prison *engagement*. He's turned the people into hirelings. Just think. If he really wanted to shove off, couldn't his Mukhabarat stop all these protests from happening?

Now the people are taking leave of the god for real. And it just so happens that the high priest in charge of Nimo's divine duties is seeing him off from the same site. Suddenly Nimo has to check her titters: there's enough irony in this coincidence that she wants to look the Newspaperman in the eye, for once. She knows what she'll say to him, too.

—:•

It is Monica Younis who is with Mouna when she arrives in Agouza. By that time a whole host, living and dead, has accompanied her. Besides Fifi and Hudhud, there was Bara Hanim, Faiza's two teenagers, and three children she taught French to in 1961. There were two of her classmates at the Sacre-Coeur, three Ain Shams University acquaintances, Faiza, and five pious mamas from the Fatah Mosque.

Later Mansour Effendi will step past her, shooting her a sad look without saying anything. There will be Semsem, too, of course, and Aziz Maher. Medhat El Tetsh, Selim El Mawardy, Sameh Khairy. And the Fop, but curiously not the Newspaperman. Fouad Qansuh will remind her of someone, she doesn't know who. At first she won't have a clue who Fouad himself is or how she knows him. Till with a flush of warmth she recognizes his stutter. Then he will remind her of someone she no longer remembers.

On the final leg of the journey there will be Abla Arwa and Hagga Hafiza. The Bey and the Omda can be seen jogging in the opposite direction, but she's not sure. Later she will encounter the Afreet with Shahira Hafiz, then half a dozen Jumpers one after the other.

But it's Monica who walks with her the longest. Petite and beguiling in baggy clothes under her headscarf, she laughs her enchanting laugh and, giving in to her lisp as she grows impassioned, she speaks to Mouna of Andrew, which she had never done while she was alive. She speaks of the way Andrew fractures and fills and makes her whole.

Her blue eyes gleaming, Monica says that her grief for Khalo Raymond was bound up with the debilitating lacuna Andrew gouged out of her spine when he left. All the while, she adds, she was *loving Abla Fifi*. Letting Abla Fifi love her, to be more precise. Letting her tenderly squeeze the magic out of her hurting body, thoroughly. So that she mothered it better than Dimyana could even dream of doing. Better than any actual mother ever could—even Fifi herself to a daughter of hers.

—You know how good she is in bed, the girl says without shame.

A longing for you suddenly pierces Mouna's chest, Shimo. Then

Monica mentions Andrew again and, thinking sadly of Amin, she feels a little jealous on top of everything else.

—Did you have to die, though, ya habibti? Mouna asks almost as an afterthought.

—But I didn't plan it, ya abla.

Imagine being called *abla*, Mouna thinks again.

—The body knows, Abla Amna. It has memory and conscience. It's the only part of you that can look to God without lying. So on my Day of Resurrection, my body did what it was supposed to.

—Hein, Mouna says. D'accord.

—It's like the journey you're on now, Monica adds. I'm here to travel with you part of the way. But you didn't plan it, did you, Abla Amna. It is happening because your body knows your Day of Resurrection has come.

—:—

So I've seen nothing of Mouna's last four years in visions, I suppose because I lived much of what happened in them anyway, and in the summer of 2014 she told me some of what I didn't know. When I arrived at that moment with Monica on the roof of Mouna's former friends' building in Agouza, for example, I already knew it had its roots in December 2012, at the presidential palace protest.

Draconian presidential decrees for the benefit of the Ikhwan had prompted the biggest anti-Ikhwan protest since the revolution started at the president's place of residence, so the Ikhwan sent in their own counterprotest brigade to discipline and disperse those *Christians and atheists,* those *enemies of Allah.*

Mouna couldn't see it while she was at the presidential palace protest, but in a video already uploaded an appropriately heavy, fifties-style gentleman—*a man who fills his clothes,* as Bara Hanim would've said—is being mobbed and mauled. Stripped, scarified, called *filthy Nazarene, koftess, infidel, blue-bone son of an unclean dog.* His gut flapping while blood drenches his walrus mustache.

She can see the look in his eyes as they push him back every time he tries to break free. The wretchedness, the utter indignity of it. But the worst part is—she recognizes the site of the incident as the first-ever street in which she promenaded by herself while living with Mansour Effendi, back in 1956, a small madame in a young neighborhood with hair like Gina Lollobrigida's.

Mouna couldn't see that man in the flesh but she saw others lined up for interrogation. Their hands and feet were tied up with cord. They were fixed with electrodes connected to portable generators and, shrieking, slapped and spat on—right there on the sidewalk.

The men who did this were lightly bearded Islamists in cheap suits, provincial types she could never have suspected of sadism. Though they were instantly recognizable as Ikhwan. And for the first time Mouna realized that as much as she loathed them, she had never thought of jihadi breeders the way she had thought of State Security. Or suspected them of being their own crime syndicate. They looked thick and baladi, like geeks. But they were armed, and no one could sensibly deny they were an organized militia working outside state structures.

Mouna couldn't believe they were filming young men while they tortured them, checking for light, for sound, calling out to each other without compunction. *And yaani how are man-of-God lies better than military-man ones, hein!* Their paraphernalia of worship, she told me, was a cover for unalloyed mafioso work.

Even more than the army, so Mouna believes or wants to, these people are responsible for the worst mass crime in Egyptian history. An epidemic of self-defenestration of the female sex. She doesn't know quite how, but she's determined to prove it.

So, after she comes home from Heliopolis, Mouna starts muttering to herself. But if you heard her that first night you'd know it wasn't about these fellahin inquisitors. It wasn't about *our children* being murdered again, assaulted and arrested and given military trials. It wasn't even about the sharmootas' sons in uniform watching said children being tortured with undisguised schadenfreude. No. She's muttering about a woman who died while it was happening.

In the course of the protests there have been twelve Jumpers—four more than the protest's actual casualties—nine of them in quick succession while the Ikhwan brigade went to work.

All will die within the week. I find out about them independently. The usual, sudden-trance trajectory of stopping whatever they are doing and heading to the nearest skyward exit. Every time there is some kind of issue with a male close one, it's true. But the only really interesting fact I discover, I decide not to communicate to Mouna.

Unlike Shahira Hafiz, the woman she's been muttering about— and the example she'll be holding up to the world as incontestable proof of the Ikhwan's culpability in the tragedy of the Jumpers—at least eight out of twelve women who died that week hail from Ikhwan-loving families. By all accounts they were happily married to pro-Morsi Islamists and felt no distress about what happened outside the palace that night.

I knew then Mouna's arcane theory about the Ikhwan being responsible for women jumping was bogus. I don't know that I ever believed anyone in particular could be responsible. But I said nothing because, even if I told Mouna, she would still be focusing on the thirty-year-old math teacher who, though a devout Muslim and a revolutionary at heart, was an outspoken Ikhwan hater.

A down-to-earth, demonstrably stable woman. *A rearer of generations* well liked by her students. She was not the type to attend a sit-in, as she reportedly said herself, but she wholeheartedly supported the palace protest. While I find out about the other eleven Jumpers, Mouna goes all out to prove that, if not for the criminal people in power, Shahira Hafiz's children would not be orphaned.

Shahira must've jumped while Mouna was on her way home. She fell head first into an enclosed empty lot behind the seventh-story apartment where she gave private classes three times a week, not far from the palace.

Leaving her two small children with her mother-in-law, in the same building where she and her dental supplies trader husband lived, Shahira had been teaching there for three years. For months she'd been having a dispute with her eldest brother—a committed protester, as it happened—over the sale of their deceased parents' house. Evidently they'd had another phone shouting match the week before.

That night she was alone marking exercise sheets and sorting lesson plans—no evidence that she spoke to her brother at all. She phoned her husband a little after eight to say she would be back by nine. He said she sounded calm, even cheerful, hoping the little ones had gone to bed without giving their setto too much trouble and discussing dinner with him. But the forensic report said she jumped within ten minutes of that phone call. She died instantly of internal decapitation.

While she looks at him on the roof of the Socialist Union, Nimo is thinking of the day the Newspaperman walked up to her at the Press Center. It was autumn then, too: beautiful weather. An indolent afternoon listening to her coquette colleague Hudhud, in her meowing tones, tell stories about the Prophet's wives. Unsuspecting. If not for Ustaz Nafi walking over to pay him obeisance, she might even have doubted his physical existence.

Not that she didn't immediately recognize him as a Mukhabarat agent, someone who was here about the secret part of her job, the part she'd been performing against her will since September 1967. That too was coincidence.

It had been a different man then. The Fop, as she always thought of him. Though he had other qualities: archaic turns of phrase, excessive gentlemanliness, honest aversion to pain. And the djinn-like ability to show up wherever she happened to be no matter the time. For five weeks after Nasser reneged on his decision to step down, she would turn around to find the Fop catching her eye.

He had a very familiar face, though she seemed to remember a younger version of it. A Brylcreemed mop covered barely half his pate, and a perpetual if instantly erasable scowl seemed to reflect his disappointment with the fact.

—Amna Hanim Abu Zahra, the low voice finally startled her one time while she wasn't looking. If I am not mistaken.

It was a mild day, for August. No sweat in the shade. And she was at El Orman Gardens, opposite the Cairo University campus. She had just taken leave of a foreign journalist she was escorting, a beautiful but loud French Canadian—quel accent, she was thinking, quel bel accent!—and arranged to pick her up again in an hour.

She didn't like to leave her, but the woman, who had a botanical guidebook with her, insisted she wanted to explore the exotic flora by herself.

It seemed incredible that such a respectable-looking elderly gentleman should be accosting her here.

—And if I am Amna Abu Zahra, wennabi, who does that make you? Bas bas, she waved dismissively. Let me pass!

But he was already bowing to kiss her hand, truly bending over:

—Forgive the effrontery, ya hanim. It is just that a great admirer of yours has unexpectedly spotted you.

—Imagine that!

She tried to make her tone sarcastic. But she couldn't help being amused, maybe flattered that he was flattering her. She would never take the Fop's compliments seriously, but they always amused her.

—Will you do me the signal honor of accompanying me for a few valuable minutes? My chauffeur-operated vehicle is at your convenience. He pointed to a gleaming black Mercedes whirring readily by the gate. Should you say no, you would not only be destroying my life's dream, the Fop winked again, ceremoniously taking her hand. You might also miss an opportunity to serve your country.

She knew him then, a full five minutes before he said, *My name, should it be of interest, is Nabil Nabil.* She knew Nasser had come for her again. And, before she consciously remembered the two big men who accompanied the Fop when he showed up in Maadi on New Year's Eve, 1959, she saw the same pair flanking him on her terrasse. Where Amin stood by the bench and shrank.

She noted the coincidence, recalling Aziz Maher at Serag and Samira's. Though surely it was the norm for the same Mukhabarat officer to deal with a given husband and wife, even if they were at opposite ends of the cooperative-citizen spectrum, and even seven years apart. Till the last time she saw him, on a rainy day the following spring, the Fop will deny he's ever heard of Amin Abdalla. But that is probably protocol.

Knowing him was more reassuring than she wanted to admit. Knowing she was in the Mukhabarat's custody. State control is the deepest wellspring of fear. But since the war it hasn't felt very substantial somehow. After you've seen the godhead without his clothes on—realized he was atrophied where he should be virile—your fear has become procedural.

A complex look sculpted Nimo's face as she thought. Grief, hatred, bottomless letdown. She had forgotten all about the Québécoise. Through an aery of poinciana boughs, a flash of sunlight suddenly looked like a pair of compound eyes. Only then did it dawn on her that she was already ensconced next to the Fop on the back seat of the Mercedes, her hand still in his while the chauffeur ceremoniously closed the door.

With its little curtains drawn, the swanky bureau-on-wheels swerves past the university and drives straight out of Cairo. Her legs classily, gingerly crossed on the back seat, Nimo senses she is being spirited away, but the feeling is less foreboding than deliverance. She loses herself to the confident, uncompromising speed only a secret-service vehicle is capable of.

The brand-new Halim song on the radio is about the Naksa, as the regime was calling defeat: *setback*. To rhyme with the Palestinian Nakba? His scowl restored, the Fop is humming along theatrically. Dead serious but so insincere he is grotesque. And the sight of him makes her wonder what will be asked.

Once a month—so the Fop instructed—Nimo was to write down all that she remembered of her conversations with the foreign journalists she accompanied. With a ballpoint pen, on as many sheets of thin letter paper as she needed. She mustn't try to be selective, she mustn't add her interpretations or views. She was simply to put down everything she remembered, including names, dates, and hours.

She was to place her monthly report in a sealed postal envelope. Stamp and inscribe it with a made-up address anywhere in Greater Cairo. And keep it on her person all through the second and third days of the month. At some point during that time, he would appear, pick up the envelope, hand her another containing her compensation, and disappear again.

Under no circumstances was she to hand the envelope to anyone but himself no matter what she was told. Should he fail to appear in any given month, she was to burn it. Should something prevent her from completing the report, she was to hand him a magazine instead of an envelope to make that clear. Any current magazine. He could not be sure how the motherland might punish her if this happened or if any species of creature found out about her new duties, but he was pretty sure it wouldn't happen, would it, now.

—They say those who let us down go behind the sun, he laughed, and she couldn't tell if he was exonerating the Mukhabarat or threatening her. The motherland is kind as a real mother, Amna Hanim, the Fop went on as she examined the envelope, wondering how to hand it back to him. You yourself will be a mother someday soon. You must know the kindness I speak of.

Now he stayed her hand, taking the money out of the envelope and stuffing it into her half-open purse while patting her shoulder and nodding.

Seven five-guinea notes, three more than her monthly salary at the Information Service, glittering and so new you could cut yourself with them.

Nimo remembers how she spent a week debating whether to confide in Amin but, finding him withdrawn, decided not to. It was a mild week—just like this one, the one during which the Zaim died—except that it was filled with fear.

Even now, thinking of what she did with her first three Mukhabarat payments in the autumn of 1967, the fear she's beginning to shed brings back the weather. By November the night chill had grown uncomfortable, but the perfect weather of the first two times has carried over into her memory of what she would keep on doing till she gave birth to me.

The first exchange of envelopes had passed with incredible ease. It had surprised her how easily the Siham-Gadesque misinformation flowed out of her as she wrote her report. Never bothering to think twice about the accuracy of a time or the intention behind a statement. Foreign journalists became exactly as the Mukhabarat wanted them. Puffed up with *the arrogance of the occupier*, curious about military and economic *state secrets*, full of *tendentious questions and demoralizing observations*.

She massaged her conscience by telling herself it was harmless. The foreign passport holders she betrayed were safe. And so would she be as long as she kept up the routine of scribbling these parodies of patriotism. She would have extra money, besides.

The first thirty-five guineas, she handed to Faiza that same day. It was time to pay the two children's school fees, and she'd been wondering where they might obtain the money without asking Amin. She fantasized about next month's thirty-five. But once the new envelope was in her purse a decade's worth of anxiety bore down on her.

It wasn't so much guilt as grief, just like the grief she felt for Fouad Qansuh. Because once again she was being rewarded for a lie and she felt unclean, unsafe from harm. Everybody knows that, until you neutralize or get rid of it, haram money will summon all kinds of evil. She was terrorized by the thought of Amin disappearing or the house catching fire.

And so, that evening while clearing up, she wrapped the envelope in one of those rubbery Heliopolis Petrochemicals plastic bags—some of the earliest to appear in Cairo—and hid it in a face-down pot left to dry. Then, during the nightly lull while Amin was working in the basement, she headed out with the envelope in one hand and the garden shovel in the other.

She chose a spot behind the mango sapling where, nearly forty-five years later when the sapling had become a tree, she would stand holding a bloodied fennec fox and cry. She dug a hole in which to drop the plastic bag and filled it up. She didn't know how to feel about the thought of the hole growing a little deeper every month to make room for one more envelope filled with cursed cash.

As of summer 1970, when she returns to work, Nimo would be able to leave Nour with Faiza in her own house. Your khalto had lived with her since 1962, but on Amin's initiative moved out two years later—to the frontiers of Tora, the small town-turned-suburb known for its prison. Since leaving the Abu Zahra house in Shoubra, Faiza had enrolled her son and daughter in a Maadi school, and her new house was actually nearer the campus. It was comfortable and convenient. But, being Faiza, she would never forgive her brother-in-law for *dropping her in a killer-convict manhole.*

All through the sixties when he wasn't working in the basement, Amin spent time reading in the attic. He would stride up there wearing only his white undershorts, with two packs of cigarettes and a small cushion. And, switching on the bare bulb overhead, with a book in his hand he would lie back in what room there was.

Amna rarely joined him, though the first two times they had sex after his release it was there. He couldn't summon up the necessary spontaneity except in the least likely spot, after midnight. When she brought him a pot of coffee and he held on to her calves begging her to sit astride him. He licked her foot like a darwish maddened with love for his sheikh. Fully erect, he cried like a baby.

He said, *How can I make amends.*

He said, *Thank God for you.*

Over and over he said, *Without your breath I'm doomed.*

Then she held on to the back of his head while, knees bent, he expired in a series of amphibian thrusts.

It didn't make her love herself and it didn't make her happy as it used to. It wasn't even bracing, but it felt intimate and real. It was something instead of silence, instead of the marah's silence. However unconsciously, it was also the possibility of the motherhood she craved.

It was something instead of silence but, once that adorable monkey finally arrived—it would take five years—she no longer wanted it with Amin. Recovering from the physical ordeal had been slow and she thought that might be the reason. Because she still fretted about him finding her desirable. Yearned for their old intimacy. Or so she thought.

In reality, of course, another impulse was taking hold of her body. A profound indifference that bordered on repulsion whenever the theory threatened to turn into practice. She resented him. His risible rhetoric and criminal carelessness. But only when he wanted to have sex. And compared to her self-disgust in the months following Aziz Maher, this wasn't a torment or even unpleasant. Especially not after that afternoon at her colleague Fifi's house, when she was reassured she hadn't lost her capacity for sensuality after all.

As Amin's need for sex reasserted itself, her own stoniness took her by surprise. Where she had fretted and felt insecure, she now painlessly denied him what was looking more and more unequivocally like his pleasure, not hers. She felt it was her mind, her mood that should determine what happened between them.

In time she'd learn to take a wicked pleasure in the sight of *her everything*, the bulbul-bearer on whose glance her life depended, constantly importuning her, abasing himself for her approval.

Even when she succumbed to his entreaties—once or twice a year until he gave up the demeaning business of *having to proposition my own wife*—she inadvertently told herself she owed him nothing. It was happening because she let it. And when she chose not to let it, as she almost always did, it didn't happen.

Amin would howl occasionally, then feel foolish and forlorn. She took very badly to being shouted at. She'd stop speaking to him indefinitely. Then he felt like a child being denied his mother's embrace. And for his sake, not hers, he would appease her as fast and as furiously as he could.

By the time he stopped trying to kiss her—that was while she was pregnant with you, and for months, for years, she had pushed him away every time—Amin had truly given up. He turned an old couch into a daybed and set it up in the basement, every so often only asking her to change the sheets.

So began their estrangement, from her recalcitrance and his self-absorption. From 1985 until 2000—and then only very briefly, for the last time—Amna Wahib Abu Zahra and Amin Abdalla Amin were never to touch again in any way.

Fifteen whole years, Shimo. And even after three weeks in the attic I don't know how they managed to be together that long without intimacy, without a shared perspective or any interest in one. But it was as if this was what kept them together, this willingness to lose interest in the other person. If they'd had real expectations of each other it would've forced them apart.

Then again, they're from a time before couples therapy and relationship goals, a time when there was no moral obligation to be happy with your spouse. Once you decided you would stay and not leave, you didn't feel the need to evaluate or improve things.

Still, in the five years before she became a mother, when she still doted on Amin's every whim, her life hanging on a word, a glance from him, they often did touch when she went up to check on him. If he wasn't sprawled with his head on the cushion—years later she could still picture it, instantly—she would find him storing or picking out volumes.

That's why it was a shock that night in September 1965. She had left him there and gone to bed, expecting him to stay till the small hours. But on her way to the bathroom in the middle of the night she noticed the attic light was out and heard a steady, thudding drone.

When she opened the door Amin was kneeling with his back to her, his hands behind him, fingers intertwined as he swayed steadily, to and fro. He was clearly doing this deliberately, as some kind of exercise. To, fro. Though it was so mechanical it looked like it was being done to him. The way he gained speed, especially.

It was very gradual, she could barely tell at first, but once she trained her eyes on him there was no doubt he was seesawing faster and faster as time passed. It unnerved her because every time he brought his torso forward, before it came back again straight as a stave—a single fluid movement she felt she had seen before—his head hit the far wall. It made an ominous, rhythmic noise slowly building up tempo. He looked like the victim of a demonic possession in a horror film. The head of the blighted family being driven to a gruesome suicide.

She knew immediately, though it would never be confirmed, that this was how he'd vented his frustration while inside.

When she returns from the presidential palace protest in December 2012, Mouna stays up all night. By afternoon the next day she is back in Heliopolis. At Shahira's house, with a lawyer and a TV crew. You can see her on YouTube even now, holding Shahira's baby and snuffling as she faces the camera. Then, with childlike concentration, she begins her disquisition:

—As a mother, as a woman who loves her country, hein, I am doing everything I can to bring the Muslim Brotherhood to justice. Of course, our deranged rulers have committed any number of crimes, but it is condemning this infant to a motherless future that I imagine we should be drawing attention to now...

The screen caption identifies her as *Translator at the Information Service—retired* and *Senior political activist*. While one of those young, illiterate announcers who've cropped up all over the web since 2011 explains how she is leading a team of volunteers to sue the Ikhwan specifically for the death of twelve women. In those days there was such discontent you accepted whatever made the Ikhwan look bad, but even then this seemed preposterous. What could the Ikhwan possibly have to do with a set of unrelated suicides?

With her hanim's Frenchy tone and her intense earnestness—*aywa, et pourquoi pas?*—that hollow-cheeked old woman in a lace-trim galabiya looks like a satirical vision of the Liberal Opposition. A badly written bit part in some future docudrama.

Mouna was so fixated she sought out young, illiterate announcers when the celebrity TV hosts wouldn't have her. Though a couple of them did feature her voice over the phone. And till even the revolutionary feminists grew tired of it, whenever she could she spoke about the Ikhwan making women jump out of windows.

The Jumpers are a fascinating phenomenon. At any other time they would've generated a furor. But right now the political scene was enough of a distraction by itself. Mouna's way of presenting the issue— her certainty of the Ikhwan's culpability, the pseudo-religious language she used—didn't help anyone take it seriously.

For a few weeks she was famous on the web. There was even a meme of her, though the perception—good-natured enough—was that she was another of the revolution's eccentric elders, well meaning but dippy. Only later did people turn a little nasty in their references to the Suicide Madame, as she was briefly called.

And maybe the Shahira Hafiz episode would've passed if she hadn't had those "Who Killed Shahira" leaflets printed and lugged piles of them around the city, placing them at strategic locations. Alongside the slogan in red, they had a picture of the woman with her family and two blocks of text telling her story, linking her suicide irrationally to the palace protest and announcing that a court case had been filed against the president and the cabinet to avenge her, then calling on the reader to *resist those religion-trading usurpers and occupiers*. Mouna designed them herself.

Eventually she would fall foul not just of the Ikhwan but of State Security too. It took a week of daily phone conversations to placate an apoplectic Abid, who felt she was embarrassing him with his superiors, even ruining his future. *Not intentionally, no, of course not. But frankly in her frail old age she needs better supervision than you're providing.* I had to wait till we met to pump him for information on how she'd provoked the ire of the old guard.

It wasn't just the arcane logic by which she blamed the Islamists for those suicides, apparently, but the way she would talk of the Jumpers sacrificing themselves to repent of the country's wrongdoing. It made her sound dangerously derailed. Like someone, whether they were aware of it or not, subverting *foundational principles*. It wasn't just vaguely haram, what she said about society's lies and the purpose of the revolution. If people took it seriously, it could potentially dismantle the official religious establishment, let alone nonreligious state structures.

—And you know there is a Shia threat from Iran as well as an atheist threat from the West, ya Nour. Aywa, ah! Not to mention the terrorist threat endorsed by the Ikhwan themselves and the threat of structural collapse they pose.

It was the first inkling I got that Mouna was onto something, notwithstanding the factual feebleness of her arguments. But I wouldn't develop a clear picture of the Jumpers phenomenon until the end of 2012. For now I just watched as her fixation mushroomed and metastasized.

One day Mouna shows up unannounced at Tante Hudhud's. She steps into the apartment with a smile and, pleading with the eighteen women she finds there to give her a moment before carrying on with whatever it is they are doing, she immediately starts speaking.

The latest theology class Tante Hudhud has been hosting at her Mustafa Mahmoud apartment is so popular each lesson is being held twice over, and Mouna times her visit for the changing of the guard. She wants to catch not ten but twenty women, forgetting—or not caring, or maybe knowing and wanting to see anyway—that this is a cloister of Wahhabi prudes who won't want to hear about the redemptive power of suicide.

In her impious galabiya, hair showing scandalously under a secular bonnet, I don't know what she is thinking.

To make them sympathetic, she starts by condemning those who *slew the life which Allah hath forbidden*, presenting the suicides as remotely controlled murders without explaining how. But who might be the murderers? they are all clearly wondering. Mouna is about to answer their unasked question when suddenly the software in her head malfunctions. And, shaken, she remembers as if realizing it for the first time:

These are people who see the Ikhwan's rise to power as the ultimate vindication. Not only will they refuse to believe the Ikhwan are responsible for Shahira's death, they will also see that death as a sacrilegious attempt to reject God's blessings and disrupt His plan.

Standing by the door, she falters, abruptly requesting a financial donation toward the future of Shahira's children before trailing off. Some of the women will later ask Hudhud where they might hand in their contributions to *the orphans your friend the magnoona was collecting for*. But for now—oddly, as it will seem to her in retrospect—none of them shows any sign of obliging.

—God protect and bless you, everyone, Tante Hudhud calls, giving

Mouna a sidelong glance so severe it seems to come straight from the late sixties. First, by God's grace, I will bring the tea, then we can start the second class, inshallah.

As the women file past, Mouna steps aside and leans against the mantel, blissfully dissociated from her surroundings. Tante Hudhud is carrying a clover-scented tea tray to the other end of the hall, practicing her usual tiptoe in a wide arc around the furniture. While she follows her progress as if through binoculars, Mouna feels weirdly philosophical about her intime.

Hudhud's beloved husband survived Amin by only three years. A well-off civil engineer who also happened to be a very gracious husband. Actually he was another former communist. He never performed salah once as long as he lived.

But how did he respond to Hudhud's born-again transformation in the midseventies, Mouna wonders for the first time in her life. How did he manage to remain good to someone who became anathema to his worldview? And did Hudhud deceive herself to justify her love, her financial dependence on an infidel?

Then she remembers: Two pious mamas are attending a women's religious lesson in 1996, cozied up, hips touching, in their own corner. The preacher's amplified voice is shrill as she shrives herself of her bareheaded past. One pious mama, small-boned and catlike, begins to sob. The other, petite and heart-faced, puts her arm around her.

But while she pats Hudhud's shoulder and nods to the strange rhythm in the mic, Mouna is thinking that women have started wearing makeup with their hijab, dressing titillatingly with immoderate amounts of makeup, and that for all her melodramatic hysteria this preacher doesn't have a problem with that.

All that matters is that the rule be followed to the letter—not how, not to what end.

For a moment—a passing moment, so terrifying it will be forgotten until that day in 2012 when she sees three people in a hospital corridor and the sight clinches something in her mind—Mouna wonders who these women think they're fooling. Don't women look less like clowns and also more God-fearing when they dress modestly without a sartorial indicator of sect?

Now too the thought of Hudhud deceiving the All-Knowing One comes into Mouna's head. But instead of terrifying her it makes her laugh. Real laughter from the heart bubbles out of her as she stands by the door, prompting even more severe sidelong glances. If they have any doubt it is a deranged woman who's come to talk to them, she thinks, cracking up even more, not even bothering to hide it, those doubts are gone alhamdulillah! Totally tara-la-li.

In 2010 Hudhud's youngest daughter left home, Mouna's thinking. All four older children already had their faraway families, and with her husband gone since 2003 she was by herself as she had never been.

Hudhud was physically fit, her body and her face alert. But for nearly a year, though there was no medical evidence for it whatever, she was convinced that she suffered from a terminal illness. It took a series of Wahhabi-flavored lectures by her friends and a hurtful argument with her firstborn to convince her the fatigue, the nausea, the abdominal pain were psychosomatic. Then she started to get better—with one difference.

Once *as cold as a British surgeon*, she had grown ridiculously effusive. It seemed to happen overnight, and it turned her into a caricature of herself, with undue, tearful outbursts punctuating a nonstop, grating squawk.

Still, her present, silent response seems to come from the pre-Wahhabi self Mouna both liked and feared so much more. Right now Mouna is in the throes of her own psychic glitch, but it strikes her how much more powerful Tante Hudhud's silent treatment was than the kind of theatrics to which, once or twice while discussing halal and haram with her, she has more recently been subject.

As the women file past, giving her quizzical looks through the eye slits in their niqabs, Mouna feels more and more dismayed and uncertain.

I used to have this image of a young working mother, quiet and conscientious, who goes about the office cloaked in secret woes. Unwilling to unburden herself.

And in the year leading up to Nasser's death she really might've given this impression on some days, but I know now nothing could be further from the reality of Nimo at a typical Cairo workplace, especially one with my two tantes in it. She might've been evasive about certain things, but the attic showed me she went about the office with the pep and circumspection of a native daughter, the newest of three new wives in the hoary homestead. More eager than anyone to unfurl and engage.

She was to polish and perfect the skills she began to develop here with Hudhud and Fifi. Opening up and being opened up to with a view to helping and being helped, pooling know-how and know-who by honestly exposing yourself, being truly vulnerable—but only within the mundane realm, the realm of money and motion. The psyche and the spirit would be there in the form of plaints and pantomime, the tone often devotional, but nothing remotely sublime was allowed to touch any instance of bonding.

Now I see her click-clacking down a long, wide corridor to her flower-filled desk, an enormous tiered cake with twenty-nine candles balanced on her palm.

I see her cozying up to a colleague while they huddle over a sheet of French verb tables, her warm tones bell-like, voicing the impossible vowels.

I see her absorbed in a five-way conversation about *Nadia*, the daily radio series with Soad Hosni and Ahmed Mazhar, about the advantages of taking the river bus to the other end of town and the best liqueur replacement in crêpes suzette, taking down a seamstress's address while defending the heroine . . .

Within three years—ready to be great wife in her own homestead now—she will have taught the piece of raw meat that comes out of her in 1969 to call her Mouna. Not Mama. Not Maman or Mummy—Maami, as middle-class and military mothers mimicking the former aristocracy affect to be called. But Mouna. And, hearing him call her as she taught, she will repossess some part of herself. However different this new Mouna is from the one she had missed being when she became the Nourmother, the progenitor, it is the same person and that person survives.

Mouna could've extended her three-month maternity leave. But by now she was choking on idleness. Her terror of losing the life that was germinating in her again had kept her housebound for much of her pregnancy. At one point she was on unpaid leave for two months in a row. It was while sorting out the paperwork at the end of that break that she first met two non-French-speaking intimes—Hedayet and Vivian, as Tante Hudhud and Tante Fifi are really called—who had been appointed within three weeks of each other in her absence.

With few foreign journalists to show around while she felt closely watched by the Mukhabarat—alhamdulillah, the Fop proved respectful of her motherly duties, but that didn't stop her from feeling watched—work had been stultifying for at least a year through her ninth month.

By the time Nour entered his fourth month outside of her body she'd grown nervous about her isolation, too. Office politics–wise it was wrong not to be seen at the Press Center for so long. *Who knows what they're concocting in my absence!* Then Amin would laugh, bleating, *My canny little capitalist.* But Mouna didn't mind.

She was happy. With Nour in her arms, she felt she had generated her own magic cloud. And, knowing she could safely leave him with Faiza while not having to live with her sister—to endure her nosiness and jealousy, her bouts of anger, her entitlement—she felt normal. She was happier than she'd ever been since her first four months of marriage. And she felt saner than ever in her life.

Thanks to a compulsive consort reading up on psychiatry, Mouna had had plenty of opportunity to think about sanity and happiness, especially the connection between the two. Mental health was the only topic Amin had talked about with any oomph since he came out. As he emerged from the mango-tree reverie, the digging and the watering, his affliction made him curious.

So he read and, his encyclopedic energy unabated, periodically explained to her the difference between neurosis and psychosis, genetic and environmental factors, what women were more prone to than men. He taught her about postpartum depression. He gave her a firm enough grasp of it that, when she had her first child, she was sure she didn't have it.

There would be a period of nearly ten years when, as the head of the legal department of the Bank of Matruh, Amin guzzled prescription drugs like popcorn: MAOIs, tricyclic antidepressants, major tranquilizers. When he was home he would either sleep like the dead or soak in coffee and tobacco smoke for as long as it took at his Olympia.

Looking like a zombified mad genius with wispy hair and toothless stubble, he spoke little or not at all.

Until he grew sick of the pharmaceutical fog. One day in 1989, he cleared his cabinet of drugs and went cold turkey. For weeks he was ill in bed, jabbering incomprehensibly half-asleep and breaking out in epileptic cold sweats.

At the end of that year he went through a spectacular breakdown—the Eighty-Nine Thing, the family would call it—but he weathered it so fast that, when he joined the Umayya Group only months later, it started to look like a pretext to leave the government appointment he'd had since 1971 for a far more lucrative private-sector job. In reality he despised the regime cronies he worked with so much that only medication had enabled him to endure their company. Their corruption and pomposity, the ideological about-face he had seen many of them do, their absolute lack of integrity. At least the private-sector people had never been pro–centralized economy.

Mouna and Amin had no intimate relations for nearly five years and she suspected he was having affairs. He probably wasn't—I can't imagine he had the time or wherewithal—but more than one attic vision hints at her suspecting it. And forcing herself not to care. Whether or not this had anything to do with their rupture, by decade's end it had deepened so much it defined their togetherness. Mouna was too far along on her journey to pious mamahood, and his new money notwithstanding Baba had very little left that might entice her back to him.

Never mind that moving to the Umayya Group meant bowing to Wahhabi capital, Shimo—objectively, it seemed to her he had come out on top. He'd retrieved his gregarious, jittery self and bought her a BMW. If he suffered unbearably from then on, it didn't show.

—:•

That meltdown at Tante Hudhud's will be the end of the Shahira Hafiz saga. It's one of the first in a chain of cognitive breaks Mouna will experience through 2013. And she is unconsciously hoping Hudhud, who by now is skidding right by her, will show some sign of support. Hudhud doesn't even look at her.

While absently picking up her leaflets, saying she'd better leave before the second lesson starts, Mouna still expects her last remaining intime to object. To motion to a seat in her supple, dainty way and, purring, swear she will not let her go before she has something to eat or drink. At least ask her to attend the lesson. She doesn't look at her.

That night when Mouna calls her—ostensibly to apologize, but really to say how hurt she is—the woman who answers the phone is neither the squawking Islamic impresario with *what's in her heart always on her tongue* nor silent-treatment Hudhud of old. She is someone else whose long, lordly silence Mouna doesn't recognize at first. And when Hudhud breaks it, it's like pellets hitting a pane, a trickle of tinkling monosyllables. They sting as they land—the withheld intimacy, the indifference—but there is something nostalgic about the whole sour soundscape.

—And yaani I just thought I'd apologize, she is saying. Not that she would've known but those are the exact same words she used over the rotary dial telephone in July 1974. I am so ashamed, hein, I am *in half my clothes* before you.

This is a version of Hudhud she's encountered only once, but it is a vital version of Hudhud. In her vulnerability and friendlessness Mouna's yearning for reunion is such that even being snubbed this way makes her pine. Streams of lukewarm liquid running down her face barely register as she remembers.

It had been a mildish week. With their children home from school for the summer and Ustaz Nafi finally, suddenly replaced by a stern new Sadat worshipper, for a long time the three intimes had been too overwhelmed to go out together.

On the one day they could all be free, a Monday, Fifi contrived to take Mouna to the Round Building cafeteria on the tenth floor to explain: those three–four hours, being precious, are better spent inside a certain Tudor-style sanctuary, with just the two of them under the Mother and Child's baraka-ful gaze. Fifi's son would be with his paternal aunt till evening, and couldn't Mouna arrange for hers to be with Faiza during that time? All they had to do was separately tell Hudhud that something had come up and neither could make it.

—Maalesh yaani, Tante Fifi giggled into the crook of Mouna's neck, whispering suggestively while, arm in arm, they entered the elevator. It's been nearly two months since we had an hour to ourselves, aha. I'm hungry, ya habibti! And immediately something softened in the Nourmother's resolve to avoid what, even though it had been happening regularly and sometimes frequently for three years, she could never deliberately so much as mention to herself.

But on that day some other colleague spotted the two of them sauntering arm in arm along the Garden City Corniche from a taxi window. And two days later when they gathered for lunch, she happened to mention it in Hudhud's presence.

—Was it Monday? Yes, it was definitely Monday. Early afternoon. I tried to call out to you but you were too far away.

Reddening, Mouna looked down while, spluttering crumbs, the dog started yelping in an adrenalized attempt to appease the cat. It was no good.

For close on six months Hudhud would stop talking to her two intimes, responding to their approaches with perfunctory grunts. Their three-way friendship wouldn't resume till her older sister died and they went to pay their condolences. She needed moral support then, badly, and nobody could provide it as sincerely as Mouna and Fifi.

It was two months before this that, phoning her to apologize, Mouna first experienced the stony, monosyllabic being that would manifest on her mobile phone again now. But there was likely to be no further death in Hudhud's life through which Mouna could redeem herself.

Mouna had never entirely forgiven her intime for being so ready to break up with her back in 1974, so she felt even more betrayed and unrepentant than she had back then. That's why her tears of nostalgia eventually segued into sorrowful sobs. She knew she had lost her friend forever.

After she comes home from wherever she's been Mouna stays up all night. It happens again and again now. Until, within two weeks of her last phone call with Tante Hudhud, she stops going out altogether.

There is a grace period when she's up anyway, sleeping only a few hours during the day. Then, aside from a bout of slower, sadder busyness between the protests of June 30 and the televised statement with which Sisi will oust and arrest Morsi on July 3, she begins to spend her evenings on the veranda. She sits still thinking of mental illness, of all the different meanings of mental illness. The time, for example, when following the birth of her second son, she did experience postpartum depression:

Nineteen seventy-seven, and she's sitting up in her four-poster bed, muffled sunlight coming through the curtains while a fan hums. She is enervated, insensate with sleeplessness. Too weighed down to pick up a diaperless toddler crawling spastically around her.

It's not as if Amin would even consider helping with a small child, but it scares her that neither he nor her six-year-old is home.

She dreams of phoning Faiza, begging her to come over. But that would require getting up and the toddler is pissing everywhere, turning the bed into a warm, noisome puddle, immobilizing her. When she summons up the energy to lift him, his tiny fingers claw at her face till, screeching louder than she could ever cry out, he draws blood.

She puts him down more violently than she thought she could, so as to nurse her cheekbone, where blood is pouring out just below the eye. He wiggles onto his back and glowers at her. For a moment, while she looks at him, he is still. The child is physically perfect, his face prettier than any she has seen. Yet she's working hard not to see how ugly he looks to her.

The homicidal hatred she feels for what came out of her belly lacerates her with remorse. But she cannot shake off the sense that, unlike her firstborn, this toddler is less of a gift than an examination from Allah. An endowment from Iblis—embodied sickness.

For there had been no comedown from being delivered of Nour. When she heard Nour cry, only a lyric melancholy overtook her.

As a baby she felt his puling presaged a hard life. It made her terribly melancholy, that's all. But with this second child she cannot shake off the certainty that she's manufactured a ghoul.

That evening in 1977, when he begins to defecate, she averts her eyes as, moist and pungent, feces creeps onto her thighs. And, shaking, breathless, she moans. The tears seem to break out of the skin on her face as she finally leaps out of bed and raises her nightie, legs apart.

A little khara has already coagulated on her thigh, the rest dripping onto the floor in thick clumps.

So our mother broods before the mango tree, the seed of the Jumpers sprouting in the soil of her being. Sometimes she talks to me. By December 2014, she is sleeping fifteen hours a day to escape *the mind-movies* into which her cognitive breaks have turned.

No Afreet will haunt Mouna again, but after a few months—the Ikhwan, the dead bodies, another officer becoming zaim—insomnia will begin to consume her for real, making her *weak and éthéré*. Beyond a doubt, she will know then what she is destined for. And, with un-believable fatalism, by January—this January, can you believe it, less than four months ago!—she will have embraced her Cataclysm.

A year after Morsi's ouster all that remains of the six months sepa-rating it from the palace protest is a haze of chaos and conspiracy. I suppose I was running around investigating Jumpers. I remember little beyond Mouna whimpering the afternoon that Shia sheikh was dragged through the streets.

Through 2013 I'm always on top of the news. I check Twitter every two minutes. But for some reason I haven't heard about this particu-lar incident. All I know is, two weeks before, this thing they called the Syria Solidarity Conference happened. A pop concert at a football court—it was the small indoor hall of the Cairo Stadium, but still—except it was Morsi who performed. With guest appearances by all the star Wahhabis, including freshly released jihadis of the nineties.

While he strutted around the court, his bodyguards around him, with the two flags of the Egyptian republic and the Syrian revolution one in each hand, hordes of fans cheered the third-rate sheikh as though he was Amr Diab.

The theme: how heretical Shias are massacring true Muslims in Syria.

That's all I know when I walk in to find Mouna at the dining table, squinting at her iPad through Baba's glasses, an ashtray brimming by her elbow. Except for the Tiffany-style lamp it is dark. Colored by the rainbow glow, plumes of smoke like dancing gas sculptures rise from an unseen point by her thigh.

She's looking trim as usual. But for the first time since February 2011, I can see that look on her face again. Grief, hatred. Bottomless letdown. For a moment it's as if I've walked in on a bad dream.

—Nour, she sighs when she notices me. There is food in the kitchen, ya habibi.

—I've eaten, my lovely. How are you?

—Comme ci comme ça, you understand. She gives a wan smile, her eyes shimmering like filled cups. Like always, son of Amin.

—You look frazzled.

—Hein, she turns away. Then her snub nose swells as the tears bubble up, rippling and breaking the menisci. I was just thinking about that sheikh.

—What sheikh?

—You haven't heard?

And, sobbing, Mouna explains to me how a self-appointed contingent of Morsi fans went to the village where the leader of Egypt's tiny Shia community lived and raided the house where he was gathered with a group of followers for some religious feast. How there ensued a kind of blockade of the house till the sheikh handed himself over. And how, by the time they left the village, his was the first of four bloodied, stepped-on corpses left by the side of the road.

—⋮•

Back in the attic, Mouna's legs are classily, gingerly crossed next to Fifi in the back of a taxi. At this point she no longer thinks of herself as Nimo. Having reclaimed it as a mother, she has had time to inhabit the name Amin gave her so long ago.

The taxi is headed to the Garden City apartment where Fifi has lived since she was unexpectedly widowed in 1965, having lovingly kept her mother's overdone decor. As Mouna's fat lips curl around a menthol cigarette Fifi is lighting for her, she becomes aware of the palm of Fifi's free hand on her thigh, clasping her with what feels like hunger. Puzzling but not unpleasant.

At one point Mouna realizes she is sitting on the hem of Fifi's chiffon shawl and starts to move. But, replacing her hand on Mouna's thigh and edging even closer, her intime unaccountably pecks her chin:

—Maalesh, ya habibti. Please stay where you are.

—But, ya Vivian—

—I like being close to you. And I told you a thousand times, ya habibti. By the life of your beautiful little Nour, aha—isn't that the name you've given him? May Our Lord's baraka fill his life with light— call me Fifi.

Mouna must be expecting a giant kennel when she arrives. For the widow's brassy farrago of comforts leaves her staring with that old childlike look on her face. The statuette of Isis nursing Horus, especially. Thick downy rugs on top of marble floors, plaid and filigree wallpaper, Formica-topped tables and puffed-up vinyl. Hardly enough room for a single foot.

It makes her own home feel austere as she reclines with another menthol cigarette and a glass of contraband Campari. The high, cream-painted ceilings of our Maadi house then, its bare hardwood and terrazzo floors. The spare beechwood furniture from Domyat and even sparer damask upholstery. The plain walls showing only the occasional nude or palm grove by Selim El Mawardi.

Even the little bedroom altar Fifi has set up around a Byzantine Mother and Child does not reduce the gaudiness. The bedroom is over-powered by an elephantine Tudor-style bed and, while Fifi tells her of the icon's baraka, Mouna realizes they are in the invisible canopy of it. They've been smoking and talking, an ashtray between them, feeling less and less answerable to the rest of humanity.

Mouna realizes with delight that she's wearing only a satin negligee that she doesn't recognize as hers, but even if she arrived in it how come she's wearing it without panties underneath like this? Djinn, she thinks to herself, without fear or loathing. This must be the work of djinn. Then, seeing her orange leg against her host's almond buttock, she notes with incredulity how naked the widow is, how breathtakingly different she's become now she's naked.

Never mind Fifi's powers of persuasion and her appetite for body fluids—infinitely greater than Aziz Maher's or Amin's—without which Mouna couldn't have experienced these internal fireworks. Never mind her smoky-smooth skin, breasts conflated, their nipples seeking each other out blindly like moles in heat. Never mind the potent lightness of her touch. Considering the seeming bulk of her, Fifi is remarkably agile.

First she lies with one arm around Mouna pecking her face, nudging her crooks and her clefts. So far, so fleet. But then she wriggles serpentine, her tongue tracing its own plaid and filigree to a locus of scarred tissue that has so far only known a fraction of the pleasure it commands. It lingers, Fifi's tongue. With what seems to Mouna like eternal energy, so unflagging it beats God, propriety, and penis-love in the battle for her psyche.

It endures till the earthquakes hit her body. And she finds herself traveling back to a rule-proof cinematic cloud she barely remembers living in with Amin. Herself in a way she never thought possible again.

Tears—gratitude, mainly—fold into sighs, moans, and occasional screams prompted by the convulsions. Though she remembers nothing, understands nothing while they bring her to herself like roaring reunions, rendering everything outside that canopy theoretical.

Now when Fifi settles back into position—firm, doughy curves and a faint scent of deer musk—her exhausted charge is as naked as she, and as unashamedly, beaming the word *djinn* over her shoulder. Orange and almond.

Mouna is in Fifi's bed while Amin's fortunes turn for real. When she returns home later than expected that day, for the first time in his life, it seems, Amin takes a strict-husband, patriarchal tone with her, *You can no longer behave in this way, ya hanim*, his admonition so convincing it takes her a while to understand he is jokingly conveying the good news:

—You are now the wife of a big government employee!

Only this morning, he explains, he was officially appointed head lawyer at the Bank of Matruh, where he's been working more or less full-time since late 1969.

His backer there, a man-for-all-seasons named Kamal Azer, had wanted him to head the bank's legal department for some time. One of three deputy bank presidents, he had managed to subcontract Amin at a cut-rate price—in return for all kinds of favors the well-connected communist used to do him back in the fifties, after they went to law school together—only to realize old Aminov's knowledge of the law and proficiency at affidavit-speak could make him look infinitely more efficient and economical.

—If only a former political prisoner of Nasser's could head a state-owned financial institution's legal department, he said.

Now he could—even though Amin's crime is communism, which like nationalism and anti-Americanism and all kinds of dignity-based concoctions of the left is now bundled with the brand-new scourge of Nasserism. But he has kept a low profile. He's been so cynical about his former comrades, in fact—he's hated Nasser with such alacrity—that the new, Sadat-appointed overlords would not have trouble approving of him.

—So from now on you'd better come home on time, he shouts down Mouna's *C'est vrai* and *Alf baraka*, cracking up as he heads back to the basement while she goes on gabbling and trembling, too overwhelmed by what happened to her at Fifi's to put together a whole sentence, or ululate.

—:•

Since the night I saw that sparrow-like, dark girl in black at Cilantro's, I haven't stopped coming up here, Shimo. Because I realized that, lying back in what space there is, I could have first-person experience of Mouna's life. I would never again touch myself in her presence—the rite quickly became holy. The Summoning of the Progenitor. But to perform it there is no need for incense or chants.

Arranged around my body at the cardinal points, instead, are her gold watch and her wedding ring, the lithograph Aziz Maher made of her and the black-and-white photo in which, hands on hips in a polka-dot dress, she sticks out her tongue. Behind her—through the balcony of the Agouza building where, on the fourth anniversary of Mubarak's stepping down, she would find her way back—the Nile flows, no concrete on its banks. Four talismans: the consecrated paraphernalia of a genuine shrine. Because I could feel the sanctity of this womblike space long before I found out it is in fact where I was planted in her belly.

It is a cold winter this year, colder and colder where my skin touches the bare floor of the attic. And it feels as though, lying here, I'm making up for the rainless swelter that is Cairo's baseline.

Every spring the khamsin dust storms blow in from the west. Every autumn coloring-book cumuli break their promise of giving us rain. Some days, it looks like it's snowing gold leaf. Or you are wading in sumptuous sludge, tires skidding, everything spattered with wet sand. But otherwise from March to December it is the same long season. Now it's as if lying here, shivering in the chilly respite, I am somehow validating all the heat and dust that Mouna lived through.

As I draw close to the end of her story—the point at which you know as much as I do anyway—I'm convinced of my own irrelevance. A man smuggling one woman's life into another's, in words. Without really being part of either. Once the procedure is over, I am no more.

That's why I called it the Cataclysm. Because, with Mouna's last act, the world that started at the Aquarium Grotto a decade before I was born ended definitively on a Nile-view rooftop in Agouza. And what I've come to realize in the process of writing you is that there is no other world for me. Outside of it I'm going to have to build myself from scratch, never mind that I'm nearing the end of my forties.

Remaining no one is a journalist's prerogative. Even with the love of my life, that is all I managed to be in the end: reporter, transporter, bearer of tidings. Aya once told me as much. *You're nothing but an echo*, she said. Except that, lying where Baba's law books are still piled like the documents in a nightmare archive, I feel more like a divine messenger than an errand boy. Somehow I've become the echo of something bigger.

All day today, every time I've thought of Mouna I've remembered her lying in her bed, unresponsive, staring at the ceiling. It happened once or twice in 2013, but those sessions didn't start for real until 2014.

Most days in the long summer of that year, from March to December while the mind-movies afflicted her, she spent her nights on the veranda looking at the mango tree. Occasionally she would have a loquacious spell. Then her confessions would be very thorough as she told me of Monica and Fifi. Of how she went through a moral rebirth thanks not to the revolution but the Jumpers. But never of what she saw in the silent sessions that—and no one knew this better than she did—were the kickoff curve in a terminal trajectory.

—:•

One more image comes to Mouna while she eyes the giant egg, on the roof of the Socialist Union the day Nasser dies:

An indolent afternoon at the Press Center. Hudhud's small voice is describing the Prophet's youngest and prettiest wife, Ayesha, going into jealous rages about his first love, Khadija, who was old enough to be her grandmother and had been dead for years—when the Newspaperman appears in front of her.

A freakishly hairless figure, with an ovoid pate so bare it looked buffed. His unblinking eyes like miniature sunglasses. His lashes and brows look fake, that's how hairless he is. And they never ever blink, those miniature sunglasses.

They ogled her breasts, looking at the spot between them where they had planted that fear. But instead of lechery in their gaze there was a void, a vacuum, a clinical indifference that disturbed her far more than being ogled. Immediately he flashed a Press Syndicate card at her, blathering about *State Information backup at the Indian Embassy*. The words, the sentences were supplicatory, but the tone was that of cold command.

Mouna didn't notice until she was at home that he hadn't given her a name. Even the calling card he handed her with the words *Outside main gate ten thirty-five* scribbled on the back was blank.

That's how he became the Newspaperman.

She remembers her crossed legs shaking. No part of her had ever shaken while one leg was gingerly, classily crossed over the other.

It was a sunless morning, not cold. The rainless gloom turned Cairo's ever-present dust from gold to silver. It made her think of the moon. A chalk-white half-moon gleaming dully in the window. She couldn't understand what or why, but she seemed to be seeing it while the lifeless body of some sad giant lay next to her.

Eerily accommodating, Ustaz Nafi had given her leave as soon as she clocked in. Mouna was relieved that the two colleagues who held the promise of being intimes kept their noses out of her assignment. In time she'll find out they had their own Mukhabarat binds.

An Egyptian-made jalopy blared toward her, blowing chalk. Within a wheel's turn of her—that's when she understood this was her ride—

the back door swung open and fell all the way out, not quite unhinged but very nearly hitting her. It flapped with feeble menace, like the wing of some ornery ornithopod run aground.

But it wasn't clear whether the Fiat ever really stopped. For all she knew Mouna jumped it while it careered past the Round Building. The door was definitely flapping for a time before she leaned over to pull it shut.

An arm like a crooked cane had beckoned her in through the frame. There were three muscular young men in the car. She could tell they were blue-collar by the deferential tone in which they addressed her, a white-collar madame they'd obviously been told to treat well. But the handless arm wasn't the only thing that felt coarse and criminal about them.

As the car barreled ahead—hitting first a fruit stall, then a motorcycle—the three men laughed and coughed. They spat and swore like baltagis carrying out a kidnapping. *Lumpenproletariat*, as Amin would say. No sense or pretense of being on the side of the law or the common good whatever, Mouna noted. And, with rather more terror than relief, she thought for the first time that the veneer of respectability the Mukhabarat had maintained since it emerged as the country's highest priesthood was peeling. What would the secret police look like in thirty or forty years?

That's why she avoided asking what the plan was in detail. Already Cairo had transformed and she felt these people were part of the new city where there were no wide shady trottoirs. And where male attention came from unknown men who might be frotteurs if not rapists or killers, horny hyenas snorting and slobbering all over her.

She assumed she was being conveyed to wherever the Newspaperman lay. The car was heading out of town, just like that other car in which the Fop escorted her. This reassured her. Even as she wondered with vague concern what might've happened to the Fop.

It was she who opened the door when they screeched to an unequivocal stop by some remote canal in the middle of nowhere. Then the man next to her leaned over and smirked as the car blew another cloud, speeding away:

—This is where you wait, ya madame. Be careful of the dust.

It was nearly half an hour before the Newspaperman's James Bondish vehicle picked her up. Like every high official's of the time, it was a German-made black sedan with curtained windows. But there was something chilling about the streamlined swagger with which it swerved into position in the dust, the seemingly self-activated smoothness of its door opening then closing behind her, and the magic of air-freshened air-conditioning. She had never even heard of a car with air-conditioning.

This, she later reasoned, must've been intentional. Making her wait alone on the frontiers of Greater Cairo, where she couldn't sit or have a drink of water, then scooping her up in this thing. For as she sat with her crossed legs shaking, the egg of the Newspaperman's head looking marbly-smooth above the headrest in front of her, she felt that scaring her was part of his intention.

For the longest time while they circled the Giza Plateau, never once glimpsing the Pyramids, nothing could be heard but the whir of the AC—until the Newspaperman spoke, telling her he would be replacing Nabil Nabil. That would be the way he spoke to her, always. Not so much averting his eyes as implying the sight of her was irrelevant. Yet she always felt that, even as he had his back to her, he could see her face.

—You will now be serving your country through me. You understand that entails certain changes in procedure.

—But I don't even have a name to call you by, she blurted, inadvertently revealing her dread, then quickly added, ya—basha?

She had addressed the Fop using the familiar *you*, adding *ustaz* only when she called him by his name. But she didn't feel she could do this with the egg-headed djinni now in charge of her life.

—Besides, she went on hurriedly, I was wondering. The Fo—I mean Ustaz Nabil, something happened to him? Or is it just that . . .

The car had sped up, deliberately it seemed to her. And, flummoxed, she trailed off.

—The man you call the Fop, he said in the same even tone after a spun-out silence. That is who you mean. He is no longer of any concern to you.

His silence physically stung. She had to consciously check her urge to break it by talking again, but already she knew better. He was skillful.

After he said, *Speak if you want*, when she began to explain that she wouldn't have enough information for two monthly reports instead of one, that there was no way she could make them more factually detailed, he interrupted her. Before she had time to request a way to hand them in other than being picked up by that felonious Fiat. Before she could consider admitting that she'd rather not have to spy on foreign journalists in the first place.

—It's important to understand what it means to be an honorable citizen, he stated. The first time in her life she heard the term. An honorable citizen serves the homeland. He wants to serve the homeland. A person who asks how or who, a person who says I can only do so much, is not an honorable citizen. Far be it from you to be unworthy of the homeland.

This clipped, one-sided hectoring reminded her of Semsem. Who, apart from that comment about attending her eldest uncle's funeral to make sure they deposited him firmly underground, hadn't really made her laugh for years. She'd been seeing less and less of Semsem since that evening at Groppi's when—chain-smoking and slugging Stella—the funny woman had affectedly grieved for the nation.

Speaking pure Socialist Union, she didn't respond when Mouna asked after her marital plans, knowing her fiancé's family wouldn't hear of him marrying an older woman of dubious lineage even if she had more money and better connections than any of them.

When Mouna muttered *But it's such a relief having Amin back, ya Semsem*, she looked away at the mention of Amin. She laughed mirthlessly at the complaint that the Mukhabarat seemed to be taking over the Press Center. Yet she glared somber-faced when, having mimed stabbing herself, she found Mouna giggling at her.

—The enemy's victory, temporary as it must be—so she had declaimed, lurching—it feels like a saber thrust deep into my flank. Plus, I believe the Zaim can put out the fire in my heart by declaring war.

Mouna quickly stopped laughing. Something frightened her in Semsem's drunken face. Together with the fanaticism and the falseness there was a kind of blood thirst, a will to murder she remembered from a scene in Semsem's early life. That is partly why she hadn't gone out of her way to see her in the last three years.

But there was something about the Newspaperman's clipped hectoring that went past even that. She tried to work out what exactly while the car completed its course, disgorging her at an equally forsaken location but within walking distance of the Giza train station.

The thing that went past terror was the sense that this osseous voice, this humanless language was the way the homeland spoke. As she realized this, the little that remained in her of the dignity-deifying patriot gave her unbearable agony.

—But I can't keep dredging up reports, she will explode the fifth time she sees the Newspaperman. There is nothing to say, bon? Besides, I don't understand how any of this is helping the country!

And without turning to her, let alone batting an eyelid, the Newspaperman will reply in even tones:

—You only have to say you refuse to cooperate one more time before you're relieved of all patriotic duties. Then the homeland will have absolutely no more use for you.

After Nasser's funeral Mouna goes home to her firstborn touched by a life-love she will not feel again until 2011. When, back from Tahrir Square, she meets him across a puddle, waving a little flag. It's true this first time the peacefulness in her face will do the opposite of what it does in her old age: it'll keep her out of her country's destiny. But the radiance presaging busy-bee behavior is exactly the same.

It's also true that she never thinks what she's feeling could have anything to do with Egyptian history. By 1970 she's seen too many ideologues blaming their marital breakups or the death of their mothers on the Naksa, all kinds of people unconvincingly playacting the nation's misfortune in their lives. It doesn't even occur to her that Nasser's death can make a difference in hers.

The relief, the euphoria of a harmless revenge exacted. Childlike justice done. That's all she's been aware of since, back on the roof of the Socialist Union, she figured out a way to reach the Newspaperman. A convoluted curlicue of tiny steps and torso twists through twenty meters from the center of the roof toward the Tahrir side, ahead of her to the left.

The night of Nasser's death, Mouna will slip out into the garden for the last time. It's actually much chillier than when she first did this back in 1967, but she hasn't bothered to wrap up. Amin happens to be comatose next to her, which reassures her all the more. As she heads to a spot so well known to her by now her feet can reach it by themselves, she is almost dancing, there is such a bounce in her step.

For a moment her nightgown swells and flutters while she sashays into the night, and she looks like that beautiful victim of Count Dracula's, Mina Harker, called out of her bed into the balmy darkness by vampiric magnetism, asleep. Except Mouna couldn't be more in control of her faculties as, Van Helsing–like, she wields a shovel and a garbage bag, humming the Sayed Darwish tune "Ana Hawet" in a marchlike tempo as she goes.

She even mouths the words as she bends down behind the slowly growing sapling, digging up plastic bag after crinkled plastic bag, dusting and stuffing them into the garbage bag she crouches over in the veranda, extracting envelopes out of bags and cash out of envelopes before she ties up and disposes of everything except the cash.

She feels she has every right to this money, suddenly. Suddenly it is not cursed or haram. It is the least Nasser could give her in compensation not just for enduring fops and newspapermen but also for her six husbandless years.

She counts 1,120 guineas while she replays that last scene with the Newspaperman, especially his response to what she finally says to him. For once some color seemed to streak his temples before he turned forcefully away, as if in flight. For once the inhuman immobility of his facial muscles broke down while, all but pushing her, he elbowed his way as far from her as he could. Even now she's delighted.

As she arrives at the empty attic to put the banknotes in the safe she recalls how she could see the egg growing bigger as she drew close, rehearsing what she had to say over and over—until she was pushing up against him and she could see nothing else. She had to raise her arm to touch it, but that didn't stop her from yanking it all the way round. For once, he was facing her.

Then, holding on to his shoulders with both hands so he didn't turn away, she raised her voice as she addressed him:

—I have been seeking you out to give you my consolation, ya basha, but also to tell you something of great national import. I hope the homeland still has use for me, hein, because I really, really want to co-operate now. Suddenly I have this ghastly need to serve my country. It is so intense it could stop my heart. Please, please don't relieve me of my patriotic duties. I know the Immortal Zaim is dead but tell me please, ya basha. How can I serve my country now?

The attic told me nothing of Mouna's last four years, but much of what it did tell me she herself was reliving by the end of 2014. The day Amin went missing, for example: 1989. For a whole week, she confided, it was playing in her head.

When she realizes he is being held at the Yellow Saraya—the state mental asylum's old sobriquet has always been a joke with them—she laughs before she remembers that people are only sent there for punishment or riddance.

Two months later, at six years old you will earnestly refer to the occasion as *the Eighty-Nine Thing*, making everyone laugh.

Something has possessed her to go down into the basement, but not until she's there does she realize it's been three nights since Amin showed up at the house. Shocked that it took her this long to notice, she starts by phoning his boss. But after four attempts it's obvious Kamal Azer won't take her call. And, for the first time in years worrying the worry of a political prisoner's wife, the bourgeois cloud she's been slowly, tenaciously gathering around herself precipitates.

Slowly she reviews the erratic routines Amin has been keeping since he went off his medication. Twice he was gone overnight, she remembers, dismissing her concern on his way back to his basement quarters with a backward shake of the head. He sleeps at the office, he tells her, muttering as he descends. And, knowing he's been marooned in the cavern of his mind though she does, Mouna is confirmed in her suspicion of an affair.

For a long time they haven't been close. Distance regulates their relationship better than the fraught intimacy of their pre-Shimo days. They sleep and eat separately, almost never seeing each other.

For two weeks at this point he's been mumbling to himself about the Berlin Wall. She can't tell if he's devastated or ecstatic, but having followed the news she doesn't understand his hysteria.

Mouna's face crumples as she stares at the mango tree. A hagga in a howdah, she is nestled in the leather bergère with the footrest which she bought herself for her fiftieth birthday. Three years into early retirement, she's been busy pooling funds to buy the first apartment she'll manage to resell at a profit, cooking and cleaning with the help of her live-in maid, Karima, and overseeing Shimo's schooling. Even Abid is grown enough to let her be in her bergère. And, though the willful six-year-old still requires hourly attention, Mouna is able to integrate her into her new, relaxed rhythms.

It's true that, driving her royal blue Mazda 929 around town, these days she often weeps in public, allowing herself a maudlin moment where no one who knows her can see. She weeps every time she remembers that Bido is a stranger and Aminov an infidel. And, sane though he is, by comparison, Nour can't make up for all that's been lost on the way.

It's true she's developed type 2 diabetes on top of a history of hypertension. But she's grown so mellow the stress lines on her face have morphed into plump pats of flesh. For a while now sleek furniture and state-of-the-art appliances have been shrinking space while mass-produced Quranic verses replace original nudes on the walls. Lavish decor ravages the stillness. She's no longer interested in subtlety.

Patriotic songs used to nauseate her. Now she weeps when she hears the celebrity she resembles, Shadia, proclaiming that *Sinai has returned whole to us and Egypt is on a feast day*. The song came out to celebrate the handover of Israeli-occupied Sinai in 1982—Mubarak's first year in power—but it's been on repeat wherever she goes since the Taba border dispute was finally resolved in February 1989.

To the sound of it, Mouna is turning the house into a consumer paradise on installment plans. Having gone full pious mama, embracing Sadati middle-class mores with a vengeance, that's what she spends her time doing.

A year from now Amin's position at the Saudi multinational the Umayya Group will be secure, his income five times higher than it's ever been. By which time one of her sons will be a university graduate, the other well on his way to becoming a police officer. And from November 1, 1990—when Amin receives his first payment, to December 21, 2000—when he imparts his final message, Mouna will be sovereign of her own new kingdom. That's when she first becomes the postmillennial Mouna that, even now, feels so much more familiar than all her other avatars. It is a subtle transformation: the opposite of what will overtake her in the fateful winter of the revolution. And, true, it won't be complete until she is widowed and spends a season, two seasons in hell. But the bulk of it happens in those ten years while she's barely talking to Amin.

When he's taken to the Yellow Saraya Amin is a civil servant still, but with her network of connections and the scrimping skills she developed in the sixties, Mouna can afford both a car and a live-in maid.

Not knowing where he is now, she retches while she picks up the streamlined, futuristic handset, a push-button plastic marvel she bought a year ago. And it's as if she really is on camelback in a Mecca-bound caravan suffering from motion sickness.

—Bas bas, I hear her whisper to herself now. One breath at a time. And she really does breathe before her panic-edged voice rises. Karima. Come here, Karima. Tell me, ya habibti. When did you last see Ustaz Amin?

But it's Medhat El Tetsh's grand, gravelly voice tumbling down the headset that follows Mouna's:

—Um, we've just contacted the health minister's office, he's saying. We have friends there who shall be doing all they can to find him.

With vague amusement Mouna recalls how—in declarative statements—he'll refer to himself using the royal *we*. Medhat never spoke Socialist Union in his life, but—like Semsem, who did speak it—he's adopted the self-important tones of a generic high official from those days. She's grateful for his support, but she can't help shuddering at the fact that neither he nor any of the other three friends she could think of has heard from Amin for weeks.

She'd hoped Amin had come home without her noticing, but soon she confirms Karima hasn't seen him either. Nor has Abid, who is berating Shimo about being unwomanly on the school bus. Nour has been interning at the state newspaper he's hoping to join, *Al Oruba*. He won't have seen his baba even if he's been here.

—But rest assured, ya Sett Amna, Medhat is saying. It's what he has half-jokingly called her since the fifties: *Sett Amna*. We will find out within the hour if he's been taken to hospital, God forbid. We will think who to call, um, at the interior ministry too.

—But, ya Medhat, Mouna's voice quavers. Kamal Azer has been avoiding my phone calls. And if anybody knows where he is, it's Kamal Azer. Amin mentioned they'd be having their board meeting this week. He was being sarcastic about the chairman. I can't remember which day it was supposed to be, but it will have happened by now. And yaani why would Kamal Azer avoid me? Whenever I've called him before he's been very courteous...

I see her standing stock-still by the bergère, a rotund form facing away from the veranda, her free hand twiddling with the edge of her headscarf.

—The health minister's office just got back to us, Medhat El Tetsh is saying after a while. Um, it appears you were right about Kamal Azer...

It was he who arranged for the asylum enforcers to come and drag Amin out of his office in one of those white straitjackets you see so often in Egyptian movies. Except Amin didn't kick and scream while they put it on. He was so cheerfully cooperative, and he proved so charming with the resident doctor—though in his rage Kamal Azer had made sure he wouldn't be allowed to contact anyone—for the duration of his stay Amin came to no harm.

Not that he doesn't weep with gratitude when he sees Medhat and Mouna with the orderly at the door of the ward.

Mouna has picked up Medhat in her Mazda. And together they visited the deputy health minister's office before heading out to the Yellow Saraya with an authorized letter. In the next few weeks Kamal Azer and the chairman will be appeased separately through Medhat's and Semsem's good offices, promising they would have nothing more to do with Amin and to leave him alone.

Smiling fondly, in 2014 Mouna will remember the story as the last time Amin made her laugh from the heart:

It had been at the board meeting, just as she suspected. Amin had behaved with impeccable decorum up to the first serious pause when, deliberately catching the chairman's eye, he suddenly climbed onto his seat. Unzipping his fly and theatrically taking out his cock, he then described a wide arc unleashing a jet of liquid straight into the faces of the besuited mandarins.

—That is all the likes of you deserve, he kept saying, his voice perfectly even, while they scuttled and scrambled.

Quick on his feet, Kamal Azer rose and, like a guerrilla in action, inched forward with his knees bent till he reached the enemy. Then, in one swift motion, he wrapped his arms round Amin's thighs from behind and started pulling—only to receive a reflexive donkey kick and promptly fall on his back.

Too shocked to complete the act of standing up, meanwhile, the urine-drenched chairman squawked inarticulately while his thighs teetered on the edge of the seat. He was a rotund former contractor with an elongated snout and a crest of downy hair, normally too aware of his humble beginnings ever to smile spontaneously. Amin said his shape and gait had always evoked a duck but, released from his stuffiness by the golden shower, now he was waddling in place, quack-quacking for real: *Ya magnoon, what's undone your nuts, ya magnoon!*

—That's all you deserve, Amin said one last time while he shook his bulbul and zipped back his fly, perfectly down-to-business. Then, winking amiably at the chairman, stepped down and returned to his office as if nothing had happened.

Mouna will be sovereign of her kingdom, hoping for a whole nation of grandchildren. But in the years after they begin to have children, Abid and his wife will deprive her of being the grandmother she imagines herself to be. Knowing her son, it seems, she accepts this with equanimity. It used to infuriate you, the way she just accepted him. How many times did you and I discuss this, Shimo. I don't know if I told you but I even asked Baba once, *Why does he have to be like this?* And, just like you and I would, every time, we came up with a myriad of explanations only to conclude that no one thing accounted for the way he was.

What pains her is that neither Nour nor Shimo will have children to present her with in the foreseeable future. There will be no nation of her own, then. And, without a crackpot communist to contend with, as of 2000 there is no kingdom. Even Karima marries and leaves her service. All that remains is the confederacy of close ones she advises over the phone like an ailing valide sultan. Together with her barricades of baraka.

No projects glitter in the distance after she leaves her BMW permanently parked by the sidewalk to wrangle with the Afreet. No idea of the future as she dismisses the last of Karima's replacements and stops taking an interest in her daughter's whereabouts. She has barely turned sixty when she begins to move with the labored weariness of a spent centenarian.

Forget grandmotherhood, though. By the time she's taken the briefcase full of banknotes that she got for her car to the bank, motherhood itself will have been flushed out of her. Unless you count piety-bonding sessions with Abid and furiously silent showdowns with Shimo.

She thought she could be the sovereign of a desert city to her measurements. Only eons of sand actually surround her in the vast, Aminless metropolis where she winds up a helpless subject. After nearly half a century Cairo is reconfiguring itself around her, a burned-out war zone. Alone, she holds on to what rituals and routines make life familiar enough to be bearable. The überpious mama shuffling back bent around the house, long johns tucked into men's socks over her rubber slippers. Watching her little télé and praying in bed.

That's why the dirt and disorder, the pollution and overcrowding that peak unprecedentedly through the millennium's first decade barely register. All she does is step out to the Fatah Mosque flashing her beatific beam, or pick up the landline speaker to order necessary provisions from the corner shop. Multi-season soap operas are becoming a thing—they're still Egyptian, not Syrian the way they would be in the winter of 2011—and she watches them. Marathons of numbing normality.

Until Hosni Mubarak steps down and—back from Tahrir Square in a moss turtleneck and an ocher trouser skirt—she stands waving a flag, Cairo will be devoid not only of motherhood but of drive. Perking up only to perform her duties—whether to God or to the womb tie He decreed—she will have been a soap-opera-watching shadow for fifteen years.

It had been all but formally announced that the all-day gathering was in honor of the leftist lawyer Amin Abdalla Amin, to celebrate his release from prison. Though the groom, as they called him—drawn, dejected, obsessed with his mango tree—had to be dragged across town to attend.

There were bound to be Nasser partisans and Mukhabarat informers among the writers and artists present at the party. The hosts knew this. But with what has always seemed to Nimo a uniquely Sudanese fearlessness—comparable only to the Sudanese appetite for liquor, she imagined—the hosts seemed unguarded as they went around quipping and storytelling, urging people to eat, drink, sing and dance, lie down if they wanted to.

There was grilled seafood and local Stella beer *in commercial quantities*, as Serag liked to joke. And for as long as they lasted, the piper and the fiddler on the guest list extemporized, having brought along their instruments unbidden.

Nimo and Amin arrived at the doctor couple's at one in the afternoon. To Amin's distress, by five in the evening politics had still not come up anywhere in the Nile-view apartment. And when he insisted on leaving Nimo didn't understand this was why his panic peaked.

He had never seen so many people in so small a space manage not to talk politics for this long.

You could count on the guests being leftist or left-leaning, though within that they ran the ideological gamut. Some were names of various sizes. Some were former acquaintances of his. Yet it didn't seem purposeful or planned, the way their conversation skipped over any possibility of dissent.

Nimo didn't yet understand that this was why he had to leave, not because they didn't polemicize but because none of them felt the need to. Over the course of five years, iron and fire had gelded the intelligentsia, he would tell her. So seamlessly there was no longer any sign of rupture. Terror had insinuated itself into normalcy. After a day among them he felt like he'd woken from a five-year blackout to a freak-show Cairo, with the city dwellers replaced by look-alike mutants unaware of their disfigurement.

But Nimo didn't understand because—even if he was suffering, even if his abruptness embarrassed her—it was a relief to see him bounce and flounce. For weeks he had been so unlike himself, so stationary.

She also didn't understand because even after three hours she was still overwhelmed, not so much by recognizing Aziz Maher the minute she walked in as by seeing her husband chat to the man she had betrayed him with—the biggest name in the house—and feeling no discomfort at the sight.

It had been all but formally announced that *the country's greatest talents* were invited. But that man's name had never come up with Serag or Samira though Nimo knew Serag to be an art collector as well as an amateur photographer, and it didn't occur to her she might come face-to-face with her single-use lover at their house.

Self-abandon was the only way she could fend off the proto-Afreet that hadn't stopped growing since it first flashed into her vision at the Aquarium Grotto. And now it threatened to manifest. So, striding forward with her hand extended, she looked straight into the painter's eyes with a big smile.

—Ahlan Ustaz Aziz!

—How are you, ya Amna?

She was glad to see he looked fatter and more stooped, less dashing than she remembered him. Her hazel eyes only slightly wider than usual while they stiffly salaamed, she took the slightly mocking look he gave her as a cue to be louder and more sociable than ever. As if to demonstrate, *Very much better than you, thanks* while she overtook him and hugged Samira.

At one point she even considered smooching with Amin within sight of him, *that poseur I met at the Round Building through Sameh Khairy, you must've heard of him, ya sayyid*, though she quickly realized this would give away her weakness. Besides, Amin was in no mood for intimacy.

So, grin-greeting Aziz whenever their eyes met, otherwise ignoring his presence and fussing over her husband, Nimo helped with the catering and the cleaning. She danced a little to the music. Exchanged jokes with the women while basking in the men's compliments. To all appearances, she was confident, almost overconfident.

The truth is—she was still shuddering when, two hours later, she puffed up her chest and stuck out her tongue for Serag to snap portraits of her in one corner of the balcony. It took resolve to put her hands on her hips, arranging her go-go boots one over the other without falling over.

But all anyone could see while Serag went crazy with his small, silent camera was her innocent mischief, the childlike look that had always endeared her to people and endeared her to them still. For the first time now I realize it is precisely this innocence that makes the other look possible, that palimpsest of grief and hatred, the bottomless letdown by which Mouna is known to me. Ingenuousness, the life-love underlying her ingenuousness, is its prerequisite.

The apartment was small but its balcony was almost as large as the hall, and as amply and tastefully appointed.

Later, three-quarters of the guests would crowd onto it, filling the seats, standing or lounging on the floor, so that from where she sat on the sill, cross-legged and drunk on beer, as the early-evening sunlight washed through them and their outlines shimmered in silhouette, their heads appeared to float at various points on the water.

But when she jumped on Serag's offer to step out there for an afternoon-spotlight photo session—his Leica M3 had been around his neck even as he opened the door—it was empty still. Even if she had to perform for the camera, it was a relief to be apart from those with whom she had been so effusive a moment before.

It was while they were crouched across from each other that, out of the corner of her eye, Nimo glimpsed Amin and Aziz animatedly conversing. Sharing a plate of breaded shrimp while they stood to one side of the swarm. Only when she had the suspicion that Aziz might be telling Amin of what happened with her was she disturbed by the sight.

That night Nimo gets her last reminiscence of Lena Qansuh. A year on she's made progress at forgetting her intime, but something about the sight of Aziz and Amin conversing over breaded shrimp brings back the image of Lena's legs shaking.

It was the last time Nimo saw her—at Café Riche, toward the end of 1962—and she never got a chance to tell her of Aziz. Wearing red capri pants, Lena sat with her back to the translucent glass of the window, so Nimo could see her legs—crossed. They were shaking, but it was obvious Lena wasn't moving them on purpose. Nimo could tell. They were convulsing independently of her will—quivering like some desperate animal striving to break free of the rest of her—while Lena lit cigarette after cigarette, teardrops neither moving nor drying on her cheeks.

Nimo had never seen anyone's legs shake that way. And it stirred her more than the belly-wringing—no, the Afreet-shaping—story her friend had started to tell.

It was about a lover, of course. A celebrated surgeon and fellow member of the Gezira Club who was happily married with three small children when they met. Nader—that was his name—was thirty-three, seven years Lena's senior, and he was devastated when she told him she'd broken off her engagement a week after they met. Her policeman fiancé had actually caught her sitting astride someone else in a car. But Nader assumed the breakup was because of him.

Later that week Lena found out Nader had punched his tennis partner in the face for calling her Kossain. A dentist by the name of Raouf whom, never mind how he talked about her, Lena was attracted to. Nimo thought it was bound to happen eventually: two—or three—men fighting over Lena. But that's not what it was.

When she broke off her engagement Lena told Nazlı Hanim not to worry, she was looking for an eligible bachelor. By which she meant she would be freely playing. There were weekends away when she and whoever she went with booked different hotel rooms and arrived separately. Or she would visit a man at his garçonnière, staying over if she felt like it. Almost every week there was someone new.

—As long as there's champagne—a lot of champagne, non?—he doesn't have to be le plus beau ou le plus intéressant, mon chou. Lena winked, her smile dissolving into an expression of such anguish Nimo couldn't help gasping. *He just has to be passable.*

At first Nader refused to sleep with her, which—ridiculously, to Nimo's mind—she experienced as a rejection, crying her eyes out before she jumped astride him in his Ford Thunderbolt convertible, where they were talking late at night on the edge of the Alexandria highway, her back accidentally hitting the horn.

—But I'm a married man, Nader pleaded with her when they were done laughing. I have a daughter of my own. And you, my darling, you are a demoiselle with a duty to your family, a reputation to uphold.

When eventually he succumbed to what she kept telling him was l'appel du coeur—it happened at the Auberge du Lac Fayoum, which used to be a luxury getaway, believe it or not—Lena didn't realize how much that weekend meant to him.

—Or maybe I did, ya Nimo, she told her friend, suddenly looking not so much serious as cruel, cruel as a cold-blooded murderer, though her legs shook faster than ever now. Maybe I knew how in love he was and I did it all on purpose.

What she didn't know was that, the day he returned from Fayoum, Nader told his wife he was in love with another whom he planned to marry, and she wouldn't let him be until she found out who. Within forty-eight hours, Nader had been divested of both his house and his children. His father-in-law promised to bankrupt him, too, which, being a powerful figure at the Doctors Syndicate, Nader knew he could. His family and colleagues were all informed that he'd proved himself unworthy of respectable society, chasing a woman of ill repute.

That night Nader decided to stay in the hospital, too ashamed to face his old mother at his parents'. And while parked by the Corniche smoking a cigarette, he happened to spot Lena coming out of the Shepheard's Hotel with none other than Raouf, who was opening his car door for her.

As Raouf's car moved Nader gave chase—all the way to the same spot on the highway where he had been with her. And when the dentist's car stopped and, slowing, Nader saw her move from the passenger seat to sit astride Raouf, he switched to the opposing lane and sped up, managing to cover some distance before crashing into a heavy goods vehicle.

Lena did not find out about Nader's death till the end of the week, slowly connecting the dots till she worked out what had happened.

—But it's not your fault, Nimo tried to say, desperate to help but not knowing how. Lena glared at her. Mon chou, I mean—

—I deserve to die and you know it, Lena said.

—But you know what would happen to me then, Nimo found her voice at last. She had no idea where that thought came from, but it was her way out of the conundrum. I would just get more and more religious, more and more respectable.

—Stop, Lena said, laughing—before she stood up and, barely giving her time to stand up in turn, threw herself into Nimo's arms.

—I would become more and more religious and respectable till I actually performed the hajj and became a hagga. No, no. You have to stay alive, mon chou, Nimo spoke confidently now, squeezing the beautiful body and breathing. Because without you I will become a hagga. And how boring would that be, hein.

I've seen nothing at all of her mind-movies in the attic. But there are moments of the revolution that feel obfuscated, like they happened while locked up inside her in the dark. The day Sisi takes office, for example: June 8, 2014.

For a little under a year Islamists have been thrashing about like the severed tentacles of a dying monster. They're being rounded up and killed even when they're not staging bombings. Whether for them or their casualties, grief is an aerosol regularly released into the air we breathe. Not in a good way, it feels like a new era. And everywhere people are focused on security and the birth of a new zaim.

Yet on the day itself all that Mouna can talk about is a fennec fox that fell on her head three years before.

—She was so beautiful, ya Nour. Her voice seems to come from across a gulf—as if, recorded in a bygone age, it was being broadcast for the first time.

—That was the day we lost the referendum, no? I'm trying to steer the conversation gently to the event of the hour. Look where we've—

—I can see her eyes, the voice cuts me off. Two perfect balls like huge black pearls set in kohl-stained wool.

Mouna begins to sound like a medium channeling someone from the distant past, a sad smile slimming her lips.

—They shimmered as she looked at me. And when she pursed her darling snout—the whiskers, ya Allah, the whiskers—I understood they could talk. Those round black pearls were talking to me.

—They can't have told you about Sisi, though, I try again.

—They were wet with tears, she ignores me.

Her smile has dissolved into an awed stare and, though her face hasn't crumpled yet, her snub nose swells while she soliloquizes.

—That was the secret of their shimmer. They were weeping for the life that was leaving them. Telling me about their death while they wept. C'était incroyable, ya Nour. The soft and fluffy thing made no sound. She just looked at me like she was mourning for herself. But her eyes spoke right into my head. And yaani what they said was ghastly. Even as they remained beautiful saying it.

Mouna sighs, then sighs again.

—That she had killed herself but not yet died, she goes on. That she had been made to kill herself. That, when she leapt over a soaring edge on the other side of this world, something—some*one*, maybe even *every*one, c'est vrai—was goading her.

And at this point it does strike me that, in a tortuously roundabout way, Mouna might be talking about the unidentified iblis behind the death of the Jumpers. As she affirms the existence of some such murderer she's grieving for Monica and Shahira, it's clear. For Ommo Sabry, Laila Samir, Mariam El Daly. For a hundred and twelve dead women she knows by name. But preternaturally she's also grieving for herself.

—She'd been chatting with old friends. Spirits and ghosts of foxes with ears as big as wings and faces so mignon, ya Allah, you just wanted to eat them. Hudhuds and Afreets jumped up and down in her head. But as she dropped through the air from that soaring edge there was silence. And in that silence, ma pauvre petite, she could see all the other foxes that had been hurled before her. And the ones that would be hurled after her. She could see them too. And she felt the helplessness of every one of them, past and future, millions of beautiful foxes. So that by the time she landed on the roof of the concrete high-rise behind our garden, the sadness and the fear had ripped two of her ribs out. One turned into a thorn and stabbed her lung, then tore a hole in her aorta. The brave little darling landed on her feet, hein. But neither the shattered bone in her hip nor the gash the old antenna on our roof made in her belly did much damage. The rib that became a thorn was the murder weapon. And that gave her more fear and sadness than anything. She was bleeding on the inside when she fell on me, and she knew it wouldn't be long before she died. But the shimmering black pearls that were her eyes had time to tell me. Whoever made her jump managed to turn her body against her. To make a part of her body the cause of her death. That gave her more fear and sadness than the death itself.

It was November 2014 when her insomnia peaked. I know because the day I found her arguing with Baba in the garden, it was beautiful out. It was the kind of weather you spend the whole year waiting for. I can see the sky again now. I can taste the dust-free air, feel the balminess on my skin. I'd stepped onto the veranda for a smoke but I'd barely lit my cigarette when I heard her. So I leaned over to look and there she was fanning herself with her block note.

In a satin negligee she would never have thought decent outside the bedroom, she was sitting on the ground with her back against the base of the parapet, her exposed and muddied legs stretched out in front of her. Like the centerpiece of some seasonal landscape, she was beautifully spotlit by the afternoon sun. I could see just how beautifully when I stood before her. But I'd had time to hear what she was saying while I walked round. I recognized her domineering cadence.

In a low, private voice, she was telling Baba off for encouraging you to leave the country when you were old enough. It sounded like he was defending himself and objecting to her petty bourgeois reaction by turns. She seemed to believe they were in bed together, which—never mind where she actually was—they'd never been since you were born. But when I called her name, Mouna looked up and addressed me as if nothing unusual was going on.

—Nour.

She caught my eye and I crouched down to look at her.

—Aren't you uncomfortable here, my lovely?

—I was wondering whether you'd gone out again, she said without blinking. Voilà, the fruit seller's boy brought over some good oranges. They're on the dining table.

—But why are you sitting on the ground?

—Hein? Sitting?

—It's muddy here, ya Mouna.

When she caught my eye again she was suddenly very agitated.

—But where else would I be?

Glancing at her legs, she tried to pull down her negligee. Then she rose with difficulty and walked back inside as fast as she could. I caught her expression as she passed. It was not so much ashamed as perplexed.

In the two weeks before, Mouna had mentioned her inability to sleep, referring to the hole in her mazag. *No more chance of filling it with sleep*, she said. *Our Lord protect us*. But it hadn't occurred to me that, when you've been sleep-deprived for long enough, REM action starts to bleed into your waking life. So that you end up doing what you'd be doing in your sleep with your eyes open and your body alert. While she interacted with me that day, I realized, Mouna wasn't seeing a mind-movie. She was not in a reverie or possessed by a visitation.

She was dreaming.

A lot of what the attic told me of Mouna's life she was reliving by the end of 2014. There was the day Amin went missing, then there was the day Nour moved out, and then the day Abid went to Luxor in 1997. Within weeks of becoming an officer, he was posted all the way down there.

He'd been wringing her belly with what felt like filial ingratitude since the age of fourteen, when he'd started calling her Mama. *Mouna is such a stupid word*, he would say. He had a way of saying it, like boring a hole in her chest. Taking pleasure in it, too. But that's how he'd always been.

Overdoing his good-boy routines with Amin and Nour while playing patriarch with Shimo. Beating her up when he felt no one would interfere. And, as Mouna also discovered, staging elaborate, deadly inquisitions for stray animals in a secret alcove within the narrow strip of garden where, some two decades later, the prettiest fennec fox will fall onto her head. Her mind could see his cruelty and craft, but somehow her mother's heart remained in denial. Though she pulled strings for him when he insisted on enrolling in the Police Academy, his appointment to State Security within a month of his graduation scared her.

Without the wasta or the time normally required for the feat, he'd managed to weasel his way straight into the police division that, in fifteen years while Mubarak proved himself the journeyman who outperforms the stars, has become even more forbidding than the Mukhabarat.

Amin emitted a bleat or two of laughter in response, making melancholy jokes about *our little sheikh the professional torturer*. For years he'd regarded Abid with a sort of amused abhorrence, not taking him seriously. Maybe, by now, he didn't take anyone seriously.

But now that he has graduated Abid could end up with a bullet in his head or—worse—the subject of an inquisition just as agonizingly deadly as the ones he used to stage for the dogs and cats of Road 9.

Five dozen tourists were slaughtered in the Hatshepsut Mortuary Temple. The women raped, the children beaten to death with rifle butts. The bodies carved with machetes and implanted with scraps of paper bearing Islamist slogans while they lay lifeless in the *holy of holies*, as the necropolis was once called. And Abid has been sent to Luxor to interrogate the families and friends of the six jihadis responsible.

Mouna has never thought it in so many words but she knows he enjoys hurting people. Besides, he's twenty-one and keen to prove himself. Wherever they go in the country, officers like him make the locals side with jihadis. Given half a chance, he'll be handed over to be made an example of.

Perversely, only while her heart eats at her out of fear for his life can Mouna admit that she gave birth to a ghoul. A creature that feeds on fear, whom the people of the valley dream of slaying. Any minute now, the time might come for the ghoul's mother to mourn her progeny.

But ten days later when he returns strutting about and basking in his superiors' accolades, Mouna is so relieved she promptly denies it all again. At first she is shaken by the change that's come upon him. For the first time in his life, Abid doesn't brag. He has done something he's proud of but, even when asked about it, he simply smirks. How ghastly, how dreadful that thing must be.

But it's the work that happens to be his lot, she quickly tells herself. If he does it well who can blame him? He's only hurting those who deserve to be hurt. The boy is upright after all, n'est-ce pas? Unlike his father and brother. At least he observes his salah.

And when he announces matrimonial plans a few months later—never mind that she's the daughter of a deputy interior minister with a reputation for both ruthlessness and corruption—it's to a virgin in hijab. To Mouna's mind that's exactly as it should be. It takes her months to figure out why she isn't pleased.

The girl is almost psychopathic in her unfriendliness, her readiness to take offense. With her father's approval, as it seems, Abid turns her into his prisoner anyway, refusing to let her work or hold money in her hand. On pain of who knows what horrors, she cannot even leave the house without his permission. Whether because of this or the martial way Abid has brought them up, the two boys—born one after the other in 2001 and 2002—only ever get to see their grandmother under strict supervision, maybe once or twice a year.

There was the day Abid went to Luxor, and then the day Nour moved out, as if to anticipate the death of Amin: 2000.

Some six years after his official appointment to *Al Oruba*, Mouna's eldest son, the light of her eyes, is besotted with a much older woman. A poet and society lady, twice divorced, with two teenage boys who don't live with her. In Mouna's wholly baseless judgment, the woman is a manipulative diva. But, pray as she might, Nour's love for Aya Mandour is not a passing fancy.

Their union is to remain childless by consensus, which to Mouna's mind is itself a matrimonial death sentence. And so by the time it is over—just in time for Mouna's estrangement from her daughter—she will feel it's a miracle that it lasted ten years. Nour's puling had presaged a hard life and now he's demonstrating just how doomed he is. Another mother might refuse to let it happen. That's what she tells herself. On pain of disowning her misguided firstborn. She'd say *No son of mine* and mean it. Not Mouna.

True, she spends a whole evening screaming at Amin for suggesting Aya might be the right partner for Nour. She won't even meet the bride. But no matter what she feels, so she tells herself, she can't commandeer a grown man's life. Not that she ever misses a chance to sit him down to try to dissuade him.

She has all kinds of reasons to experience Nour's marriage as a disaster. But what is moving her is the knowledge that it will drive them apart. *Mais non, nothing can take my Nour away from me*, she keeps telling herself. But just as she knew the Eighty-Nine Thing would be the start of a new ten-year phase of her life, she knows Aya Mandour will make her a stranger to her firstborn.

It is not the distance separating Nour's new house from Road 9 that troubles her, not even what of his love and loyalty will pass from her to Aya. Only the fact that, being this woman's husband, he can never be as close to her. And it's true: until he moves back in with her, a divorcé, in 2010, they will be all but estranged.

—Ya Mouna, ya habibti, wennabi don't look so glum.

The third time she starts putting forth on *this marriage of catastrophe, of dark catastrophe*, he cuts the conversation short and starts doing his mock tai chi to diffuse the tension. But the hard look in her hazel eyes doesn't change. Apart from overtones of anger with her, she can see he's happy. He hasn't been this happy in years. It infuriates her.

—C'est vrai! When you marry an older woman, she's pleading, you practically hand over your freedom. Then, sitting up in her bergère, she picks up a magazine and starts fanning her face agitatedly. You won't even have a proper wedding!

—Seriously? Nour tries not to shout while, fumbling with a cigarette and a box of matches, he heads for the veranda. You're seriously upset about the lack of wedding?

Because he knows she didn't have one either. What he doesn't know is that, though moving in with Amin had actually felt like a release from the Abu Zahra irons, at some point between Abid's birth and Shimo's, she got it into her head that Amin had robbed her of every young woman's rightful dream. Somehow she managed to pass over the weeklong festivities of her marriage to Mansour Effendi. She also passed over the fact that, while Amin would've enjoyed a large reception, it was she who categorically refused anything more than a tiny get-together for their katb kitab.

—Just like your unfortunate mother, she mumbles, looking past Nour's head at the mango tree.

For a moment she recalls the image of Amin on his knees in the dust, planting it. It feels unexpectedly heartrending that he hasn't so much as stepped in the garden for years. It is midsummer and the fruit has begun to ripen on the branches. When was the last time she tasted it? For as long as she can remember, every year the tree bears fewer mangoes and, of those, fewer edible ones. She can't think who will even pick them this year.

Nour, the Nour of 2000, is smoking with his back to her, out of earshot. But I see her. I see the anger stiffen her jaws and I hear her muttering, the words becoming more and more indistinct as she furiously fans:

—He shoves a debauched divorcée in my face and wants me to

smile and nod encouragement. Two children, she has! And yaani I spent all those years bringing you up so a chameleon sharmoota like this can lick your brain?

There was the day Nour moved out, and then the day Shimo became a junkie: 2004. Shimo didn't really become a junkie but, stepping in the garden late one night, Mouna noticed an unusual, acrid smell.

Mouna is retracing her nocturnal route to the Mukhabarat money's hiding place, after midnight. Surveying weeds and bird droppings in the scant lamppost light. Gradually she becomes aware of a smoky, vegetable odor. It's the odor she will smell again on coming home from the Fatah Masjid on the fateful night of your twenty-seventh birthday. Without being unbearably offensive it is ugly in a dangerous or evil way. Immediately it brings back a crow-like flying insect with translucent, fluttering wings and a proboscis like a deer horn dagger.

This is not so much an image as a presence, its only definite sign an icy fear in her chest. For a moment Mouna suspects that, dreaming up an olfactory stimulus, she is traveling in time. Then what started out as an idle stroll becomes a mission to prove the odor real.

Slowly she traces it to the narrow strip behind the house where years before she discovered Abid's animal interrogation alcove—and onto the tip of a conical, hand-rolled cigarette like the ones in which people used to roll hashish.

At first that's all she can see. Then she spots two fingers and a thumb raising the object to a vaguely familiar face with a glazed look and headphones over tousled hair. There is barely enough light to make out who it is, and Mouna has to bend over and stare from various angles before she's able to process the scene.

With a Discman in her lap, Shimo is cross-legged in her underwear, grime all over her thighs. Eyes closed, she is nodding rhythmically, playing air guitar as she mouths the lyrics to "Nothing Else Matters." Smoking what Mouna quickly identifies as bhango.

That, then, is what hashish's cheap new substitute smells like. In reality bhango is not so different from the traditional aromatic resin, which has been in short supply since civil war broke out in Lebanon.

But in her pre-Afreet pious mamahood Mouna bundles it with *heroin and hallucinogens* among the things that turn young people into corpses or zombies.

—Shimo?

She's having genuine difficulty processing the sight of her favorite child like a trampy sharmoota damaging her brain in the dust. The one she has loved more delicately, cared for more diligently than the other two.

—You dog's daughter! Softly, she stretches a hand toward her face. Don't pretend you can't hear me now.

But, clearly secure in her solitude, the girl is oblivious even as Mouna's hand brushes her chin. That's why Shimo is startled nearly to death when, slipping before she has had time to stand back up, Mouna falls headfirst onto her like a diver in a cartoon. *Ah, ah, aha, aahaaaa,* her scream sounds inadvertently like the Metallica the girl was so blissfully immersed in. Now, while the headphones come undone and silence strikes her like a gong, Shimo reflexively punches the head that's colliding with hers.

—What the—

—Dog's daughter! Mouna flails wildly as she lands, trying to get up and slap Shimo at the same time. She remembers nothing of Aziz Maher's sebsi or *Ne me quitte pas.* What are you doing in my garden, you misbegotten dog's daughter?

Now they are both growling. When, raising herself on the flat of her hands, Shimo slips from underneath her mother, the hem of Mouna's viscose nightie snags on one of Shimo's elbows and Mouna's lower half becomes uncovered, too. Her thighs are just as soiled by the time she and Shimo are sitting opposite each other in the narrow space. Hands behind butts with their legs stretched and their feet almost touching, they are both panting.

—Deen keda, ya Mouna, what are you doing?

—Bas bas, what am *I* doing?

As she registers the impiety, the impropriety, the im-baraka of the scene, Mouna remembers neither her revolt against sharaf nor her devotion to dignity, neither the cinematic cloud she inhabited in her first four months with Amin nor the canopy of Fifi's Tudor-style bed under the benevolent gaze of the Mother and Child. She thinks only of disgrace in this life and torture in the next, growing more enraged by the second at the thought of a bright and blessed young woman willfully embracing both.

—You nearly made my heart stop, ya Mouna. I was just listening to music.

—Music, hein? And what's that you're smoking, then? If you want to ruin your life, alors! But don't think I'll let you turn my house into a drug den.

—Mouna! For God's sake, Mouna. It's only a joint. Surely—

—You curb-born vagrant! She lashes out, starting to slap her again before gathering the strength to rise and straighten her nightie. *Only a joint*—have some shame, she rasps while she marches out of the narrow strip of garden on her way back to the house. You shameless, curbborn vagrant. Shame.

For weeks Mouna stops talking to you. On my visits during that time, while she pretends you're not there, I try to explain that you mustn't expose her to what you and your friends do. Not to be dishonest but to avoid a clash. And in a way, I try to explain to you, to protect her.

Eventually, while I stand in the shadows nodding my encouragement, you go over and promise never to touch bhango again. But it isn't just that you don't intend to keep your promise. More than I could ever suspect, the fracas has taught you to protect your privacy savagely, revealing less and less to the mother you can't forgive.

Because at fourteen the precocious computer whiz has already turned into something Amna Abu Zahra cannot countenance.

Never mind your having absolutely no time for either housework or religion. Beyond your clothes and your manners, the profanities that string your sentences together and the subversive views you're always voicing, you have an unquenchable thirst for the world. And what this thirst is turning you into is a person who owes nothing to anyone.

Another girl might be vulnerable to premarital sex, you're simply keen on it. You feel no shame or remorse about doing the things you're not supposed to, only anger with people who think they can tell you what's right. So that as it cools that anger matures into alienation.

And, from now till the day Mouna opens the attic door to find your knees above your breasts, a smooth silver object buzzing between your thighs, you will grow only more resentful of the country you were born in and the lies that people tell there.

Soon enough, unbeknownst to me or anyone, you'll hatch a plan, ya Shimo, a plan that at your age—though she had been married and divorced and married again, maimed and molested and made to fend for herself—Mouna could never have conceived of:

To go to Stanford.

Of course, you tried and failed to make that happen when you graduated from high school, and again when you got your university degree. But I guess you'd acclimated yourself enough to being here that you could wait.

And in the six years separating your graduation from the day you leave, Mouna knows. I have been up in the attic and I can tell. Cowed by the Barra and the Arwa within her, keen on living out the Sadat-era persona she's taken on—the better to refute Socialism in her unconscious, lifelong battle with Amin—Mouna doesn't have the courage to admit or confront it.

But in her heart she knows all that her girl is keeping from her. The highs, the orgasms, the Jahannam-worthy heresies. The life that's there to live and the fight to live it. And, what you don't know but should, virtuous sister, is that in her heart she's proud.

That's why she becomes Afreet fodder once Amin dies. Because all that she's consciously lived for since she took early retirement in 1986, all that she's believed since she started wearing the hijab in the wake of Sadat defeating Israel, is nothing more than a way of dealing with her husband and her family background.

It's how she ends up retreating into her Bara and Arwa, presiding over a small tribe so as to help folk live out their lives exactly as they were going to.

Watching her exotic flower seed grow into a powerful pitcher plant— beautiful but deadly, invulnerable if not to the vagaries of history then at least to those of gods, omdas, nassers—she still can't help being scandalized and worrying, it's true. And yet she secretly suspects her life might be redeemed by the fact. Never mind that she's too tired or proud to behave accordingly. What you told me that day across a kitchen table at Zengy's is true:

She knows she has produced what she could never be.

Now I see Mouna as she briskly approaches the riverbank, Shimo. An emaciated figure in a lace-trim galabiya with a look of grief and hatred, of bottomless letdown in her eyes.

I see her but I also see the world as she sees it. And the two together feel like a summary of my being. Everything I've ever encountered or experienced, inside my head or outside—everything in the world as I know it—has its unacknowledged root in her suffering. It is eye-opening and liberating and incredibly scary to know this, but the joy of it is that I might have an answer for you after all:

The femicide you say I'm predicating salvation on, I no longer have any doubt that femicide is happening to me too. Even if being a man I'm also somehow causing it, Mouna has turned me into a kind of Jumper.

For a while after she glimpses the sluggish water now Mouna is aware she is alone. Even the passersby seem fewer and farther away. They grow smaller in size, while the birds, the insects look larger than humans. The orange-washed blue of the sky has given way to a tight mesh of blackness, as if a translucent niqab has been laid over the city's face.

Now the noise, muffled, transforms into an awful cawing. That sound used to paralyze her with fear. Now it reassures her that she is on the right—the only—trajectory. Just as Monica was telling her, that this cannot be otherwise.

Listening carefully to the cawing, she can make out the chant that so delighted her four years ago to the hour while she walked on the opposite side of the river: *Hold your head high, you're Egyptian.* Sayed Darwish returns, too, this time in a normal tempo, but while she opens her mouth to murmur the tune Mouna notices that the perspective has changed:

She's looking on everything from an impossibly high point now. She can see the Nile for miles ahead, winding down like some dark gray leak in the indistinct fuzz of that cosmic niqab.

Only the facade of the building she's headed for looks bright, as if bathed in floodlight in the midst of darkness. And, looking at it from the opposite side of the road, Mouna has supernatural resolving power.

Every crack in the veneer registers on her retina, every variation in the texture of the AC units jutting out of the wall, every blotch on every window.

This gives her the impression of a tunnel as she crosses the street, which she feels is something she must do alone. That, she reasons while she glances at the elevator, is why people have stopped showing up. The elevator would be quicker, she knows, but the exertion of climbing the stairs is part of how she's been envisioning her homecoming.

By the time she reaches the first landing—five stories to the roof where the metal door, as she hopes, is open—Samira has her arm in hers. In her Sudanese-accented Egyptian Arabic she is praising Serag's photographic talent and the twenty-five-year-old Nimo's beauty.

At every landing someone new appears. And, panting, Mouna listens more than she talks. Progress is very slow, but she doesn't stop for a moment.

It is Nour she phones when she realizes what has happened, back in December 2000. Shimo isn't home and all she can think is how to keep the news from her for as long as possible. The thought of Abid or Faiza is too unpleasant to consider.

—Karima, she calls out to the maid who has been with her for nearly twelve years now, and her voice is so even it shocks her.

She tells the maid, then she is silent. She thinks of Fifi and Hudhud. She thinks momentarily of Semsem, the way Semsem's humorous compassion pulled her out of the pit of Barra Hanim's passing. But it is for a beautiful, moneyed friend she does not remember having that she longs the most.

While Karima emits the inevitable scream—a generic, almost stylized cry of grief, though in this case not insincere—Mouna unconsciously misses a girl who might have helped her flee her destiny of pious mamahood. A girl who, though totally ta-ra-la-li, can be both confidante and counselor. Who can be her envoy to the sophisticated classes and her initiator into erotic secrets. None of these qualities are in any way relevant to her needs now, but it is for a someone, anyone who possesses them that she longs.

Looking depressingly middle-aged a year before she marries, Karima stands immobile by the bedroom door, grunting inarticulately whatever Mouna says to her, not moving. Slowly Mouna walks across to her leather bergère to pick up the Ericsson GH 688 phone Abid made such a show of gifting her with a few months before. This poor girl isn't even related to him and look what's happened to her, she is thinking.

Nour is his favorite son. But Nour has a duty to know. Mais bien sûr. It is really only he who should be contacted. Because, so she tells herself, Amin would have wanted only him.

But really it's because, beyond the company of that spectral friend, only the sanity she associates with her eldest son is desirable. And for the first time since they became cheap enough for everyone to have, she is grateful for mobile phones.

She hasn't phoned Nour since he moved out. What few times they spoke, it was he who contacted her. They met maybe once a fortnight, when he came to the house—often briefly, always alone—and said little to each other when they did. The tension that's built up this way makes her even more strident than she would've been, though as soon as he hears her breath it is clear to Nour this is an emergency.

—Mouna—

—Your father, she snaps tersely. Then, giving in to the ecstasy of tearfulness, she's inadvertently keening. You need to be here now, d'accord? You can't leave us like this, ya habibi—

—I'm on my way!

The sound of the line going dead jolts her back into sobriety, and for the first time she realizes she is still in the throes of the gift she was given. That endmost vindication. It is the certainty that this gift marks the beginning not of an indefinite but of an infinite absence that afflicts her. Gradually taking on form, in time it will prick and burn and knead her, plant hexes under her tongue. But, even at the worst times, the memory of the gift itself will always be a comfort of sorts.

It starts the way the Eighty-Nine Thing started. Once more she hasn't seen Amin in days when an intangible tug tells her she should check on him. Back in 1989, when she went down into the basement, she might've had a spring in her step. There was nothing eerie or ominous until she registered his four-day absence.

Eleven years later she shudders while making her descent.

There has been no premonition of anything terrible, no giant housefly circling her head. But, prompted to seek out her husband, she knows. The way she has known what Shimo is keeping from her. She knows without knowing. And the knowledge makes stepping down like boarding a locomotive tomb along a blood-spattered riverbed.

For a moment Mouna remembers a distant day in 1965 when, half standing over his Olympia typewriter, Amin responded with crushing tepidness to the breathless news with which she came running. That HADETO leaders had agreed to liquidate their organization only to be betrayed by the regime.

There was no daybed in the basement then. The architect's lamp light gave the space shape, however uneven. Apart from coffee and cigarette traces, there were no smells either.

This time it is like wading into musty gelatin. Till, past a certain distance from the door, the blackness engulfs her. Seeing nothing, she is guided by his groans. At least he is here, someone is here to emit those small, bleat-like exhalations. Could he have been calling for help?

Panicking, she rushes forward and trips over something—his clogs. It occurs to her only then to switch on the lamp, and so she does, retracing her steps. She's comforted to realize he's asleep.

She calls his name, loudly. Quickly he opens his eyes, moaning a long *Aywa* as he struggles to raise his head. While she walks toward him Mouna inadvertently catches the digital wall clock next to the lamp. 17:21, it reads. She will never forget this. When she walks back out the wall clock will read 17:25.

—What's the matter, ya Amin? She can see his eyes wandering, jumping up and down until they focus on her face. Why are you sleeping at this hour?

—Not sleeping, he says, and in his voice she can hear not just infirmity but submission—a level of resignation she didn't encounter in him even when he'd stopped being jittery on his release from prison. I was just resting a little. I need to rest. I think I'm ready for a rest.

—But are you ill? She is confused, helpless, though she instinctively channels her mounting alarm into practical suggestions. Did you not eat today? When was the last time you left the basement, son of Abdalla?

—I've needed a rest for too long, he says, with what will later strike her as prophetic lucidity. I've been hurting myself, I've been hurting others too, for too long. Remember the first time I talked to you, ya habibti? Remember how young I was? You were even younger of course, you were practically a child, but remember? It's been nearly half a century since that day but even then I'd already been hurting myself for too long. That must be why I'm resting when I'm not supposed to be.

—But what do you mean? Ya Allah, what's wrong with you, ya Amin? She's visibly panicking now. Let me phone a doctor, hein. I'll just—

—Mouna, he cries, beaming. My Mouna.

The first time he has called her that since the sixties. And his voice is so warm with it, it comes so naturally, the name stuns her into silence. All she can do is stay in one piece.

—I'm fine, he says. I'll be fine. Just come over here for a minute. She obeys hypnotically. And by the life of your children don't look so sad. What's sad about a man needing a rest after half a century?

They haven't touched once for fifteen years. For fifteen years he has given no sign that he appreciates or respects her. Not that she ever thought him unthankful, but she could never forget all that she'd been through since they married. All that their marriage had done to her.

For fifteen years they haven't touched. But when she leans over his daybed now Amin Abdalla Amin takes hold of Amna Wahib Abu Zahra's hand. With rough and awkward grace he brings it to his lips. And, mumbling *Thank God for you, how can I make amends*, he plants one, then a second kiss on its back.

After fifteen years, ya Shimo, the humblest gesture of gratitude within the last four minutes.

And even before she knows he's no longer there Mouna is too stupefied to make an utterance. Rooted, she stares at the hand he has kissed, gazes into his eyes. Looks away, then attempts to rouse him. Till it finally dawns on her there is no life in his face.

A Vision of Amin

And after five years five decades five centuries all that remains is a scar. It is the shape and size of a strawberry nestled perfectly in the small of Amin's back. It has the color of aubergine, a many-hued darkness gleaming, with three ashen points marking the edges. Mouna dares not imagine how it came to be. In the ground outside Dekernes where they left him at the end of 2000, she doesn't know if enough of his flesh remains for it to show still. But it was there when, without the decency to give Amin so much as a stroke by way of advance notice, with neither heart trouble nor tumors to announce his approach, Azraeel made his call. Having let him head the Umayya Group's legal department for ten tantrum-free years. Having spared the family the vagaries of scarcity and Socialism, Our Lord suddenly moved to take him. Until the moment Nour drives Mouna to the Amin family cemetery, Amin never lets her see it. He remains as silent as the day he returned in May 1964, when abandoned by the bathtub she was terrified of his thinness. All through that summer Amin busies himself with the mango tree, toiling like the salt of the earth, determined. For weeks he visits every orchard he can locate in Cairo until he has selected the pit of an Alphonso mango he's tasted and approved of. He cleans and scrubs the pit. He dries it. Then he carefully cuts and pries it open to get at the large bean inside. The seed. At first Mouna protests, laughing, *But it's not an easy thing, ya sayyid*, she says. *Besides, you can get a shrub to plant in the garden instead.* But no. He has to do it with his own hands, a skin-on-bones peasant's son who has never in his life touched hoe or harness. He pots and waters the seed. For two weeks he waits for it to germinate where he's placed it in the basement, patiently going down twice a day to tend to it. Once it has sprouted he takes it out in the garden to become a sapling. He spends hours in the soil with his back bent digging and fertilizing and planting it where it will grow. And still he is silent. Even in 1966, while the Comandante himself is in Cairo for the second time—by then he's back at work joking and talking, no longer emaciated and still—all he says is, *He was here while we were being beaten. In July 1959, godlike Guevara was here* to meet the Immortal *Zaim. Just like that Negro boxer who named himself Muhammad Ali. He came the year they let us out, didn't he? The Comandante had to confer with Gamal Abd El Nasser as well. If not for the sake of world Islam, then for the sake of world revolution.* Then he lets loose that unbelievably bitter titter, a bleat that signals hysterical laughter but sounds like a wail. And maybe the Comandante believed it, Mouna's thinking. That doctor. That killer christ. Maybe he believed that by beating Amin Abdalla and Selim El Mawardi and Medhat El Tetsh the local sickle of world revolution was removing *the factor of individual interest, and gain, from people's psychological motivations.* That he was forging the desired new type of human in the hearth of pain. Even in 1999 when Abid joins State Security, Amin's own son—born the month they ate the fruit of his mango tree for the first time—Amin jokes to hide how distraught the news makes him. For a while he taunts Abid with his quips—*So how do you like the electroshock interrogation kit you've been issued, then?*—but only because he'd rather not disappear into the basement immediately on finding out. That time he comes into Mouna's bedroom late at night and whispers in her ear in the dark, *Any idea why it might be that I don't feel like a proud father?* His tone is mischievous, but she can tell he's crying. Now he takes up the whole back of Nour's little Volks while she huddles in the passenger seat and all three of them trundle through the gloaming, the Afreet in her lap still hiding, and Shimo not driving up with Abid in his Jeep Cherokee till evening. Without tearing her eyes away from the pink-and-orange yonder Mouna sees Amin lying on his back behind her, with his stiff eyelids and his unmoving hands, and she senses him telling her how he got the scar, and calling her Mouna again, for once confiding in her in the same wordless language he used for their last communication. Godlike Guevara, who *swore before a picture of the old and mourned Comrade Stalin,* who had no qualms about shooting his fellow *in the right side of the brain* and then proceeding to remove his belongings. Maybe he did believe in the Nasser he was visiting. *But how—no, what—to tell you, my Mouna? There is no explaining what it is to lick a man's boot,* Amin is saying. *You do it willingly, but why? Not because if you don't you will be made to stand stark naked with your face to*

*the wall and your feet in sewage in a room full of restrained dogs ready to
eat you alive. To be punched in the head for hours on end or given electric shocks in your balls. Not because when you do you have a small chance
of getting a bowl of lentil soup made with no stock to eat with your bare
hand. Unless there's a bite of pebble-flour bread to scoop it with. Not even
because, having had an alleged doctor you've never seen before thrust a
rusty goad in your anus on the pretext of a health inspection, laughing
at your frailty and lack of balance, asking where in the world you've hidden your cock, you now need what reassuring intimacy you can have with
your regular jailer. But no, my Mouna. You lick a man's boot because
over the weeks or months or years this has become your function and your
purpose. Believe me, ya habibti, the man whose purpose and function is to
have his boot licked doesn't like it any more than you do, not really. But
it is a destiny to which you must both submit. It was a kick, a hard kick
that toppled me face forward to the dust. An interrogator had demanded
it while I cowered half-naked with my arms around my knees. What neither I nor the jailer who delivered it paid attention to was that the boot
I was looking forward to licking had a steel toe and, with its leather fray-
ing, some of the metal was sticking out. So that the blow that might've
broken my spine ended up branding me with the strange strawberry you
wonder wordlessly about.*

The roof is exactly as Mouna imagined it: the low brick railing canopied by rows of satellite dishes, the patterned, blue-and-yellow cement tiling, the vents and water pumps whirring. The beautiful view of the Nile.

At the door is Amin, waiting to take her hand. His face is lit by the bulb, but when he steps forward to meet her it is obscured. His grip is rough, awkward, but there is such grace in his voice that, like a teenage sweetheart, she rests her head on his chest.

Whispering *Mouna*, he gallantly takes her arm and walks her to the broadest break between the satellite dishes facing the Nile as if taking her to a café table. He helps her sit with her legs dangling over the edge before taking his position next to her, lighting a cigarette.

—So you have to go again, son of Abdalla?

—I know you deserve better than this, ya Mouna. He sighs, blowing smoke. Anyway it won't be six years this time, I promise.

She nods.

—You don't believe me, do you? He gives one of his bleat-like laughs. And, before she finds herself alone again, it makes her truly happy to hear it.

Looking up, she can see a nearly full moon dipping closer and closer to where she's sitting. It is silver, unusually bright and very large. As she stares at it, Mouna begins to murmur "Ana Hawet," her voice rising gradually as she slides her buttocks closer and closer to the outer edge.

—Mon chou, someone cries suddenly. I heard all about Aziz Maher.

—Lena! Mouna gasps, taking the beautiful figure suddenly sitting next to her in her arms. I've missed you so much, mon chou.

—That's why I came to see you, ya Nimo. I've been keeping up.

—But where have you been? Mouna rasps.

Because less than a minute before her buttocks scrape the edge and she takes off like a bird leaving its perch, inexplicably rising in the air before gravity takes hold—by my love for you she rose and, as if she had wings, she even fluttered there for a moment—what's been erased from her memory comes back to her.

She remembers Susanne. She remembers El Maître. And she remembers that her intime did precisely what she is doing now, a whole half century before.

—I became a hagga because you were gone, Lena.

—I know, Lena laughs.

And she looks prettier than anyone or anything Mouna has ever seen in her life.

Do you see how I've become the echo of something bigger, then, darling sister? How I've managed to unburden myself not just of our mother's story but also the revolution's. From here to where you go about your life oblivious of the Jumpers, seven thousand miles away, do you see how I've managed to ship seventy years of pain?

Because echoing Mouna doesn't just make me the revolutionary man, the male disappointment to be found in every one of those dead women's lives without exception. It also turns me into the prophet whose message gives all of their deaths meaning. And there is no longer any other function I can serve in the world where they lived and died.

The truth is I've already put the house up for sale. Once I send this off, I will be ready to move out. I've taken out a six-month contract on an apartment in Zamalek, and packed most of my stuff. The new apartment is right behind the Aquarium Grotto, in that part of the island you like so much. The plan is that, by the time I'm due to leave there, I will have bought a place from my share of the sale.

That house off Road 9, with a circular sliver of a garden and a spacious basement—with a disused attic on the way to the roof, Shimo. The house that started out as a signpost on the road to Helwan, the only residence within several kilometers' radius. Contractors can't wait to raze it to build a high-rise that will bring in billions. And just as you might expect Abid is very keen. He has probably sent you the papers you need to sign by now, though I'm sure the lawyer will find a way to finalize a deal without your approval too, if necessary. It won't be long.

Four years after the revolution I can't wait to get rid of the house myself, is the truth. Let it go, for God's sake. May it be offered like those savory biscuits handed out at the cemeteries, called *mercy and light* because that's what offering them is supposed to bring the dead, no? For Mouna, I mean. May the house be mercy and light.

What else could I say about it?

I am no longer enraptured at all, but nor am I disconsolate. Coming off the boat that took me down the river of the revolution I feel I'm stepping into a space beyond history. No longer at sea. And there is something lovely about being on land but—to my surprise—it turns out to be without desire. Without a mother to desire in the form of a country that could've been. Or a sister who could've lived in that country.

It might be too late for my release to mean much. I'm probably past the time when I can build my personhood from scratch. And maybe you're not convinced by what I've told you, either. But I have summoned you to mourn Mouna, and it's enough to think of you thinking of her as my words come through. If not lovingly or fondly, then at least with a sense of wonder. It's enough to think of me reaching you without the business of living between us, and you knowing the stippled story you were so reluctant to listen to at last.

I think of you thinking of her as the tips of my fingers touch the keyboard to type this. And I think how she possessed me and I managed to exorcise her. Along with history and desire. How I did it with words that are neither French nor Arabic but in your language, the language you and I share, which neither she nor Baba spoke.

I think of you thinking of all she had to endure to spare a husband or a son, of all you had to reject to be free of her, and of the time that lies between the two of you like air space. And I think how, to perform the exorcism, I became an air traffic controller directing all kinds of flying conveyances in and out of time.

Then, while the tips of my fingers touch the keyboard, her face forms in front of me on the screen. Grieving widow, secret agent, career woman, reborn mother—nonstop, she is reincarnating. Until, through a moment of peace when she looks unsullied, she rests on the gleeful apostate avatar.

Eventually the look of grief, hatred, and letdown begins to reconquer her lineaments, and as I gaze into it—for the first time in my life—I know that look is all I've ever been. Yet I also know that, having gone up to the attic to tell you of the Jumpers, Shimo, I will no longer be that look now. Even if I end up nothing at all, I won't be that look on Mouna's face.

Yours, in this life and the next,
Nour

Timeline

1948: The Arab armies are defeated in Palestine, where the state of Israel is declared as a result.

1952, July 23: The Free Officers stage the July Revolution forcing King Faruk (Muhammad Ali Pasha's heir) to abdicate, and kick-starting moves to abolish the monarchy and parliamentary life and to disinherit the feudal aristocracy.

1953: Egypt is declared a republic and General Mohamed Naguib becomes president, only to be ousted and replaced by the true Zaim ("Leader") of the revolution, Gamal Abd El Nasser (a.k.a. Nasser) in 1954.

—Radio Sawt El Umma opens, directed by Sameh Khairy.

1956, July 26: Nasser, now president, nationalizes the Suez Canal, leading to the Tripartite Aggression (a.k.a. the Suez War).

1962: Establishment of the Soviet-style Socialist Union to replace parliamentary democracy.

1967: Egypt is defeated in the June War with Israel; Sinai is occupied.

1970: Nasser dies; his deputy Anwar Sadat takes over.

1971, May: Sadat stages a Corrective Revolution purging Nasserist (pro-Soviet and left-wing) government and security figures and introducing free-market, pro-Washington policies.

1977: President Sadat visits the Knesset, in the buildup to the Camp David Accords a year later.

—The Bread Riots and the Student Movement protest Sadat's making peace with Israel and adopting free-market economics.

1981: Sadat is assassinated; his deputy Hosni Mubarak takes over.

1982: Most of Israeli-occupied Sinai is returned to Egypt.

1989: The Taba border disagreement with Israel is finally resolved in favor of Egypt.

1997, November 17: Hatshepsut Temple massacre.

2001: 9/11.

2005: Mubarak wins first-ever contested presidential election to serve an unconstitutional fourth term in office.

—Mubarak's son Gamal begins to emerge as a political leader.

2011, January 25–February 11: Tahrir Square demonstrations that result in Mubarak's stepping down.

—March–April: Referendum on Constitutional Amendments gives power to the army and the Islamists (led by the Muslim Brotherhood, or Ikhwan) through the first interim period.

—October 9–10: Maspero Massacre.

2012, June 30: The Muslim Brotherhood candidate, Mohamed Morsi, is elected president.

2013, June 30: Demonstrations against the Brotherhood and Morsi.

—July 13: Morsi is ousted by the army commander, Abd El Fattah El Sisi, and the second interim period starts.

—August 14: Rabaa Massacre.

2014, June 8: Sisi is sworn into office as president, having run practically uncontested.

Acknowledgments

This book would not exist if Noor Naga and Madeline Beach Carey didn't conjure it along, and it would not be what it is without all that Anni Liu did for it. Felicity Trew was the person who first planted its seed in my mind. Jessica Williams-Sullivan helped pick it up. Carol Sansour, Hilary Plum, Miriam McIlfatrick, Luciana Erregue, Josh Calvo, and Akin Akinwumi played significant parts in its conception or evolution. Except for the last two names, all of these people are women. The book's subject is a woman. It was inspired by a woman. Before I started working on it, I had never imagined I could work that way with a female character. I want to thank everyone who has come in contact with the book at any point since it started to take shape back in 2017, even—especially—those who were indifferent or uninterested.

YOUSSEF RAKHA is an Egyptian author of fiction and nonfiction working in Arabic and English. He is the author of the novels *The Book of the Sultan's Seal* and *The Crocodiles*, which have been translated into English, and *Paulo*, which was long-listed for the International Prize for Arabic Fiction and won the 2017 Sawiris Award. *The Dissenters* is his first novel to be written in English. He was among the thirty-nine best Arab writers under 40 selected for the Hay Festival Beirut39, and his work has appeared in publications such as the *Atlantic, Bomb*, the *Frankfurter Allgemeine Zeitung Quarterly, GQ Middle East, Guernica, Internazionale*, the *Kenyon Review*, and the *New York Times*.

Youssef is the only child of a disillusioned communist and a woman who struggled against incredible odds to go to university. He lives with his own family in Cairo, where he was born and raised. Among other things, he has worked as a photographer, cultural journalist, literary translator, and creative writing coach.

Graywolf Press publishes risk-taking, visionary writers who transform culture through literature. As a nonprofit organization, Graywolf relies on the generous support of its donors to bring books like this one into the world.

This publication is made possible, in part, by the voters of Minnesota through a Minnesota State Arts Board Operating Support grant, thanks to a legislative appropriation from the arts and cultural heritage fund. Significant support has also been provided by other generous contributions from foundations, corporations, and individuals. To these supporters we offer our heartfelt thanks.

To learn more about Graywolf's books and authors or make a tax-deductible donation, please visit www.graywolfpress.org.

The text of *The Dissenters* is set in Garamond Premier Pro.
Book design by Rachel Holscher.
Composition by Bookmobile Design & Digital Publisher
Services, Minneapolis, Minnesota.
Manufactured by Sheridan on acid-free,
30 percent postconsumer wastepaper.